"A devious, delectable historical spy confection in which an icing of lavish-court intrigue slyly masks heady doses of ripe feminism and lethal social commentary. *Milady* snared me in its web from the first pages, and I'll be first in line for the film premiere."

—Lyndsay Faye, author of *Jane Steele* and *The Paragon Hotel*

"A woman's place is no longer in the subplot and Milady de Winter is a seventeenth-century heroine destined for the twenty-first century. With bold, witty writing, and a narrative that rips along, Laura L. Sullivan crafts a compelling novel for a character deserving of her own story. I loved it!"

—Hazel Gaynor, *New York Times* bestselling author of *The Lighthouse Keeper's Daughter*

"As sharp and merciless as a Musketeer's blade, *Milady* is the historical adventure I've been waiting for, one that will leave you gasping to the very last page. Adventuress, assassin, and provocatrix, Milady de Winter is an unforgettable heroine, more than a match for any adversary. This is the story Dumas should have told."

—Deanna Raybourn, *New York Times* bestselling author of *A Dangerous Collaboration*

MILADY

LAURA L. SULLIVAN

BERKLEY

NEW YORK

BERKLEY
An imprint of Penguin Random House LLC
1745 Broadway, New York, NY 10019

Copyright © 2019 by Laura L. Sullivan

BERKLEY and the BERKLEY & B colophon are registered trademarks of
Penguin Random House LLC.

LIBRARY OF CONGRESS CATALOGING-IN-PUBLICATION DATA

Names: Sullivan, Laura L., 1974– author.
Title: Milady / Laura L. Sullivan.
Description: First edition. | New York: Berkley, 2019.
Identifiers: LCCN 2018023852 | ISBN 9780451489982 (trade pbk.) |
ISBN 9780451489999 (ebook)
Classification: LCC PS3619.U4357 M55 2019 | DDC 813/.6—dc23
LC record available at https://lccn.loc.gov/2018023852

First Edition: July 2019

Printed in the United States of America
1   3   5   7   9   10   8   6   4   2

Cover art: *Woman with knife* by Lee Avison / Trevillion Images;
Buildings by Liubomir Paut-Fluerasu / Arcangel
Cover design by Sarah Oberrender
Book design by Elke Sigal

*For Buster
and Luis*

The things a woman has to do to make her way in this world . . .

Mrs. Fox's whorehouse attracts a peculiar clientele. Oh, to most women, any man who will pay for heartless amours must be a little bit peculiar. We women, you see, are polar creatures, careening wildly from one extreme to another, either wholly romantic or entirely practical. Love-making, for us, must either be about devotion or commerce. Never both. We don't mix the two, although myopic men believe we do.

I have known many prostitutes, and not one of them has ever fallen in love with a client. Few indeed harbor anything but dislike for them, though occasionally a twinge of pity might creep into the most sensitive houri's heart. Which is not to say that whores don't fall in love. They do, harder than most. Just not with the men who pay them, no more than a blacksmith will fall in love with his bellows.

Somehow, though, men always believe that their whores secretly love them. They cannot be content simply to pay for pleasure, as they might pay a chef to prepare a sumptuous meal. No, they insist that the woman they rent must *feel* something. That, they think, is their right, and they feel cheated if their money cannot buy more than physical release. The best of the customers hope their gold will buy affection. These men are at least harmless, if deluded.

Others, however, insist on sharper feelings.

The marquis enjoys what his confreres call *le vice anglais*. Here, on the outskirts of Paris, the English Mrs. Fox is happy to provide all variations of vice. The English and French are in a constant state of agitation with each other, their royalty alternately bickering and intermarrying, their religious sects quibbling about minutiae they are willing to die over. And yet through peace and war (and war was threatening now at the Huguenot fortress city of La Rochelle), Mrs. Fox found that national relations were always cordial enough to keep her in business. Here, Frenchmen can conquer their traditional English enemy on comfortable feather beds rather than on the battlefield. Or, more often, yield.

For most of her customers like to be on the receiving end, whipped by a beautiful English wanton. Not the marquis. Few of the high-end girls will take him on, and he does not care for the ladies of the street, poxed and desperate. So you can imagine his glee when he spies me among Mrs. Fox's bevy, an innocent young widow fresh from the English countryside, with hair as golden as ripe wheat at sunset and eyes like English bluebells.

Forewarned of his presence, I hide behind the more experienced girls, but this only serves to attract his attention. My fear acts like oysters and Spanish fly to him. Even through downturned lashes, I can see his breath quicken in excitement.

"Step forward, Charlotte," the procuress says in her silky voice. "Let the gentleman see you." I hang back, and she gestures to two of the other whores to guide me forward. "A new girl, not a virgin, true, but fresh to the trade. Her only lover was her husband, mangled in a mill, alas."

I feel a tear tickle my cheek, but when one of the girls nudges me in the ribs, I look into the marquis's eyes and manage to twitch a smile at him before dropping a curtsy. "Milord."

"Yes," he says ravenously. "Look at that skin. Your husband was a prosperous man, eh? You never had to work, I can tell." He nods to Mrs. Fox. "She will do. She will do to a nicety."

When the girl beside me whispers into my ear exactly what he intends to do, though, I balk and pull away from his reaching hand. Behind him, I catch a glimpse of Roger, who sails under the flag of "nephew" but is Mrs. Fox's young lover and bully boy. He keeps the customers in line . . . and also the girls, if necessary. The marquis follows my terrified eyes, and we both watch as Roger clenches and unclenches his meaty hands, conveying a multitude of meanings. *If the marquis gets too rough,* that gesture tells me, *I'll step in. But if you refuse to please your first client, these hands will make you hurt in ways the marquis never dreamed of.*

And so, I accept my fate. What else can a poor English widow do?

Feigning courage through my trembling, I lead him to a room that smells of, well, the sort of things a brothel is known for. But this isn't an ordinary pleasure den. There is a propped ladder, a sturdy wooden X, a bench, and the sort of stand usually used to hold saddles. On the wall are paddles, short and thick, and long and slender. A sweating bucket full of birch rods waits in one corner, and a braided cat huddles in another, tossed aside by someone in the throes and forgotten. The walls are painted in roses and peonies, and the other furniture could be found in any middle-class English merchant's parlor. The floor is oft-scrubbed wood, and the rugs are red.

He gestures to the crossed beams, and I know he means for me to pliantly place my hands in the thongs affixed to their capitals. He is a large man, a soldier and an expert swordsman who could easily move me into whatever position he chose, force the most abject submission. But that I would meekly thread my hands into the restraints myself excites him.

My will is the first thing he will break. After that, my skin.

I move to the X, then pause. "Will you take wine, sir?" I mumble.

"What?" he demands.

"W . . . wine, milord. Mrs. Fox said I . . . should offer you wine." He laughs as I seek to delay the inevitable by shuffling up to a low table.

While I pour a single cup of wine, he smirks, and turns to examine the birch rods.

I don't spill a drop.

"Thank you, my dear," he says as he takes the cup, just exactly as if I were a lady worthy of respect and not an English whore he means to thrash bloody. Down it goes, and he wipes his lips on the lace at his sleeve, then gestures me to bondage.

I face the X and slip my hands in. The leather is rough on the tendons of my wrists.

"The other way," he says.

Slowly, I turn all my softest parts back toward him, and he secures my hands high above my head, spread wide. I assume he'll buckle them to the tightest hole, but no. I can't escape, but my hands are held loosely. I can wiggle and struggle. The pulling will chafe my tender wrists raw. Oh, he has done this before!

I'm still clothed. The marquis takes a knife from his belt. Mrs. Fox has factored the cost of my gown into my price, along with the inevitable doctor's fees.

"Milord, I beg of you, wait a moment." He pauses. There is no script for this—Mrs. Fox left it to my natural instincts—but if there were, I'm sure I commenced begging exactly on cue. "I am a widow, alone in the world. For the love of God, have mercy on me."

His weapon is erect as he advances on me. "Alone," he says. "Helpless. Will you scream, my pretty? If you don't, I'll give you ten livres for yourself. We won't tell Mrs. Fox, eh?" He smiles at me, then a shadow crosses his face as he doubles over. In a moment, he has collected himself. The marquis wouldn't let a pang of the guts interrupt his pleasure.

The blade touches my throat, just above my high bodice. Other harlots reveal their charms, but I know the thrill for him is that they are hidden, that he is the one who can unveil them. Down the knife presses to cut through my costly fabric, and I feel the honed edge kiss my skin beneath the layers. Did he cut me? I can't tell, for the knife is so sharp I can't distinguish pressure from pain. He will not be the first man to mark me.

I hear the breath of parting silk as he slices my gown further open . . . and he staggers back. His hands clench in a spasm, then open uncontrollably. The knife clatters.

Now? No, too soon. But it will not be long.

"Milord!" I cry out. Whore that he thinks me, he won't believe I care about his well being. The creature he has tied up only fears anything that might keep the madame from getting her coin. This day will be taken out in my skin one way or another—if he does not pay to flog me, the bawd will flog me for his lack of payment.

He tries to straighten, but then vomits over the red rug.

No matter. The poison in the wine is already deeply into his system. He can purge all he likes; his doom is still clear.

My frightened visage fades, and I stand calmly with my buckled arms widespread high over my head. I am bound and he is free, but only one of us is afraid now.

"You shouldn't have defied the cardinal," I say in my low purring voice. "Once, perhaps. Audacity amuses him. But never twice."

"Gar!" he chokes out, looking at me in confusion.

"Is it a novelty to you, milord, having no control over your own body? I imagine so. You enjoy taking away others' control. How do you like being helpless and in pain?"

He topples to his side in his own vomit.

"Can you hear me, milord?" I wish he were near enough to kick to attention, because I would particularly like him to hear this last part before he expires. "Cardinal Richelieu sent me to kill you for matters of state, but I have reason enough of my own to be glad to see you wiped from the earth. Your wife did me a kindness once. She was too good for the likes of you. I know the world believes she drowned, and pities you for your tragic loss. But I once saw her swim past the end of the pier at Nice in high waves. She would not perish in a horsepond. Admit that you drowned her, and I will give you the antidote."

With the last of his strength, he rolls to his fallen knife and makes a pathetic lunge at me. Then with a guttural groan of agony, he stiffens in one last convulsion, and his eyes stare, forever unblinking, at the nothing that is his due.

I sigh. A confession would have been nice, if only so I could laugh as he begged for the antidote to the poison. But no matter.

A bit of simple acrobatics brings my ankle up to my bound hand, where I retrieve a knife—one of many; vital systems must have redundancies—and cut myself free.

Mrs. Fox peeks in the door. "Done already? That was fast."

"My poisons always are. I would have liked him to linger a bit longer, but his heart was in such palpitations at the thought of violating me that the poison spread more swiftly through his veins than I'd anticipated." I rub my wrists. Good, there are no welts this time. Other times men have tied me up, I have not been so lucky.

Mrs. Fox looks with distaste at the marquis. "I don't suppose you'd care to tell me what you used. It could come in handy one day."

"If you ever tire of Roger?"

She throws her head back and laughs. "When I tire of him, I'll pension him off like I have the others. No, killing is not for me. You keep your poisons, Milady. I'll keep men under control with my own methods."

"They've worked well for you so far. Business seems to be going splendidly."

She nods. "Thanks to your timely loan."

"What would Paris be without Mrs. Fox?" I ask. "I couldn't have you going back to England."

She sighs. "Ah, the fog, the sunless skies. I miss it, times. Do you?"

I narrow my eyes at her. "Being a born Frenchwoman, I am happiest in my mother country."

She chuckles again. "Of course, of course."

Damn, but she's a shrewd woman.

"Care for a cup of wine after your exertions?"

I glance at the emptied cup on the table. "I don't care much for strong drink. It hides a multitude of sins. Shall I send someone to take care of that?" I gesture to the thing that was the wicked marquis.

"No, Roger will dump him in the river after moonset. You rest easy. No one will even know he was here tonight. So"—her eyes even craftier— "does this sufficiently repay the loan?"

"Hmm . . . How about some of your raspberry tarts? For the road. I won't overstay my welcome. Then we'll be square."

"No, love, stay a bit. It isn't often I get to talk with someone as witty as you." She takes my hand, and we walk downstairs to her private parlor, gossiping about her girls, the local magistrate, the price of butter.

Women, you see, can combine affection and commerce with each other, if not in their relations with men.

I might say that my opinion of men is low. But then, my opinion of mankind is fairly poor to begin with. It is only that men generally have more scope for mischief and malice.

At home—the home only four people know about—I strip off clothes that carry the faint stench of brothel and splash my face in the basin. Ah, to wash the world away in a cold cascade! Off comes the kohl from my eyes, the cinnabar from my cheeks, the false flags that give whatever face I want to the wide world. I always have a mask on.

Everywhere except here.

I hear a step behind me and whirl with the instinct of long training. Water beading on my lashes blurs my vision, and I only vaguely make out a large masculine form bearing down on me. In an instant I'm overpowered, my arms pinned, helpless.

Helpless beneath his kisses.

I can hardly breathe. My heart is wild. When at last he releases me, I blink my eyes to clarity and gasp, "Darling!" and wiggle free enough to throw my arms around his neck. Pulling him close, I unbalance us both, and we go down on the carpet in a tangle of limbs and laughter. There's a quick, violent tussle, and I end up on top, straddling his chest, my hands on the tender pulse of his throat.

I kiss that pulse, his blood thrumming against my lips.

Here, in this house, are all the things those who think they know Milady would say I don't deserve. A prison cell, the torments of hell are more fitting for one such as me, many believe. My name—my title, rather, for no one knows who I truly am, and even in Paris I have many guises— is whispered in the dark as furtively as some speak of the devil, as if to breathe my name would conjure me up in the flesh. And oh, what flesh! My beauty is part of my legend. Deadly beauty.

But I am not so beautiful as they think, nor yet so deadly. I have some natural gifts, but above all, it is my training and practice that make me what I am today—the cardinal's creature, the most feared assassin in France.

In comes the third part of our ménage, carrying with her the minuscule fourth. She looks down at our combative posture with wry eyebrows. "Mission successful? As if I have to ask."

I unstraddle the Comte de Wardes and slip into a linen robe before taking the cooing little bundle from Madame Bonacieux, or however she styles herself at the moment. Another spy, she gained a position as the queen's seamstress, secured through a false marriage to an elderly, influential merchant. The queen, of course, is charmed with her amusing, insinuating prattle, and tells her practically everything as she is fitted for her embroidered undergarments. And it all goes to the queen's enemy, the cardinal.

I look into the cherub's face, mostly because when he is in the room, I cannot seem to turn elsewhere, such is the strange gravity of motherhood, but also so I don't have to see the swift pained look that I know will cross my lover's face at the thought of my mission. We both know, rationally, that such indignities and dangers are part of the job. That does not make it any easier for the heart to bear. I know I am in an ecstasy of nerves whenever he leaves on a mission.

Any small slip, the tiniest betrayal, an accident of chance, might tear all the happiness in this little house asunder.

And now, here comes another chance for fate to have its way with us. Madame Bonacieux has a message from our master. A new assignment.

My lover moves our child onto his lap as I take in the details. It skims by me, mere trivia. That Gascon boy D'Artagnan who appeared out of nowhere and, almost accidentally, thwarted two of the cardinal's plots already—I am to befriend him. Easy enough. If I cannot make a nineteen-year-old bumpkin my devoted servant, I have lost my touch. Madame Bonacieux, too, had been tasked with seducing him in her own tricksy way, and already has the boy half mad with her feigned kidnappings and royal schemes. But the cardinal always prefers two strings to his bow. It is one of the easier assignments of my career. I breathe a weary breath, almost, but not quite, like a sigh, and ask my friend, "Why?"

"His Eminence is interested in the upstart gadfly, and wants to co-opt him for his own uses. The young man has made fast friends among the king's Musketeers, and seems to be everywhere. It is he who brought the queen's diamonds back from Buckingham, saving her honor."

My son, all apricots and cream, makes a sound very like a snort. When I look over, though, he has only spit up on his father's chest, a thing that both of them seem to find extravagantly amusing.

"It was a stupid plot to begin with," I say, peevish, "if a goat from the country could thwart it. But I didn't mean a small *why*. I meant a rather larger one."

The three of us, spies all, fall silent. We had come to the cardinal as vessels, not empty, perhaps, but supremely porous, absorbing all his tales of duty and justice and peace. One strategic death can prevent thousands, he always said, as a daub of mud can save a dike. We do this for the widows, for the children, for the young soldiers.

I have done more for the widows and children out of my own pocket, my own will, than the cardinal has. As I look at the cruel and ravenous world around us, the best that can be said for our job is that, without us, it might all be worse.

That is a far cry from making the world better.

In the shorthand of long acquaintance, we repeat a frequent conversation with a mere glance. We know all the arguments. We know we cannot leave.

"We should leave," I say, the milky scent of my son driving the smell of sex and vomit from my memory, making me weak enough to speak my wish aloud.

The comte nods, but says what we all know. "He wouldn't let us. He would kill us, and everything we love."

I would like to argue that we are his best spies and assassins, that we are a match for the cardinal. But the world is not like that. Lions are torn apart by jackals, and desert sand can wear away a colossus. If I was alone, I could risk it. But look at what I have to lose.

I dress, very carefully, donning my clothes like a costume, like weapons. Last of all, I put on my rosary of red and black beads. For one can always use a little extra help.

If you had told me ten years ago that spy work could be tedious, I would have laughed. But any job, performed not with love but of necessity, becomes drudgery. Ferret out this secret, kidnap that prince, forge one missive and steal another . . . It is all so much housekeeping now. However well you scrub the floor, it becomes dirty again. Ten years make excitement dull.

Almost without thought, I catch D'Artagnan's eye, make him follow me, stage a scene with Lord de Winter (my supposed brother-in-law; I've had as many sham husbands as Madame Bonacieux). Predictable as clockwork, the impetuous Gascon challenges de Winter to a duel. Spilled blood sharpens a young man's appetite. If he wins, he will be so inflamed for me in his victory that he will do my bidding in exchange for promises never fulfilled. If he should be the one pinked by de Winter's blade, I will play the loving nurse, and twist him to my ends just as easily.

My lover has taken our son to the countryside to roll in clover and no doubt try to befriend and embrace a bee, which will end with a sticky sweet to distract him from the pain, to everyone's satisfaction but the bee's. With nothing better to do, I disguise myself as a woman just poor enough to not be robbed, just well-off enough to not be mistaken for a streetwalker, and stroll off to see the duel.

There is quite a crowd behind the Luxembourg tonight. The combatants have brought seconds . . . and thirds . . . and fourths! It is usual to have a comrade to ensure fair play, or to take the duelist's place should cowardice prevail. But to have three seconds? D'Artagnan's friends are all in Musketeer uniform. They all negotiate in the shadows, and I see one of the Musketeers lean in to whisper something to de Winter's man. Once they've determined the rules of casualty and mortality, they move into a circle of light cast by their torch-bearing lackeys.

Though I'd never laid eyes on them, I had learned something of D'Artagnan's friends, those Musketeers with geographic sobriquets that obviously hid something. Portly bon vivant Porthos; lean Aramis with his holy, romantic air.

And then my breath stops as the third Musketeer's face becomes clear. Taciturn Athos, older than the rest, deadliest of the three even when deeply in his cups, as he often was.

Athos. He took his name from the monastic mountain where all women are forbidden. Even female animals.

I should have known. But how could I? The man I trusted so long ago is dead.

Yet here he stands before me, absently chewing on a bit of braided gold looped on his shoulder, alive. And in that moment, everything I ever felt for him lives again, too. The affection. The betrayal.

Once, I was innocent. Once, when I bore another name, I had a credulous and open heart ready to embrace love. As I watch him, my hand flutters again to my throat. Along the left side, always hidden by a lovelock, is a smooth cicatrix, just barely differing from my own skin in color and texture.

Fury rages in me—fury and fear, one begetting the other. For anger can push someone to rash acts. I want, more than anything, to walk casually up behind him, an unnoticed and unimportant woman, and open his throat, let his blood spill on the thirsty earth. But his friends would end me on the spot. Therein lies the fear. Not of my own death, which has always hovered over me like a kestrel. The fear of losing what I have finally found.

And so, with a wrung and twisted soul, I step back and let Athos fight, let him hide behind his assumed name.

Part 1

Chapter 1

1615

I don't think my father, Lord Paget, had any idea he had a daughter until I became a woman. I wasn't useful until then.

My mother had the rearing of me in our country estate near Yorkshire, a grim and beautiful land that filled my days and my dreams. When I recall my natal home, I envision not the banquet hall nor Maman's sumptuous bedroom, but rather a crenellated speck on the horizon, an anchor in the vastness. We were always outside, Maman and I. She abhorred walls. She told me once that each life has cages enough around it without adding stone and mortar.

She named me Clarice, a prettier version of the old family name, Clarick, which for centuries had been used for boys and girls alike. The Yorkshire folk sometimes called me Lady Clarick when I walked or rode about the countryside. I made no effort to correct them. Nothing changes a Yorkshireman.

When I wasn't with Maman, I romped with the children of the castle. I knew from whispers that some of them were my half brothers and sisters, from the rare but fecund times Lord Paget visited his lands. We ran together over the moors and dared one another to creep into the caves that riddled the dales. Denys, the falconer's son, was an especial favorite. A bit older than me, he was hero and rival all at once. He was bolder even than I, and once got lost in a cave for two days.

Though I was allowed to mix freely, Maman kept careful watch to be sure I didn't pick up their northern accents. She never struck me, never so much as raised her voice at me no matter what mischief I got into, but if I let loose with a *dunna* or *owt* or *nowt*, her eyebrows would dip down and I'd correct myself. She made sure I spoke either rarefied court English, or the elegant French of her own homeland.

By the time my playmates were eight or nine, they were put to work in the fields, the piggery, or household service. When I bemoaned their fate to Maman (with, I must own, a touch of superiority at my own free state), she told me there is nobility in service. Just be sure you only serve the cause of your choice.

For the most part, after that, Maman was my only companion. I still saw Denys, for Maman enjoyed spending time with the old falconer, his father. He was of French birth like herself, and had traveled with her to join the household upon her marriage. Our mews was a pathetic remnant of what it had been in generations past, and our falcons and hawks were old and rarely flew. Still, we were one of the few families below the rank of duke to have a gyrfalcon (though she was half bald and half blind), and we kept the ancient birds comfortable for the honor of the house.

Maman and I were so close that at times I hardly knew which thoughts were my own, and which were hers. Inside the castle, she was mostly silent. Outside, though, in the gardens and across the windswept fields of heather and thyme, she was forever talking to me, teaching me everything under the sun. Knowledge, she counseled me, is a weapon. I laughed, replying that as I had no enemies, I needed no weapons. A woman always has enemies, she said. Gossip, time, loneliness, regret . . .

Then she would brighten and take me through the herb garden where she grew the plants she used to physic the household. The blacksmith drew teeth and sawed off limbs, and my mother, like the lady of every estate, took care of the rest. One day, when I was chatelaine of my own lands, I would do the same, so Maman made sure she passed on her knowledge to me.

On the morning that my life would change, foxglove was in bloom. "Foxglove is very poisonous, *ma chère*," Maman began. "It slows the heart. A handful of leaves in a tisane will calm a racing pulse, such as the stout and the elderly often have. Two handfuls brewed in a decoction will kill the strongest man within an hour. His heart will beat so." She tapped out a rhythm on her thigh, first brisk and healthy, then growing slower. She ended his life with one resounding clap. "And la, that's the end of him."

I bore it patiently, for she'd been teaching me the same things since I could speak sense. She always began with dire warnings about how all these helpful herbs could kill a man if they weren't used exactly right. I supposed that was only natural in a healer. I shouldn't like to poison my patients by mistake.

"Comfrey," she went on, "resembles the foxglove before it is in full flower. It is taken in a tea to help with chest complaints. I often make Lord Paget a brew of comfrey and catmint when the northern cold disagrees with him. But you must never confuse the two."

"Then why do you have them planted right next to each other?" I asked. It seemed that even an experienced herbalist like my mother might make a mistake one day.

She only laughed and said, *"Pour l'amour de la beauté."* The two blossoms looked well together, nothing more.

This was peculiar, too, for unlike the formal gardens on our estate, this one was jumbled, with innocuous treatments like rhubarb and rue growing in disorderly clusters beside hemlock (whose lesson always came with the tale of Socrates) and wolfsbane (which we could not touch ungloved, for its poison could seep through the skin).

It was made for function, not appearance, Maman told me. These plants, she said, are like the finger of God. With them, she could touch any man or woman to the very quick, to their inner parts, and do with them as she pleased. That, she said, is what makes the garden lovely. I wouldn't have called it a beautiful garden, but like all things connected with my mother, I adored it.

We went riding after that, racing across the moors. I had a new mare, a dark bay roan who was proving difficult to handle. Her mettle-someness gave her speed—so long as I gave the mare her head—and for the first time, I beat Maman and her big gray gelding.

"Well done!" she shouted, laughing. I loved to hear her voice big and bold like that under the mauve sky. Inside the castle, she barely spoke above a whisper. I don't remember her *ever* speaking the few times my father was home. Out here, though, she was herself. Even from my youngest days, I understood, dimly, how some of us have to be two people, or three.

We dismounted and loosely hobbled our horses so they could graze. My eyes absently picked up all the things they had been taught to see— the crowberry and hair grass, the winking asphodel in a low boggy spot. I saw the telltale spray of feathers where a hawk had taken down some unfortunate bird, and the rocky crevice that might conceal an adder. I saw the gathering of clouds like a mackerel's speckled sides that told of a storm come evening. Maman said that most folk go through life half blind. She wished to give me the gift of clear sight.

You will think I was a savage, with all this talk of racing and beasts and physicking. Behind the castle stones, Maman taught me the skills a lady needs, too. I didn't have the patience for embroidery, preferring my scenery ready-made and natural, but I had a neat hand and stitched well when I had to. I had an eye for beauty, and though neither my mother nor I cared for weaving, we collaborated on designs that she set her lady's maids to crafting. When I married, I would take them to my husband's house and call them mine, for the genius behind them was my own, if not the menial labor.

She made me spin, though, for endless hours, because she said the distaff and spindle teach patience. People are undone by impatience more than by any other sin, she told me. Greed, lust, anger, murder—they are all the fruits of impatience. Women, above all, need patience.

Further, I could dance, sing, declaim poetry, and strum an adequate tune on the fifteen-string lute. I discoursed upon the latest literature, and partnered with Maman to read the plays of Jonson and Shakespeare aloud for our own amusement. We put on pantomimes of dress-up, wearing her old court gowns and adding assorted frippery to emulate the clever maidens and dashing young men of the dramas and comedies. Once a year, in late spring when the muddy thaw cleared and the roads were passable, we watched the touring actors under a tent at the village fete. Side by side with enthusiastic cottagers, we laughed at the men dressed as women dressed as men in *Twelfth Night*, and thrilled at the court scheming of *Hamlet* and *Macbeth*. This was my glimpse into the world, and I dreamed vaguely of excitement in iambic pentameter.

As the years went by, my body began to fill out Maman's old gowns more completely. I learned to move as a lady moves, to mince in heeled slippers and twitch my fan just so. It was formal and constrained, but it was all acting, and at that age, I thought it fun. I didn't know that every time a man's eyes are on her, a woman has to be acting. She is only herself when she is alone.

I was, my mother said, prepared for almost anything life might fling my way.

Which meant, of course, marriage. What else could there be? Marriage or the nunnery. Even in plays, there are few other options for women, though the lucky ones have some adventure on the road to matrimony. Perhaps the poorhouse, or a tangential existence in some relative's household, but I was not meant to be a maiden aunt.

Marriage was the only choice for me, and I knew even then that I didn't want a marriage like my parents had. Theirs was cold and unfathomable. I craved a marriage of warmth and sunlight, of laughter and conversation. At that age, I firmly believed I was the equal to any man alive, and I wanted a marriage that reflected that.

We sat in the scratchy heather like any Yorkshire milkmaids, our legs outspread, bonnets off, the sun kissing our cheeks. "I have something for you," Maman said, and I clapped my hands in delight. There was still much of the child about me then.

Maman was always giving me presents. Once, it was a lamb to raise; another time, a strange glass she bought from a peddler, which when gazed through made my hand look immense, the lines of my fingertips a geography of valleys and hills. Mostly, though, she gave me things of her own, objects she had kept to herself for many years, things from her childhood in France. Old books, a porcelain figurine, a small jewel. She bade me keep them safe and, as far as possible, secret. From who, I did not know. I knew no one beyond Maman and the castle servants. Our nearest neighbor was a two-day journey away, and some old feud kept us from civility.

Now, Maman drew a small wrapped bundle from beneath her cloak. I felt my excitement growing. I hoped it was a book. I'd read the collection in the castle a hundred times. *The Faerie Queene, Piers Plowman,* and *The Canterbury Tales* in English, and *Gargantua, Pantagruel,* and *Daphnis and Chloe* in French. Her present might be some just-published tale of adventure.

I was deeply disappointed when I saw it was the wrong shape for a book. Maman peeled back the layers of fabric: a rich brocade on the outside, but beneath that, rough oiled cloth.

"*Zut!*" I gasped at what she revealed. A slim dagger, no thicker than my thumb at its widest point, winked in the sun. She drew it from its scabbard, and I looked in amazement. Double-edged, it tapered to a cruel point. The unadorned hilt flared slightly.

If a book gently offered me a phantom of adventure, this weapon seemed to thrust endless possibilities upon me, whether I willed it or no.

I was no stranger to knives. Like most people in the north country, be they man, woman, or child, I carried a blade that I used for everything from paring my nails to spearing my meat at the dinner table. Maman had introduced the Continental habit of forks, but as I've said,

Yorkshire customs are a long time dying. The lady's maids and hangers-on of our small household stabbed at their food as if it might run away. I also had a smaller single-edged knife with a blunt tip that I used for cutting herbs. They were tools, used for benign ends.

This knife my mother held so caressingly in her lap was something else entirely. The moment I saw it, I knew it had one purpose only: to kill.

I felt repulsed by that blade. And yet . . . my finger reached out to touch the deadly edge. My mother shifted to keep it from my reach.

"Do not touch the blade except to clean it. Its sharpness is for other flesh than yours." I had never heard her speak in this tone before. My skin prickled, and I reached for the hilt instead.

Something in me thrilled when I touched it. I held the dagger up before my face. My own reflection, thin and distorted, gazed back at me in the highly polished steel.

"I've taught you about the insides of man," Maman said. Though we were alone with miles of moors between us and the nearest humanity, she spoke in a very low voice, as if she didn't want so much as the dirt beneath us to hear her words. To me they were sharp and clear, burned on my memory.

"You know where the heart lies, and the kidneys. You know where the body's rivers bring blood near the surface." Lightly, she touched parts of her own body: her throat, the hollow of her thigh, the soft curve of her stomach near her navel.

I nodded. Pigs were butchered for the castle weekly, and Maman had taken me to see when they were cut open. Their parts, she'd explained, are very like a man's. And whenever she was called upon to physic one of the servants or villagers, I helped her. She might stitch a wound, slice a vein to purge ill humors, or cup their backs with hot glass. As she worked, she taught. I knew just where the heart nestled warm and snug beneath the ribs, where the thrum of blood pulsed under the skin.

"This blade will reach them all, *mon cœur*," she said, her eyes strangely vivid. "It will slip past bones and slice through meat. It is a fine and subtle instrument."

"But why do I need a knife such as this?" I asked, knowing all the while that I could never abandon it now. Already, it seemed like an extension of my body. Without it, I would be bereft. "I thought you said that knowledge is the only weapon I'll ever need."

"This blade is another form of knowledge," she told me. "When you know you hold the potential of life and death, and other people don't, it gives you power. The best kind of knowledge is secret."

We rode home shortly after that, galloping without speaking. I could feel the chill of the scabbard against my belly, where I'd concealed it beneath my skirts.

Maman couldn't have known what was coming. There had been no message, and he wasn't expected. Still, I cannot quite think it was a coincidence that she gave me the dagger that day. Maman had a way of knowing things.

When we rode our lathered horses into the courtyard, the steward informed us that my father was home from court.

"*Merde*," my mother said under her breath.

In peasant homes, long-absent fathers are greeted instantly with embraces and tears of joy, with heartfelt benedictions and thanks to the maker for their safe return. In our castle, and in other noble households, the master's rare homecoming is a signal for everyone to run to their chambers to make themselves presentable, a panic of propriety. Previous homecomings had been formal and cold, and this, I was sure, would be no different.

Maman summoned her ladies and set them to work. "Never mind about me; see to Clarice. She smells of the stables."

It was true, there was a distinctly horsey air about me. But why did it seem to worry her? Lord Paget had never paid attention to me. I don't mean only that he didn't ask after my little cares, or consult me about affairs of state. I mean that, to the best of my memory, he had never spoken a single word to me. His life was elsewhere. He visited often enough to plant a child in Maman, until my rather difficult birth put an end to that. Afterward, he came to his northern estate but rarely, taking away first one brother, then another, to set them on their way to being soldiers or lawyers or courtiers. But not me. Never me.

I was nothing to him, but overall happiest that way. He frightened me, as children are frightened of pale-eyed bogeymen. When I saw him at lengthy intervals in my childhood, I would watch him from across the hall, or at the far end of the banquet table, and thank my stars he was not the sort of papa to dandle me on his knee. I would have screamed.

Court business must have been pressing, for he had not been here for nearly five years. Still, my suspicion of him lingered. I can't say why. My mother never spoke ill of him, and the servants didn't bear tales. He had done no crime, committed no sin, other than absence, to earn my suspicion. I suppose it was because his coming temporarily stopped all my pleasures, robbed me for a few days or weeks of my mother's close attention.

Or was it the disturbing way Maman transformed when he was here? She seemed to bury her true self somewhere deep within. When we were alone in the castle, Maman was everything—the sun, the stars, the lady of the estate. When Papa arrived, she became nothing. It made me feel sick whenever he came. Yet Maman was strong, clever—there must be some reason behind it that I couldn't fathom at the time.

Or perhaps I feared my father simply for those cold blue eyes that raked over me without seeing. Like death or the devil, he had a way of turning me, too, into nothing.

My mother's ladies stripped me so fast, I scarcely had time to hide my dagger in my bedclothes. They fairly threw me into a clean linen smock, tugging it low over my breasts. I was to wear an old gown of Maman's, nipped in to fit my waist. It was a tedious process for one used to wearing no more than a hastily fastened skirt and bodice over an unlined corset. My body wasn't accustomed to being squeezed in such an undignified manner. Whenever I wore these sorts of clothes before, it had been a masque for my mother's amusement and mine. Now it felt in earnest, as if I were a knight girding on armor.

When I was dressed, Maman came in to examine me. For an instant, I saw her eyes flash with pride and approval. Then she shook her head. "What am I thinking?" she asked herself. "Take it off, all of it." She consulted briefly with one of her ladies-in-waiting, who left and swiftly returned with another dress, neat and serviceable, a lady's dress, but drab brown and unadorned. The bodice snugged high against my throat, and my chest was pressed flat.

"Did I do something wrong, Maman?" I asked, but she did not have time to answer.

Before I knew it, I was standing in the great hall with the rest of the household. The servants lined up in fidgety rows at the lower end, while my mother, in the full court dress of twenty years ago, waited patiently at the head of the hall. I started to go to her, but she shooed me with a gesture back to the line of her ladies-in-waiting.

You'll think a lady-in-waiting is a grand thing, and so she is at the king's court. There, the queen's ladies are the daughters of dukes, and foreign princesses. Their duties are light—holding a fan, aiding a love affair. Mostly, they are there to converse with the queen, bear the brunt of her occasional spite, and provide lovely foils to her grandeur, until they are married off.

My mother's ladies-in-waiting were much more humble specimens. The loftiest of them was the sister of a knight who spoke of little more than the age of her family name and the current decrepitude of the family fortunes. There was the ruddy-cheeked daughter of a yeoman farmer whose loud, infectious laugh and good nature made up for her garish manners. One was a lawyer's daughter, another a pretty and penniless orphan, niece of the estate's steward. Their title might have been impressive, but in truth, they were mostly maids, airing Maman's bedding, mending her clothes, and drawing her bath. At dinner, they would sit near Maman and me and chatter with us; so, as is usual in the country, the servants were midway between slave and family.

I thought I would be unnoticed among them. Lord Paget was here to see Maman, and to be certain that all his acres were providing the most income possible. He would care for me no more than for my mother's women, I was sure.

When he stepped into the hall, everyone fell instantly silent. I hadn't seen him for at least five years. I had been a veritable child then, scrawny and wild. My father had changed, too. The acres must have been providing, for he'd grown infinitely finer in clothes and manner.

He moved with studied grace through the center of the chamber. He was dressed in the most stunning garments I had ever seen. His tightly fitted doublet was a shimmering white that gleamed like mother-of-pearl, embroidered all over with golden sunbursts. On his legs he wore the kind of short puffed breeches I'd heard about but never seen. They were the lush black of a midnight forest, stitched with silver flowers and vines. His hose were an alarming crimson, the hue of fresh-spilled blood. Fine Flanders lace made clouds at his wrist and throat. He looked more costume than man, a walking wardrobe.

But no, there were those pale blue eyes, sliding critically sideways over his assembled household. However fine the clothes, the man was still inside. He had never dressed so well before. He must have had some promotion at court.

Halfway across the room, my father made a formal bow. The rapier belted at his waist swung up provocatively erect, challenging the room. Maman returned his greeting with a deep, graceful sweep of her skirts, sinking almost to the floor and rising with her head demurely bowed. She looked physically smaller, weaker. It was hard to believe this was the same woman who had only this morning galloped across the moors like a Valkyrie. I didn't understand how she managed the dramatic change, as if her very nature had shifted. When I examined her, I couldn't see any tension in her face. She didn't look like she was acting. She had simply *become* different.

I wondered if I could do it, if I tried.

He walked toward her again, lifting his feet in a peculiar affectation like a cat on ice. There was a little sneer on his mouth as he glanced right, no doubt noticing that Denys's shoes had splashes of falcon excrement on them, then left, toward the ladies-in-waiting and myself. I held myself still, prepared to be ignored, or at most briefly noticed and as soon dismissed. Five years ago I'd been an adolescent, coltish and pimpled. I hoped I made a better impression now.

Lord Paget stopped abruptly. His eyes locked on me. Not on my own eyes, but simply on me, wandering over my body as if it were a specimen. I lowered my head self-consciously, and in a panic made an inventory of my person. Were my shoes clean? My hair tidy? Had my petticoat and skirt hem accidentally caught in my bodice fastening, showing the world my drawers? All these years, and he had never acknowledged my existence.

Timidly, I raised my head to meet his gaze, which lingered lower for a moment, then finally found my eyes. My heart beat wildly. My father! For the first time, I felt a tentative surge of affection. Perhaps he was not so scary. That was just childish fancy, the fear of the unknown. For now he was looking at me, smiling. I ventured a small smile in return, making myself be bold.

But he held my gaze, and though I couldn't describe what I saw there, it made my flesh creep. It certainly wasn't paternal love.

He regarded me a moment longer, then continued to Maman. He kissed her hand, and then they retreated together. The entire banquet hall exhaled in relief. I was left with a curious dread in the pit of my stomach.

The servants dispersed, but Denys strolled up to me with a grin. He was near twenty, but my milk brother. His mother, a Yorkshire woman, had nursed me when Maman's milk failed. (She perished of the white plague a few years later.) As children, we would play from sunup to sundown, me always a step behind my hero as I struggled to keep pace. Other lads might have slipped away, annoyed at a young, female burden. Not Denys. He showed me snake's eggs and four-leaf clovers, and how to tickle trout in the stream. And he always, always waited for me when I fell behind. When I grew older and left most of my peasant playmates behind, I'd still seek him out in the mews.

Lately, though, I almost never saw him. Weeks, months would pass without us meeting, and I decided he was avoiding me, too caught up in adult concerns these days to care about playing with a child. It was bound to happen, but I both yearned for him and resented his desertion.

Now, though, we slipped easily into our old childhood camaraderie. I remembered how he could switch from the most elegant French to almost indecipherable Yorkshire dialect, and always had a joke for me. Like my mother, he used to make me little presents—the glossy feather of a rare black stork, dark with a green and purple sheen; a pebble with a winking bit of opal; a chubby baby dormouse. I still kept them all in a box in my chamber—except the dormouse, of course. That wee greedy beast all but lived on my shoulder and gorged himself to death on hazelnuts and marzipan within a year.

"Would you believe it?" Denys said as we walked out of the hall, my wide skirts brushing his leg. "Isolde laid an egg."

I forgot that strange feeling my father's look had given me, and burst out laughing. "At her age?"

"The old biddy has a bit of life left in her. It's unfertilized, of course. Unless Robber got to her." Robber was the only male in the mews, a little merlin who thought very well of himself.

"Could they really?" I asked. I tried to picture the petite gaudy bird atop the dignified old matriarch, and laughed again.

"No. Some birds can crossbreed, but not those two. Come on, Isolde wants to show it off." He took my hand and pulled me along to the mews. My bare skin had hardly been touched by a male since my rough-and-tumble days of play with the servants' children. Even the stable lads who helped me mount took care. Denys grabbed my fingers as though it were the most natural thing in the world, and it felt like flint striking steel, making a spark that leaped from my hand to my heart.

It was a day of odd sensations. This one, though pleasant, was no less baffling.

In the mews, I praised Isolde for her egg. She'd crafted a makeshift nest of her own feathers and a bit of bone she'd regurgitated from some prior meal. There she hunkered with her speckled breast puffed, protecting a chick that would never be. She snapped at me when I tried to touch her, though she was usually very gentle. She'd known me all my life.

"I'll take it away in a few days," Denys said. "But for now, she deserves to think she's accomplished something."

"How sad, to lose a child," I said. "Even one that's just an empty egg."

"You're so tenderhearted," Denys said. We stood as close as my skirts allowed. I looked up into his face. I was tall for a woman, but he was taller still. I was so used to that face, the green jasper of his eyes, the fine features framed by shaggy, sandy hair. I knew that countenance as well as my mother's, and better than my own, for we had only one mirror in the castle. It was a face to be easy with.

"I've always loved that about you," he went on. "The care you lavish on small animals, your generous way with the servants, especially yours truly."

"Which are you?" I asked with a smile. "Servant or small animal?"

"Your humble servant, of course," he answered, then gave a crooked smile. "Though, do you remember how Sylvan used to perch on your breast while you fed him sweetmeats?" Sylvan was the dormouse.

He said no more than this, but something seemed to give way within me, so that I felt suddenly weak and dizzy.

"I . . . I should go." I picked up my skirts, suddenly conscious that the fine material was scraping a floor full of straw and guano.

I felt his eyes burning on me as he watched me leave.

When my father found me in the passageway just outside the mews, I was flushed and flustered.

"What have we here?" he asked. His voice was higher pitched than I would have imagined. I thought he would loom intimidatingly tall, but we were of a height exactly. Both of us were wearing heels.

"My lord," I said, bobbing a curtsy. I couldn't bring myself to call him Papa.

He stepped closer, and I could feel the wall at my back. Was he going to embrace me? Why was he suddenly noticing me after all these years?

I should have been glad that he was finally paying attention to me, but instead I was suspicious.

"I heard that Lady Paget had a new handmaid," he said. His breath was stale.

"Y-yes, my lord." I was thoroughly puzzled. It was true that the steward's niece had entered my mother's service only a month ago, but why was he talking with me about household affairs?

"You are so sweet," he said, stroking my cheek with the back of his hand. "So fair." He twined a lock of my blond hair around his fingers and stepped closer, a feat I had not thought possible. I was now pressed flat against the stones, and our garments were touching all along the front of our bodies.

"Are you a good girl?" he asked. I had to make myself not turn away from his breath. I dared not cause offense. "If you are a good girl, I'll give you a gold coin. Would you like that?"

It occurred to me that after five years' absence, he must still think of me as the thirteen-year-old I was, pimpled and scarcely out of short skirts. It must be hard for him to suddenly strike up a conversation with a grown daughter. He might even feel guilty about showing me so little attention before now.

I almost wished he had continued his old habits. I was decidedly uncomfortable.

"Do you know what a good girl does?" he asked me. "A good girl never tells."

He put his hand on my bosom, rubbing with the palm. I can't imagine he got much joy of it, as my corset and wooden busk made a hard, flat line, and the bodice of my old-fashioned dress rose to my throat.

"Lord Paget!" I tried to cry, but then his mouth was upon me, lips like worms and stinking breath, and I was crushed.

Suddenly, he was ripped away from me. I saw Denys wrestling with him. Denys was stronger, and he easily heaved my father across the passageway.

"Insolent varlet!" my father cried. "You'll hang for laying hands on me!"

"Lord Paget, this is your daughter," Denys said firmly.

My father gaped, his mustachioed mouth working like a whiskered carp. "She . . . I . . . she's not a lady-in-waiting?"

"No, sir. She is Lady Clarice, your only daughter."

"But my daughter is . . ." He counted up on his fingers, his face pale. Then he forced a hearty laugh. "Of course she is! That was only a test of her virtue. She has passed admirably. Her mother has raised her to be a proper lady. She'll make some man an honest wife."

He pulled Denys aside, and I could plainly hear him offer the lad gold for his silence. Apparently, a good boy never tells, either. To my surprise, Denys accepted. I heard the coins clinking, then my father stalked away without a backward glance at me.

You will notice that even then it was the men who conferred and schemed. Though one was a lord, the other a mere assistant falconer, it was the men who made the decisions. I was not considered.

Alone, I panted against the wall. "What just happened?" I asked Denys.

"Your fool father mistook you for a servant ripe for seducing," he said.

"You mean he intended to . . ."

"To do what Robber would like to do to Isolde, if he were able."

Foremost in my mind was not the question of incest. It was natural he did not recognize the face of a daughter he had never spoken to. That wasn't his crime. But to think that a lone virgin in this household could be so accosted. What if I had in truth been a servant? He would have almost absolute power over me. At the very least, I would be cast out, penniless, for refusing him. If I truly vexed him, he might trump up any charge he liked and see me flogged in the village square, or pilloried, or hung. He might never have exercised it, but he held that power in his fist, and any servant would know it.

They could not have said no. Many men would have considered him a gentleman for offering coin for what he could have taken for free.

My father was a monster after all.

"And you took his gold?" I asked Denys with bitterness. I thought he at least would have been better than that.

He shrugged. "He had my silence anyway. Why not take his gold in the bargain? It might be useful one day."

"What will Maman say when she knows?" I felt more sorry for every other woman than for myself.

"Clarice," he said gently, laying a hand on my arm, "everybody knows what your father is. Half the children in this castle are his get, and a fair number of the village brats, too. Telling your mother about this particular incident would do no good."

"Poor Maman!" I said. "But something must be done to stop him. He can't go about . . . violating women."

"What shall I do, eh? Tell the village priest? Perhaps you'd like me to murder Lord Paget in his sleep? Talk to him, man-to-man? Oh, Clarice, this is what the world is." His fingers brushed my cheek, wiping away the memory of my father's vile touch. "Only know that all men aren't like your father. Far too many are, but not all. It shouldn't be like that—coarse and brutal, coercion or transaction."

He touched my hair. He kissed me lightly on the lips.

"Love should be tender. You should be willing."

I should have screamed, or slapped him, or called for our elderly castle guards to haul him away.

But I didn't.

Not even when he kissed me again.

My mother wasn't there when I entered her chambers, so I sat on a velvet cushion to wait. I had resolved not to tell her what my father had attempted. And yet, I needed the comfort that only she could provide. Maybe I could awaken her from the staid, demure state my father's visit seemed to have put her in, and we could scheme to keep him so occupied he had no time to foist himself on the women of our house.

Or perhaps a concoction of valerian and chamomile. If he was busy during the day, and slept soundly after dark, the castle girls would be safe. Oh, but that would be a weak formula. Perhaps valerian with a pinch of something stronger. I ran through all the herb lore Maman had taught me. Dosage was all, she often said, the difference between cure and poison. A leaf or two of belladonna, perhaps, or the most minuscule bit of wolfsbane would put him out for the night.

I gasped. I was thinking of poisoning my own father!

No, I corrected myself. I was contemplating giving him an unsolicited medical treatment for his disease.

I heard voices outside Maman's chamber. One of them was Lord Paget. Like Polonius in *Hamlet*, which we once saw staged by a group of traveling mummers, I scurried behind a long hanging tapestry and hoped I would not meet Polonius's grisly end.

"She's a woman grown, Victoire," my father said. "I've never seen such glowing golden hair, such a flawless complexion. And her figure! She will set the Thames afire. She'll be the toast of Whitehall."

"My lord, she is scarcely more than a child, untutored in the world's ways." Mother's voice was soft and reasonable, but I could feel the tension in it thrumming like the strings of a viol.

"She's eighteen, and at court they say a woman's past her prime at eighteen, and a positive medlar at twenty, rotten before she's ripe. I warrant she'll secure herself no less than a duke before she's there a fortnight. Perhaps she can even aim higher."

"Higher than a duke?" Maman asked. "That's a very small number of candidates, most of them already wed, I believe."

"The best one isn't, though."

"You can't mean Charles?" Charles was the younger son of the king, heir to the crown now that his elder brother, Henry, died a few years ago. "He could only marry a princess, and a foreigner at that to cement one union or another."

"Perhaps," my father owned. "But he is fifteen, and all fifteen-year-old boys are like bucks in rut. A marriage made in secret may be legitamized later. At the least, its annulment might buy a duchy."

"Your ambition flies high," Maman said. "She is but a baron's daughter."

"You've been away from royal courts too long. You forget the power of a beauty as exquisite as Clarice's. Yours certainly charmed me against my better judgment all those years ago. My sons have served the family well. Now it's her turn. A good marriage will lift us higher. A great liaison might do even more. She's old enough to marry. She's coming to court."

"But, my lord! Please, give me another year with her. There is so much she doesn't know."

I thought he would be angry that she was opposing him. But my father's voice when he answered was soft and lazy, as if he were talking about the weather with a farmer. There was no need to have an argument when there was no chance of him losing it. Whatever he decided was law for the family. "What she doesn't know, I will teach her."

"Then let me come to court with her. I was one of Marie de' Medici's ladies. I know how to navigate the intrigues of a royal court."

"A woman's place is in the home," he said.

"*Précisément*," Maman replied. "And so Clarice should remain here, educated by me, unsullied by the world, until she is ready to take her place as wife to a man of our choosing."

"You would marry her to some bumpkin of a baron with hundreds of acres and thousands of sheep, whom His Majesty has never heard of? There are many kinds of wealth in this world, my dear, but the only one that matters is the trust of the king. I have that now—in part. Soon, I hope to have more. In time, I could be one of the rulers of the land, one of the powers behind the crown."

I heard him leave.

"Clarice," Maman said, "you can come out now."

"I'm sorry I eavesdropped, Maman," I said in a small voice.

"*Quelle absurdité*," she replied. "A woman has to know where she stands in the world, and all too often no one is willing to tell her. You have to find out for yourself, by whatever means necessary." Her voice had an edge to it.

"I have to leave you?" I asked, tears welling.

"*Ma souris*, children always have to leave their mothers. It is the curse of being a woman, one of the few we can't overcome with cleverness. I'd hoped you wouldn't have to marry for a few more years at least, and then . . ." She sighed, and I saw her hands working nervously, squeezing at each other as if each were a small struggling animal she had to subdue. I realized she wasn't just sad to be losing me. She was angry. Furious. She tried, but she couldn't hide it.

"I had so many plans for you, Clarice. All your life I managed to turn his eyes away from you, to make him forget you. Ill favored, I called you whenever he asked, or sickly, until he stopped asking. This time I tried to hide you among my ladies-in-waiting, hoping he would pass over you. I hoped to have another year or two. But some fool must have told him who you were, curse it. I should have sent you away the moment I knew he was here!"

"Plans?" I wondered aloud. "Did you have a man in mind?"

She looked just the slightest bit scornful, which was another way I could tell how distraught she was. "Is there no higher ambition on your mind, my love?"

I bowed my head, chagrined, but thought, What does she mean? She had taught me so much . . . except what, exactly, to strive for. All of my lessons had practical implications for a role as wife, mother, chatelaine, herbalist, healer. I had come to realize that doing any one of those things well was an accomplishment in itself, and beyond the scope of most of the people Maman and I helped each day. To do them all superbly, as I was trained to do, would place me in a sphere beyond that of most women.

But that, I thought, is not what she meant. I had never before marveled that she took such care with my education, but assumed that every mother schooled her girl-children so. And yet, it now began to tickle my mind that she might have some other plans for me. I thought of Viola shipwrecked, of spirited, plotting Portia, and felt a frisson of anticipation jolt through my shock and sorrow. I wanted to ask, but seeing her so upset, my foremost thought was to soothe her.

"Don't worry, Maman. I don't want to go, but just think of everything you've taught me. A daughter of yours can survive anything."

She threw her arms around me. "I know you can, Clarice. But there are things I haven't told you. Things I don't even know if I *should* tell you. I've spent my life . . . But no. You deserve a better life than mine."

"Have you been unhappy, Maman?" I asked.

"Never with you, *mon bijou!* But my life has been spent waiting, always waiting, for a call that never came. I married to serve a cause, my child."

I thought she must mean that her family was impoverished, that she had married my father for money. It is a common enough tale.

"Ah," she went on, "maybe this will be for the best. Mayhap at court you will find a man worthy of your love. A man who will cherish you and protect you. A marriage, when it is a union of loving equals, is not such a bad thing."

"I don't want to leave you, Maman!" I cried, and held her tight, weeping.

And yet there was a certain allure in my new future. Much as I would miss my mother, I had begun, vaguely, to think of other things. That kiss from Denys meant nothing, of course, because he was only a commoner. But it sparked piquant fantasies.

Maman had been everything to me, but the *only* thing, really, all of my life.

Soon I would be in a world I had only read about, seen on a makeshift stage—a magical realm of light and music, of witty conversation and politics and poetry.

And so, though my grief was unfeigned, there was an adventuresome spark beneath it that I didn't let Maman see.

"I have another gift for you," she said. I watched her press a panel of her wall here, there, and then a little hidden cabinet sprang open. It was so cleverly constructed that when it was closed, no one could know it was there. I saw papers inside, a glass vial, a small pile of jewels. Maman left these things and took out a piece of ivory, closing the door swiftly.

"It's a busk," I said as I examined it. I had worn one when dressing up for practice. I wore one today. It was meant to be placed in a pocket at the front of my corset to keep my stomach and chest in that firm, flat shape fine clothing demanded. It pushed my bosoms up almost to my shoulders. In my high-necked gown, it made little difference, but Maman had told me that in more fashionable circles, dresses were worn so low that the bosoms would all but hop out, ballooning upward with each breath.

The busk was marked with three carved fleur-de-lis, the stylized lilies emblematic of France, Maman's mother country. There were words, too.

"*Un pour tous*," I read. "*One for all*. What does it mean?"

Maman closed her eyes for a moment. "In the tide of great affairs, it is not the many who make the crucial choices, but the individual. Mobs do not decide the fate of the world, nor even armies. It is always one man—or one woman—often unknown to history, working in secret, dedicated to a greater good, who shifts the tides."

Her words made me feel strange—grand, somehow, but also small.

"I'll speak more of that tomorrow. We'll have a week or two at least, and there is a great deal I must tell you, secrets I had meant to keep until you were married. But for tonight, this is enough. This busk is made for a particular purpose. Do you see the opening here?"

She tilted it so I could see the top. For a moment, I was puzzled, then my eyes opened wide. "It's just the right size for my new dagger."

Maman nodded. "I had them made together, before I was wed. The busk will hold your blade perfectly secure and concealed. But you will know it's there, close to your heart, should you ever need it."

I still couldn't imagine why I would ever need it, or why, in fact, Maman had needed it before her marriage. But it comforted me to know I would have a piece of Maman near to me no matter how far away she was.

I burned with curiosity to hear the secrets she had to tell me. I thought they might have something to do with the wedding night. I had asked Cook about it once, and she'd told me to watch pigs in springtime. That experience hadn't left me much enlightened.

I'd thought to have more time, to get used to the idea of leaving Maman, and to get to know my father, to see if there was any good in him after all. But when I woke the next morning, I found that the servants had already packed my things and readied the coach.

"You can't take her yet," Maman pleaded as I was bundled, all unprepared, into the creaking carriage.

"Why let moss grow on my plan? The Howard faction needs to go, so the Paget and Villiers families can rise."

"And you will use our daughter to achieve your ends?"

"Why else have children? A woman, however limited her abilities or empty her brain, can achieve some things a man can't. She can ferret out secrets with a giggle, or inspire jealousy, even duels. Using her beauty, I can contrive to twist half the men at court to my particular ends."

How cold and calculating he sounded as he discussed my fate.

"Do you have a specific plan?" Maman asked more sharply than she usually spoke to my father. I was intensely curious, too. How could I possibly do any of those things?

"I have a few ideas, and will consult with my allies about others. Now tell me, is Clarice a resourceful girl? Obedient? Can she think, and speak without simpering?"

"She is clever," Maman said. "More clever than she knows, I think."

"Clever enough to hide what brains she has, I hope."

I embraced my mother then, clinging as if I would never let go. I felt numb.

"I will follow as soon as I am able," Maman swore as she pressed a rosary into my hand. My tears fell on the rosary, and I saw it in a blur. It was a curious thing, made of what looked on first inspection to be red beads with tiny black staring eyes.

"Keep your secrets," Maman whispered fiercely in my ear, "for they are your treasure. Keep your knowledge, for that is your weapon. Speak softly to your enemies, and make them love you. And when you strike your foes, be sure they never know who wielded the weapon. Men fight with swords face-to-face, over stupid quarrels. When you do battle, do it quietly, in the dark."

I took in her words, stored them like precious jewels in my heart, beneath the dagger. I didn't fully understand them or realize how they would guide my life. But they were her last gift to me, and precious.

Chapter 2

And then we were rolling away, and I was alone with my father for the second time in my life, praying it would go better than the first.

I had more leisure to look at him now as I sat across from him. He was slight of build, with hair a shade or two darker than my own, graying at the temples. He wore it in long curled locks. Though he was dressed for traveling today, his small mustache was impeccably curled, and his beard combed to a merciless point. He wore pearl studs in his ears, and a cloud of heavy perfume wafted off him, tickling my nose.

In short, my father was what the fashionable people of the time called a fop.

I didn't know what to say to this stranger who had sired me. After an eternity of jostling, he spoke first.

"While you are with me, you must obey me in everything. The reason behind some of my commands might not be clear to you, but still, you must always do exactly as I say if you want to succeed at court. It's a dangerous place, full of whispers and intrigue, but with my guidance, you can go far."

"You intend me to marry?" I asked, secretly running my fingers over the beads of Maman's rosary.

"Eventually," he said. "There may be more important things to do first." Then, as casually as if he was inquiring after my health, he asked, "Are you a virgin?"

I blushed and looked down.

Striking like an adder, he grabbed my wrist, grinding the bones together as he squeezed tight. I gasped. "This is a matter of the greatest import, Clarice. No games with me, as you value your life. Are you a virgin?"

His grip hurt, and frightened me. I had never been roughly handled. My first thought was for my knife, but I quickly dismissed that notion. What, slay my father in his coach with his retinue all around us? A moment later, I realized I could very likely shake him off. Though he was hurting me, I could tell he wasn't all that strong. I was his size, and what's more, years of riding and working in the garden had left me strong as a peasant.

But I did nothing. My strength and will were a secret I should hide. My treasure. I let him manhandle me until he thought I was cowed and released me. "I am pure," I whispered. The word felt false. Why would it make me impure? Were all married women impure, and all virgins destined for impurity? I found it hard to see my mother as a soiled and sullied creature.

Still, it was the answer he was looking for. I rubbed the red marks on my wrist until he patted me on the head and apologized.

"We have to be a team, you and I. No," he corrected himself, "we are an army. A small army. I, the general, and you, my only soldier. We are going into a great battle, and you must follow my commands if we are to win it." How frightened a soldier must feel when he doesn't trust his commander. "The prize for victory is the kingdom itself. Well, perhaps not the kingdom, but such land, and influence, and titles as are overall better than a kingdom. You will see that kings are but sorry creatures, at the mercy of their minions."

"And we will get the king in our power?" I asked.

"You're a sharp little thing," he said.

I stared out in the other direction, willing myself to think clearly, but my brain was all in a whirl. Thanks to Maman, I knew so much. Philosophy and poetry, languages and healing. Maman had taught me how to observe the world, and she always pushed me in her gentle and loving way to think, and think some more, about every question I encountered. Would any of those things be useful in this intimidating place known as court?

As I was looking out, lost and alone, I was surprised by a familiar face riding with the guards and servants behind the coach. It was Denys, his sandy hair blowing in the wind. Isolde perched, hooded, on his gloved fist.

Without weighing my words, I almost asked, "Why is Denys traveling with us?" But some new awareness taught me I should learn to think before I spoke, so instead I said, "Why is Isolde traveling with us?"

"Who?" my father asked.

"The gyrfalcon." I pointed out of the coach. "There, on the fist of that lad." I pretended I had no idea who he was. My father would probably not expect a lady of his family to be able to distinguish among the servants.

"The king's last gyrfalcon died, and none of his falconers have managed to find a wild chick to replace her. Ours might be ancient, but she is a gyrfalcon, and the province of kings. I thought a gift of her might win me favor. *Us* favor." He smiled and patted my hand, and I managed to not recoil from his touch.

"And the boy is her caretaker?" I asked carefully, as if I didn't recognize the one who had saved me from my father's misguided advances.

My father shrugged. "Your mother recommended he go with the fowl. She said he has a rare way with the bird, and it wouldn't do for her to die along the way, or as soon as she is presented. Besides, the lad wanted to see London. He's a likely enough boy."

One who can keep your secrets, you suppose. If it had been me, I'd have kept anyone with a secret about me as far from London as possible. Not that he had anything to fear from Denys, but had he been inclined to gossip, he would have just had a wider and more influential audience.

From the carriage, I watched Denys under pretense of observing passing scenery. However hard I gazed, though, Denys never looked back at me.

Though his clothes were rough, Denys rode like a knight, and looked like a king with Isolde on his fist. I remembered that kiss, soft first, like a petal brushing against me, then harder, as if his mouth demanded something from mine. Surely, there was no harm in a kiss.

There would never be another, though. My father meant me for something else—for some*one* else. As we bounced along the rutted road to the clomp of horses and the creaking of carriage chains, a shadowy figure seemed to loom before me, shrouded, faceless. He was my future, and I didn't even know him yet. How strange to realize there is a man out there somewhere in the world whom I would one day belong to.

We stopped that first night at an inn. My father and I each had a room, while the servants made do with the stables and hayloft. Dinner was kidney pie and small beer, served by the innkeeper himself. I had never eaten in a public place before. I felt the eyes of other travelers on me, and looked down at my greasy pie.

"Now you begin your education," my father said in a voice too low to carry. "Do you know anything about love?"

After a long while, I said, "I've read stories of love."

"There are two kinds of love," my father told me. "Storybook love, the love you feel for another, is the kind that makes you weak, a slave. Never let yourself fall in love, Clarice."

"Do you love Maman?" I asked abruptly. He ignored me and went on.

"There is another kind of love, a love that is power and control. The love *others* have for *you*. That's the love you have to master and use for your family's best interests. A man who fancies himself in love will make fatal missteps. Do you see that moth?"

He pointed to a dusty-winged creature helplessly circling the candles in the iron chandelier above our heads. "Which would you rather be, the moth or the flame?" As he asked, the poor little moth immolated itself in the fire, crumpling and falling in a tiny toasted heap to the floor.

I thought of Denys's kiss. It had felt strangely like a flashing fire inside me, as when dry leaves touch flame. It felt as if I had lost myself in one blazing instant.

"The flame," I said, pushing aside the odd desire to be consumed.

He nodded. "You know nothing of the nature of men, the way they will lust after what they cannot have, pay any price for possession. And you don't know the nature of women, how they will feign innocence and yet sell themselves to the highest bidder. It is the way of the world, and as we live in this world, we must participate."

Much as I disliked my father, I noticed that he was talking to me almost as an equal now. I felt proud. I didn't realize he was sharpening me, giving me an edge as if I were his sword.

"At court," he went on, "you will make men love you. They will give up state secrets, abandon their legal wives, neglect their children, all for your sake. Some will gladly die for you. You can do this easily, because you're beautiful and of a good family. But I will tell you a secret: any woman with half an ounce of sense can do the same. There is power between your legs—as long as they remain closed."

Maman had spoken of power, too, and this made me pay even closer heed to my father's words.

"I'll show you how easy it is for a man to get what he wants from a woman untrained in the ways of power. Watch, and learn." He raised his voice. "Innkeep!"

The man came tableside, wiping his hands clean on a rag. "My lord?"

"My child has need of a lady's maid for the night. Have you a daughter fit to attend her?"

The innkeeper wrung the rag tightly in his hands, looking nervously over his shoulder. "My lord, my good wife could attend you," he offered.

"Nay, someone younger," my father said, giving the landlord a meaningful look. He drew a money bag from his belt. "Someone fresh and delicate, as befits my girl." He nodded to me.

"My eldest daughter lives with her husband a mile from here. I could send a lad on horseback . . ."

"Younger," my father said, drawing out a coin. Having never made a purchase, I had little idea of the value of money, but the innkeeper's eyes lit up. My father added another coin, shining silver.

"I . . . I have another daughter."

"Fetch her," my father commanded. When the innkeeper left, he turned to me and said, "Innkeepers always have another daughter. They keep them in stock, and borrow 'em from a neighbor when they run short."

Before long, a pretty little maiden came up to our table. She was finely built, with wrists that looked like they would snap as easily as sparrow bones, and a twist of russet hair. She must have been my age, but her tiny build made her seem younger. She couldn't bring herself to raise her eyes to my father, but sneaked a shy glance at me.

My father regarded her for a long moment with that same look he'd bestowed on me yesterday, before he knew who I was. The look that made my skin crawl.

"Yes," he said at last in a caressing tone. "You will do nicely. Please go upstairs and wait in the room on the right."

He waved her away before I had a chance to say, "But mine is the room on the left. I thought you said she was to serve *me*."

"Oh, she is, sweet child. To serve as a lesson in what *not* to be. You see, any man can find a willing woman. When I am through with you, you will appear to men as the unwilling woman who can't help herself, the pure maiden overcome—almost—by a man's love."

He took my wrist again, more gently than in the carriage, though the old bruises hurt beneath his fingers. "But whatever your own desire— and women have desires, too—you must never give yourself to a man. Never, without my express permission. If you do . . ." His fingers tightened. "Together, we can make you next best thing to a queen. But if you betray me by giving your favors without my approval, I'll kill you, or lock you in a nunnery. You are my property until I give you to another man." His voice sweetened. "And even then, dear girl, I'm sure you will always serve your father well."

He patted my hand, and rose to teach me my lesson on the body of the innkeeper's daughter.

I fumed with rage, and with a feeling of utter helplessness. Willing? That child wasn't willing. She'd been sold by an avaricious father to a lord too powerful to be denied. Her virtue would be ruined. Purity might count for little in my philosophical brain, but reputation certainly did. She might fall pregnant. All because my father wanted to teach me a lesson about the world. (I was too naive to realize he would have done the same thing that night even if he'd been traveling alone, though with less thought and pontification beforehand.)

But what could I do? How could I defy my father? I pictured storming into the room and denouncing him. He'd laugh and have me hauled out. Could I drug him, as I'd thought to before? I had no herbs, no potions. I could burn the inn down, I thought wildly . . . and destroy a man's livelihood, and possibly kill all inside. Was it worth it, to save a girl from violation?

Yes! something screamed inside me. I eyed the candles with their leaping flame. I felt reckless with anger.

Then another voice, like my mother's, spoke calmly in my head. *There is always a way to achieve your ends. All it takes is cleverness, secrecy, and boldness.*

First, I hurried outside to the unkempt kitchen garden that sprawled in the back, plucking a common weed with my hem and stuffing it into the pocket that hung beneath my skirt. Then I ran to the stables and called Denys's name.

He crawled out of a pile of hay, rubbing his eyes. "My lady?" His formal address reminded me the guards and other servants were listening.

Making my voice haughty, I said, "Boy, my father asked me to check on our most beloved gyrfalcon before we retired for the night. Pray bring me to her." I held my head high, and wrinkled my nose slightly at the stable stench, as though I hadn't spent some of my happiest moments amid the smell of horse droppings.

"At once, Lady Clarice. Step this way. If you would take my arm?" Gallantly, he guided me around the prone men and steaming horse pats to the perch where Isolde sat, puffed and sleeping. I squeezed his arm with gentle pressure, hoping he understood and would play along.

"I have heard tell of a fainting sickness among falcons," I said loudly enough for those nearby to hear. "A most terrible condition where they fall into a fit, stiff on their backs with their beaks hanging open." I gave Denys my most eloquent look. "My father is in such fear of that disease that he insists he be summoned immediately should there be the least sign of it. Kindly check Isolde for any symptoms."

Denys, you see, had such a way with the birds that he could charm even the fiercest. Isolde, his special pet, would allow him to stroke the soft feathers of her breast until she went into a sort of trance. He could tip her on her back and rock her like a baby, stroking her into calm. I had never seen another falcon act that way. Perhaps it was only because she was half dead anyway.

He gave me a questioning look, and I nodded. With a little shrug, he began stroking the snoozing bird. She stirred in her sleep, then sighed and let her body go limp. I cried out in pretend alarm. "No! Not our precious gyrfalcon! Do your best, and I'll fetch Lord Paget."

I now had my excuse in hand and my ingredients hidden away as I ran to my father's room and pounded on the door.

"God's eyeballs!" he roared. "This better be important, or on my life, I'll flay . . ." He opened the door and saw me. Behind him, weeping on the bed but mercifully still dressed, was the innkeeper's daughter.

"Papa!" I cried, using that term of endearment for the first time in my life. "The gyrfalcon is dying. You must go at once." He hesitated, and I reminded him, "The king's favor depends on that bird." With copious curses, he pulled his disheveled garments around him and quit the room.

Instantly, I was at the girl's side. "My father means you harm. Do you know what he intends to do?"

She nodded, great tears rolling down her cheeks.

"Do you want to let him? Is this your choice?"

She shook her head. "My father . . . the silver . . ." she stammered.

"Then you must do exactly as I tell you. Quickly, before he returns." Then, wincing at the burning pain, I handed her the cluster of stinging nettles and told her what to do.

For a moment, her pretty eyes glowed with relief and she looked on me as a savior. Then her face clouded again. "But my father will beat me if I don't return with the silver."

I had no coin myself, nor any jewels to give her. Then it struck me. "I know how you can have my father's coin after all," I said with a smile, and gave her more directions.

I returned to my own room. A quarter hour later, my father returned. I heard sounds of muffled protest, a feminine squeal, my father's laugh . . . Then he shouted, "The pox! Get out of here, you vile strumpet!" A moment later, I heard the girl bundled into the hallway, and the door slammed behind her.

The angry redness and huge lumps caused by applying stinging nettle to the nether regions couldn't be pleasant, but the symptoms would subside within the hour, unlike the deadly pox they imitated. My father would think he had a lucky escape, and the girl was safe. As instructed, she would then go to the stables and tell Denys that Lady Clarice commanded he give her one gold coin—one of the three my father had given him the day before.

My own hands still burned like fire when I lay my head down on the pillow, but I didn't care. My heart sang with triumph. My father had indeed taught me a valuable lesson: any manner of opponent can be defeated.

"I ought to be mad at you," Denys whispered as I mounted the coach the next morning. "Giving away my hard-earned gold like that. Luckily,

Lord Paget gave me three more for saving Isolde's life." He gave me a secret grin, then ignored me for the next three days.

The next night, we stayed at the home of a baronet my father knew, and the night after that, a viscount. Perhaps my father continued his usual habits, but he didn't tell me about them and I didn't discover them. At those castles, I slept with the daughters of the house, sharing a bed while they gossiped about their amours and quizzed me about mine. They were prodigiously jealous of my going to court, but their envy didn't make me think more highly of myself. Instead, the easy camaraderie of sisters made me miss Maman more keenly, and made each night away seem like a curse. The sense of adventure was tinged with a deep ache.

On the fourth night, though, we came to Brooksby, in Leicestershire, and there my life changed forever. You'll think it changed when my father clapped eyes on me, but no, that was just the first gust of wind far out at sea. It was at Brooksby Hall that the tempest struck shore.

Unlike my own home and the other places we'd stayed, this was an elegant manor house, not a castle. Even in a time of peace, my castle was prepared for siege. While my home had high walls, crenellated towers, and arrow slits, this was a low-spreading abode with many glass windows and an undefended approach. It was a place for gentle living, and I felt the difference as soon as I entered the flowered grounds. Brooksby Hall was like a sigh.

We were greeted by the lady of the manor herself, Mary Villiers, a charming widow of about forty. She seemed to know my father well.

"This can't be your daughter!" she exclaimed. "You told me she was sickly."

"She's improved," he said dryly, and allowed Lady Mary to lead him to a small, elegant dining chamber. Our banquet hall served scores, from the lord to the menials, and was carpeted in rushes and, often as not, dogs and old bones. This room was reserved for family and guests. It was warm and intimate.

Lady Mary looked me over with a friendly smile. For the first time on the journey, I felt a bit at ease. Here was a mother, not my own, true, but from her smile I thought she must be a kindly woman. I was too young to recognize the appraisal of a skilled procuress. She was a thousand times the schemer my father ever was, and far more capable. "What a charming thing you are!" she said. "And so your papa is taking you to court? How lucky for you. You're sure to be a sensation." She took my father's arm. "My lord, we have much to discuss. I believe there shall be a change of plans, all to the better. My sweet, will you excuse us? Perhaps you would like to stroll around the gardens."

She waved me graciously away and bent her head in close conversation with my father.

I'd thought travel would be more exciting, but as the long hours had worn on, jostling in the coach with my father, I found that even my fears gave way to absolute boredom. One can only reread Rabelais so many times, and my father's conversation was limited to the occasional wry remark or bawdy joke I only half understood. By that fourth day, I had been longing even for a highwayman to break up the monotony of travel.

At least here at Brooksby I could stretch my legs properly. We'd stopped earlier in the day than usual, and the afternoon sun was slanting golden rays through the French doors. I stepped outside, and in an instant my weariness was gone, all my loneliness momentarily banished.

I had stepped into a paradise.

Bowers of golden roses arched over carpets of forget-me-nots and sweet thyme. All around me were flowers in a delightful jumble, a haphazard arrangement that looked as if some bountiful goddess had simply strewn all of her favorites in a blessing upon the earth. I felt like I had stumbled into a magical place, a land of dreams. It was the same feeling I got when, on some dreary Yorkshire day, Shakespeare transported me to sunbaked Italy. The real world was suspended, and I found myself in a place almost as real, and infinitely more beautiful.

And oh, there was the hero of this paradise, reclining like Adonis on a bench beneath an arch of trellised pink clematis. His eyes were closed, long dark lashes resting on the peach of his cheek. I stopped, afraid that any sound might wake him. He was so beautiful lying there. Perhaps men don't care to be called beautiful, but there was no other word for him.

His hair, curling and bright chestnut, tumbled around his sleeping face. He had a noble nose, a long, full mouth, fine arching eyebrows a shade darker than his hair. He must have been twenty at least, but unlike most men, he was clean shaven, and so looked younger. His skin seemed to gleam in the declining sun like a pale golden pearl.

You mustn't think that I was such a ninny as to be in love with a handsome face, even though it was by far the handsomest I had ever seen. I knew that I lacked a great basis for comparison, for the only men in my life thus far had been guards, servants, and peasants. If he had woken and opened his mouth and said something foolish, or belched, my fascination with him would have evaporated. But for now, as he lay asleep under nature's benediction, I found him irresistibly fascinating,

Then his eyes opened, the clearest, brightest hazel eyes. He wasn't at all startled, but seemed like it was the most natural thing in the world to wake to a young woman's stare.

"Do I dream?" he asked, in a voice that sank into my soul like spring rain on moss. "Are you a goddess, a fairy, come to enchant me?"

Again, you'll believe me a fool to be charmed by such language. But I was inexperienced, and lonely, and it warmed me. It made me think of Titania and Oberon, of Puck and Peaseblossom.

He rolled to his feet, tall and lithe, and had my hand in his in an instant.

"No, your flesh is warm, not cold and otherworldly. Goddesses are marble, and fairies fear the sunlight. But you, gentle maiden, are a creature of flesh and blood."

My mouth trembled, and my thoughts fled. Had Maman called me clever? I was a tongue-tied imbecile under that boy's caress. I could only stare, and do my best to remember to breathe.

"Not a goddess then," the beautiful young man went on, "but worthy of an offering nonetheless." He released my hand, and it fell, nerveless, bereft at being deprived of his touch. He turned to the nearest flower bed and plucked a pale pink rose. "Which is the perfect blossom for a rare beauty such as yourself?"

"Not a rose," I said. I'd found my tongue at last, only to voice words that were stupid and rude.

He looked at me in mild surprise. "I thought a rose was a classic love token."

Love! He couldn't mean it—and I didn't want him to, for even in my confusion, I knew a love so easily bestowed must be cheap. But no one besides Maman had ever said the word to me, and it kindled a sympathetic spark.

He was waiting for an answer. "A rose is insipid, predictable," I said at last. His lovely brow furrowed, and I had to soothe it instantly with spoken balm. "I mean, a rose is perfect. Thank you." How tempting it is to change one's beliefs for just a chance at love. I didn't feel the danger then. Oh, how young I was!

But he'd already tossed it casually over his shoulder. It lay, bruised and crumpled, on the gravel. A thorn had pierced his finger. He sucked at the little wound and said, "No, you're absolutely right. I'm sure you've been offered hundreds of roses by unoriginal swains. We must find something exquisite for you, something that really suits you. Let's see." He snapped off a sprig of lavender and looked at me questioningly.

I reached for it, but he pulled it out of my grasp at the last instant, making me stumble almost into his arms. "Is it truly the right flower for you, my lady?"

"Well," I admitted, "I've never cared for the scent." The lavender joined the rose on the ground.

"Hmm . . . perhaps a marigold?" He plucked one and sniffed, wrinkling his nose at the slightly rank odor. "No, the gold reminded me of your hair, but the scent is good only for bees. Mayhap a lily? No, they make me think of death. A primrose? Too commonplace. Sweet William? No, that might make you recall some other sweetheart."

He turned his back on me, scouring the garden for just the right flower. I allowed myself a smile at last. "There it is," he said when he turned around. "My earthly goddess smiles, and so I know I've made the right choice." He held the flower cupped in his hands so I couldn't see it. "I don't know what this one is called, but it makes me think of you. A deep purple blue like your eyes. The blossom looks to me like a mysterious lady with a deep hood hiding her beauty. And you are a woman of mystery, I can tell. I don't even know your name. Will you tell me, lovely lady?"

He looked at me with his hazel eyes sparkling, his mouth eloquent between mirth and hope. Slowly, as if revealing a precious thing, he uncupped his hands to show me the flower.

I shrieked, and with a strength and speed I didn't know I possessed struck the deadly blossom from his grasp.

"What on earth?" he began, but I'd already captured his hands and was lifting my skirts (immodestly high, I'm sure) to wipe away whatever touch of that fatal bloom might remain on his hand.

I only knew we were being observed when I heard a laugh behind us. "Oh, my dear George, you were doing so well! I would have sworn she was yours for the plucking, but what a sorry end to your attempt."

He made a sweeping bow to his mother. "I was using the Flower Technique, just as you taught me, madam. I can't see where I can have failed." He bowed again to me. "Your servant, my lady."

I felt like I had been shaken roughly out of a dream. Had his entire romantic conversation been a ploy?

"The garden is an ideal setting for it, my son," Lady Mary said, "but perhaps the Zephyr Maneuver might have been more appropriate. Where the breeze caresses, so can you. I trust you'll do better at court. Now, my lovely child," she said, turning to me, "what has my lout of a son done to offend you?"

"Wolfsbane!" I cried. I'd forgotten for an instant. "He plucked it with his bare hands, and oh, he was cut! The wound from the rose thorn! It might have seeped in." I looked his hands over carefully to see if they were flushed. "Do you feel any pain, like pinpricks?" I looked around wildly for belladonna or devil's trumpet, dangerous in themselves but the only possible antidote to wolfsbane poisoning.

Lady Mary threw herself on her son. "Poisoned! My son! My plans!"

But a few moments later, when no symptoms appeared, I pronounced him safe. Lady Mary eyed me narrowly. "So you know of poisons, do you, my dear?"

I opened my mouth to make one answer, then snapped it shut again. "No, only of healing herbs," I said after a pause. "My mother taught me."

"And so you should tell all and sundry. Very well, you might do quite nicely." She took me by the arm and led me through the garden, a little away from the men. I wanted to look over my shoulder at the young man—George, had she called him?—and see if there had been any truth in those pretty words he'd charmed me with. But she held me firmly, guiding me with small steps along a fragrant path of thyme. The scent rose as our feet bruised the leaves.

"I am concerned, my sweet, to find you so gullible and openhearted. When my son spoke those tender nothings to you, did you really swoon? Or was yours an act, too?"

I blushed and bowed my head. (That gesture and flush of color came naturally to me then; later, when I was past blushing, I would learn to feign it when needed.)

"So in the space of three minutes' idle chatter you were heels over head in love? That won't do." She tut-tutted. I could not properly contradict her, because I wasn't sure what I felt. Not love, of course, but a yearning for . . . something. There was a vast chasm where Maman had been. My closest connection had been ripped away. Adrift, I wanted to latch on to some person.

"If our families are to work together, I must be able to trust that you are made of sterner stuff. *Act* in love when it suits, but, never tumble into it. You need fortifying, girl, before you can be my son's partner."

"Partner? What do you mean?" The idea made me unaccountably giddy. To have someone I could rely on, talk with as I talked with Maman! I vow for all his beauty, having a friend was the first thing on my mind then. I was painfully stricken with solitude, and he was a possible cure.

Lady Mary didn't answer me, only smiled. I was to learn a little more from her as the days went by. But not everything. Never everything.

That evening, while my father and Lady Mary retired to the fireside to scheme amid the dancing light and shadow, I found myself a book and a quiet nook. I tried to read, but all the while my ears pricked for George. Just after dinner I'd seen him talking to one of the household pages, and then he'd disappeared. I'd hoped he would seek me out, not for more of that flowery nonsense, but so I could ask him about his mother's plans for me. For us. But the evening dragged on, my candle subsided to a nubbin, and he did not come.

Make them wait, or make them come to you. I soon learned that lesson myself, but that night he practiced it on me. I alternately hoped and chided myself for hoping. He was a pretty boy who spoke well, no more.

Then, when my candle guttered and died, and he came upon me in the darkness, I caught my breath and realized he was no mere pretty boy, but a man. A man with luminous eyes that shone in the faint moonlight coming through the window. A man with a strong hand he placed at the tender nape of my neck, making me shiver.

I shouldn't be alone with him, I thought wildly. Beneath the innocent longing for a friend, his touch brought out something feral in me, something I should flee from. Part of me hated this odd feeling. Suddenly, I lacked control, as if my very body was at the mercy of another. And yet the sensation was exhilarating. If someone had force-fed me a delicious syllabub, I could not be more confused. Could I enjoy something if it was thrust upon me against my will?

George seemed unconscious of my confusion, and sat down beside me. He held something in his palms.

"Give me your hands," he said, and I held mine out, cupped. What would it be? I was startled to feel something warm and fluttering against my fingers, and pulled back, but George closed my hands around it. I felt the shape of a small bird, struggling, its tiny wings flexing ineffectually as it strove to fly from its prison. I opened my hands and in the dim moonlight saw a drab little bird with a speckled breast and an olive-yellow head.

George leaned his head close to mine. "Can you feel his wee heart beating against your hands?" he said in a low voice that reminded me of the wind over the moors.

I could feel the wee bird's thrumming pulse, hammering away so fast it was almost a continuous vibration, the swift beats barely distinguishable.

"Tonight, you hold his life in your hands. Feel how he trembles? Today, you held *my* life in your hands. You held my heart . . ." He broke off, and I raised my eyes from the bird to his. "You saved my life," he murmured, and stroked my cheek with his fingers as gently as if I had been the small-boned songbird.

"I didn't," I protested, confused. "I only . . ."

One finger touched my lips, silencing me. That feather touch took my power away.

"You saved me," he insisted. "Now my life is yours."

He placed his hands over mine and scooped up the quivering bird, retreating into the darkened room like a beautiful wraith. I sat alone in silence, my hands still warm from the tremulous little life I'd held within them.

He was wrong, though. I learned later, oh, much later, that when you save a life, the obligation is always the wrong way 'round. You would think that the person you save would be devoted to you. But no, saving a life is like feeding a stray cat. The object immediately feels they are entitled to all of your love and care, and you, foolish you, feel obliged to nurture them evermore.

For the first time since the journey began, I didn't fall asleep on a tear-damp pillow, missing Maman. The next morning, I found a cage of the same little songbirds hanging up in the corner of the kitchen. They were crowded, and their cacophony of shrill whistles made the cook complain. "It is their one morning of sun," her assistant said, and the cook shrugged. "Weeks of gluttony, and a drunken night," she said mysteriously. "There are worse lives."

I did not understand any of this until that night when we were served the costly delicacy of ortolans, force-fed songbirds drowned in Armagnac, roasted, and eaten whole. As I heard Papa crunching their toasted heads, I made myself believe that George had released our little bird, and it was even now cooing itself to sleep in the garden.

We stayed at Brooksby Hall for weeks. Denys and Isolde traveled on to London ahead of us. I think my father was terrified that his gift would keel over before she was presented to the king.

Lady Mary put me through my paces while my father amused himself with the kitchen staff. (He sampled the more delectable young servants first before settling on the cook herself, a bosomy comfortable woman his own age. I've since learned that though men like excitement in the beginning, most yearn for comfort in the end.)

Lady Mary and my father, who'd long been cronies, had decided that George Villiers and I would work together to achieve our ends. According to Lady Mary, George needed to please the king and I must marry a fortune. Of the two, George's mission was clearly paramount. Once he was in a position of power, he could use his considerable new influence to negotiate a great marriage for me.

Innocent though I was, I knew it had to be more complicated than that. Every parent schemed for a good match for their children. That was commonplace. From what I could gather, this scheme was more devious and far-reaching. My father and George's mother spoke to each other in animated whispers, with frequent sidelong glances in my direction that told me there was more than met the eye. Even my keen eye.

"How can we help each other?" I wanted to know.

"In a thousand ways," Lady Mary replied.

Sometimes it is as simple as a word in the right ear, a secret kept or told. Other times, all a lover needs is the prick of jealousy to spur him on. Two working together were always exponentially more powerful than one. She had thought to ally George with another young man of good (but not noble) family, but then there would be a risk of competition. With a female ally, our goals would be different, and so we would never stand in each other's way.

When I pressed her, she told me more of court life.

"Imagine a jungle," she told me. "A dark and savage place teeming with hungry creatures. Every one of them has fangs and claws. Every one of them is clever and strong and swift. Who will survive longest, grow sleekest, do you imagine? The lone leopard scrabbling through the wilderness by herself? Or the wolf pack, the loyal partners who guard one another's flanks at all times? At court, there is always someone ready to stab you in the back."

My hand went to my hidden dagger, which even Lady Mary didn't know about. But then I realized she wasn't speaking literally.

"Everyone is vying for the top few positions. Some of them have actual titles—duke, or groom of the bedchamber. Others are informal, based on friendship, or shared secrets, or fear. For example, my family and yours are united by old friendship and mutual interest. We're also allied with the Jermyn family based on mutual hatred of the Howard family, particularly Robert Carr, who married into that clan."

It was the first time I'd heard that name, which was to play so prominently in my fate.

"Why do we hate Robert Carr?" I asked. Unwittingly, it was already *we*. Lady Mary caught it, and looked smugly satisfied. I had committed myself to her side, a player in schemes I didn't yet understand.

"He rules the kingdom," she said with a little shrug.

"Him? Not the king?"

"Well," she prevaricated. She seemed to be considering how to answer. "Carr is the king's favorite, so he has a lot of influence over His Majesty."

"His favorite?" I asked. "You mean, his friend?"

"Yes, and other things. Favorite is a title, as much as earl or duke— though not such a permanent one. Government is a large thing, and kings are smaller than they seem. They like to have someone at their side to help them. Not a minister, who might have his own agenda. A favorite is a friend, adviser, secretary, confidant, spy . . . a host of things."

I thought for a moment. "And you want to oust him," I reasoned. It seemed to me that court politics were similar to the plot of a novel. Only think what would be the most shocking story to read, and there you have the most likely scheme. There are some fools who believe novels have no application to real life.

"And replace him with someone of your own choosing," I hazarded further. "But who?"

Lady Mary smiled mysteriously.

"George?" I asked incredulously. It seemed an impossible leap to go from third son of a minor lord to the de facto ruler of England.

"Why not?" she asked defensively, bristling at imagined insult to her son, or perhaps her plans. "Carr is no more than a jumped-up Scottish knight's son, a mushroom that sprouted overnight from a lump of dung. A clever man like George can easily take his place, with friends like you and me to pave the way."

She looked at me slantindicular. "You *do* want to help George, don't you?" she asked in a low, insinuating voice.

I did.

I might have rebelled against this cynical, ambitious, heartless world I found myself in . . . if it weren't for George.

Oh, how we laughed together at his mother's schemes! When we were alone in the garden, he would strut like the most dandified courtier, making a leg to the delphiniums, gallantly kissing tulips. "What a great lord I have become," he mocked to an imaginary court of flowers. "I have been appointed the Chamberlain of the Royal Underthings. You, sir? Chancellor of the Privy Pot?" He bowed to a patch of foxglove with a tornadic twirl of his plumed hat. "Why, you outrank me, indeed! I strive to reach such lofty heights!"

And I would collapse in a jelly of giggles. How ridiculous he made this quest for position sound. He entertained me with pantomimes of pettiness and scheming, as good an actor as any of the traveling mummers who visited Yorkshire.

"Why do it, then?" I asked him as I reclined on a marble bench carved into the likeness of a sleepy leopard.

"Because it is the way of the world," he said. "Because it is better to have money than not, respect than not."

"Better to have power than to be powerless," I added, nodding.

"Exactly. Everyone is acting thus. If we can do it more swiftly and with better effect than anyone else, why not? If we do as our fond parents wish, we can have the greatest rewards for the lightest exertion . . . and then when Fortune has been won, cast aside that mistress and choose for ourselves." He flopped down beside me on the leopard's rump, inclining his head toward my shoulder. "And think what a romp it will be!"

He leaped up again, reaching for my hands. "Dancing until morning . . . flirting just for the fun of it . . . playing cards—for money!"

"Scandalous!" I cried as he whirled me into a lively country dance.

"Better than staying in the country where nothing, absolutely nothing ever happens, when even the parties are based on the ripening schedule of some bit of produce or stupid sheep."

He pulled me close. "Aren't you sick of waiting? You have been taught about the world, as I have—I know it. Your sapient eyes tell me all! All of that learning . . . and yearning. Now, or soon, it is time for us to put our knowledge into practice. And what fun that you will be there with me!" His eyes were alight, his lips so close to mine. Then we heard Lady Mary's foot on the garden path, and we separated, demure children ready for her tutelage.

For before any of that adventure George and I laughed at could commence, Lady Mary said she had to teach me certain things. "A bumpkin—even a lovely one—is no use at court," she told me. First and foremost, I had to learn the art of love. Or rather, the art of seduction. Love, it seems, had nothing to do with it.

Lady Mary had a regular scheme of seduction training, and she set us up as antagonists in feigned lovers' games. In short, George would woo me, and I would woo him, according to scripts she set for us, as she looked on.

"No, no!" she'd exclaim when I let my eyes look too dreamy. "You aren't a lovesick mooncalf. You're a lady of high birth who is being won half against her will. Always keep a man in doubt of his success."

Or, "Stupid boy, you press too fast. She's not a strumpet to cajole into a tumble behind the hedgerow; she's an heiress who has her pick of any man."

Then she would stop us and make us begin again, until we had our lines down exactly. And not just our lines. She schooled our very faces, the palpitations of our hearts. Lady Mary would hold mirrors for us at all angles so we could study the effect of our expressions.

When I was a little girl sitting in the audience under a gaudy tent, watching the redoubtable Rosalind parry and scheme, I dreamed of being her. I envied Lady Macbeth (until the end, which I rewrote in my head). At that tender age, though, I didn't understand which I longed to be—the active, interesting woman, or the actress. I could hardly separate the two, and each seemed equally exciting. Now, it seemed I would get both. It made me giddy. Maman had been wrong to fear for me so.

Under Lady Mary's tutelage I learned how to entice a dimple to appear in my cheek without a smile. I perfected the art of gazing up through lowered lashes. My pouts became legion, differentiated to a hairsbreadth of nuance. Lady Mary turned the moue into an art form. I had never been so aware of my own body.

Whether that was all her doing, or George's, too, I cannot say. My skin felt like it tingled all through the day, and burned all through the night.

It isn't possible for me to feign without feeling. I've been called cold and heartless, a spy without true emotion who can cozen her dupes and then betray them. But I swear to you, when I played at lovemaking with George Villiers, I learned that I can never quite kill my emotions. The false becomes the true. All those hours when I acted as if I loved him, practicing for the real thing with someone else . . . they befuddled my heart until it didn't know what it felt.

Petit à petit, l'oiseau fait son nid. Little by little, the bird makes her nest. In bits and pieces, my affection for George was growing.

What had first been attraction to a handsome face, then balm for my loneliness, and eventually the novelty of having a man pay attention to me with gentle words and secret touches, soon deepened and strengthened. He felt it, too, I was certain. We never spoke of love outside of playacting, and yet the most banal word seemed to hold a secret meaning, as if we had developed our own secret lovers' language.

"Are you well today, Clarice?" he would ask over our small beer at breakfast. It meant, I was sure, that he had been thinking about me all night, as anxious for my happiness as he was for his own.

"Yes, very, thank you," I replied, with the hidden pronouncement that I was as joyous as angels on high, because he was near to me. Who has need of love-words spoken aloud when they ring so prettily in the head?

One day, after I'd been at Brooksby for about four weeks, George and I sat side by side in the garden. We perched close together on that same bench where I'd caught him dozing in that first mad meeting. We'd been hard at work for hours, and his mother had finally pronounced our performance passable and went inside for a cup of chocolate.

"Alone at last," he said with a sigh.

"Is that flirtation?" I asked. Familiarity had let me find my voice with him.

"Do you want it to be?"

I slapped his arm lightly with my closed fan, then snapped it open with a flourish. I half hid my face behind it, and let the lace brush against my right cheek. Lady Mary had taught me the codified language of fans, and that gesture meant *yes*.

But aloud I only said, "Of course not. We are a corporation, a single body devoted to a single cause—advancement."

"'Flesh of my flesh,'" he quoted, and I laughed so I didn't sigh.

But George's eyes were serious. "Clarice," he said, his voice low and a little hoarse, as if speaking my name pained him somehow. I looked a question at him. "You must know by now," he said, sliding closer so that I felt the warmth of his leg against mine.

Was this the moment for bald truth? Could it be? I thought he had spoken veiled and coded words of love before, but I suddenly felt the gulf that could exist between what I imagined he might feel, and what he truly felt. I was all in a panic, quickly certain that I must be wrong, that I couldn't be worthy of him. I'd imagined all of those hidden meanings. Love was one-sided, a fantasy, an impossible dream. I wasn't being a coquette when I said, "Know what?"

"That I love you."

He said it flatly, finally, and somehow, that made it all the more powerful. Another man might have added flowers and curlicues to those bare words, ribbons and gilt to make them more beautiful. But George, who had been well trained in the many flourishes of pretended love, only said the simple, unadorned truth. Seduction schemes were for other people. For us, truth was enough.

I melted. I had been feeling something I tried to deny ever since laying eyes on him. His beauty was captivating, but more than that, he looked at me like he knew my inmost heart. I imagined being looked at like that all my life.

Suddenly, I saw the possibility of just that: a life together. We had spoken of a future together, helpmeets against the world. True, it was a most mercenary joining, for the purpose of individual gain. But what if we were to cleave to each other as man and wife? How many unions between men and women begin as a partnership like that? A respectful meeting of equals. The exact opposite of my own parents' marriage. I blessed my father for taking me away from the home I love, for that wrench had brought me George. But my analytic mind would not let me grasp at happiness quite so easily.

"What about your mother's plans for you? And my father's for me? They want rich and powerful people for both of us." I bit my lip suddenly, realizing that he'd said love, not marriage. The two were very different. I was assuming I knew his intentions.

George looked at me tenderly. "You dear little goose. Once I become the king's favorite, I *will* be rich and powerful." He took my chin gently in his hands. "Your father will happily give his blessing. And as for me, I'll be free to marry whomever I choose without thought of money or title."

Then he kissed me, and my small world seemed to explode into a grand universe of myriad delightful possibilities, of strange colors and angelic music and . . . Oh, I know I sound like the dimmest little turnip that ever went to market, but I was young, and dreamed of love, and there it was in the most idyllic form proposing marriage and kissing me.

"Tell me that you love me," he murmured against my mouth.

"I love you," I said helplessly and truthfully. Fleetingly, I remembered my father's words. Being in love puts you in another's power. But I didn't care. I was his thrall. I was the moth, and I knew my wings would never singe.

"Swear it," he urged, his eyes passionate. "Swear that you'll love me and no other."

"I swear," I told him. "I swear on my life."

"And you'll save yourself for me?" he asked.

I wasn't immediately sure what he meant . . . then it dawned on me, and I felt a warm flush creep up my neck and face.

"Yes," I managed to breathe, without meeting his eyes.

"We'll both be pure for each other," he said, and as little as I knew about such matters, I understood that this was somehow a greater thing, coming from a man. I was expected to be a virgin on our wedding night. He wasn't. But for me, he would remain untouched.

He kissed me again, but very quickly, not lingeringly like the first kiss.

"Then we understand each other." He smiled sweetly. "Only, it must be secret for now. My mother has such lofty plans for me that she would object to any union not of her own choosing. And your father wants a duke for you, I'm sure. If they knew about our love now, they might try to part us. So you can't say anything, to anyone, until we've gotten rid of Carr and I'm installed in his place. Once we do that, we can live happily together."

I felt almost dizzy. To be understood, and cherished! This must have been what Maman wanted for me.

"Will you help me, Clarice?" he asked. "Will you do anything in your power, absolutely anything, to help me succeed?"

"Of course," I said, without a single thought of what that *anything* might entail. "I won't just be doing it for you. I'll be doing it for us. For our future together."

I tilted my face up for a kiss, and he complied, in a way that put that kiss from Denys to shame.

Chapter 3

Under Lady Mary's tutelage, I began to understand human nature. She took George and me to rich neighboring estates or to humble village markets, letting us watch people interact. She quizzed us at great length about who was in love, who had some long-standing grudge, which man was guilty of selling sick sheep. The hardened lip, the shifty eye, the softest sigh—this was the language I learned to translate. After a while, whether through Lady Mary's instruction or my own knack, I found I was able to read people, even strangers, quite accurately.

Maman had taught me to observe, but Lady Mary taught me to make connections, to feel the separate sticky strands of each human web. *Stupid girl*, she would call me whenever she was dissatisfied with my performance. And yet, it was during the months at Brooksby that I first began to believe in my own cleverness.

I longed to test it. I was tired of all this acting. I wanted the real world, with its challenges and dangers. And I wanted George at my side.

He did not speak of his love again, but counseled caution. If either of our parents knew, they would separate us. I followed his lead, and dissembled disinterest. I knew discretion was our friend, and that silence and secrecy now would help our cause later. It was piquantly delicious to have the certainty of his love locked securely in my heart.

During our training, we spent nearly every waking moment of every day together, acting out the various scenarios and ploys Lady Mary had devised. She had a veritable syllabus of seduction schemes, categorized and cross-referenced by gender, age, even season, so that George and I would never be at a loss.

They were mostly simple, but at the same time fiendishly clever. Each had a name. The Elegant Stumble, for example, played on a woman's desire for protection, and a man's compulsion to offer it. It had countless variations, and Lady Mary put me through my paces like a horse in a ring. Again and again, I practiced tripping without looking like a buffoon. I mastered everything from the Tipsy Sway (which gave a man hope that wine had weakened my defenses) to the Outright Swoon. The Swoon was problematic both because it risked sullying one's gown and also because it might imply that a woman was sickly. On the other hand, it sprawled her out in a most suggestive fashion, and Lady Mary said a clever woman could reveal a flash of any body part she liked to a single person in a crowd.

My favorite version of the Elegant Stumble threw me right into George's arms. I feigned clumsiness so I'd have to perform that maneuver over and over. (Any fool can trip, or pretend to trip. It takes a master and much practice to fall beautifully and naturally.) Every time, George's strong arms kept me safe, and pressed me fleetingly to the warmth of his chest. "No, I don't think I did that quite right," I'd say. "Let me try again."

I can vouch for these techniques. Though I was acting and knew they were all manipulation and craftiness, they worked on even me. My love for George deepened daily.

Then one day Lady Mary announced that the Villiers family was in danger.

She didn't entrust me with the details, but it was the sort of thing that I've seen hundreds of times since. In fact, I've practically made a living off of people's ridiculous compulsion to put things in writing. Treason should be whispered, never put on paper. A person may be discredited or killed far more easily than a wily slip of parchment may be recovered once it has fallen into the wrong hands.

The long and short of it was that some sprig of the Villiers family tree had written something indiscreet about a secret alliance with France that circumvented the king's wishes. Lady Mary had word through her astounding array of back channels that a Frenchman sympathetic to the Howard clan had stolen the incriminating letter and was sailing to Dover, to meet with one of the king's agents and pass proof of Villiers's treachery on to the king.

"But *did* your stepson betray the king?" I asked.

"Oh, kings come and kings go," she said. "England is what matters, and what we do is in England's interests, whether the king realizes it or not."

That was a new way of looking at things.

"Usually, I'd simply hire a thief or even an assassin to take care of the problem," Lady Mary said with a nonchalance that shocked me. I didn't know which was more surprising: that she could so casually resort to crime, or that she actually knew criminals to hire. I glanced at George, but he seemed unperturbed.

"But in this case that would be disastrous," she went on. "The problem with felons is that, well, they're felonious. It would all be fruitless if the man I hire decided to steal the letter himself and sell it to the highest bidder. George, I thank the heavens you aren't as foolish as your half brother."

Lady Mary was the second wife of the late Sir Villiers, George's father. George had two older half bothers by his father's first wife. One of them had been busy on Villiers business in France.

"And so," Lady Mary said with a resigned sigh, "one of us must go and take care of it."

She didn't like to send such an untried cub as me, but she couldn't go herself, or send one of her trusted allies like my father. They were too well-known. The Howard clan had spies, just as Lady Mary had. (Some were probably even the same people.) They would know if the Villiers family was onto them, and flee.

I, however, was a nobody.

"Still, we'll have to disguise you," she admitted. "Your target frequents court, and you'll be there eventually yourself. Unless, of course, you fail me in this."

Did she mean she would veto my presentation? I wondered. Or would I never make it to court because I'd be dead? Once she spoke of assassins, this mission had begun to seem all too real.

After hours of dithering, she decided to send George, too. He hadn't been presented at the English court, and though he had spent some time in France, he would probably be unrecognized. What's more, he would recognize our target, having seen him once in Paris. In any case, the bulk of the work—and danger—would fall to me.

And so, by nightfall, George and I were in a carriage on our way to the eastern port city of Dover. My hair had been stained with walnut juice, which Lady Mary assured me would wash out. "Beware of downpours," she called after the carriage as we rolled away.

You'll want to know why I did it. Why did I submit myself to her dangerous machinations? For all the talk of great matters—dukedoms and grand marriages, political power and affairs of state—this still felt like a game to me. George and his merriment made it so. As when I raced Maman over the moors, thinking only of the thrilling speed, not the danger of a broken neck, so was I then. As when Denys and I crept into the caves, daring each other to go farther, farther . . .

What joy to dash into devilment with a friend at your side! Having a companion multiplies bravery, sharpens confidence. Alone, I think even my rash spirit would have been cowed. But just as dogs in packs are fiercer than a solitary cur, I found such strength in George's camaraderie that I thought I could do anything. As he sat beside me on the plump carriage cushions, distracting me with card tricks while I tried to come up with a plan, I did not think of danger and treason. I thought of days and nights alone with George, working side by side. I did not even think of the romance of it, only the shared labor, the partnership as we strove for a future together.

I remembered holding hands with Denys when we were young, creeping deeper into the darkness, the chitter of bats above us and the dim sunlight fading fast at our backs. Our fear was a sham fear, delicious to us. We scared ourselves for fun, not really believing we could be lost in those endless caves forever. As I faced this, my first assignment, I felt much the same. I was young. Prison, death, and disgrace were abstract notions. George was in the flesh. Which would you have chosen?

Lady Mary didn't give us concrete instructions, because she didn't know the exact situation we'd find ourselves in. The burden of my task, though, was simple. Seduce the agent with the letter, and relieve him of it.

As we jostled along the rutted road, I practiced my technique. Now that it would be in earnest, though, everything I said felt false, every gesture contrived. He saw my hands nervously fumbling with my rosary, and held them to still my nerves. "What ails you, sweet?"

"I couldn't seduce a schoolboy," I moaned.

"My dove, speaking as a former schoolboy, let me assure you that a sheep in a dress could seduce most red-blooded schoolboys." He kissed my knuckles lightly.

We arrived at the port city the next afternoon. Dover stank. There is no delicate way to put it. Fish, dung, offal, and every stench that horrible humanity can produce. Sewage trickled through the gutters, and I saw a man relieving himself in an alleyway (and I don't mean pissing against a wall). You will remember that I spent a lot of time in the stables, and had smelled more than my share of festering wounds, yet even I say Dover reeked to high heaven.

The city was almost frighteningly busy, thronged with Continentals newly crossed, and every manner of monger come to deliver his goods to ships. George pointed out women I'd first thought simply poor and sloppy, and identified them as the lower sort of prostitute. Then there were others, fewer in number, bold and glittering and looking like my exact idea of fine ladies. They wore scarlet and canary and azure, and jewels (paste, I decided later) sparkled in their coiled hair.

"Oh, I hope I can be like that lady someday." I sighed as I admired a beauty in lace over periwinkle silk picking her way daintily through the ordure.

To my chagrin, George laughingly informed me that she was simply a more expensive whore.

I knew right then that I could never succeed in seducing anyone. This wasn't my world. I might be the daughter of a baron, but I was for all practical purposes a peasant.

"I'm not a great lady, and despite all your mother's tutelage, I can't pretend to be anything other than a country girl who's spent her life with dirty fingernails. I might not look it now, but any gentleman will see clean through me. I couldn't even spot a prostitute!"

George had faith in me, but I knew it would never work. "This target is a man of the world," I explained to him. "What's more, he's carrying something dangerous, something that might make his fortune or cause his death. He's ready for someone to try to thwart him. If a strange fine lady approaches him, batting her eyelashes, what will he think? Of course he'll know in a heartbeat what I've come for." I covered my face with my hands.

Then it was as if the cloudy skies of my mind suddenly cleared in a blaze of sun. I beamed at George.

"What?" he asked, smiling back with no idea why.

"I can't pass myself off as a great lady," I said with a mischievous grin. "But I can play a Yorkshire lass to perfection."

"And how will that seduce a lord?"

"I don't know many lords, but I've seen my own father's tastes. Barmaids and serving wenches and cooks."

A look of distaste crossed George's face, and I thought, at least I don't have to worry about him pestering our servants. I did not often let myself think about a concrete future with George, and now I beat it back quickly. It was too distracting, and I needed my wits clear.

"Trust me," I told him. "A lady will attract his suspicion. A peasant wench will be so commonplace that he'll never see me as a threat."

"But mother's techniques are for the nobility," he protested. "They're meant for ladies in silk in a flower garden, with servants fetching sylla-bubs. They don't work for the lower classes."

"A servant doesn't need technique," I told him with growing confidence. "She's practically there for the taking. A low-hanging fruit. I don't have to be a seductress. I just have to be prettier than the other servants . . . and available."

My father had taught me more than he knew. While my gut roiled at the truth of the world, and I wished it wasn't so, I knew I could turn the world's depravity to my advantage.

Though George was still dubious, I positively tingled with certainty. We stopped at a carriage house, and I dickered with the hostler's wife to buy some things I needed for my disguise. My hair was already a nonde-script brown, and dull from the walnut juice. I tied it beneath a kerchief, but coaxed a few curls out to twine fetchingly over my cheeks. She let me buy her third-best dress, a sack-like thing in washed-out blue. The ma-terial, a blend of wool and linen, was surprisingly soft, though, and the dress was very clean. Once I cinched it in at the waist, I looked charm-ingly rustic and ready for hard labor. My hands were still calloused from spades and reins, despite Lady Mary's best efforts with pumice and lan-olin. With a theatrical smudge of dirt on my cheekbone, I was perfect.

"But how are you going to get near him?" George asked. His source had told him my target was staying in the Sprightly Cony, an inn and tavern near the docks. He'd be waiting for his contact, who would be arriving within the next day or so. I didn't have much time.

"Leave that to me," I said.

I didn't approach the tavern owner because my target—if he had any sense—would have already paid him to inform him of anyone asking questions, or anything out of the ordinary. So instead I lingered around the back of the tavern until a weary-looking wench emerged carrying a big basin of slops.

"Looks heavy," I said in a light version of my Yorkshire accent. (The real thing would have been all but indecipherable to a southerner.) "Let me help."

I took one side of the basin and helped her carry it to the pigsty.

"Thanks," she said, though she looked at me suspiciously. "What do you want?"

I laughed. "What every woman wants. A good man to work so I don't have to. Until then, does your master need another wench?"

I could tell she took to me. "Master's a miser, and hardly pays me enough to keep me in ale."

I winked at her. "Lucky thing any man with eyes would buy you a flagon for a kiss." That made her giggle and blush, though she was older than me by a good few years. "I just came to Dover, and I'm in terrible need of work. Can you ask your master?"

She thought a moment. "I don't know . . ."

"Please. He don't have to pay me. Not at first anyway. I'm fearsome hungry. If he could just give me my dinner, I'd be happy."

She looked at me skeptically. "You'd work for no pay?"

I shrugged. "There's other ways of earning coin. Do you get some nice gentlemen here?"

Her eyes widened in comprehension. "Oh, you're one of *those*."

"Might be, if anyone makes me an offer," I said offhand. "What do you say? I'll split anything I make tonight, if you help get me in."

"Split for the next week and you have a deal," she said, and spit into her hand. We shook, and she brought me inside.

"This here's my cousin," she said casually, jerking her thumb over her shoulder at me. I bobbed a curtsy like I'd seen country girls do. "Might be she'll do a bit of work here if you give her scraps." She pressed her hands to the small of her back, arms akimbo. "The *Gabrielle* is docking tonight, and you know there will be a rush. Could use another pair of hands."

"What's your cousin's name?" the surly-looking owner asked as he eyed me up and down the same way my father had.

"Annie," she said without a pause. "My ma's sister's man moved the family north to try sheep, but they died—sheep and her parents both— and now their daughter is back. I do what I can for her, but . . ."

I looked at her in amazement. The lie came so lithely and naturally off her tongue. I made a point of remembering her name—Jemima Brock—and in later years I looked her up and put her to use. Even without a Lady Mary to tutor her, she was one of nature's born deceivers.

"Very well," the owner said. "Keep her in line." He returned to his pipe in the back room.

And so I became a tavern wench for the evening, pouring ale and cider, wiping down tables, serving chops and potatoes. Among my duties, apparently, was allowing men to pat my rump. The first time, it made me jump and squeal, which the man seemed to like. Jemima gave me a look that clearly said she knew I was faking innocence, but it was a nice performance.

My target might have already been there, but I had no way of knowing. George was supposed to point him out. After I had been working for about an hour, George came in, dressed as a sailor.

"There's a likely prospect," Jemima whispered when we crossed paths. "Just off ship, pockets full of pay." She was eager for her fifty percent share of my debaucheries.

I walked over. "The man in brown velvet," George whispered.

I nodded as if taking his order. "Tripe and onions on the side, sir?" I asked loudly enough for my voice to carry.

"Please," George said.

Under my breath I murmured, "Smack my bottom."

He looked briefly alarmed.

"People will think it strange if you don't," I said as I pretended to wipe up nonexistent crumbs.

And so I got my first intimate touch from George that was not choreographed by his mother.

Jemima chuckled and made a gesture as if slipping coins into her pocket. I retreated behind the cider barrels to examine my target.

He was a well-made, soldierly-looking man with a long, chiseled nose and dark eyes that seemed both sleepy and bright, like a lizard's. The longer I looked at him, the more handsome he seemed. There was an arrogance to him that I found fascinating. It is only a charming trait when it seems to be justified, and as I watched him, I picked out clues that made me think it might be. He didn't wear a sword, but he sat slightly askance at his table, as if used to making space for a weapon at his hip. He was dressed like a merchant, or a sailor on leave, but I could tell from his haircut and neat, buffed nails that he was used to much finer garb. He'd been one of the fellows who'd taken liberties with my posterior when I took his order. What's more, he was French, though he spoke English well enough to fool many.

He scanned the room lazily, and only the tapping of his large fingers on the table belied his complete ease.

I was in the tavern, I'd spied my mark, but now what? It would be easy enough to sneak upstairs to his room while he ate. He'd ordered a large meal of mutton, eggs, and potatoes, which Jemima should have been frying up, though she was currently chatting with an elderly merchant captain.

But he wouldn't leave something that important unguarded, would he? No, it would be on his person, and Lady Mary hadn't taught me a thing about pickpocketing. I'd have to get him alone, perhaps even undressed.

I shuddered. I didn't think I could do it, even to help George's family, even if I had no intent of following through. I hardly even thought of doing such things with George yet! It seemed a sacrilege to pretend such a holy feeling with a stranger. I didn't even know enough about the physical aspects of love to fully comprehend what my target would expect of me in his bedroom. Beyond kisses and caresses there were other things, I knew, delicious, frightening things that both attracted and repulsed me with their strangeness and intimacy.

As I slyly watched him, he stroked his shadowed jaw with an absent sensuality I decided made him particularly susceptible to feminine charms. But which maneuver to use? I ran through a litany of all of Lady Mary's ploys. Could any work here? The Virgin's Gambit? The Spilled Milk? The Elegant Stumble might get me a caress, but I guessed a man engaged in high-level political scheming would defer his pleasure until after the deal was done. Someone from court would soon arrive with a sack of gold in exchange for the incriminating letter. After that was concluded, he might welcome a tumble with me, though not before.

I racked my brains. The Ignorant Female? No. Perhaps the Thorn in the Palm? Lady Mary said men will always take advantage of an injured woman. I began to feel a rising panic. None of those things would work for a servant. I made the wrong decision. I'd fail this mission and prove that I was the bumpkin I knew Lady Mary expected me to be.

Then I had an idea. Lady Mary had touched on one other ploy, but we didn't practice it because it relied on fate. The Fond Physician. One of the best ways to win affection and loyalty, she said, is to care for someone through injury or sickness. During the malady, they'll be at your mercy. Afterward, you'll have their gratitude.

Sickness, she said, depends on the will of God, and so that technique was unreliable. But hadn't Maman taught me how to play God, how to reach inside of people's bodies and make them do my bidding? Perhaps Maman's teachings were more valuable than Lady Mary's.

I would make him unwell! Then, in the throes of misery, I'd take him to his room and comfort him. Perhaps even comfort him to unconsciousness. Then it would be easy to steal the letter back.

I stopped cold. Maman had taught me about plants and herbs so I could heal, not harm.

But you won't be killing him, a little voice in my head argued persuasively. Maman taught me dosage, so that I could know the fine measure between cure and kill. How many times had she given some servant or farmer an emetic or purge? They'd become violently ill for a time, but then were cured of whatever evil had beset them, be it worms or colic or ague.

I wouldn't be poisoning him, exactly. I'd just be treating him for a disease I wasn't entirely sure he had.

But what could I use? I knew half a hundred things that would work, but I couldn't lay my hands on any of them. The wayside inn on the way to Brooksby where I'd saved the girl from my father's lust had been in the country, between field and forest, so there were plants everywhere. Nettles had been easy to come by. But aside from a few straggling weeds and timothy grass, I hadn't seen much greenery in Dover.

I needed more time to think. In the meanwhile, Jemima was starting to fry up the Frenchman's dinner. Whatever I used, I'd have to slip it into his food. I needed to delay her.

The Elegant Stumble came in quite handy as I lurched toward the stove, flipping over the cast-iron skillet with a cloth-wrapped hand.

"You stupid scullion!" Jemima shrieked as the grease stained her skirts and blistered the bare skin of her ankles.

I apologized, groveling, and offered her one hundred percent of whatever I earned that night. "That sailor flashed gold," I told her.

She sniffed, and said, "You'll cook this order afresh, too. Scrape up what fell. That can be your supper tonight." She stormed off.

As I'd never cooked a thing, I decided to wipe off the mutton, and douse the eggs with pepper to camouflage any dirt from the floor. The potatoes, already highly spiced, didn't show any dirt, but as I examined them, I found one chunk with a green patch, and without thinking tossed it into one of the slops buckets along with the night's potato peelings. I'd spent enough time with the Paget family cook to know that green potatoes can cause sickness.

Then I caught myself, and felt stupid and brilliant all at once.

In a trice I'd dug through the half-full trash for the bits of discarded green potato peelings that are found in any kitchen garbage, and added them to the rest of the fried potatoes to cook. When potatoes grow too near the surface, the sun makes poisonous green spots in the otherwise wholesome flesh. A bite or two might not cause more than a twinge, but by the time I brought my target's meal out, at least half of the potatoes had green spots. I concealed them with a generous helping of gravy.

"*Merci, mon petit chou-fleur*," he said as I beamed at him, and dug right in. I was so grateful I left my rump in easy reach, and he took advantage.

Half an hour later, when the vomiting started, Jemima was all too grateful to have me help the customer up to his room. When the delirium and partial paralysis set in, I searched him and found the incriminating letter tucked inside his vest.

George and I were soon on the road back to Brooksby. I was still breathless and giddy from my success. I asked if we could send money to Jemima, but he didn't think it would be possible. Money sent by a known messenger could be traced back to us, while an unknown messenger would simply steal the coin. It was the one sour note.

"Will he die?" George asked after a while. After too long, now that I think on it.

"No," I said, with slightly more certainty than I felt. He'd probably make a full recovery within a day or two from the poison that closely resembled that of deadly nightshade. It isn't poisoning unless someone dies, I told myself. That made me feel much better, even self-righteous.

After we'd been on the road a little while, George said, "Clarice, I don't think we should tell my mother exactly what happened."

"Why not?" I asked. I wanted to show Lady Mary how clever and resourceful I was.

"She might think what you did . . . unladylike."

I was instantly chagrined, and frowned at my lap. Would it have been more ladylike to have lured him into his room with lascivious promises, stripped, and hit him over the head with a poker when he was enjoying himself? I couldn't think of any other way.

"What if I just tell her that you distracted him, and I stole the letter? She won't ask many questions, as long as our family is safe."

I agreed, albeit reluctantly.

"*I* know what you did," George said, squeezing my hand. "That's the important thing." When the carriage turned, I let myself sway into him, and stayed against his shoulder until I dozed off. I dreamed of him, oh, such a lovely dream, a haze of kisses and flowers. But at the end, the dream changed its tenor, and I thought I saw George prone and pale, dying, while I stood over him with a potato in my hand.

When I woke with a jolt, he was sitting on his side of the carriage, I on mine, a world of cushion between us.

Chapter 4

1628

*A*thos, sprung from my past. I cannot dwell on him or I will go mad. Only the job at hand—that has always been the cardinal's advice. The mind is a mettlesome horse, after all. Early training and a firm hand later will keep it perfectly in check. I file Athos away for another time, and ignore the nauseous cannonball that has taken up residence in my gut.

I predicted the duel's outcome to a nicety. Combat is a boost to camaraderie, and after having soundly beaten de Winter, D'Artagnan declared him a true gentleman, tho' English, and shook his hand. So as planned, my faux brother-in-law took his erstwhile foe home to meet his sister. After an appropriate interval, the young Gascon took to calling on me alone. Though pining for his kidnapped Madame Bonacieux, he is a stoic, and plows ahead on the vital business of seduction.

I confess it makes me feel young to hear his filigreed blandishments and curlicued compliments. He sits across from me now, struggling to bring pretty praise naturally into the conversation. When he shades his eyes and swears the firelight glinting off my golden hair nearly blinds him, I laugh, feeling almost as though I weren't engaged in spy work, but simply indulging some young protégé, a cousin of the Comte de Wardes, perhaps. When he leaves, he attempts the slightest liberty, which I lightly rebuff. He is eager and pliant, but cannot possibly truly believe he will secure me. On his next visit, I will broach our true business, and turn him to the cardinal's ends.

The moment he leaves, though, I forget him, and pen a quick note to my lover the Comte de Wardes. I have vacillated these last days over whether to tell him that Athos has emerged from my past. They are both dangerous men, and should my lover take it upon himself to protect me, there is a chance, however small, that things would not go in his favor. Still, he has learned in our time together that I prefer to protect myself, and tend to do a fine job of it, too. And so tonight I opt for truth. I crave his counsel, and perhaps more important, I need the solace of his touch, his laugh, the easy understanding of long years.

Come tonight, I beg, and send my maid, Kitty, to deliver the message. She knows nothing of my business—a simple creature, competent though often lazy. She is charged to give the note to a lamp-boy on the corner, one of my regular couriers. When she comes back sooner than expected, I am pleased with her new alacrity. Perhaps she will improve in my service, I think as she draws my bath and I prepare for my lover.

Clean and unadorned, I command her to extinguish the outside torches and snuff all but a single candle in my bedchamber. The Comte de Wardes is not known at this address, to myself in this guise, and I would rather he is not seen by prying eyes. Kitty dismissed to her own amusements, I await my lover's advent.

We've been apart for many days, and I lounge half-clad in anticipation. I've managed to steal a few precious hours with our son, who is under the care of a trusted nursemaid, but now I yearn for another sort of love. What a splendid world it would be if we could be together, all the time. Though from what my married friends tell me, all they want to do is escape from their husbands and children. Wretched world, to always taunt us with what we cannot have.

There is a knock at my door, and like a country wench, I leap up to welcome him myself, into my house, into my arms. I know the house well and navigate easily through the blackness. When I fling the door open onto the darkened stoop, I can't see more than a large masculine shadow, but with a laughing welcome I pull him into my dark cave and entwine myself around his body.

"Oh, my love," I breathe in infinite relief, so overwhelmed at the respite he carries with him that at first I don't notice anything but my own sensations. His hands are all over me, one delving down, the other climbing up, mountaineer-style, each achieving their goals at the exact same moment, eliciting a squeal and quiver. I kiss him hungrily . . . and feel the tickle of a mustache on my lips.

My lover is clean-shaven, and not enough time has passed since our last meeting for him to grow such an accoutrement.

His smell is wrong; his taste. This unseen, unspeaking man in the dark is as tall and well made as my lover, but the contours are different, the texture incorrect.

A stranger is groping my most personal parts.

Immediately, I shed the mantle of woman and don the armor of assassin. The only outward sign I give is a gasp, easily disguised as pleasure, but the probing fingers caressing all the right places may as well be ice. They numb me.

And then I know all at once what happened. That lazy wench Kitty didn't feel like traipsing down the boulevard to deliver my letter. When the charming D'Artagnan offered to carry it for her, she accepted. That vile man read my letter to the comte, and thought he could thrust himself into his place and violate me all unknown.

He almost has—I'm clad only in a silk robe knotted at the waist, and his hands are everywhere.

But I don't scream, and I don't fight. I cannot let him know I've seen through his deception. He'll have nothing to lose then, and take by force what he hoped to take by stealth.

"Easy, my love," I say with a chuckle. "We have until dawn, and I have opened the finest wine, which will quite breathe itself to death if we leave it until we are sated. Let me up and we will toast each other. A little wine will only make our amours all the keener."

It is a gamble, for the bird is in the hand . . . but he releases me, and I stumble to the little table where I keep my wine, and a few select additives. My heart is thudding. I am afraid! I note that sensation because of its oddity. Who would not be afraid when attacked in the dark? I, perhaps alone of all women in Paris, who has not been afraid for nearly a decade, should laugh at this treacherous bumpkin thinking he can rape me under my lover's guise. And yet I tremble, and when I pour the wine, half of it sloshes out with a clumsiness I cannot blame on the utter darkness.

He's on me again, unspeaking, thinking his terrible deception complete. "Wine!" I gasp, but his mouth is on mine, disgusting because it is not my love's, and my hand flails behind me for the hidden compartment in the cabinet. I cannot slip it in the wine. I am almost undone! He bears me to the ground. The floor is bruising against my shoulders and spine as he pins me. I grit my teeth, hold my breath . . . then he is choking and sputtering as I slam a pouch full of fine powder into his face.

"What the devil?" he begins, but gets no further. He has breathed a great deal of it in, and Datura works fast. With my limbs almost failing me, I drag myself out from under him and shove his insensible bulk off of me.

Then, it is like I've become another person, a small and fragile creature, utterly unlike the notorious Milady. I weep! Crumpled in a heap just a few feet from my stupefied attacker, I dissolve into a trembling puddle. My thoughts run to wild *what ifs* that are worse than the fate I just escaped, tormenting me even more now that the danger has passed.

When I was bound and helpless before the marquis in Mrs. Fox's whorehouse, I knew not a jot of fear. When he lay dead at my feet, I chatted blithely with the procuress, unconcerned. Thus it had been through every danger in my life. Why has this attack undone me? I look at my trembling self like a disembodied spirit, feeling contempt for my weakness.

The wild mare of my brain has thrown its rider, broken its leathers, and now gallops unchecked! Some unheeded voice that seems to come from outside me urges calm and circumspection, but inside there is nothing but turmoil, instinct. Every urge tells me to flee, to gather my child, my lover, to my bosom and do whatever I can to keep them safe.

"I cannot do this anymore." I hardly even know it is myself speaking. It sounds like the utterance of an oracle, a profound, eternal truth.

Speaking it plainly aloud is the spell that calms me. Hysterics and tears have been cathartic, but I vow they will never happen again.

Then, in a sudden saltation, I see clearly what I must do. Drying my tears, crawling to D'Artagnan's side, I whisper into his delirium all the things he longs to do to me. His body twitches as he dreams with wide, staring eyes of slaked lust. Come morning, his befuddled brain will believe it all true.

I let him come to me again the next day as his own self, as gaily welcoming as if I have no idea what a lustful monster he is. I flirt; I entice.

I let him think I have fallen in love with him.

But when he presses his suit, I demur. I am too shy to give myself to him. Ah, but I love him so thoroughly! I would forgive him anything—anything! Will he forgive my reticence?

Then, as a token of my love, I give him a ring. Pale sapphire, clear and heartless and cold like Athos's eyes when he betrayed me.

D'Artagnan slips it on his finger with a smug look. Then he, predictable fool, falls on his knees and tells me there is no need for shyness. Unbeknownst, I have already yielded to him, so there can be no cause for caution. "I know you will forgive me," the idiot says, "because your love is pure and trusting and forgiving, and you are too noble to condemn me for what was, after all, only an excess of passion for your lovely self."

For all his swaggering airs and deadly fighting skills, he is only a young man after all. He really believes that love conquers rape.

He believes it somewhat less when my dagger slips between his arm and ribs, slicing both. He thinks I miss a killing thrust accidentally. All of the fury I felt when he attempted to violate me, the volcanic eruptions I somehow managed to keep in at the time, come out now in perfectly choreographed passion. This inflamed face, these molten eyes, were practiced in the glass before this anticipated moment. Hoarse, guttural—rehearsed—accusations rip from my throat as I swear I will kill him and torture anyone he loves. "I know of your seamstress slut, whoreson! I'll make you watch her die!"

He evades me, angling for his sword cast carelessly across the room, but I close with him, allowing him to catch my wrist before I stab him. We grapple, me appearing weak, and as he casts me off, protesting his love all the while, I let him tear at my bodice.

Combat ceases. We both stare at the same place: the faint pink but unmistakable scar on my bosom. His heavy Gascon jaw gapes. My eyes widen with the realization of what he has just seen. Then with a savage scream I launch myself at him, calling him gutter names, and he just escapes behind the door connecting to Kitty's chamber.

And where will he run with the tale of my scar, with the sapphire ring? To whom but his mentor, most renowned of the Musketeers, Athos.

I know he lives. Soon he will know that I live. Then my plan for escape from this life will begin in earnest.

"**K**ill him!" I say in a voice as close to command as I dare use to the cardinal.

"Care to tell me why?"

"Does it matter? D'Artagnan offended me!"

"And he may yet be useful to me." He considers. "Very well, I won't ask you to interact with him. The little Bonacieux seems to have him scurrying well enough."

"I want him dead!" I repeat in a surly, sulky tone.

He looks at me quizzically. He has never heard this edge in my voice, and I can see him try to identify it. Is Milady afraid? "And yet you cannot slay him yourself?"

I bite my lip, and his eyes widen slightly. Are his suspicions confirmed? "He is one of the most dangerous men in France," I murmur reluctantly. "And what's more . . ."

"Yes?"

"He has friends. Three Musketeers, each more deadly than the last. The worst is Athos." I shudder, and drop my head, letting my lovelocks hide my face. "I . . . I would have no hope against him."

"Athos, eh? Have I heard of him?" asks the man who knows everything that passes in the realm, from the affairs of the queen to the falling of a sparrow.

We are at La Rochelle, the besieged city. My work goes on, as ever. There was a captain to kill, a message to sneak past enemy lines. I performed this official business, the cardinal's work, in the most perfunctory manner. In the meantime, I sent a bottle of poison wine to a certain Gascon acquaintance of mine. The concentration was low enough not to kill, but I heard that a greedy servant swigged down the lees after pouring out a glass for D'Artagnan, and as the poison was concentrated in those dregs, the servant died most horribly. No matter. My ends were achieved, whatever the unfortunate means. The three Musketeers were warned that someone was trying to kill their friend. They would be clever enough to point the finger my way.

"If you've not heard of him, Your Eminence, you are remiss. Cold, deadly, with singular purpose . . . none can stand against him!"

His eyes gleam with interest. I, his favorite weapon, seem to be losing my edge. Now this new blade looms on the horizon, and he is piqued.

"I would not challenge Athos for a king's ransom!" I cry.

"You are paid almost that much for what you do. The price of kings is in decline of late." He sighs, and looks out the window of our inn to the distant fortress. "Very well. Although I would like to get this D'Artagnan for myself, and though I would prefer not to aggrieve the king's Musketeers at this delicate time, I will arrange for the man who offended you to die. But there is a price."

Isn't there always?

"A death for a death."

It is interesting that the cardinal is so intrigued by D'Artagnan, because, thanks to an unsigned note in a disguised hand, the young Gascon is almost as interested in His Eminence. In fact, he and his three friends are in a room just below ours at this very moment, listening through the connecting stovepipe flues as the cardinal makes his demands of me.

Kill a man, His Red Eminence commands. That is easy enough. Oh, but that man, of all the men in the world! Another resurrected ghost. I will not do it, I think, even as I nod and smile and tell him how it can be done. After all, I have an audience.

"But I will need a letter of marque on this piratical expedition," I tell the cardinal. "A note in your own hand, signed and sealed, giving the bearer leave to act as they see fit, at your command. In short, I need preemptive absolution."

He laughs and makes the sign of the cross. "Of course, my dear. Go forth, child, and sin no more . . . until the next time."

The cardinal gone, I adjust my bonnet in preparation for embarking on my last great mission. I don't yet know if I will comply, but I must seem to. He has asked me to kill a man I swore I would never see again. Quite a dilemma, particularly when my mind is fixed so strongly on other things.

I hear a step without, but don't turn when the door eases open. It must be the cardinal, having forgotten some bit of information, or his embroidered red silk handkerchief. Staring at my face in the glass, trying to decide if my son will inherit my nose, I don't turn.

"Yes?"

But when there is no reply, I sigh, expecting something to be added to an already onerous assignment. When I turn, a shrouded man stands in the doorway. A cloak covers his body; a hat tugged low shadows his eyes. He shuts the door and slides the bolt into place.

"You live," he says.

"You live," I breathe, and though I was forewarned, it still feels like a ghost has manifested in my room. Up close, I see that the years have not been kind to him. He is still handsome in his way. Men can get away with a great deal of self-abuse. But his hair is graying, and his nose shows signs of the bottle. His forehead is deeply lined; his eyes and mouth are not. There has been little smiling in the last dozen years, I believe.

Buried in that ruined vessel is the man I once trusted.

"Are you a demon?" he asks.

"No more than I ever was." He makes a sound like a choked laugh. Yes, I suppose that turn of phrase would smite him.

And then there is a long silence, and I honestly do not know if his next action will smack of love or murder. In him, the two are inextricably intertwined. "I heard your conference with the cardinal. I don't care a fig for your plan to assassinate the Duke of Buckingham. The English are my enemy now, and one perfidious Englishman's life is of no consequence to me. But you will not harm a hair on D'Artagnan's head."

He is devoted to his friend. Oh, take care, young Gascon! This man's love is a dangerous thing!

"He offended me," I cry. "I will have my revenge."

His face flushes, and at last there comes an emotion I can understand. But too soon, alas, too soon! If it happens now, the fiction will become truth. I must rein him in.

He pulls a pistol from his belt, cocks it, and points it at my face.

"Demon woman! What is there left on this firmament that can offend you?"

And so I reveal how his friend violated me, telling the truth as D'Artagnan believes it. Athos blanches. The lines in his brow crease to new chthonic depths. The primed pistol wavers, and I step forward to caressingly push it even lower.

"Not my face, if you ever loved me. My heart . . . because you loved me once."

Oh Lord, it is as good as a play to see the flickers of love and lust and memory and fury dapple his face like sunshine through the trees. He knows not what to feel. Dare I heighten his confusion?

I pull down my bodice, showing luscious breast and damning scar. "Better still, shoot me there." I press the cold muzzle against the scar.

He is all atremble, and I think I will die, if not by will then by accident. His finger makes minute convulsions on the trigger.

Finally, he steps back. "Give me the letter."

"What letter?"

"I heard all, remember? Hand over the pass His Eminence gave you,
excusing your every action." I hesitate, and the pistol returns to my face.
"Now, or I swear by God, you'll make a hideous corpse."

What choice do I have? Overwhelmed by masculine force, I give
him the letter.

Exactly as I had intended to do all along.

He does not kill me, but leaves with a look of confused anguish, and
I know he has not exited my life for long.

Jointed marionettes on strings. That's all most people are. And I know
this all too well, because I was a puppet once . . .

Part 2

Chapter 5

1615

I had been told I was beautiful. It never occurred to me to believe it until I was presented at the court of King James I of England.

Under Lady Mary's guidance, I had improved my natural gifts considerably. Under her care, my hair burnished like sunlight and coiled in copious curls. My skin was bathed in May water every morning, soothed with witch hazel every night, and felt its first touch of cosmetics. Light powder took the shine from my nose, and a touch of kohl darkened my lashes. Lady Mary judged my lips plump and pink enough on their own, but encouraged me to bite them, and pinch my cheeks whenever I was unobserved, to give them added color.

And my clothes! Maman's finest gowns were rags compared to the lovely garments I acquired when we arrived in London.

I knew that my father never lacked money, and Lady Mary seemed comfortable enough. When we got to London, though, I learned that we had many backers who controlled the strings of very liberal purses. I had spoken truly—George and I were a corporation, and there were many who wanted to invest in us. I learned that they, too, were enemies of the king's current favorite, Robert Carr, the Earl of Somerset, and his allies the Howard family.

With money from our faction, George and I were outfitted magnificently. For him, slashed doublets in velvet or silk, sewn all over with gold and silver, dotted with jeweled buttons. He had yards of lace, silken hose in a rainbow of hues, heeled shoes with bows and great pomposities on the toes, aigretted hats, garters stitched with mottoes about love. Once he went to be fitted for a garment so special, so secret, that even I was barred from seeing it. He and his mother whispered about its glory, but I was kept in the dark.

My clothes were made of just as expensive material, but were of an altogether plainer style. "A beauty as fresh as yours needs no embellishment," she told me. I was used to such loose and simple clothes that I didn't much care what they dressed me in. The gowns Lady Mary chose were quite elegant enough for me.

On that great day I was to be presented to King James and his good wife, Queen Anne, I was dressed in a close-fitting gown of deep rust-red stitched about the breast with golden vines, which Lady Mary said made me look like a fairy in autumn. The bodice was cut so low that I feared for my modesty, and I was sure I would trip over the trailing skirts.

"Who is that glorious creature?" I heard some male voice ask. The hall was thronged with people, all of whom seemed much more glamorous and important than I.

"God's tripes, what a bosom," said another.

"Idiot, every cow has udders," someone else pronounced with scorn. "But that face! Like an angel!"

Not every comment was complimentary. "Minx!" a woman hissed.

"That looks like a dress I gave my waiting woman last season," another quipped.

Then a man's voice with a faint French accent rang through the others clear as a bell, stating in unnerving detail exactly what he would like to do to me if he had me alone in his bedchamber. Later, Lady Mary said she knew when she heard those comments that I would be a crashing success.

I didn't dare look around me, but their remarks both alarmed me and gave me strength. I felt like I was feeding off their gazes, their thoughts, growing larger and more important with each step I took.

I knew the king and queen were on their thrones, their son Charles at their side, but they were so far only blurs to me. I had to focus on walking. Lady Mary led me slowly through the presence chamber, and I arrived at the foot of the dais without mishap.

At last, I looked up into the eyes of the king.

I didn't see my future heartache there, the end of all my fondest dreams, the death of love and trust. I only saw a man a little portly around the middle, perhaps fifty or a bit less, with a tired face and light brown hair brushed smoothly back. There was nothing particularly royal about him, and I started to relax, smiling up at him.

Lady Mary pinched me, and I remembered my duty. Gathering up the fullness of my skirts, I sank low to the ground in deep obeisance to my monarch and waited for him to acknowledge me. I felt like I was there an eternity. A woman giggled. I counted my heartbeats as my legs began to tremble. Thirteen . . . fourteen . . . fifteen . . .

Why hadn't he spoken to me? Had I committed some terrible blunder? I suddenly remembered my dagger, locked as it always was inside the busk at my chest. Had the hidden knife peeked out of my low-cut bodice? Did he think I was an assassin? I placed my hand to my heart, as if swearing fealty. The knife was still secure and secret.

Finally, I looked up, to see what was wrong. The king didn't even seem to know I was there. He was gazing over my head to the back of the presence chamber. A little smile played on his lips. If I *was* an assassin, how easy it would have been to slay him there in that moment of distraction. Whatever he was looking at, it commanded every particle of his attention.

Lady Mary cleared her throat, and Queen Anne touched the king's arm.

King James shook his head as if to clear it of some fantasy. "You may rise," he said in a sonorous voice with the faintest trace of a Scottish burr. I remembered that he had been reared in Scotland, son of Henry Stuart (assassinated by his wife) and Mary, Queen of Scots (executed by her cousin Queen Elizabeth).

I clasped my hands in front of me. "We are pleased to welcome you to court, Lady . . ." An attendant behind him whispered my name into his ear. "Lady Clarice, daughter of our good and loyal servant Lord Paget." The attendant whispered something else. "You have delighted us with the gift of a kingly gyrfalcon, and we thank you for your kind generosity. He is a splendid bird."

"She," I blurted out. "The largest and fiercest are always female." Mary hissed at me to hold my tongue. The king frowned down at me.

"You are female, I believe, and you are not so large."

The prince, young Charles, laughed and said, "I think she only referred to falcons, Your Majesty. Or perhaps not. She seems to be fierce enough for this court."

I glanced his way, while Lady Mary made faces at me. The prince was a pleasant-looking young man, fifteen or sixteen, with a little wisp of down on his chin teased into a point, trying its best to be a beard. He smiled at me, and, forgetting all the subtlety of seduction I'd been taught, I grinned in return, a toothy smile without a trace of artifice. I heard Lady Mary sigh beside me.

"We are amused," the king said, without a trace of that emotion, and nodded to me, which was my signal to make my curtsy to the queen and the prince.

The queen gave me a sympathetic look, the prince a wink, and my performance was done. I had no idea whether I'd succeeded or would be tossed from the court.

As I walked away, a man accosted me, grabbing my hand in a proprietary way and kissing it moistly. "Allow me the pleasure, my lady. Armand Jean du Plessis, Bishop of Luçon." While his head was still bowed

over my hand, I recognized the voice that had called out the lewd sugges-
tion, and I jerked my hand away.

Then he raised his face to mine, and it was all I could do not to scream.
It was the French agent I'd poisoned in Dover. A bishop! And here in
court!

For a moment, I couldn't breathe. My tight corset squeezed the air
from my chest, and the hard busk pressed my heart to stillness. I would
faint, I was sure of it. Then I managed to gasp a breath and look at
things more closely.

There was no recognition in his penetrating brown eyes. Naked lust,
mild curiosity, amusement, but not a trace of anger or suspicion. He did
not know me!

It was then I realized another great truth of the world, one that
would serve me well in years to come. The lower classes, I discovered in
that moment, are a different species entirely from the aristocracy. This
is not a truth of natural history, but an absolute of human belief. He
would no more conflate the barmaid and the court lady than he would
think a house cat could turn into a leopard.

My hair and clothes and setting were different, but my face was un-
changed. He should have known me in an instant. I had half killed him,
and thwarted his scheme. He might not know for a certainty I was the
one responsible, but it would be a natural assumption.

And yet he saw my fine clothes and perfect coiffure, and looked no
deeper.

"I'll allow you no pleasure, monsieur," I said in Maman's court French.

He gave a Gallic shrug. "Then the pleasure may be all yours, mademoiselle. At least, the first time."

I didn't understand him, and hurried away, the weight of his eyes
upon me all the while. I felt strangely powerful, to have this new knowledge, to know that my very person and body were a secret so deep that
no one else could plumb their fathoms.

Lady Mary and I retreated to the wings to watch the rest of the presentations. As it turned out, there was only one after me. I finally learned what had commanded the king's absolute attention. He commanded *everyone's* attention.

My appearance had drawn comments and catcalls. When George Villiers entered the presence chamber, the room grew still. I swear not a soul was breathing. This, then, was the sartorial secret he and his mother had kept so well. He was all in black, soft and deep as night. Instead of the short, puffy breeches that were a la mode, he wore pants that fit close to his shapely legs and reached to his knee. Black hose, black shoes, black garters all made him look slim and solemn. But upon that black was Poseidon's own bounty of pearls.

They hung from him in lustrous ropes, from shoulder to wrist, from chest to hip, twisted around his throat and descending to his legs. He positively dripped with pearls. With a look on his face that I would almost call demure, he approached the king, and the gleaming pearls rattled like the chains of the most elegant ghost. My father, his sponsor to court, walked beside him, but no one had eyes for Lord Paget. I, who had caused a quick sensation, was already forgotten.

At the king's feet he bowed, the practiced flourish of a courtier, and the pearls swept to the floor, bouncing with a pleasant melody. The pearls must have cost thousands, tens of thousands, but he treated them as if they were mere tinsel. Appear valued, and you will be valued. He was a young man without title and with hardly any rank, of a middling family, come to beg at court. But he looked like an emperor offering his very empire to King James.

His face, though, was all boyish charm, and unlike most who had been presented that day, he never lowered his eyes but stared at the king. There seemed to be some secret communion between them. I saw the king mouth a word, but I don't think even those courtiers closest to him could hear what he uttered. George, though, must have, because his smile deepened, and his eyes crinkled.

The king spoke some rote public words, and George moved on to the queen and prince. As casually as if they were school friends, he asked

Prince Charles a question about stag hunting, and the prince responded at length.

Then it was all over, and the world of the court regrouped to assess its new members, to plot our downfall or co-opt us into their own cliques.

"Did I do well?" I asked Lady Mary.

"You most certainly did not. There may be a time for a lady to be saucy, but in the royal presence, you are to be demure and virginal, always. Correcting the king! It's a wonder you weren't clapped up in the Tower."

She held a conference with my father, while I stood with George, looking out over the curled and feathered heads, the sea of silk, the roaring ocean of gossip. He looked perfectly at ease. But then, he had been to the court in France for a year, where he learned all sorts of fine and easy manners. This was so new to me. The crowd alone, the sheer number of people threatened to overwhelm me. I was used to my mother, a maidservant, a gardener . . . no more. How did my father and Lady Mary expect me to accomplish anything in this mass of people? I'd felt beautiful and powerful while they watched me approach the king, the cynosure of their eyes. Now I saw the sidelong looks, couldn't quite hear the whispers, and felt uncertain.

"It is decided," Lady Mary said a moment later. "You're unsuited to this sort of work. Your father will send you home, and we will continue our plans with George alone."

"No!" I cried, causing nearby heads to turn.

When I first left home, I would have given almost anything to remain there safe in my patterns and habits with Maman. Now, though, being sent home from this dazzling place and this great wide world would feel like a crushing defeat. Yes, court frightened me . . . but so had galloping on a horse at first. Soon afterward, it felt like racing the wind. Court would be no different.

"Again, you make a scene," Lady Mary chided with a hennish clucking. "Haven't I taught you that you should be noticed, but not notorious? You'll ruin all our plans with behavior like that."

"I'll try harder," I swore. "Please, let me stay."

Lady Mary and my father exchanged a look. "Hmm . . . perhaps there is something you could do," Lady Mary said. "It's difficult, and I doubt you could manage it. If you do, you'd show us what you're capable of, and I'll consider letting you stay."

The spark of a challenge ignited in me. "I'll do it."

Her mouth stretched in a slow, spreading smile. "Very well. You know who our enemies are. Carr, and that French bishop. If you want to stay, find some way to cause either man to suffer disgrace. Do you think you can do that?"

I had no idea how, but without hesitation, I swore that I could.

We left the presence chamber shortly afterward. Both my father and Lady Mary had rooms in Whitehall Palace, and George and I were given small chambers nearby.

Before we parted for the night, I asked him what word the king had whispered when he beheld George in all his pearls.

"Ganymede," he said, and kissed my brow.

Outlandish plans swirled in my head, but in the end, I had no need of them. Opportunity came to me.

"There's to be a masque next week," Lady Mary informed me. "If you are here—*if*—then you must participate. I will be portraying Venus, and you will accompany me as Cupid."

The servant lay a set of men's clothes on my bed. They were quite drab and ordinary. Obviously, Venus was to be the star attraction. Only a little gilt bow without a string marked me as Venus's child with his arrows of love.

On edge, I tried on my masque costume. Although I could only see a tiny portion of myself in my little mirror, I was surprised at the transformation. Once my hair was tied back in a tucked-in queue, it was even more amazing. The padded doublet concealed the curve of my breasts and broadened my shoulders, and the short, puffed pantaloons made my hips irrelevant. The entire costume was black, with the sleeves pricked to show a white shirt beneath. Once I wiped away the trace of powder and kohl from my face, I looked like any ordinary beardless boy, one of a hundred pages or younger sons of noblemen swarming the palace.

In the mirror, I could scarcely see my own self. Even knowing of the feminine soul that lay behind the cloth, I still saw the boy first.

It made me wonder at the way people only see what they expect to see. Boy's clothes; therefore: boy. I had fooled the French bishop even in the same gender by changing from poor to rich. He'd probably be no more astute if he saw me in these clothes. I bet that even George wouldn't recognize me at first, though I was the woman he loved.

What great fun it would be to swagger up to his door and pretend to be a man. How long could I pull it off? Half of me hoped love would help him instantly see through my disguise. The other half, prideful, wanted to be so successful that even he was duped.

It felt strange to stride through the palace in men's clothes. They showed off my body in unaccustomed ways. With my legs on display but tightly encased, my lower half felt positively naked, and yet strangely bound at the same time. For the first time, I wondered why men, who have no fear of rape and who will whip out their privities to pass water or fornicate whenever they will, wear such binding nether garments that take such a struggle to remove. We women, on the other hand, who live in fear of violation, wear skirts that can be easily lifted by any passerby. It should by rights be the other way around.

I suppose the rules are made by men, who want to protect their own precious jewels while leaving ours convenient for filching.

Feeling the need of one touch of femininity, however hidden, I slipped Maman's rosary into my pocket and went hunting for George's door. It was slightly ajar. I heard low voices within.

"There's no need for us to be enemies," an unknown man's voice said.

I heard George lightly reply, "I have no enemies," in the dreamy woodland faun tone he liked to use in our seduction games. I always thought that voice was silly. I preferred his voice when it grew husky and passionate.

"You know what I mean. I know the Villiers, Paget, and Jermyn factions are all plotting against the Howard interests."

"I'm sure I don't know what you're talking about," George said in his silky voice. "Plots! You make us all sound like Bill Shakespeare's peculiar families, hating each other in iambic pentameter."

"I know your game," the unknown man went on. "It's one you'll never win. The king is loyal to me. I've been his favorite for nearly ten years."

"Oh, as long as that?" George drawled. "What an age!"

The king's favorite! I realized that George must be ensconced with the notorious Robert Carr. Lady Mary had given me a quick recitation of this most formidable foe's history. He came to London with his friend Thomas Overbury. They said Overbury was the brains, and Carr the beauty. With Overbury pushing him, Carr rose quickly in the king's favor. Soon, he made a scandalous marriage to Frances Howard, daughter of the Earl of Suffolk. The only problem was that she was already married. She sought an annulment on the grounds of non-consummation, and Carr and Frances married, much to Overbury's displeasure.

She was an ambitious, manipulative woman, and Overbury did his best to prevent the match, unearthing scandals and condemning her reputation to anyone who'd listen. The newlyweds got their revenge, though. Soon, Overbury was imprisoned in the Tower of London on some trumped-up charge, and he died there a few weeks later. All this happened some two or three years before I came to court. Now, Carr ruled unchallenged and supreme as the king's chief friend and adviser.

"You'll never take my place," Carr assured him. "But as I serve the king, so you might serve me." His voice dropped. "Those I honor with my favor can rise to great heights."

A heavy silence followed, and I had the impression something was happening in that deliberate silence. Then George said a bit breathlessly, "I assure you, great heights make me dizzy. I've come to court for one reason alone—to marry."

I pressed against the wall, my heart pounding in my chest. We hadn't spoken directly of our plans since his early declarations, so sometimes I half thought it had been a dream. Only in rare moments did he find a chance to murmur precious love-words, crumbs to sustain me. But to hear him speak to another person of our love! That made it more real somehow. Of course, he wouldn't reveal my name—but that he was making his intentions clear to this outsider buoyed my heart.

"I'll be watching you, Villiers," Carr said.

I heard the door shoved open, and I sprinted down the hallway, desperate to not be caught eavesdropping. As I ran around the second corner, I crashed hard into a man just emerging from a room.

"*Ventrebleu!*" he cried, grabbing me by the shoulders and holding me at arm's length. "What right have you to spy on me?" He shoved me away and pulled a hood over his face.

It was the French bishop. I could see in a flash that his goal was concealment. Was he emerging from some married woman's bedchamber? Was he on another secret mission? He was obviously up to some devilment, and unwilling to be caught.

Had I been sensible, I would have simply run. But George's words had elated me, and my costume gave me a false confidence. I looked into his face, searching for the second time in a day for recognition. I found none. It would please me to rub my own recognition of him and his situation in his face as he squirmed. I had no fear for myself. I thought only of a moment of fun, never imagining the consequences. It was exhilarating.

"Spy, Bishop?" I asked piquantly, my voice going from feminine to masculine mid-sentence as I remembered my clothes. "That's funny, coming from you," I said meaningfully.

He looked momentarily alarmed, but quickly regained his composure. "And I suppose you know whose rooms these are, *mon petit fils de pute?*" he asked sharply. "Who sent you to bear tales of me?"

I fell into my role easily. It was vastly entertaining. "I serve none and answer to none, sir. But as for tales, there's no harm in the truth." I didn't know whose rooms I'd caught him leaving, but it was obvious he thought I did and wanted to keep it secret.

Then I realized with delight this might be the very thing Lady Mary had asked me to achieve. I didn't know the identity of whoever he was visiting, but Lady Mary would surely understand the full implications. I'd simply remember the door, pass the word on to her, and she'd be pleased enough to let me remain at court.

But what if I could provoke him further? This thing I caught him at may be no more than a dalliance, and nothing Lady Mary could use. If I angered him, however . . .

Lady Mary had tutored me on the finer points of men's honor. Although duels were illegal, and technically punishable by death, most of the time the authorities turned a blind eye to combat. King James, though, was adamantly against dueling. He'd even written a treatise on the subject. I could tell from the bishop's offended agitation that he would only need the smallest push to send him over the edge. If he was caught participating in a duel, his reputation with the king would plummet.

I smiled. As a woman, that smile would have been teasing and irresistible. As a boy, it was infuriating. His face grew red.

Before I knew it, he'd peeled his glove off and slapped me across the cheek.

No one had ever struck me before. Another woman might be cowed, but in my boy's clothes, I felt a boy's privilege to stand up for myself, to strike back boldly instead of meekly submitting. I rose up in a fury and struck him with my open hand with all my strength. I was pleased to see him stagger back—but not so pleased when he drew his dueling sword and pointed it at my flat, bound chest.

"You will meet me on the field of honor and fight to the death," the bishop said.

And to think, I wanted to tell him, that only this morning he had looked at that breast with hunger. He'd propositioned me (his intentions were clear, even if I didn't understand their nuance), and now he wanted to kill me. I was angry at him for his lascivious comments earlier, for thinking he had any right to accost me like that. And of course, had he but known it, he had good reason to feel murderous. But my blood was hot, and it was the offended woman who answered his challenge, not the counterfeit man.

Playing my part for Lady Mary's schemes, I shouted, "Gladly, sir, if a man of God dare!"

"I was a soldier before I was a priest," he growled. "The meadow in St. James's Park at dawn, then. What is your name, varlet?"

"Clar . . . Clark," I stammered. "John Clark."

He nodded, turned on his heel, and left.

From inside the room I heard a giggle. A disheveled head of brown curls peeked out. "Bravely done, fellow," she said. I vaguely recognized her from the crowd at my presentation, though now she had on far fewer clothes. "If you survive the morning, come to my rooms tomorrow night." She blew me a kiss and closed the door, letting her robe slip at the last instant so I caught a glimpse of the lush thicket between her legs.

What strange creatures they breed in court. I vowed I could never become like them. A man so blind he can't recognize the woman he wanted to seduce a few hours hence just because she's changed her clothes; and a woman so indifferent to affection she'll simply bed the winner of a pointless duel.

A duel! I had no fear for myself. All I had to do was go back to my room, strip off my clothes, and John Clark would disappear. But the bishop would show up at the dueling ground. Lady Mary could arrange to have the king's guards waiting. The king was dead set against dueling. If he found out that Armand was involved in one, he might well be thoroughly disgraced. Surely, he'd be dismissed from court, sent back to France, and there was one of our enemies gone.

I had to tell Lady Mary at once. She only had until dawn to prepare.

The palace was huge, bigger even than the Louvre and the Vatican (though at that time I hadn't seen either place), and it wasn't long before I was lost. I wandered through the hallways, skirting servants (or hosing, or breeching them, I suppose, in my masculine garb) and searching for

Lady Mary's rooms. I thought I'd known the way, but in the confusion of my earlier flight, I'd become hopelessly lost.

I turned down a corridor I thought was hers . . . and ran smack into a boy about my age, dressed in a bright green doublet with silver braid, and high riding boots. He smelled of horses, that old, familiar stable scent that reminded me of home. With a sudden stab of guilt, I realized I'd hardly spared a thought for Maman in the last few days. The excitement of court had overwhelmed me. Now the missing returned with a fresh pang.

"God's eyeballs!" he cursed, scowling at me. He looked familiar, but I couldn't place him. He'd probably been among the throng at the presentation, too.

"I'm not going to fight a duel with you," I preempted him at once, backing hurriedly away and holding up my hands in surrender. "You have my most sincere apologies for bumping into you, but I'm no swordsman and I've had enough of duels for one day, thank you all the same."

His scowl vanished. "You've seen a duel? How I envy you. No one will ever tell me where or when they are."

"I haven't seen one, but there's one tomorrow morning," I said without thinking.

"Perfect. I command you to take me," the boy said, and with that regal voice, I recognized him, and in my shock and terror, I curtsied before I knew what I was doing. It's an ungainly thing to do in breeches, I discovered.

"Are you . . . ?" Prince Charles began, frowning in puzzlement as I desperately tried to convert it into a masculine bow. "Take off your hat."

"Your Highness, I . . ."

An upward twitch of his eyebrows was enough to remind me that as the heir to the throne, he all but held my life in his hands. Seeing my future quite clearly—disgrace, spinsterhood, exile—I dragged the high crowned hat from my head, letting my hair tumble free.

"I thought as much," Charles said, looking inordinately pleased with himself for having discovered my secret. I was impressed, too. He seemed slightly more observant than most court men. "You're Paget's girl, right? The one who corrected my father before all the world?"

I hung my head, but he lifted my chin with his fingers. "It's not often the presence chamber is so lively. Between you and George Villiers, you caused quite a sensation."

I snuck a look at the prince. He didn't seem shocked. Lady Mary's voice lectured me in my head. *Some men will like a bold wench—within reason. If you judge your mark to be so, let him think you daring. Just never more daring than him. Then seem to regret your hoydenish ways.*

"Your Highness, I made a terrible mistake dressing in these clothes. It was all for a childish prank. I just got so overwhelmed in the excitement of court. Life at home in Yorkshire was so placid." I made my eyes luminous with unshed tears. (I didn't let them fall. I knew that while imminent tears are enticing, fallen tears just leave the eyes puffy and the nose red.)

"It sounds like my life here," the prince said wearily.

"Oh no, Your Highness," I gushed. "I can't imagine anything more exciting than being the prince."

"It's a charade occasionally enlivened by a parade," he said, and I laughed, though I was sure he'd rehearsed that quip and probably repeated it a dozen times. *Men's jokes are always amusing*, Lady Mary taught me. *The richer the man, the funnier the joke.*

I took a chance, and gave him the shy, seductive glance through my lashes that Lady Mary said was an especially effective maneuver of mine. "It must be hard to be a prince," I said with warm sympathy. "Someone watching you all the time, your fun as carefully choreographed as a masque."

"You understand me," he said. "Everyone else looks at me with dread or envy. Except the king and my tutors. *They* treat me like a dunce. But you— Can you really know how my life is?"

I just smiled, that sphinx smile that tells all and nothing.

I was astounded at my calmness. The prince, within my grasp! He had to marry a princess, so an affair was the only possible end he might seek. Both my father and Lady Mary had made it abundantly clear what would happen to me if I gave away my virginity, even to the prince. It was my choicest treasure, and like my very person, belonged to my father to spend as he pleased. Still, this was exactly what Papa and Lady Mary had envisioned for me: cozening the loftiest nobility to gain favor for our family and our faction. I don't think either of them quite dreamed I'd aim this high.

If I could keep on the prince's good side, he might use his influence to help George. Money, an earldom—I might be able to help George get anything, if I played my cards right. And then . . .

"I long for excitement," the prince went on. "A duel would suit me perfectly. Can you arrange for me to attend?"

"But your father has declared dueling illegal," I protested.

"Then we'll just have to make sure he doesn't find out. I know how I can sneak past my retinue and out of the castle."

"Surely, anyone who sees you will recognize you, Your Highness," I said. He was pulling me into deep and dangerous waters. "Anyone but a country bumpkin like myself. Why, your costly clothes alone . . ."

"True," he said, musing. "I don't have a single outfit that doesn't mark me as a prince." He snapped his fingers. "You'll give me yours, then. The clothes you're wearing now. They're decent and serviceable, and won't mark my rank. You'll have no need of them."

I fairly sighed with relief. For a terrible moment, I'd thought he was going to make me don boy's garb again and take him to the duel. I'd happily give him directions—and clothes—and send him off to enjoy himself as he may, though I could have told him it would be a disappointing, one-sided duel indeed. Perhaps George could take him to a better duel on another day, something more exciting that would cement their camaraderie . . .

"Because you'll be wearing your own gown when you accompany me," the prince went on blithely, unaware that I almost died then and there. "And a mask, of course, and a deep hood. That should suffice to protect your reputation, no?"

"But, Your Highness, I can't!" I cried.

His lighthearted manner changed abruptly, and he was once again every inch the sovereign-in-training. "You *will* accompany me, Lady Clarice."

And that, it seemed, was that.

Lady Mary was so proud of me. She called me her little chicken, her chuck, and gave me a box of almond sweetmeats. "And to think, I almost sent you home," she said, with a sly wink at my father. Lady Mary reassured me. "I'll arrange for the guards to arrest the bishop on his way to the duel. It will all be over by the time you and the prince get there."

"And George," I added, for she'd promised he would accompany me, both for my safety and my honor. "Won't the prince be angry when there's no duel for him to see? He has his heart set on it."

"He won't care—it will be an adventure. As long as he sneaks out for a frolic, he'll be content. And think what fun the three of you will have laughing about it afterward! It will make you all fast friends. I couldn't be happier with your success." She kissed me on the cheek, and I blushed, immeasurably proud of myself.

Whenever I voiced other worries about the plan, she tut-tutted and told me to trust her. "Do as I say, and both you and George will rise like . . . like smoke."

I didn't like her analogy. Smoke may rise, but it can also be puffed away with a breath.

Chapter 6

I never slept, but was scrubbed and dressed and ready long before the prince was expected. I wore a gown borrowed from Lady Mary, too light for the season and very revealing. She lacked my lavish curves, and my body strained at the thin ruby-colored silk. I slipped my busk—and dagger—down the front. I couldn't imagine needing it while dressed as my proper gender, but I remembered Maman's words and kept it close.

When the tap finally came at my door, I'd been pacing for the better part of an hour. I hoped for George, to steady my nerves, but it was the prince. He was dressed in his finery, but I had the borrowed outfit waiting for him. I curtsied low, and had the pleasure of feeling his eyes skim appreciatively over me.

"God's eyes, but you are lovely," he murmured, all but eating me up with his intense gaze. Then he unbuckled his sword, and started stripping off his clothes.

My hand flew to my breast, my fingers on the hidden hilt of my dagger. I was certain ravishment was at hand. I nearly cried with relief when Charles only dropped his fine garments in a heap, leaving on his knee-length shirt, and began to struggle into his disguise. He might intend ravishment eventually; there was time enough for that. This might be his only chance to sneak away to a duel. The sheltered prince had his priorities.

We crept out into the deserted hallway. I wore a mask tied securely around my head with a red silk ribbon. The eye holes didn't quite line up, so I had to keep shifting it to see properly. It wouldn't seem too strange. Masks were in fashion just then, to add piquancy to a woman, or, more practically, to protect the face from London's omnipresent soot and grime.

I was frightened, but I told myself over and over that this was for George's sake, and for our future together. When he'd risen sufficiently high, we could convince our families of our match.

"George Villiers will accompany us," I told the prince as I tapped on George's door.

"Is that necessary?" he asked. "I need no distraction from my charming companion." He made me a little bow.

I flashed a winning smile, but quailed within. Why wasn't George answering my knock? I rapped more loudly, hurting my knuckles, but still, there was no answer. I didn't dare call out.

"No matter," the prince said. "You can be my guide, and I your defender." He put his hand on his sword hilt. The fine filigree of the guard was a striking contrast to his borrowed clothes, and marked him as either a noble or a thief. I wanted to tell him that the sword ruined his disguise, but didn't quite dare. I'd already corrected enough royalty for the season.

"But he promised he'd go with us," I protested. "He's practically a cousin, and it wouldn't be proper for me to . . ."

The prince was having none of that. "If you were worried about propriety, you wouldn't be here now. Come, I don't want to miss it." I hesitated. "Are you disobeying an order from your prince?" He asked it archly, but I heard the veiled threat and hastened down the hallway, my hand lightly on his arm.

Oh, George, I thought as I looked desperately over my shoulder. *Where are you?*

As we rounded the next corner, I heard footsteps behind us. George! I whirled with an expectant smile beneath my mask . . .

"Your Highness, my lady," Robert Carr said with a bow. When he rose, there was a little smirk on his face.

"What are you doing here?" Charles asked Carr petulantly, sounding like a little boy in the schoolroom.

In his suave manner, Carr replied, "Word came to me that you and your charming lady of mystery were planning an outing of dubious legality." His own spy network must be even more extensive than Lady Mary's. "I've come to offer my services to make sure your royal person is unmolested."

Charles looked supremely annoyed. I knew the one thing he longed to do was escape his minders' watchful eyes and have an adventure of his own, free from the constraints of court life. And now his father's chief courtier had come to be his watchdog. I could tell that he'd like to dismiss Carr at once. But that would mean the end of his adventure. Either the king already knew, and would allow it only under Carr's supervision (which, given His Majesty's abhorrence of duels, was highly unlikely), or the king didn't know yet, but would if Carr wasn't allowed to go and keep him safe.

The poor prince could only have an outing under the care of his handlers. I could see Charles grinding his teeth, and I put my hand on his arm. He might be disappointed, but I meant to salvage the excursion if I could. I leaned my cheek against his and whispered, "Mayhap we can slip him."

Charles perked up at once, and said, "Very well, Carr. Let us away."

Outside the scattered torches of the palace, it was a wet wool morning, gray and damp. I wished I had a cloak, or George's warm arm, for the chill seemed to slither up my legs.

Uncertainly, I picked our path through the nearby St. James's Park, trying to find the open meadow of the dueling ground. I would have gotten lost, perhaps even on purpose to avoid the coming awkwardness, but the prince heard a commotion ahead of us and quickened his pace, dragging me at his side. How many women, I wondered, would delight in being on the prince's arm? They could have him as far as I was concerned.

I saw figures in the center of the field. My pulse began to speed. That wasn't right. The French bishop was supposed to be arrested on his way to the park. The place should have been deserted. This was supposed to be a dawn stroll, no more. I slowed, trying to check the prince, but he said, "Ah, here we are."

"There you are, you blasted nuisance!" the bishop cried. He was dressed in civilian clothes, and looked quite comfortable with the sword at his hip. There was nothing ecclesiastic about him this morning, and I had the impression there rarely was, unless it especially suited his purposes.

Some choice Yorkshire curses slipped free of my lips sotto voce as he stalked up to the prince. "I didn't believe you'd have the cods to show up, you varlet," he said to Charles. "But as you have, prepare to meet your end, Mr. Clark. Is this your second? And your harlot come to bid you adieu as you expire?" It was only then I remembered that the prince was wearing the same clothes I had last night. I'd been blinded by the pride in my plan! The bishop thought the prince was me—or rather John Clark. I gave a hysterical laugh. He had no idea he was challenging his prince to a duel. Treason heaped upon mere crime.

Charles, though, didn't seem to see the joke. Offended by the bishop's familiarity, he bristled and drew his own sword. "How dare you address me in this fashion? On your knees, sirrah!" The bishop only laughed.

"This is ridiculous," I said, stepping between them. "You can't possibly fight your pri . . ."

Suddenly, there was a shout from the surrounding woods. "Surrender in the name of the king!"

The king's guards rushed into the clearing, their heavy swords hemming us all in. Damnation! Lady Mary's plan must have gone awry. Instead of catching only the bishop en route, they'd surrounded the lot of us. We were trapped.

My first notion was simply to tell the truth—that His Highness wanted to see a duel. They were so used to seeing him in cloth of silver that they never recognized his rather commonplace face in ordinary clothes. Once they knew who he was, the guards would drop their swords, fall to their knees, and do their master's bidding.

But as I drew breath to reveal all, I realized that this would be disastrous. If the king knew the prince was at a duel, he'd punish him, and anyone associated with the rash caper. That would certainly further my designs against Carr, but the penalty would also fall on me, and anyone connected with me.

My heart sank. I had to do something to keep the prince from being captured and identified.

But what could one woman do against a dozen soldiers armed with swords and muskets?

I had an idea, and it seemed like a good one. "When I distract them, you run," I whispered to Charles. Then, as generations of women before me have done when placed in a trying situation, I screamed. I ran for the soldiers, looking my most pathetic and terrified (which wasn't at all difficult just then), and begged for their help as if I were an innocent maiden there against her will.

All of the soldiers looked to me, but whether to help me, or because they thought I was a madwoman, or because my perilously low dress had been pulled even lower by my feigned hysterics, I didn't know, or care. The important thing was it gave Charles a perfect opportunity to run into the forested section of the park and escape.

Except, he didn't.

That stupid, arrogant boy, who ever since his elder brother died had been taught to believe he was the second most important person in all Christendom, stood there in his drab peasant clothes and expected the king's guards to recognize and obey him.

"It is my will that you retreat from this assembly, and allow us to carry on our private pursuits," he said haughtily. Which, as I could have warned him, didn't sit well with the soldiers. The captain of the guards, looking bored and exasperated, didn't say a word but came at Charles with his sword. The prince did his best, and I must say he looked pretty doing it.

His fencing master must have spent hours teaching him how to thrust elegantly. It was nothing to the soldier's brutally efficient style. He simply knocked the prince's sword out of his hands with his heavier weapon and put the tip to his throat.

Carr, who like myself had evidently been looking for a way out of this that kept his reputation intact, stepped up and began, "Captain, I insist that you . . ."

The soldier didn't seem to like someone approaching so near his flank. He reversed his sword and bludgeoned Carr with the heavy pommel. He sank like a stone.

I had dashed toward the soldiers before, and now I ran back to Charles. No one tried to stop me, though the bishop, his second, and the surgeon were disarmed and held at sword point by now. I wasn't worth their notice. They didn't believe I was a threat, and in my flimsy shoes and filmy dress, I couldn't outrun them. Eventually, they would corral me and question me, or do worse if they thought me a harlot. But for now I was negligible.

I realized then that great power lay in being underestimated.

No one stopped me when I walked up to the captain holding Charles prisoner. He didn't even glance my way as I drew my slender dagger from my bosom. Standing behind him, unnoticed, unimportant, I had time to both be afraid and conquer my fear. I had time to consider, and dismiss various targets. Not the heart, the throat, or the kidney. It wasn't this soldier's fault that he was accidentally threatening his prince. I didn't want to kill him. And not the tendons of his leg, or his career was over.

I stabbed, hard and true, into the meat of his thigh.

When he turned, I whipped the knife behind my back, and I'm not sure whether he truly believed at first that I was the one who had stabbed him. A woman? Impossible. Too stoic for his own good, he bought us time by not yelling, but whirled on his one good leg as if looking for his attacker.

I grabbed the prince's hand and pulled him into the forest. To hell with his royal whims. I would save him whether he wanted it or not.

When I ran, the captain must have seen my knife, slick with his own blood, because he cried, "After her!"

The fog was thick that morning, rising off the lake and making the park a grim fairyland. Within a few steps, I could hear the soldiers behind us, but couldn't see them, nor they us. I think we would have gotten clear away had not the contrary prince insisted on being princely.

"'Tis shame to run from an enemy," he panted as I dragged him along. I paused only long enough to wipe the knife on the moss underfoot and slip it back into my busk.

"They're not the enemy," I said through gritted teeth, wanting more than anything to strike him. "They're your own soldiers. But they can't know who you are!"

He tried to carry on an argument as we ran, and finally, he jerked away from me. "You, being a lady of delicate sensibility, must of course flee from conflict. I bid you return to the palace. I will proceed at a pace and in a manner befitting my rank."

I learned later that he'd had rickets as a child, and hadn't been able to walk properly until he was six. Though he was much stronger now, and an avid hunter, he did most of his sports on horseback, sparing his legs. I think he was embarrassed to have me see his legs weak and trembling.

"But, Your Highness," I pleaded.

"Go," he said, panting. "I command you."

I had no choice. To disobey was treason.

I've since learned that strategic treason is sometimes in everyone's best interests, provided you're fairly sure the monarch in question can be brought around to your way of thinking in the end (or will never know about it). That early morning, though, I just ran into the fog and hoped for the best.

Unfortunately, in my confusion, I ran in the wrong direction, and came face-to-face with the captain, limping through the woods. Wounded though he was, he managed to grab hold of my arm before I could flee. I pulled away and slapped him across the face with my free hand, but he gripped my other arm, holding me like a vise and pulling my sleeves off my shoulders. As I struggled, half naked, we both tumbled to the ground, but he never released his grip.

Now he had his knee in my stomach, digging in, pinning me agonizingly to the ground. "Who are you, you damned jade?" he asked, and I realized with utter relief that I still had my mask on. That relief was short-lived as he tore it from my face. There was no recognition in his eyes, but by the time he'd dragged me to prison, someone surely would have identified me. I was close to naming myself, in hopes he'd go easier on a lady of gentle birth.

Whatever he believed me to be, he was not inclined to mercy. The deep wound in his leg was bleeding onto my belly. I could feel the blood, hot and viscous, seep through the fine raw silk.

"Sir, please release me," I begged, hardly able to breathe with his weight on top of me. He loosed my arms, and I began to hope.

Then his hands closed around my throat, and I tried to scream, but I had no breath. There was to be no prison, then, no trial, just sure and swift punishment. He thought me a harlot, no doubt, and a loose woman at a duel who stabbed a soldier of the king's guards deserved no better. It would be a footnote on a report, and an unmarked grave for me.

Already my vision was hazy, my thoughts fogged as he squeezed the life from me. He didn't feel the fists I beat against his ribs, and my pleading eyes (no doubt bulging by then) had no effect on him. Death nipping at my heels, I had no other choice. I reached for my dagger. The vein I'd marked in his throat stood distended with his effort to kill me, throbbing.

My fingers brushed the hilt, but his choking grasp half blocked me, and my head was cloudy, my strength fleeing. I didn't think I had the strength to save myself, and the world seemed to ebb in one final tide.

"Let her go," a low voice said from behind.

He wouldn't have, I think, if the command hadn't been followed by the slick, sharp sound of steel being drawn once . . . twice. The captain's hands unclenched from my throat, and he stood awkwardly, favoring his wounded leg. He drew his sword, still straddling me as he searched for the interloper.

I heard him laugh. "Is this a game for children?" he asked. His boots crushed my gown. "Is every duelist this night a peach-cheeked youth? And what are those weapons you wield? Even your blades are child sized."

My vision was still hazy, but as the blood rushed back to my head in deafening pulses, I saw a figure standing near, a tall, slender form that seemed to hold two slim weapons. Too small for swords, too big for knives, they looked like children's playthings, skinny and flimsy.

But when the captain advanced on the stranger, I learned for the thousandth time that looks can be deceiving.

A Musketeer could describe the artistry of the fight, how the captain used a parry of the Viggiani school, a thrust favored by Saviolo. To me it was all speed and savagery at first. The captain lunged, confident in his skill and power, going for a kill right away. He looked surprised when the other man flicked his sword to the side with the left knife, then danced inside his guard to slice the captain's wrist with the right.

"Who are you?" the captain bellowed as he circled his opponent.

I was deeply curious, too. At first I thought it might be George come to rescue me, but the build was wrong. This man was taller, lighter. And while, like any man of his age, George knew how to fence, it was clear, even to me, that this man was a master at his unusual style.

But the stranger didn't answer, only stepped lightly, searching for an opening. Enraged, the captain charged again. The blades joined and parted, the men advanced and fell back, in such frenzied motion now that I could scarcely follow it. I had no idea who was winning. As they whirled and countered each blow, I could barely tell them apart.

It should have disgusted me, frightened me. And yet . . . I felt some-how more alive than I ever had before.

The fight became beautiful. The stranger was almost dancing.

Then the captain got a lucky strike that seemed to pierce the other's arm, though I saw no blood. The man with two knives dropped his guard and cringed. Laughing, the captain lunged to kill his opponent.

I screamed.

Then at the last second, so fast I could scarcely see what happened, the stranger straightened and turned slightly so the rapier blade passed without touching him. The captain, overbalanced with his overconfident assault, stumbled forward, and the stranger slipped behind him. One knife stabbed up under the captain's armpit. The other stabbed down in the hollow of his throat.

The captain fell heavily to his knees and didn't rise again.

The stranger came at me swiftly, his knives in his hands. I scrambled backward on the wet grass, skidding and desperate.

Then I heard a soothing Yorkshire voice speaking to me as if I were a restless falcon.

"Denys?" I gasped. How was that possible?

His hands, gentle enough to smooth the softest down of a bird's breast, eased my bodice the rest of the way up over my bosom. "Come," he said, and offered me his hand. I grasped it like a lifeline to a drowning man. He pulled me to my feet, and when I staggered, he swept me into his arms.

"We have to hurry," he said. "If the other soldiers find us, we're done for. Luckily, your gown is the color of blood. You have so much on you. Thank heaven none of it your own."

I rested my head against his chest. For a second—and a second only—I hardly cared how he came to be there. I only cared that I was safe. Soon enough, though, curiosity (which I've found to be a close cousin to self-preservation, despite the old adage about cats) took over and I asked him, "What are you doing here?"

He smiled down at me, nestled against him. "Saving you. Didn't you notice?"

"I mean . . ."

"I know what you mean. Don't trouble yourself about it. Only know that when you need me, I'll be there."

"You followed me?" I pressed.

"I just happened to be here," he said.

"And how did you know how to do . . . that?" I gestured at the dead sergeant and all it implied.

"Just got lucky."

I didn't believe him for a moment. That was the fighting of someone who had trained his whole life. How did Denys know that? As far as I was aware, he'd trained in nothing but falconry.

He'd arrived at the palace long before I had, settling in with Isolde while I was learning the art of seduction under Lady Mary's tutelage. I'd meant to pay him a visit in the royal mews, but hadn't had the leisure. And truth be told, the intoxication of court and my feelings for George had eclipsed my thoughts of my old friend—and my brief, unwise infatuation with his lips.

Still, as I looked up into that kind, familiar face with its constellations of freckles, I had to admit that at that precise moment I treasured him more than all the world.

He snuck me into the palace and left me without answers.

When Lady Mary found out that her gown was ruined, she was furious.

It was nothing to the way I felt when she sat me down and told me how successful our plan had been. The plan I had not been completely privy to.

I was perched in her bedroom, cleaned of blood and clad in a loose sea-green morning gown. I'd hardly had time to put together a coherent thought, and I had a feeling that when I had leisure and solitude, I'd give way to tears. I was fending off the memory of the captain's hands squeezing at my throat, of his body falling lifeless to the ground. Eventually, I feared, I wouldn't be able to fight it anymore.

"Where was George?" I demanded. Though relieved he'd not been caught in the mire, I couldn't help but think that somehow everything had gone wrong because George had not been there. In a way I was right. Lady Mary would never have permitted her precious son to be endangered. Me, on the other hand . . .

"It was necessary that he not join you this morning," Lady Mary said evasively.

"But why?"

"First, tell me everything that happened."

I did . . . almost. I told her about stabbing the captain to help the prince escape, and admitted that someone later fought and killed the captain when he tried to kill me. But I swore that I had no idea who his murderer was. I owed Denys that much, at least. Again and again, the nagging questions sounded in my head: Why had Denys been there? Had he been following me? Why?

Lady Mary owned that she was impressed by my pluck and quick thinking.

She wasn't satisfied that the endeavor had been a complete success until she heard a scratching at her door. She opened it, and a kerchiefed head poked in. The servant whispered something quickly, and Lady Mary handed her a coin.

"I believe you've proven you can be trusted with our complete plans," she said. Whenever someone announces that they're telling you the whole story, assume there's still a half—usually the better half—untold.

"I've gotten word that the prince is safe," Lady Mary said. "Apparently, he slipped into the stables and everyone believed he'd been out for an early morning gallop on the palace grounds. That was my only worry in this whole scheme. If the prince had been injured . . . Ah, but you saw to it that he was safe, bold girl!"

No worries about *my* safety, you see.

"This morning," she said, "you went a long way toward securing Carr's downfall. He was arrested, exactly as I'd hoped, and the king is livid."

As it turned out, she'd arranged for one of her spies or agents to drop a discreet word about the prince's early morning plans to Robert Carr, in the hopes that he would decide to accompany the prince. She knew that though Carr and the king were the closest friends, a king is mortal, and the friendship of his heir is almost as important to cultivate.

Carr had been trying for the past few years to earn the trust of young Charles, so far unsuccessfully. Whether the prince resented the way Carr stole his father's attention, or noticed his weaselish ways, Charles had made his dislike of Carr abundantly clear. Carr had hoped that accompanying the prince to something as exciting as a dawn duel might bring them closer.

"It might have worked, if the soldiers hadn't shown up at the dueling place instead of arresting the bishop on the way," I said, still not grasping Lady Mary's plan.

Lady Mary said nothing, only smiled that slow, stealthy smile of hers, and suddenly I realized.

"You never just wanted the bishop arrested on the way to the duel. You ordered the guards to go to the dueling ground . . ." My voice was loud even to my ears.

"Hush," she cautioned. "Of course I didn't give that order." For a second I felt guilty for suspecting her. "It can never be traced back to me. I had one of my agents do it."

It had been her plan all along for Carr to get caught at an illegal duel. That would be profoundly embarrassing for the king, because he had spoken often and at length about the sin of dueling.

"And what if the prince had been captured?" I asked.

She shrugged. "Even worse for Carr, because he'd not just be corrupt himself, but corrupting the prince. That would have been perfect. I bet Carr would have been dismissed on the spot. As it is, the prince will surely keep silent, and the burden of the king's displeasure will fall on Carr."

"And the bishop," I pointed out. "And his second. What will happen to them?"

Lady Mary seemed unconcerned. "Nothing much will happen to

any of them. A French bishop languish in jail? He'll make a hefty dona-
tion to the royal coffers and the whole thing will be forgotten."

"But . . ."

"Carr is toppling now," Lady Mary went on, ignoring what she surely
saw as my childish concerns. "All he needs is a good shove, and he'll tumble off his high pedestal for good. If we're lucky, he might even get his
head lopped off in the bargain." I shivered at the casual, almost gleeful
cruelty of her words. "And then George will rise to fill his place."

Why George and not some other? I wanted to ask. Many other courtiers had been there longer than George, were older, with more experience, were already better friends with the king. But Lady Mary, intent on
her schemes, didn't have time for questions.

"Carr has been under suspicion for years," she confided to me. "There
is a rumor about Overbury's death."

Thomas Overbury, Carr's erstwhile friend and first sponsor, had
been dead more than two years. There were rumors aplenty. Even I, at
court for only a few days, had heard murmurs. Overbury had stood in
the way of Carr's marriage to the already married heiress, Frances. Carr
got the king to offer Overbury an ambassadorship to Russia to get him
out of the way, but Overbury refused it, preferring to look after his friend's
(and the king's, and the country's) best interests at home. Refusing a king
is treason, and he was locked in the Tower of London. It should have
been a symbolic incarceration, a brief object lesson. But Overbury died
in prison a few weeks later.

Now, Lady Mary whispered a single word that, if proved, would spell
the end of Carr's reign.

"Poison!"

"He didn't die a natural death?" I asked. "Who poisoned him?"

"The agent isn't as important as the commander," Lady Mary said.
"I don't know whose hand actually tipped the poison vial, but I know
who ordered them to do so."

"Carr?" I guessed.

She nodded. "And his wife, that slut Frances." I've since learned that almost any woman another woman doesn't like becomes a slut.

"And you can prove it?"

"Ah, there's the rub," she said, starting to pace her bedroom. "If only I could find absolute proof of Carr's guilt and present it to the king, Carr would be gone and George could slip easily into his place. But how? I'm at my wit's end, Clarice. I've bribed half the court and blackmailed the other half, and still, no one can hand me definitive evidence."

She stopped pacing across the flagstones and shook her head as if to clear it. "Don't fret, child, or you'll ruin all your beauty, and I still have need of it." She seemed altogether lighter now, carefree. "Tell me, how do you like court? Have you acquired any beaux? Perhaps the prince himself, eh? Remember what I taught you, and don't ever give away more than the tips of your fingers. If anyone offers you familiarities, come to me. We can put our heads together and decide if he needs to be punished—or pushed to propose. When we're all done here, we'll find you a pretty husband, never fear." If only she knew she didn't have to hunt for a husband for me. I'd already picked one out, and she was already doing everything in her power to bring the match about, though she didn't know it yet. Her mighty ambition for her son suited us perfectly. She was as good as arranging the marriage for us.

She patted me on the head as she left, for all the world as if I was a child, and not a woman who had stabbed a man, seen him die, saved a prince . . .

When she was gone, the tears and the terror pounced, and I threw myself on her bed, dissolving. But after that catharsis, I found myself more angry than afraid. Had George come sooner, he would have found me curled in a moist little ball. No doubt I would have meekly flung myself into his arms and let him comfort me. But he delayed, and by the time he found me, I was fuming.

"We are partners!" I railed at him, and watched the smile fade from his face. I was pacing like a caged panther, and I whirled on him with my claws out. "I trusted you. Not your mother, but *you*, George. How could you let me walk into that trap without foreknowledge? Why was it only my neck on the block, not ours? What became of our corporation?"

He stood, to all appearances dumbfounded.

"I was so scared, George," I said, though I didn't sound at all frightened then, no more than a Fury. "He grabbed me . . . and he pulled down my dress . . . and he *hurt* me! And I . . . I saw him die! I was covered in blood!"

Aghast, he took me in his arms, but I pushed away and pummeled his chest with my fists. "How could you do it, George?" He let me go, and I hugged myself, my own arms wrapping around my body, cold comfort because they weren't his.

"My mother said everything went well. Didn't it?"

"You weren't there! You were supposed to be there."

"What happened to you, my love?"

With those words, I felt something melt inside me. I wanted to believe in him. As I told him the story of the night, his face shifted from concern to shock to anger.

"It was well the Lord thought to make the fifth and sixth commandments, for I vow I could well murder my mother for what she has put you through. My poor lamb. I would give anything to have been there to protect you."

"You didn't know?" I asked.

The truth is found in the silence before the lie.

"I never dreamed!" he answered smoothly after the barest pause. "She told me I had to stay behind, that there was a change of plans, but I didn't imagine she would put you in such terrible danger. Oh, that is her way, so bold herself she thinks everyone else she favors is as capable. And yet, you were, Clarice! I would never for worlds have let you test yourself like that, but look how you succeeded. Come here."

He held out his arms again, and this time I entered them, let myself be enfolded.

"I would never have agreed to it—and, naive fool that I am, I should have questioned her more closely when she told me to stay behind. But it is hard to argue with success, is it not? Oh, Clarice, my angel, look what you have done for us! The meddling bishop routed, the prince your friend, and most important, the insolent Carr in deepest disfavor with the king. This night might be the making of me. Of us."

"But why couldn't Lady Mary have told me in advance about her plans? I could have gotten away as soon as Carr was in position."

He looked into my eyes. "Let us for a moment forget about our love, and about the fear you felt, and instead pretend that we are speaking of other people. If you had known, would you have given away the game with your nervousness? Might you have run too soon and spooked Carr? The entire plan could have been ruined if she'd trusted either of us with the information. For if she'd confided in me, do you really think my sense would have overruled my care for you?"

"You could not be involved," I admitted. "If anything had gone amiss, you couldn't risk having your reputation tarnished."

He nodded. "I grieve that you have gone through such torments. But I would sacrifice anything to achieve our ends. Would you not?" He kissed me lightly on the brow. "Particularly now that it is over. Come now," he cajoled, "admit it. Now that it is behind you, wasn't it fun? In a way, I envy you the excitement of the night. We planned such capers in the garden at Brooksby, did we not? And here I am doing little more than smiling and simpering where Mother directs me. But you! What an adventuress you have become!"

I was smiling by the end of this speech. It was true. Fear survived becomes adventure. Secure in our partnership, I nestled against his shoulder and let him spin dreams of our future together. "Your wedding gown will be cloth of gold," he said. "Our house will have forget-me-nots and pansies."

"But not a sprig of wolfsbane!" I added.

"We'll have three sons and three daughters," he said with his arm around me. "We'll be happy for the rest of our days."

And I thought to myself, *It was all worth it.*

Chapter 7

❧

*C*arr, to no one's surprise, was released by sundown, and he attended that evening's royal assembly, dressed as finely as ever in a turquoise suit with a flashy jeweled peacock pin on his breast. But though he mingled and danced and talked gaily with all of the beautiful women in the room, he didn't talk to the king. His Majesty seemed morose, and few courtiers dared approach him.

To my alarm, Prince Charles singled me out for a dance. It was a stately *contrapasso* for two couples, and we paired with Carr and his pretty wife, Frances. I could hardly remember the steps as I searched their faces for signs of murder. I saw only beauty and grace.

It wasn't a dance such as we had at home, with whirling and jumping, but a courtly promenade of mincing steps and slow turns designed to show off a man's well-turned leg, a woman's elegant lines. There was a great deal of bowing and trading of partners, and after a while, I found myself standing close to Carr.

"You look fresh and well rested," he said, before turning in a pirouette.

I curtsied to him, and stepped in a circle around him as he held my fingertips.

"I've found that early hours don't agree with me," I replied. "I renounce them evermore."

We separated, and I didn't know if he thought me complicit in his arrest, or if he believed it to be mere bad luck.

The two men began a movement of their own, each prancing stiff and formal as they circled each other in the dance, leaving Frances and me to ourselves. She smiled at me sweetly, and I returned her smile. Lady Mary hadn't taught me how to read women as she had men. Frances didn't mince her words. "If you interfere with my husband again, I'll pay a beggar with smallpox to embrace you. And that pretty boy of yours, Villiers? He'll find realgar in his soup if he and that bitch mother of his don't cease their schemes." All the while looking like Aphrodite herself. Frances Carr could give me lessons in brazenness even today, a match for Milady at her prime.

I was trembling by the end of the *contrapasso*. Charles bowed to me. All through the dance, he hadn't spoken one word. I suppose the honor he bestowed on me with his presence was my thanks for his little adventure.

When we separated, that vexing, oblivious, lascivious bishop (who had either escaped or been released; I wasn't sure) tried to secure a dance with me, but I shook him off without ceremony. He looked after me hungrily with his dark, sleepy eyes and said, "Someday, *ma petite choupinette* . . ."

As soon as I could, I found Lady Mary and George. "She all but admitted she's a murderer," I told them breathlessly. "She said if we don't leave Carr alone she'll poison you!" I recognized the name realgar as a kind of poison, even if my own knowledge was limited to plant poisons. Realgar was common enough, and often used to kill rats.

Lady Mary and her son exchanged a look. "I see we're hitting to the very quick," Lady Mary said, obviously pleased. "They're scared."

"What if she tries to poison George?"

"Easier said than done," Lady Mary assured me. "Overbury was in prison, and could only eat what he was given, or starve. He would have been easy to poison. George, for the nonce, only eat what I give you, just to be safe." He nodded.

Frances Carr's blatant threat didn't make me fear for myself, for I'd had smallpox as a child (with the good fortune of the only mark being a small cluster of scars near my hairline, easily covered with a curl). But poison was a real threat. Once, it had seemed almost an adventure, this scheming for power. A game, or a horse race. The Carrs had seemed no more than a hedgerow to be leaped over on our mad career to the top.

Now, though, I was both terrified and spurred to action. After the initial fear passed, I felt fury rising within me. A sense of allegiance to our group and an indignation that these people would play with the life of the man I loved for their own selfish ends surged within me. That night, I swore to Lady Mary that I would find a way to prove Carr's guilt. She seemed amused by my new adamance. "Many have tried, child. But I applaud your loyalty to the cause."

I quizzed my father, drawing him away from the voluptuous pleasures he preferred and making him tell me every detail that he knew of Overbury's death. He told me that shortly after Overbury's arrest and imprisonment in the Tower of London, a new Tower lieutenant was appointed, one Sir Gervase Elwes, a friend of Carr's. I learned about Frances Carr's crony Mrs. Anne Turner, a doctor's wife who had made a name for herself patenting the bright yellow starch used on ruffs, and evidently knew something about chemicals and elements. Today, she was the chief of costuming for court masques. Mrs. Turner's former employee, a man named Weston, had been Overbury's servant in prison, and was thus one of the few people allowed to have regular contact with him.

Even I, inexperienced as I was, could draw a line of suspicion directly through those people, marking their probable guilt.

My father, though, didn't seem sure. "Vomiting and flux and fever are common enough, particularly in prison. Lady Mary is convinced, but she grasps at straws and chases will-o'-the-wisps to help her son. Admirable, but occasionally misguided. As I recall, it took Overbury some three months to die. Does that sound like the work of a poisoner to you?"

Not if I was the poisoner.

For all of a day, I was uncertain. Then the next evening, I saw a servant, one I'd never noticed before, hand George a glass of wine. I thought the man's eyes looked shifty. I struck the goblet violently from his hand. He looked annoyed, and since there were so many people around, I couldn't tell him my suspicions. I thought I saw Frances Carr smile at me from across the room, her cat eyes narrowed.

Something hardened in me then. I was haunted by images of George poisoned, George dying. I remembered his near-miss with the wolfsbane. Life is so fragile, I realized, and to love someone makes them a hostage to all the terrible ills and cruelties of the world. I pictured George wasted, pale, perishing, and the steel grew strong within me. It was something cold and unfeminine, something that never quite went away afterward.

When they threatened what I held dear, I changed.

Le cœur a ses raisons que la raison ne connaît point. The heart has its reasons, of which reason knows nothing.

I chose my target carefully. Carr and his wife were already suspicious, and a poisoner's greatest ally is secrecy. The Tower lieutenant might know something, but I could hardly visit the Tower of London on my own. I asked casually after a servant named Weston, but as servants were generally beneath notice, no one had heard of him, and I didn't dare press too closely.

That left Mrs. Turner, who was quite well-known to everyone at court. I sent a message to her, saying that I dearly wished to have a spectacular costume for the upcoming masque, and begging her to please come to my assistance. I could, I hinted, make it worth her while.

I got an answer back almost at once. She'd be delighted to help, and invited me to her chambers.

No, I replied by messenger. Could she come to my room? Though it was far too humble for an artist as renowned as herself, I was anxious to keep my scheme secret. When I revealed all, I wrote, I intended to create a sensation the likes of which England had never seen.

Flattered, she agreed.

I told no one of my plan.

The next morning, Mrs. Turner came to my bedroom. As soon as I saw her, I had misgivings. She was a plump, motherly woman in a simple flowered gown. Her cheeks were as rosy as a country milkmaid's, and her eyes bright and without guile. I'd been expecting someone dark and twisted, a subterranean imp of a woman. But Mrs. Turner made me think of baking bread, warm and wholesome.

What if I was wrong? What if I did this terrible thing and I was wrong?

But I was all graciousness as I invited her to sit in the one chair in my room. I sat on the bed, my feet tucked under me, secretly counting the beads of my rosary to calm myself. Then I jumped up as if only just remembering my manners.

"May I offer you a dish of tea?" I asked. "I'm afraid I only have chamomile and peppermint, not China, but I have a lump of sugar if you like." I'd heated the water in a brazier over my fire earlier, and now the tea was steeping in a pot on my dressing table.

"Thank you, Lady Clarice," Mrs. Turner said, dimpling. "You are most kind."

I crossed the room and with my back to her pretended to pour out two cups of tea. In reality I'd already made my own separately.

I handed her the pretty cup, porcelain painted with pink rosebuds, and took my own, sipping first. It was strong, more peppermint than chamomile. If there was anything else in the brew, it would be virtually undetectable. Particularly since only a very small quantity was needed.

She drank at once. It had been sitting awhile, and was cool enough to consume quickly. A good hostess, I immediately offered her more, and this one she sipped more slowly as I started to talk.

"Whitehall Palace has exceedingly lovely gardens, does it not?" I asked, regarding her over the delicate rim of my cup. It was there, of course, that I'd gotten my poison.

She seemed puzzled, then brightened. "Ah, do you want to model your costume after the king's pleasure gardens? Many women before you have chosen a floral motif for their costume, but perhaps we could give it a novel approach. What do you think of real flowers sewn into a mantle?" She was warming to her topic, and I felt a pang of regret for the rude awakening that was in store for her.

But she needn't fear. If she did as I bid her, all would be well.

"The labor would be costly, because several seamstresses would have to be on hand to attach the blossoms mere minutes before the masque began. You wouldn't want to appear in wilted flowers, would you?"

She chuckled . . . then clutched her stomach as if stricken by a sudden sharp pain. She smiled in apology. Gas, she no doubt thought.

"You could have golden bees, suspended on wires to give the illusion of flight," she went on. "Or brass bees. They'd be cheaper and the effect just as nice." I could see beads of sweat bloom on her forehead, but she pressed on. This dress would bring her a hefty commission. "What are your favorite flowers?" she asked. "Roses? Lilies?"

I stared at her until she grew uneasy and had to look away.

"Wolfsbane," I said in a breathy whisper.

She looked at me, confused. "I'm afraid I don't know . . . oh!" She clutched her stomach and doubled over.

"It burns, doesn't it?" I asked, forcing myself to be calm and cold even though I wanted to run to her, comfort her. She looked like our cook at home in Yorkshire. "You'll vomit soon." I snaked a foot under the bed and pulled out a chamber pot. "In here, if you please. Vomiting won't rid you of the poison, though."

Her eyes grew impossibly wide, and she mouthed the word back to me: *Poison!*

"You know something of poisons, don't you? Not too much, I warrant. It took Overbury weeks to die from whatever you gave him. With the wolfsbane tea you just drank, I'd say you'll be gone in two hours. Two excruciating hours."

I took a sip of my own innocuous tea, hoping she wouldn't see my hands shaking.

She stared at me in a panic, then bolted for the door. She didn't make it halfway across the room.

"Your body isn't your own anymore," I said. "It belongs to me. Your muscles are growing weak; your heart is all aflutter. The burning pain is spreading through your body, isn't it? Tell me what I need to know, and I'll give you the antidote. Fail me, and you'll die." I imagined myself on stage, an actor reciting those powerful lines of malice. It wasn't me, only a character.

"If I die, you'll burn!" she choked out.

That *was* a worry, but I schooled my expression. "Your body will be carried out of here by my agents," I lied, "and next anyone sees of you, you'll be a bloated corpse in the Thames, violated by eels."

I impressed myself. My novel reading was providing me with ample fodder to terrify this woman. Inside, though, I felt a self-disgust that gnawed at my vitals as painfully as any poison. I am not this person, I swore to myself.

For George, for the life we've planned. Just thinking of this gave me fresh courage, and I stood over Mrs. Turner where she lay sprawled and writhing on the floor.

Very clearly, I said, "Tell me what you know of Overbury's death. Tell me everything, and I swear to you I'll let you live."

Weeping, she finally did just that. I even made her write out her confession, signing it in a shaky scrawl, before I gave her the brew of angel's-trumpet and belladonna that would quickly reverse the effects of the wolfsbane.

As she lay on the floor, recovering, I slowly poured the remaining tea into the leaping fire, where it sizzled and sputtered and eventually evaporated. I made sure every leaf was burned to ash.

* * *

I knew what a terrible thing I did, holding a woman's very life in my hands to make her do my bidding. But I didn't think of what would come next. I threatened death and then withheld it in the end, and so absolved myself. The king and the swift justice of the high court, however, showed no mercy no matter how much the guilty confessed. At least, not if they were lowborn.

After getting Mrs. Turner's signed confession, I brought it, victorious, to Lady Mary. "I have it!" I told her, waving the paper under her nose. "Carr is finished." She didn't believe me at first, but when she realized what I'd accomplished, she positively danced for joy, taking my hands and whirling me around.

She took the confession to be delivered by a trusted third party. She didn't want the accusation to come directly from her. The king might have already been annoyed with his old favorite, but that didn't mean he would think kindly of anyone who snatched him away. Carr's fall had to look like his own failing, not the result of an attack.

Once the word was out, things moved with dizzying speed. Though I gave her ample time to flee if she chose, Mrs. Turner was arrested the next day in her rooms in the palace. I don't know why she didn't run. I suppose she thought her friendship with Carr, and her money (besides the yellow ruff starch, I learned she owned three bawdy houses and half share of a merchant ship) would protect her.

It didn't. The trial lasted eight hours. She was found guilty and hanged two days later, as were some days later her former servant Weston, his son, the apothecary who had compounded the poison, and Lieutenant Elwes.

I went to Mrs. Turner's execution, wearing a black dress and the mask I'd worn at the duel. I felt I had to witness the results of my actions, the closing act of the terrible play I'd orchestrated. She'd dressed herself very finely for her last day on earth, wearing yards of costly lace, and a huge golden ruff starched and colored with her own patent saffron treatment. (The fashion died with her.) It made her head glow like the sun. She looked regal as she mounted the gallows at Tyburn. I had to remember that she'd played a role in a murder.

So had I.

The bloody ghost of the dead sergeant seemed to float around my head, jeering at me as I watched the hangman slip the hemp rope around her neck. She dropped, and in the sudden silence, her neck snapped with an audible crack.

Now a second ghost joined the sergeant, a plump, rosy-cheeked face twisted and contorted, its eyes bulging, its lips blue. For her death, too, was on my hands.

Robert and Frances Carr, the Earl and Countess of Somerset, were arrested and brought to trial. Carr pleaded not guilty, and was sentenced to be hanged. Frances confessed—confessed! And yet, though she, too, was sentenced to death, both were instead imprisoned in the Tower. I imagine they took great care about what they ate there. After an interval, both were pardoned and released, ordered to live in exile far from court.

The nobles who had ordered death to win power for themselves had escaped with their lives. The underlings who had done the deeds, who had mixed the poison, delivered it, and poured it into Overbury's food, paid dearly.

We were just alike, the Howards and Carrs, the Pagets and Villiers, stopping at nothing, stooping to anything to get what we wanted. The only difference was that our side had played the game better than theirs.

I tried to put it behind me. Late on the night of Mrs. Turner's execution, I found George in his room and threw the bolt behind me. Then I kissed him with a passion that surprised us both.

"None of it matters!" I cried. "I did it for you, and now we can be together." He didn't know what my part in the affair had been, and looked confused. I didn't care. I kissed him again and asked when we could be wed.

"Soon, my love," he said, thrusting me gently away. "There are things yet to be done before we can declare ourselves."

"Of course," I agreed, becoming demure, a little embarrassed by my passionate outburst. "How goes it with the king?"

He looked away, and took a breath that made no words. Then he seemed to gather himself. "I'm moving quarters today," he said. "To Carr's old chambers."

I squealed with delight. "That's a good sign. Have you been seeing a lot of His Majesty?"

"We played cards last night," George said. "And I'm to join him on a stag hunt tomorrow."

I clapped my hands. Everything was working out perfectly. "Then soon you can speak with your mother about marrying me!"

"Very soon indeed." He paused. "That is, if you will still want me." I felt a flash of dread, then noticed his eyes crinkled in amusement. "After we are wed, I'll still have a courtier's duties. Will it vex you if I am called off at all hours to the king's service? You might expect more from a newly wed husband, and charge me with neglect."

"Oh, George, I know the price we have to pay to be together. If you can bear to be apart for a time, I can bear it, too."

"And only think of our reunions!" he said, nuzzling my neck. "And now I must away. His Majesty is expecting me."

"So late?" I asked. It was long after midnight.

"You see? You shall throw me off, I know it! My only hope is to get you properly married before you get too annoyed at me. Then it will be too late for you to be quit of me."

"Oh, George, I'm so proud of you! *Je t'adore!* I can't wait until we're married." I pressed him to me, once again forgetting all modesty as my body crushed his. Although we'd promised to keep ourselves pure until marriage, I wanted to give myself to him, then and there. I only understood the bare mechanics of lovemaking—Isolde and Robber, pigs in springtime—but my body felt such an urge to join his. He disentangled me with an embarrassed smile and reminded me he must wait upon the king's pleasure.

I'd just have to wait for the wedding night.

As he left, a last wisp of uncertainty prompted me to call him as he was at the door. "Promise me you love me. Promise we'll marry."

He smiled, lightly and boyishly, and said, "Clarice, I promise." Then he was gone. I curled up in his bed, wrapping myself in the sheets that smelled of him.

I promise, he told me to my face. Tell me, after speaking those words to me, who is more the criminal, him or me?

It is George Villiers who made me what I am today. Without George, there would be no Milady to strike terror into the hearts of men.

I dozed for a while, there on his bed. It wasn't at all appropriate, but as we were to be married, I didn't fear a scandal. I awoke before dawn, and despite so little sleep, I rose clear-eyed and refreshed. Love is a tonic.

George had never returned to his room that night.

No matter, I thought. He said he was moving into Carr's old chambers. Perhaps he was there now, sleeping in a far more luxurious bed, and would have his belongings moved from this small room later. A book of Ovid's poetry lay on the table beside his bed. He would be wanting that today, I thought, smiling at myself as I admitted I was coming up with the flimsiest excuse to see him. I'd take the volume to his new chambers, surprise him as light-fingered dawn touched his face. After taking a moment to splash water on my eyes, I slipped into the hallway and navigated the halls until I found the king's wing. The guards let me through with a cursory glance. They were used to assignations, I supposed, and since I was an accepted member of court, I wasn't suspect.

After questioning a servant, I discovered which rooms had been Carr's. I knocked softly, but when there was no answer, I didn't scruple to let myself in. I couldn't bear to be away from George for a moment longer. The marriage litany sounded in my head, oaths I had already sworn in my heart. *To have and to hold*. Oh, how much I wanted that! An indecent amount, I'll own. I felt warm all over, tingling in unexpected places as I searched for him.

It was a large suite of rooms. He wasn't in the first, a sort of antechamber. *Till death us do part*, I chanted in my head. He loved me. Nothing in this life could separate us now.

He wasn't in the bedroom, either. The huge bed had been stripped, and the stuffed feather mattress sat naked on its board. There were a few pieces of furniture, but the room showed quick and thorough evacuation of every sign of Robert Carr. His star had fizzled out, while my George's was ascending.

There was one more room, a dressing room with an empty wardrobe and a clothes press. A large mirror stood in the corner. I paused, regarding myself. Most mirrors I'd seen were small, and I rarely had the chance to contemplate my entire body. I wanted to see if I was a fitting prize for George.

I was. I can say with all modesty that my body was lush, my hair spun gold, my lips a pink pout, my skin alabaster. But my eyes . . .

I gasped and stepped a pace back from the mirror. My eyes didn't seem to belong to me anymore.

They were the same deep blue. They were just as large, wide spaced, with long, dark lashes and a languishing look . . . but they were different. There was some new spark glinting in them. Was it fire, or a shard of ice?

I don't know if anyone else would have noticed the difference, but I certainly did, and it alarmed me. Were they different because they had seen so much since I'd left Maman? Or was it because an altered soul looked out from them?

I squeezed my eyes shut and backed farther away, when I heard sounds.

Laughter. A low moan. A gasp. A rhythmic sound I couldn't place. It sounded close, but there were no more rooms in George's new suite.

But what was that? The tapestry on the wall moved when there was no window, no breeze. I lifted one corner, and found a hidden door, carelessly left ajar.

Though every instinct screamed at me to leave, some compulsion made me slip into the narrow passageway and cross to the adjoining room.

The king's room.

I saw them together on the king's magnificent bed. King James, and my beloved George. Naked, sporting. At first I didn't quite understand. It didn't *look* like pigs in springtime. It was supple and athletic. Hadn't the Greeks . . .

But no, this wasn't Greek wrestling. Laughing, George pinned the king to the bed and kissed him.

Clarice, I promise, he'd said.

The *who* wasn't important, you understand. It was the *what*. That was the betrayal. To love me, and then be naked and joyously intimate with another, whether king or empress or scullery maid.

There was, even in my grief, a part of me that watched in detached fascination. Maman had taught me to observe, and I was seeing something I had never before witnessed. It was an absolute novelty. It was pure, somehow, as fiercely beautiful and changeable as a storm sweeping across the moors, the gentle caressing raindrops giving way to violence and thunder, then fading away again to calm.

And the flesh, exposed, animal, sublime. I had seen more of mankind, and certainly more of man, than most females my age, because I had helped Maman physicking the servants and tenants at home. Even then, though, only the pertinent realm had been exposed. Here before my eyes was a vast new country, the hills and declivities laid bare like undiscovered geography, and I stared at the spectacle of thighs and buttocks and arms, of flesh soft and strong, of two becoming one.

For a brief moment, lost, I forgot myself and marveled. Then it all came rushing back, and I saw again not a curiosity but my own true love betraying me with another.

I made a little muffled sound. The sound of my heart breaking.

George turned, cursing when he saw my face. He sprang up and came after me. I ran through the secret passage, through his dressing room. He caught me in his bedroom, gripping me cruelly by the shoulder. When I struggled, he flung me onto the bare bed and pinned me by the wrists.

As he loomed over me, I looked into his beautiful eyes and searched for the man who had held me in his arms hours ago.

And then, like the heavens breaking clear after a downpour, I thought I understood. Like me, George would do anything to be together. I had demeaned myself by poisoning a woman, by condemning her and others to death. I had done it for him, for us.

He must be doing the same thing, making the ultimate sacrifice so that we can be together. He must be yielding to the king's demands only in order to gain the money, title, and power he needed so that we could wed. And yet a voice in my head asked: Could I have done that, giving myself to one person while loving another? I didn't think so. But George was better than me. If giving in to the king's desires could win him his love, he was willing to do it. Oh, noble George! But before I could ask him, his eyes flashed with a peculiar light. "You saw nothing," he snarled in a strange, bestial voice.

"Of course," I said, forcing myself to smile weakly. I was miserable, but I tried to tell myself that this horrible thing was for the greater good. And it wouldn't last forever.

"If you breathe a word, the king will have your head."

"George," I soothed him. Poor man, he looked traumatized. This must have been terrible for him. "I know, I understand. It will all be over soon, and then we can be together. We can plant our garden of forget-me-nots . . . We love each other, that's what counts . . ."

He let me go abruptly and stood up. It was only then I realized he was completely naked. I blushed, tried not to look at the wedding night parts, and utterly failed. This didn't matter. Nothing mattered except being together in the end. Any sacrifice was worth it to find the happiness we'd imagined for ourselves.

And then I discovered that for all my cleverness, for all that Lady Mary had taught me, I was no more than an infant, a dupe, a pawn.

"Love you?" He laughed, then his voice softened. "You child, there is no such thing." Then he drew himself up, and if it was an act, it was a perfect one. "Marry an insipid little nothing like you?" he asked with poisonous contempt. "When with the king's blessing I can marry a duchess? I've seen everything you've done, are capable of. Why would I want to marry a scheming, villainous woman like you?"

His face went blank, his eyes dead, and he stared through me. "I've got everything I ever wanted now. What further use do I have for you?"

They had used me, he and his mother, my father. They made me love George Villiers so that I would do anything for him, so he would rise to be the king's favorite. In my laughable naiveté, I never knew the king's favorite was also his lover.

I ran, hoping he would call me back, explain that his cruelty was all a ploy toward some greater scheme I didn't understand, that he loved me.

I had risked my honor for him! I had all but killed to protect him. I stabbed a man, poisoned a woman, sent five people to the gallows, all for love of him and the partnership he'd promised. Because I believed he loved me in return. Yes, love is selfish. I wouldn't have done it for my love alone, only for our mutual love.

I raged, and I wept, and the ghosts of my victims jeered at me, and a little voice in my mind asked, *And what did he ever do for you, foolish girl?*

Maybe a moment ago that strange spark in my eye had been fire, forging a life of love. Now I knew it was truly ice. My heart was frozen.

I had almost reached the safe solitude of my room when I stumbled into a man. He caught me up gently, saved me from falling, and that tenderness in the moment of my pain made me sob. "How now, my pretty maiden?" It was the French bishop, the man who had seen me in three guises, and only desired me in this one.

In that moment, I looked at him with new eyes. I was broken inside. Not just my heart, but my will, my strength, my dignity. I wanted to hurt George. I wanted to hurt myself, to do something so terrible it would bury this rage and grief, if only at the bottom of an abattoir or sewer.

My father and Lady Mary had wanted to make me their instrument, their weapon, using me for their own ends without care for my tender heart. My most precious possession, my virginity, was to be bait for my victims, to destroy them.

I will not be their pawn any longer, I thought, black rage welling up through my sorrow the way pitch may impregnate a gushing spring. I will take away the weapon they seek to wield. I will rob them of my virginity, and make myself of no further use to them.

I will give freely and cheaply the jewel I had saved for George.

When the bishop held me against the garnet satin of his doublet, I pulled away . . . but only to lead him to my room. His face betrayed some surprise, but he did not hesitate.

I was ready to be seduced. No, I was ready to be ravished, taken, to have all control stripped from me. I had tried to control my destiny, yet other people had manipulated me like a puppet. What was the use of trying anymore? In anger and sadness, I stood beside my bed and prepared to be used. What else, I thought in my utter dejection, is a woman good for? Best to be used, be broken, be ruined, and have done with it.

I wasn't in my right mind, you'll see. Had it been any other man, I would have been taken in a trice and left weeping on my bed. But the bishop—Armand—was not a mere seducer. The French spy, the lascivious schemer, servant of God and Mammon, the man I'd poisoned, was a true lover of women.

I have met one or two such as he since, and they are a rare breed. True, he would fornicate with almost any woman who would say *yes*, or *no* with a giggle. But he took his fornication seriously, and practiced his craft, his art, his passion, in ways I could not then begin to imagine. I had been taught seduction, not sex—everything that would lead me to the very edge of that mysterious experience, but as I valued my life, no further. I knew the fundamentals of cock and cunt, those gutter words bandied about by peasants and nobles alike. I knew the penetration, the grunting, of pigs in springtime. I knew the spurt, the sigh, the gravid risk. I had heard hints of pain, of distaste, of tedium. When Armand approached me, I braced myself for a hard chore to be struggled through, at most a battle to be fought, and lost. I was sacrificing myself, and did not expect enjoyment.

He kissed me, and though I did not care for him at all, it was a kiss that thrilled me to my core. There was hunger in it, need, combined with an artistry as precise as a great painter's finest brushstrokes on his masterpiece. His hands touched my shoulders, my throat, and he was not a painter but a sculptor, carving my flesh into life with the press of his fingertips.

We were near my bed, and he knelt before me like a supplicant. I gazed down at him, flushed and baffled, watching him grasp the hem of my skirt in both of his hands and raise it. I thought he would kiss it, for he bent his head, but he only inhaled deeply as he bundled up my skirt and shift and drew them slowly up past my knees, my thighs.

"Lay back on the bed," he said. "Don't be afraid. I won't hurt you."

"I don't care," I said miserably. "I don't care if it hurts." Maybe a new pain would distract me from my broken heart.

He pushed me back gently onto the down-filled mattress, his big, calloused hands scooping under my hips, shifting me backward. Then he climbed onto the bed after me, kneeling as he kissed the hollow at the top of my thigh, and pushed my skirts higher, pressing his mouth against my belly. He rubbed my skin with the roughness of his cheek.

Then he slid his hands under my thighs, parting my legs in one supple move, and kissed me again, oh, a kiss I never could have imagined! Every touch of his tongue between my legs seemed to drive me farther up a mountainside, to the breathless Himalayas, to rarefied Olympus, and I gasped. I was on the very pinnacle of something magnificent, and Armand kept me poised there for a blissful and tormenting eternity. This was not the pain I was expecting, and yet it was agony. I cried out some incoherent words, the burden of which was *please!* I looked down the strange exposed terrain of my body, and Armand glanced up at me, his luminous dark eyes crinkling at the corners to see my distress. The rhythm of his peculiar kiss quickened, the pressure deepened . . . and I was tumbling heedlessly down the mountainside, my body overwhelmed with a bliss that killed all other things.

Had someone asked at that moment, *But what of George?* I would have answered, *George? Who is George?*

No, that is not strictly true. I am certain that for some long moments

I utterly lost the powers of speech. I lay on my back in a daze while the Frenchman held my hips through the last of their trembling. He kissed my belly again, then rested his cheek there with a sigh of his own particular enjoyment.

"As I told you, mademoiselle," he murmured against my flesh, "the pleasure will be all yours . . . the first time." He told me in his low, French-tinted voice that he did not deflower virgins. "Widows were my preference, before I was ordained," he admitted. "Twice widowed, even better. No cuckold to threaten my life afterward, and the lady, praise God, is so sick of husbands that she lays no traps. But now, *mon Dieu*! Whelps and pox and all sorts of concerns! With the tongue, all achieve pleasure without risk. And there is artistry in it, no? Any lout can *thrust thrust squirt*. But to coax a lovely woman to the highest pleasure and hold her there, to grant her relief at the moment of my choosing! And then . . ." He looked up at me where I lay sleepy eyed and spent. "To have the same delight in return. After a decent interval, of course."

He was in the process of teaching me to grant him that delight, praising my natural aptitude, when Lady Mary's maid walked in on us, gave one quick survey of the scene, and retreated with a look of scandalized malice.

"Ah yes," Armand said sadly as he caught me gently but unequivocally by the back of my head and finished in a trice. "With virgins there is always that danger, too. The angry papa shall come anon, no?"

He wisely fled, and my sorrow and rage came flooding back. I was not given time to dwell on my problems much longer. Lady Mary ran in screaming, my father hot on her heels. He struck me, called me a whore, locked me in my room, and the next day, I was bundled in a wagon. I thought I'd be sent home, where Maman and the moors could ease my grief. But we rode east, to Dover, and thence onto a ship. When I tried to flee, I was bound hand and foot. The only possession I was allowed was the red and black bead rosary Maman had given me. My knife, as ever, was concealed in my busk.

In this manner, I arrived at the Convent of St. Ursula.

Chapter 8

1628

We sit in soft, flickering firelight, so that the years may be kind to us. A dozen years and more have passed since I first met the woman who now styles herself Madame Bonacieux. We both have taken care to ensure that time touched us as little as possible, but we have also been trained to observe, and I know her keen eye detects the same subtle aging I find in her.

"It went well, then?" she asks.

"As well as can be expected," I reply dryly, and she cocks her head.

"As bad as all that?"

Even she, my dearest companion, knows almost nothing of my life before we met. And yet she knows me as well as anyone save the Comte de Wardes, and can tell from the weary inclination of my body that this was more than a typical assassination. This death has touched me.

"Do you wish to speak of it?"

I don't, but I know it will release me, and after the end of this night, there will be no one she can tell even if she wished to. This is a night of endings, one way or another.

"I loved him once," I whisper, slipping my hand into my pocket in that old nervous habit, fondling my rosary and saying prayers not to God, nor the Virgin, but to the memory of my mother.

Her eyebrows rise as she reads an epic in those few words. "And you killed him?"

"Not with my own hand. I found a man to do it for me, but he was my instrument, as surely as if I made the thrust into Buckingham's heart. Felton was his name, a man with the repute of a Puritan but as susceptible as any to feminine charms. Buckingham had slighted him in a question of promotion, and it was a simple enough matter to goad him to violence."

We sighed in chorus. "At times it astounds me that anyone is left alive in this world, easy as it is for men to fall into murderousness. Swayed by a word, they are."

"Mere weather vanes and shuttlecocks," I agree wearily.

It is a day of disillusion, fading into a long night.

Looking into the hearth instead of at each other, we reminisce. Not the earliest days of our acquaintance, but the middle point of our career, when we had just risen to the top of our game, when it *was* a game, full of challenges and sharp joy. Of course, we only know it is the middle because this is the end.

Do you remember . . . Do you remember . . . ?

We have masqueraded as sisters, as rivals, as mistress and maidservant. "Somehow it seems more often to be me who takes the place of the grand lady, while you, my friend, assume the place of underling. Why is that?"

She shrugs, not at all offended. "You were born into the nobility. I was born to a merchant family."

"How do you know?" I ask her, confirming her suspicion with my question. "I never told you about my birth, my family." I'd been ashamed of my past when first we met, and though I told her a few things, I'd passed myself off as a Frenchwoman, and never corrected the matter. I'd gotten into the habit of secrecy, and it was a hard one to break. Now, though, it didn't seem to matter.

She smiles softly into the firelight. "We've had the same training. We see past the surface, the artifice, into the truth of people. I know you are English, though no one else could tell that from your voice or demeanor or habits. I know your father must have had a title, that you spent time in the English court before we met."

"And you never said a word!"

"Why should I? Your secrets are your own."

I chuckle. "Apparently, they are not such secrets. I'm sorry I never told you about my early life. You are my most trusted friend. I should have told you."

She shakes her head. "No need. I understand you. I love you. With or without complete disclosure."

We stare into the fire in silence for a moment, letting the memories wash over us, through us . . . leave us.

I catch my breath and say suddenly, "I wish there was another way."

"He would never let us go alive." We've said it over and over, my lover, my friend, and I. The cardinal is very partial to us. If we were not so clever as we are (or as he made us), we might believe that we are his friends. He shares affairs of state with us, consults us about the cares of governance. We drink wine together, neither of us sniffing the cup first. There is trust between us. He sees that we are honored and wealthy and safe.

And yet there is no question about who is master, who is servant. He is the spymaster, the secret-keeper. We are his creatures. We have trust and status because we please him. But none of us have any real doubt about what would become of us should we fail to please him.

There is no swifter route to his displeasure than to leave our comfortable position under his thumb.

"You've known him longer than any of us," she goes on. "Tell me, what would he do if you marched up to him one day . . ."

"I would slink. It is more effective, even on cardinals."

"Very well, you *slink* up to him and say, what? Your Eminence, I have heard all your secrets, I know things about king and country that could send you to prison, devastate France, destroy the economy, make every lord a cuckold and every lady a harlot . . . but I grow weary of this mode of living. Would you mind if I take my very dangerous secrets and retire to some place where you have no hold over me?"

"He would smile, bid me think on it . . . and then kidnap my son until I agreed to serve him until death. Which, after such a revelation, would surely not be far off."

She nods and says flatly, "If we try to leave, he will kill us all."

"Or more likely, kill one of us to try to compel the others to stay. Even rebellious, we are too valuable resources to cast off lightly. But we would lose his trust, and sooner or later he would decide we were too much of a threat to live, and he would send some other assassin after us."

"What a pleasant man he is, under other circumstances," she muses.

"Indeed," I say, and because of what will happen before the sun rises again, I decide it is safe to tell her of the first time the cardinal and I enjoyed each other's company. Well, the first time that led to mutual satisfaction, if only for a few moments. He still has no idea that I'm the tavern wench who poisoned him with green potatoes so long ago, back when he was a mere bishop.

She pitches forward in mirth and utter astonishment, and I smile. It is rare that either of us can surprise the other.

"You and Cardinal Richelieu—lovers?"

"In a sense, though by the letter of the law, my virginity was intact."

"How long did it last?"

"Only that once. After he trained me so well in the art of poison and knife-play, I don't think he felt inclined to be so intimate."

"I imagine not. What a guarantor of fidelity you and de Wardes have, knowing what each could do to the other in the event of betrayal!"

I smile at her jest, but it is not like that with de Wardes and me. I would not tell her this, for in this case, I think even to her practiced observation the truth would sound like a lie, but neither he nor I have ever had another lover since we committed to each other. I have done . . .

things . . . which I believed were necessary at the time. Both of us have the reputation of consummate seducers. But we all know how important the surface, the appearance of things is, and it does not take much to make the world believe that he and I are profligate, unscrupulous lovers.

Besides him, I have had only one other lover.

I take no prudish pride in this, nor would I feel shame if 'twere otherwise. Madame Bonacieux has, at any moment, a veritable stable of lovers. It suits her.

Fidelity, devotion suit de Wardes and myself.

Here in France, de Wardes, Madame Bonacieux, and myself have made up a trusted, treasured triad for so many years. And now, because we have knotted ourselves up inescapably, it must come to an end. Not, as with the Gordian knot, by way of a sword, but (for Madame Bonacieux at least) by the assassin's more subtle weapon.

"Let me brew you some tea," I say, rising, tucking my skirts away from the flames as I swivel a little pot on its jointed metal arm over the hearth.

"D'Artagnan and his Musketeer friends ride swift steeds. They will be here before long, and the deed must be done betimes."

She nods. "It is the only way."

"It is the only way," I repeat, and with my back to her, sprinkle choice herbs into the pot. It will require a strong decoction.

"And he will come?" she asks. She sounds as young as when I first met her.

"He has been told of your kidnapping, your imprisonment in this convent by the wicked Milady. He loves you. He will come."

"He loved you, and he tried to violate you."

"Yes, men love strangely sometimes. But we have created in you the ideal victim, the tender dormouse who needs to be protected, the baby bird who must be saved. Every man wants to be a hero in a romantic tale. We wrote this tale specifically for him. He will come to rescue you from my clutches."

I pour the tea, straining the bitter herbs through a cloth, and cup it in my hands as I kneel before my old friend. She reaches for it. "It's too hot!" I say sharply as I pull it to my belly. *Not yet*, I think. *Not yet.*

Buying time, borrowing it, begging it, I blow on the tea, sending pungent steam wafting to her. She pulls a face, but reaches for it inexorably. "Quickly! I need to warm my insides, steady myself." She takes a quick sip, testing the temperature, then swallows it down. I close my eyes.

It is done.

In a life of betrayal and vengeance, of hate and murder, of darkest peril, this is the hardest night I have known. I am afraid.

A rap at the door tells me a watcher far down the road has heard hoofbeats charging through the hushed forest, and lit a signal fire.

"So soon!" she cries, smacking her lips at the bitter aftertaste.

"You will need a longer tale to hold them off," I say, as brusque now as if none of this mattered to me in the least. Facades and fronts for the world, even for my friend who can see through them.

She looks at me in sympathy, and I let one final flash of concern color my countenance before I am the consummate spy again. Did I get the dosage right? I would not like her to linger, nor yet . . . I had gauged it to her size and weight, but now that I look, her brave face looks more gaunt than usual, her dimples vanished. Has she lost weight in these harried last few weeks? What if I miscalculated the amount of foxglove and wolfsbane?

There is no time for doubts. Done is done.

With a lingering backward look I quit the cozy little room and leave her to her fate. Met by a bevy of nuns, led by a youthful Reverend Mother with a faint harelip, I have a habit thrown over my gown, a wimple over my hair. Sister Marie Claire tucks in an errant curl, and we exchange a quick look of simultaneous memory. "No one holding you down this time," she quips, then dashes off to ready my carriage. They will be coming by the main road that winds through the forest to the front of the convent. I shall leave by the back. I don't have far to go.

"Will we see you again, Milady?" the Reverend Mother asks. I have been a great benefactor to this place.

I consider lying, but these girls and women have been lied to so many times in their lives, promised that marriage would make them happy, that men were made to protect them, that God is just. "No, Reverend Mother. I will not be coming back again. Tonight I embark on a journey from which there is no return."

She embraces me. "You have made this place a paradise."

See what money and goodwill can do? Every convent should be like this one, a marvel of industry and education. The women are here of their own free will, and although I gave gold aplenty in the outset, the convent is now entirely self-supporting. It is *my* convent, the first boon I ever asked of the cardinal after completing a particularly important assignment. Milady: patroness.

I am sad to leave, but anxious to go. Then . . . damn those Musketeers! Who is provisioning them? Their horses fly as if on wings. They are here, tumbling off their beasts, clanging their weapons, shouting without thought of stealth or surprise, hammering on the convent door with their steel-nubbed mitts. I dare not leave just yet. I must hide, and wait for an opportune moment. If discovered, perhaps my nun's garments can buy me time as I wait with the other women.

I hide in an adjoining room, and peek through the keyhole to watch my dearest friend's final moments.

With tears welling in my eyes, I marvel at her consummate skill. I know the wolfsbane is starting to make her extremities numb. I know the foxglove is slowing her heart so much that her body is growing heavy, her vision dim.

Oh, the tale she weaves! Spun of gossamer and steel, her fabrication is the stuff of troubadours' dreams. The sighing love, the trust, the fading doe eyes turned toward D'Artagnan as she confesses her love, breathlessly plans a future in his arms. Then confusion as the poisons take effect. "Do I swoon with love?" she whispers to the weeping Gascon. "Why does my body feel so weak when my heart feels so strong?"

And then, the realization of her doom. They find the emptied cup, smell the poisoned tea dregs, tell her the worst. Oh, the tragic angelic quaver in her voice! We rehearsed that, she and I, in the first year of our apprenticeship. She was always better at it. Too much weakness always made me feel a bit ridiculous. But my tender friend built her career on strategic weakness, on reluctantly yielding to the things she always meant to have in the first place.

Then, as the end is near, she gathers her strength to condemn her assassin. Hearing her, I fully understand how lies can outlive truth. No one who heard her that day could ever be convinced that the story was other than what she said.

She tells of her loyalty to her queen, and her persecution by the cardinal and his minions because of it. Kidnappings, threats, all endured out of love for the monarch she served, and for France. Only say your action is for your country, and how people will fawn over you. She has D'Artagnan tearing out his hair at the injustices his little love suffered.

And what a monster she makes me out to be! The noblewoman who befriended her in this convent, who got her secrets, pretended to comfort her, and in the end poisoned her to avenge herself on D'Artagnan.

"I drank it down in all innocence, and afterward she laughed and said I am dying for my lover's sins." She reaches a hand to his cheek, then lets it fall as a spasm hits her. "Why does she hate you so?" she gasps, her face contorted in agony.

D'Artagnan has the decency to blush, but Athos steps in and says, "Milady hates any enemy of the cardinal, any friend of the king and queen."

My friend looks around with her big, baffled eyes. Her vision must be clouding now.

"How can any woman be that evil?" she asks. "May God forgive her for what she has done."

D'Artagnan only wails and buries his head in her bosom, but Athos, predictable Athos, says, "God may forgive her, but here in this life she shall be punished!"

I know that look on his countenance. Time and drink and memory had changed him enough that he didn't kill me on sight the last time we met at La Rochelle. Grown wise and kind, even philosophical, he would be useless to my ends. But here is the old Athos roused, the man who can't see past the surface of things.

"We will avenge you, my child," he says to my friend. "Do you know where the demon woman has gone?" In his agitation he has caught up a teaspoon and is worrying it between his teeth. Necklace, braid, quill . . . all find their way into his mouth when he is vexed.

"D'Artagnan! D'Artagnan, where are you? I'm so cold!"

"Tell me where she is!" Athos barks, all but shoving the young Gascon aside.

She whispers the name of a town, and Athos throws down the spoon, stiffens, with his hand on his sword. The other Musketeers consult with him briefly, along with another man who has heretofore stayed in the shadows.

My supposed brother-in-law, the Englishman Lord de Winter.

"It must be an act of law, not of personal vengeance," de Winter councils. "We have learned her secrets. She must die, I agree, before her poison spreads any further. But we must not cut her down as we would a dog in the street. No, if this is to be done the right way, in a manner that does not trouble our honor, we must have a trial, and a proper executioner."

Athos and the others nod, and the Englishman continues, saying what I have paid him handsomely to say. "After I got proof just a few days ago that she killed my brother, her husband"—a bit of improvisation that only adds to my wicked reputation—"I took pains to discover her true history. And if you truly wish justice to be done, there is only one man who can properly carry out the sentence we know shall befall her after trial."

They wait, thrilled by this drama that will be embedded on their souls forever, until de Winter intones in an ominous voice, "The executioner of Lille."

How annoyed Madame Bonacieux must be to have the attention dragged away from her at such a crucial moment. Every actor knows that the death scene is the most vital. She makes a mewling sound, arresting their attention.

"My love, my hero!" she breathes, barely audible, making everyone in the room bend to her like flowers to the sun. "What happiness I've had in this life has come from you. Kiss me, beloved. Let this be our marriage day, to be consummated in heaven."

He kisses her, and a story for the ages is born.

Her heart slows, her breathing grows ever more shallow. Then, quite prettily, my dear friend dies in D'Artagnan's arms.

She does it for my sake.

I can't let her sacrifice be in vain. They mourn now, but they are men of action. Soon they will commend her to the nuns and pursue me. I must flee.

Part 3

Chapter 9

1615

I must say, one of the best things about the Convent of St. Ursula was the clothes. Surfeited on silks and breathlessly tight stays from my sojourn to court, it was a relief to be given a loose woolen habit with no more than a rope belt to cinch in my waist. Beneath that, my body was utterly bare to the scratchy fabric.

I did not care as much for the head-shaving, though.

I've since learned that there is a proper order to things. When a girl enters a convent, she is at first a curious visitor: a postulant. She is allowed half a year at least to learn her way to the privy, as it were. She meets the sisters and other young girls, participates in daily life, while she considers her calling and the nuns evaluate her potential to bring them either profit or disgrace. If all agree, she then becomes a novitiate and receives her habit. Only after a few years of that apprenticeship is she allowed to make formal vows of chastity, poverty, and obedience.

Or, alternately, realize that that triumvirate of virtues is neither desirable nor possible.

A true nunnery that selflessly served God or the poor or whoever should be the true receiver of earthly piety would not want a woman who was unwilling or unsuited. The Convent of St. Ursula, however, was a cistern for the discarded dregs of womankind.

I had been untied somewhere mid-channel, probably so that I could more conveniently vomit. My handlers—two stout and stupid men, and a stout and clever woman—no doubt realized that if I purged in my bonds, the stink would follow us all on the remainder of our journey. So they cut the rope, put a bowl under me, and left me to my misery.

Which lasted all of ten minutes before the pitch of the craft became customary and I began to think of escape. Misery had alternated with clearheaded scheming since the moment when the bullies clapped hands on me. *George*, I would moan, so full of sorrow. And then I'd see his mocking face, Lady Mary's . . . my father's. The three of them set me up with devilish precision, careless of my heart and soul. Wicked Lady Mary, and wickeder still my father, whose ties of blood should have stayed even if love did not. To use me as his instrument, heedless of the cost, and then cast me aside! I seethed with plots of vengeance. All told, it was as good a way as any to pass a tedious journey. I may say my mind was never unoccupied.

I plotted escape . . . but to where? Maman. If I could but get to her, all would be well. We could flee together to parts unknown, away from this unclean world to a perfect feminine paradise of our own. In my weaker moments I thought, *If only she had come to court in time to save me from myself.* But in my heart I knew I couldn't place the blame on her absence. It was all my own doing. I thought I'd been so clever, and I'd been duped. Blame the world or blame myself—blame did me no good. Better to plot in the moment, for the future, than to dwell on the past and make accusations to excuse one's own failings.

An easy truth to philosophize, if hard to follow in endless hours of introspection.

Would Maman be on her way to court even now, as she'd promised? Surely, she would come for me as soon as she heard of my plight.

Or would she learn what I had done, and disown me for the treacherous, murderous harlot I was? But I am not those things, Maman, I longed to tell her. I came to this pass through tricks and mistakes and innocence. Left in our Yorkshire bower, I never would have poisoned anyone. Even wolfsbane harms no one if it is only left alone.

Yet the poison lies within it still. Was the poison in me all along?

They were a silent crew, those ruffians tasked with my abduction and delivery. The men only leered at me, the younger one lasciviously, the elder with a sort of sympathetic, confused curiosity, as if he couldn't quite understand how he'd gotten into this profession of dragging girls to nunneries. The woman, though, said just enough to confirm the destination I had already assumed. Beyond that she spoke mostly in abstract and terrifying homilies. "They'll beat the sin from your arse afore the devil can burn it in deeper," was a favorite, told with her chubby hands clasped piously. She further opined that beauty is a cause of misery, but that years of hard work and perhaps a soapmaking accident involving undiluted lye might make me chaste through necessity. "Smallpox is handmaiden to chastity," she said. Her own face was liberally pitted with scars, but I believe it was more her manner than her face that kept her chaste. I have known homely women, loving and charming and intelligent, with a dozen men prostrate at their feet.

She did not give me much encouragement to discourse on these matters, though. When I asked her any questions, she replied with a pinch and a twist. My tongue, ever hopeful, won me a battery of bruises before I resigned myself to silence.

Once on the Continent, we bounced for days on rutted roads, stopping now and then to eat tavern slop or piss behind a hedge. At long last, the carriage took a woodland path, and after another half day of travel without hearing the barking of dogs or seeing the smoke of cottage fires, we came to a lovely building of golden stone on a hill surrounded by scattered open forest.

The woman rapped on the door, and a little grate opened at eye level. I saw no more than a glittering behind it. "You'll have gotten the message from Lord Paget by now," she said.

The door creaked open on protesting hinges. Here was a door that thought itself above such trivia as ingress and egress. It obviously considered itself a more stable and permanent thing, a wall. Still, it opened to let me in, then shut behind me with heavy finality. I was alone with the abbess.

I had been contemplating this moment for much of the last few days. Should I resist, scream, weep, and generally make such a nuisance of myself that the Reverend Mother would either cast me out or, for preference, summon my mother to remove me? Or should I cozen her with affection and soft words, win her favor and wheedle what I want from her?

One look at the abbess told me that neither would get me far. She was a large woman, made more imposing by her vast black habit. The heavy hemp belt girdling what passed for her waist was knotted three times at the end, and hung to her knees. Perhaps those threefold knots were to help her contemplate the Holy Trinity, but I rather thought they might double as a cruel bludgeoning whip.

Her clothes were the simple, rough material I'd expected, though her wimple was as white as new lambs and starched into a cornette so preposterous I felt an immediate urge to knock it from her head. An urge I luckily resisted, or I would now be lacking several of my teeth, I'm sure.

In startling contrast to her humble clothing were the sigils of her office. On her breast lay a pectoral cross that would make a pope feel ostentatiously dressed. Six inches across, made of beaten gold and set with rubies, hanging from a chain as thick as a baby's arm, it looked heavy enough to make a lesser woman a hunchback. The tall and sturdy abbess was unbowed.

In her hand she held the other symbol of her rule within this cloister: the crosier. Meant to mimic a shepherd's staff, as she was the benevolent tender of her flock, it curled at the top like a ram's horn, around a figure I first took to be the traditional sheep, but on closer inspection proved to be a fat and sullen-looking pig. The rod was made of ivory and gold, and even if the gold parts were mere gilding, it still looked like a king's ransom. Like the cross, her crook was set with large rubies.

And here I thought I would have to take a vow of poverty.

She looked at me for a long time, and, uncertain under her regard, I made her a deep curtsy. When I rose, my head collided with her outstretched crosier. Not quite a blow, more an interference resulting in pain.

"None of that," she said in French with faint traces of peasant accent almost but not quite overcome. "You've left courtly life behind, never to return. Why do you think a Protestant slut like you was sent to a Catholic convent, hmm?"

I hadn't even considered that aspect before, but it made sense. If I managed to leave an Anglican convent in England, I'd still be considered an acceptable member of English society. But my deeply anti-Catholic homeland would be loath to welcome back a Catholic convert, however unwilling my conversion had been. To the barriers of distance and stone and sin, yet another wall was being raised between me and my return to England.

She used her crosier to lift my chin, and then my arms, examining me head to toe. I remembered that a shepherd's crook is used not only to guide sheep and defend against wolves, but also to catch young lambs by the heel and flip them over so they can be castrated and grow up to be nice, tender mutton. It is used to hold down a reluctant hogget so that she may be tupped by a randy ram. It is a device of control as much as it is one of protection.

"Pretty," the abbess said. "Too pretty by far. Women should be homely and simple. Let me see your hands." I held them out, and she evinced some surprise. "You have done work." She made a sound like a snort, and I think she hated me then, because all of her assumptions about me were not played out to the letter. "You will do more," she said, and rapped my fingers with the crosier. I jerked them back and hid them in the folds of my skirt.

"You will learn obedience," she went on. "Humility, chastity, piety." She punctuated each with a blow to some imaginary devil, striking the air with her staff. "But as you are no doubt too foolish a chit to learn those last three on your own, we will focus on obedience. The sisters will prepare you tonight, and after a night of prayer, you will say your vows at dawn. You will do exactly as they instruct you, on pain of . . . pain." She smiled, showing large, even teeth, crushing teeth like Jack's giant must have gnashed when he smelled the blood of an Englishman. "We are a flagellant order."

She turned on her heel, commanding me to follow. So much I obeyed . . . but not a great deal of the orders that followed.

I had no faith in force, and she did not strike me as a woman susceptible to flattery, so I tried simple politeness.

"I have had a long and tiring journey, Reverend Mother," I said with what I fancied a simple, humble grace. "If I could retire to my chambers for tonight to rest . . . and pray . . ." How clever I thought myself to throw that in. "A simple meal would do. Then in the morning perhaps we can speak of my future."

It would give me the night to get the lay of this place. Perhaps by morning I would be gone.

She did not even acknowledge me. I trotted behind her long strides to catch up. "You spoke of vows," I said to her back. "Surely, tomorrow is too soon . . ."

She stopped so abruptly that I almost crashed into her. Slowly, she turned, and when I saw the cold gleam in her eye, I knew I was lost. The smallest smile twisted her lips, the smile a man may make when he draws back his bow today, thinking of rabbit stew tomorrow. I saw in a flash what my future would be: bowing to this woman and others like her, or else suffering.

I say with pride that I chose suffering that first night.

The abbess didn't answer, but marched on, and I perforce followed. She took me to a bare room with a grated drain in the center, as in an abattoir. There she left me to stew in the cold, my stomach rumbling as I paced for more than an hour. Finally, a small army of women came in, carrying a copper bath and several buckets of water.

They gave me orders in calm, firm voices. *Take off your clothes. Step in the tub.* When I refused, they manhandled me into compliance. None of them were as big and stout as the abbess, but they were like jackals on a lion, and overpowered my body if not my will. I don't know if the thick stone walls blocked my screams, but I did my very best to be sure the entire convent was aware of my displeasure.

The sisters flung me in the water—cold water that raised gooseflesh all over my body—and scrubbed me with boar bristle brushes that left my skin raw. The older ones whispered like witches as they worked. *Sinful baggage. Useless wench.* Their little maledictions stung me like gadflies. *Scrub the sin off her.* A brush tangled in what they hissingly called my shame hair, and a wimpled harridan jerked it painfully free.

The younger ones just pushed up their sleeves and got on with it. One or two gave me fleeting sympathetic looks. A girl who couldn't have been more than fourteen, so small her oversize habit pooled at her feet, stroked my golden head as if I were the family cur and looked sorrowful.

When I was clean—and what can be cleaner than removing the outer layer of skin—they hauled my shivering body from the tub and pulled a rough black tunic over my still-wet flesh.

"Kneel," one of the elder nuns I later learned was Sister Marie Agnes commanded. Another handed her a pair of heavy shears.

"No!" I cried, wide-eyed, and started to back away. The humiliation of being stripped and scrubbed was bad enough, but not this!

The young girl who had petted me stepped forward. "Please," she whispered, "if you don't, they'll sit on you, and they won't be so careful." She pointed discreetly to her temple, where I saw the angry pink of a not-long-healed slash.

But I didn't kneel, and they did sit on me, and they weren't careful.

When they dumped out the tub, it washed my blood neatly down the drain. My shorn hair was tied up in twine and sent to be made into a wig for some countess. Virgin nun hair commands a high price.

Connie.

She whispered her name to me the second the door shut, then dared no more until the footsteps echoing outside the chapel died, and the world went quiet.

"They'll be back to check every hour or so until midnight, but after that they sleep until matins. I vow these nights of penitence are the only peace I get here."

I'd been sent to this chapel to kneel the night away, praying, preparing my mind for vows on the morrow. The sisters left me with terrifying descriptions of what would befall me if I rose from my knees for so much as a moment.

Connie, though, had no compunction, and stood, stretching her arms high above her head with a feline grace.

"You'll be whipped!" I said in horror.

She shrugged, a supple movement I soon discovered was typical of her. She had a way of moving that made the simplest gesture like a dance. "If they want to flagellate you, they'll find a reason." She stretched out a leg, pulling up her tunic to show bruises like the marks of clutching hands on her calf and thigh, evidently from the Reverend Mother's knotted girdle. "Better to go to the pillar without sore, creaking knees." Still, I noticed she dropped back down almost immediately, glancing over her shoulder at the door.

I snuck a look at her as I pretended to pray to the hideous wooden Christ nailed to the front of the chapel. She was my age, or perhaps a year or two older, with bonny brown curls just peeking out of the white cap that was supposed to conceal them. Her eyes were large and bright, and merry when they caught me watching her. She winked at me.

"What are you praying for?" she asked, sidling a bit closer to me.

"Release," I said. "Escape."

"Those are not possible," she said, her mouth pressed in a serious line. Then the corners of her lips start to twitch. "However, it is both possible and satisfying to place a serpent in the Reverend Mother's chamber pot. Perhaps you could pray for that?"

"Is that why you're being punished?"

She smiled demurely, making a dimple pop into existence. "I should be rewarded for my virtue," she said, making a little moue. "It was only a grass snake. It could have been an adder."

Without thinking, I replied, "An asp would be better, perhaps. The bite of an adder is painful, but rarely fatal. Also, they are sluggish and not prone to biting unless picked up or trodden upon. An asp is a much more temperamental beast."

I found her looking at me wide-eyed.

"I hadn't thought to kill her!" Connie said.

I felt my cheeks start to burn, and my chest became so tight I feared I'd never breathe again. I was tainted! This girl, a hoyden to be sure, meant only a joke on the oppressive Mother Superior. Immediately, *my* corrupt brain went to murder. I began to fear that I was irrevocably broken, that even Maman would never forgive the person I had become.

Then Connie said with a laugh, "But now I'll think of nothing else! Oh, if only I were brave enough! But then Sister Marie Agnes would step in to take her place, and I'd have to fetch another asp. There are very few asps in the cloister gardens, and no end of nuns . . . and only one door, and only one key. No, my friend, we are well and truly trapped."

She sounded quite cheerful about it. Her dimples rarely left her cheeks, I would find.

"My mother will be coming for me," I said with more confidence than I felt. She hadn't come to London, despite her promise. Why would she come here after such a disappointment of a daughter? Perhaps my perfidious father had not even told her where I was. Perhaps he said I died of a quartan ague. But I would go mad if I did not believe in salvation. It would not come from that wooden man in agony, his red-paint blood falling in chips, mouse-gnawed, on the altar.

Connie shook her head sadly. "No one's mother ever comes for them, once the door is barred. Nor their father, nor their lover. When people are sick of their women, be they daughters or mistresses or dowagers, and have the means to make them disappear but not quite the morals to make it permanent, they do the next best thing—send them here."

In this peculiar religious order, women were not called, but sent. It was a repository for difficult, complicated, awkward, or unlucky women.

As I came to know the nuns and novices, I learned their stories. Every one was different, but they had a common thread—these were superfluous women who had in the mysterious commerce of gender somehow lost their value.

Sister Marie Bernadette was the youngest of six daughters, and the dowry money ran out at number five. She kept house for her brother until he decided to marry a woman who didn't want to compete for the keys to the pantry, so she was encouraged to either find a husband of her own or become a bride of Christ. Christ, apparently, demanded less money to take her on, so a bargain was struck, and her sister-in-law retained unchallenged mastery of the household larder.

Sister Marie Teresa came from a good family and was lovely . . . except for the mild harelip that marked her as cursed by a witch. When little boys started throwing stones at her, her family decided it was easier to send her to a convent rather than teach the boys the basics of civility.

There was a dowager who had too many opinions on how her son should run the estate. A woman whose firstborn too closely resembled her husband's captain of the guards. Another whose childless state made it clear she was an unfit wife. The little girl who warned me I'd be sat upon—Sister Marie Claire—was nearsighted and bookish. The first might be an attractive quality in a woman—keeps the eyes from wandering, you see, and makes a husband's paunch and bald pate less noticeable. The bookishness, however, was deemed insurmountable. All had been sent to the Convent of St. Ursula.

Connie's was a story so common even the fairy-tale spinners would blush to tell it: beloved mother dies, clueless father marries a horrid woman with children of her own, father dies, leaving his girl to her stepmother's tender mercies. In the stories, stepsisters are the problem. I think Connie would have gotten along quite well with the most evil step-sister, either co-opting her or giving as good as she got, if not better. No, Connie's undoing was her stepbrothers.

That night as we knelt side by side, alternating between numbness and pins and needles, Connie told me how her brothers' ham-handed attempts at seduction began the night of her father's funeral. While he lived, she was a protected woman, the property of a baron, and they would no more violate her than they would one of her father's sheep. When he lay in his coffin, though, she was a coney ripe for the hounds to run down if they could.

"I never did more than smile at them, and that in the barest civility," she said of her younger self. "I vow I did nothing to encourage them. Still, Philippe would accost me in the buttery, and Jean-Claude in the hall. If there was a billowing tapestry, I would be pulled behind it. Even little Bernard, just thirteen and covered in spots, had to compete with his brothers and creep into my chamber."

"How horrid!" I said with warmth. To think that they who were practically brothers should accost her!

Some impulse made me tell her about my father's unwitting assault, and she nodded sagely. "What man can get away with, man will do," she said with that sinuous shrug of hers. "As soon as he knows he won't swing for it, he will do it, whether it is murder or swiving where he's not welcome. Morals are only consequences in disguise."

"So your stepmother sent you here because she thought you were seducing her sons?"

Connie laughed, then stuffed her knuckles in her mouth just as the door creaked open. A sour-faced nun entered and glowered at us for a moment. "Let me see your knees," she demanded. We stood and hoisted up our coarse woolen habits. She bent to scrutinize, and deemed them red enough before retreating with a yawn.

When the danger had passed, Connie continued, "No, she didn't care a fig about her sons' morals, or even mine. Penniless girls are only a danger to young men when they are marriageable. As a stepsister, I couldn't get my hands on their money by tricking them into marriage. No, she only objected when her new husband made eyes at me."

"And when she caught him propositioning you, she found you at fault," I surmised.

"Well . . ." She giggled again, and proceeded to tell me that not only did she concede to her stepbrothers' seduction, but to her stepfather's, too.

"You poor thing!" I began, not understanding.

"Not at all! It was a diversion. What else is there to do in the countryside?" She very matter-of-factly told me that although the idea came from them, she had no very strong objections. "And once I had learned all there was to know from Philippe and Jean-Claude, how could I in good conscience withhold my knowledge from poor young Bernard?" She winked at me, all the while looking as pious as a nun.

"And your stepfather?" I asked, hardly knowing whether to be scandalized or entertained. There was something so happy and pure in Connie's lasciviousness, like a vixen romping in a flowery meadow.

"Ah, he was a handsome devil. But weak. He didn't fight to keep me. And so I ended up here." She sighed, but seemed strangely unaffected by her troubles. I wondered if she was a bit touched. There was something undeniably wild about her, a fey sort of separation from the expectations of the world. She was like an ocean wave that lashes against the shore, is sucked out to sea, but never discouraged, smashes the shore once again and forevermore.

She was, besides my mother, the most vital creature I had ever met.

I didn't confess all my sins as we knelt that long night in the chapel, yet I believe that she would not have judged me harshly. Needing a tale to share, lest my first friend turn against me for secrecy, I told her about my episode with Armand. I mentioned neither name nor place, and spoke as ever in French, letting her believe that seduction was the only thing that led to my being sent here.

At her insistence, I explained that interlude in some detail. She sighed and said, "That sounds delightful. And much less sweaty than the things Jean-Claude and Philippe taught me. I wonder when I shall get an opportunity to try it."

"I thought you said no one ever leaves this convent."

She looked at me sidelong and said, "Perhaps not, but you seem so sanguine about your chances, you give me renewed hope. Who knows what the future may hold? Besides, though this is a chaste sisterhood, you must not think that there are no men about." She pronounced the word *men* as if they were a rare confection, held temptingly just out of reach.

"I thought a nunnery was just . . . nuns." My religious education was a bit lacking.

"The Reverend Mother thinks she is the next best thing to God, but being a woman, she cannot perform Mass. There is a friary not far from here, and a church in the village some five miles off. Priests come daily for Mass. And then there are the merchants, the carpenters, the shepherds . . . A clever woman could find a man, in a pinch. Perhaps not her ideal man, but desperate times, my friend."

"You want a man?" I asked her. "Just any man?"

She shrugged, making the rough cloth hanging on her shoulders seem a sensuous living thing. "One gets in the habit, I suppose. Some might call it a fault," she went on, keeping her face altogether serious. "But then, I am told it is a virtue to be loyal to a fault. And so I am loyal to all of my faults."

I burst out laughing at the unfortunate moment the Reverend Mother came in to summon us to the first of what was to become an endless cycle in my life while I remained there, the Liturgy of the Hours. After morning lauds, I was to take my vows.

She stood in the doorway regarding us for a long, severe moment. "Stand up," she said at last, looking only at me. Which, although I had every desire to protect my new friend, didn't seem quite fair. The joker is surely as much at fault as the laugher, if not more so. One does not chastise the stabbing victim for bleeding on the carpet while ignoring the man with the knife. (Although I suppose one must be wary of criticizing men with knives.)

In any event, I bore the brunt of her wrath. She said some very un-nunnish things in a rough dockside voice and described in some detail the torments that awaited me in hell. Not even a caveat, mind you. No mention that I might escape eternal suffering if I mended my ways. Pure condemnation. I could have taught her that people are much more malleable when given hope, however false.

As she spoke, she caught up the trailing knotted hemp rope that served as a girdle and began beating me about the legs.

You must remember, I was in a peculiar state at the time. Betrayed, bereft, scheming escape . . . and yet buoyed by this quick camaraderie with Connie. Add to that a hard journey and a sleepless night on my knees. In short, I was so confused and bemused I hardly knew what to feel, and so felt almost nothing.

She was expecting me to dance a jig when she beat me, a dance with squeals and tears. But I was so overwhelmed by my very existence, and so unused to such treatment, that as the heavy bludgeoning rope lashed my legs, I just stood there. It hurt. Sweet Jesus, but it hurt! And yet some part of me said that it simply could not be happening, and it took my brain a long time to muddle through the facts and realize I was actually being beaten by a huge, angry nun.

I believe, despite my extensive training by Lady Mary in schooling my expression at all times, I may have even smirked. Just a wry twist of lip at the bizarre way my life had come to this pass.

Had the Reverend Mother but continued a moment, kept on beating me, the hysterical tears she was hoping for would have come, copiously. But for a woman who no doubt spent a great deal of time in prayer and contemplation, she had remarkably little patience.

"You wicked girl!" she said, her face getting redder by the moment. "Have you no shame?" Perhaps when one has stabbed and poisoned and well-nigh murdered, one feels less shame for such things as laughter. "*You* are one who dooms all women to hell." I could see the spittle flying from her lips. "You are the receptacle of original sin, the one from whose loins springs . . ." It was there I stopped listening, because really, the weight of the world's woes on my shoulders? I had done great wrong, but not more than thousands of other people, I was sure. I think her hypocrisy and faulty logic were what first gave me an inkling that my actions were not so bad in the grand scheme of things. In condemning my sins without having any knowledge of them, she pushed me to forgive myself.

Besides, nothing had yet sprung from my loins, and I was quite sure then that nothing ever would.

This happened all in a flash, and I didn't quite think it through with such clarity until I had leisure, on my knees the next night for another midnight prayer vigil. This night, though, her words only made me stand a little bit straighter. A mistake.

"Prideful slut!" she cried. I did not know Reverend Mothers were allowed to use such words. "Unrepentant Magdalene! Lift your skirt!"

And, woe is me, I had the audacity to smile as her words brought back a memory of Armand creeping up my hem. How can a person feel despair and amusement and fear and arousal all at once? What strange engines we are.

I suppose she thought the thin weave of my tunic was sparing my legs, and so she wanted better access. But finally, I was brought to action. I shrank away and said, simply, "No."

Her beet face turned aubergine, and she came at me, a great holy hulk of a woman, her eyes aflame with conviction. When you see such certainty, beware.

She took hold of me, and though I am not particularly small nor weak, she dominated me with ease. I didn't even fight her; I just struggled to get away. To where? There was no away. I was trapped in the walled convent.

She grappled for my tunic with one hand, flailing her whip with the other, catching me in the ribs and arms, anywhere she could reach. Finally, I lost my footing and she flung me bodily across one of the pew benches. It toppled, knocking over two others, and I heard Connie scream. The Reverend Mother was muttering, Bible verses or maledictions, I don't know which, and a look of triumph sprang to her features as she finally caught hold of my skirt and flung it up over my head so she could commence properly whipping my bare thighs.

I was weeping, pleading, just as she wanted, but her holy ire was properly inflamed now. She shook off Connie when she tried to come to my aid, and all I could do was try to protect my most vulnerable parts.

It was then, in a surreal suspended moment between blows, that I looked to the chapel door and saw a man. A youth, rather; a hobblede-hoy. There I found yet another example of the myriad emotions a person can feel simultaneously. On the face of this young priest was shock and mortification and anger and curiosity and terror . . . and a lust as naked as my thighs.

I wonder, if I had not caught his eye, whether he would have looked his fill and departed before the show was quite over, no doubt to rehearse it later in his lonely priest's cell. He was a fellow who hemmed and hawed over decisions, slow to act. But I was to discover that where he had once committed himself, he was a veritable juggernaut.

He stared at me. He blinked, as if waking up from a troubling dream. Then he cried out, "Stop! This is unseemly in a house of God."

The masculine voice rang through the little chapel, freezing the Reverend Mother mid-swing. She rose and faced him, and it was strange to see that, although in bulk she made three of him, and was twice his age, she seemed to quail under his gaze. Just for a moment, though. His masculine power in this feminine haven could only go so far.

The Reverend Mother gathered herself up and said evenly, "She is an unrepentant novice, due to take her vows after lauds."

"'Do not let kindness and truth leave you,'" the young priest quoted. "'Bind them around your neck. Write them on the tablet of your heart.'"

I thought he would come forward and gallantly help me up. Some storybook yearning that lingered in my heart thought he might even scoop me up and carry me out of this place, set me before him on a swift charger, and carry me home to Maman . . .

But of course he only tried to look wise and ended up looking like a young boy dressed in his father's clothes. He'd interrupted the Reverend

Mother in sudden attack, but he was no match for her in pitched battle and so had to be content with what he had accomplished. My tunic covered me to the ankle once more, the beating was over, calm was restored in the house of God. Looking pious and skinny and ridiculous and sweet, he bowed his head and left.

Without, I might add, a backward glance at me.

The Reverend Mother glared at us. "I will return within the hour, and you, miss, will take your vows. If you balk, you will learn the spirituality that long fasting can bestow."

She swept out in a whirl of habit that would have done a countess proud, and Connie and I were back on our knees.

"I won't take the vow," I declared in a quavering voice. My entire body from the shoulders down seemed to throb from the blows. I felt like I'd been pinched by a hundred imps. "She can't make me. If I say the words, I'll be trapped here."

"You silly goose," Connie said kindly. "They're just words. An oath is only an oath if it is sincere in your heart. Do you think Jesus is so desperate for brides that he'll latch on to a lie just to trap you? He is not a filthy old merchant buying himself a convent-bred wife. He is the son of God!"

"I am less concerned with God than with man," I whispered back. "The law must surely keep me here once I take the vow. If my mother comes, they will be able to say that I have sworn, and must remain."

"If she comes, it will be a miracle," Connie said. "Once miracles start happening, I doubt anyone will care much for law."

The next morning, bleary and weary, I took my vows of poverty, chastity, and obedience. As if we were given any choice in that holy trinity. I had no possessions beyond my tunic, and a pair of sandals they gave me that morning. The golden earbobs I'd been wearing when I was snatched away had disappeared somewhere on the road, pawned by now, no doubt. My kidnappers had left me my rosary, thinking the seeds strung together must be of no value, but the nuns had taken it, along with my clothes, down to my very corset, when I arrived. To my knowledge, they hadn't discovered the dagger in my busk. Surely, there would have been more screeching and beating if they had. Connie told me they tossed all the clothes novices brought with them into a chest that would go to the ragman when he came by every few months. A casual glance would show no more than a piece of wood, so it might have been overlooked.

Poverty accomplished, I was faced with obedience. The Reverend Mother's hempen girdle made sure of that, and if that didn't suffice, hunger and sleeplessness made up for the lack—flagellation, fasting, and nocturnal vigils. Fortunately, the commands were simple, if tedious. As soon as I had spoken my vows, I began taking part in the Liturgy of the Hours, in which every division of the day and night was made holy with my off-key singing. As a novice, I was tasked with the latest and earliest parts of the breviary, and nodded off at my luncheon. Fortunately, the gruel was not stout enough to choke me even if I fell face first into it. For the most part, obedience was easy. There were few diversions other than Connie's charming chatter to lure me from compliance.

That left only chastity.

Ah yes, chastity.

For all her queening, the Reverend Mother was still a mere woman, insignificant in the eyes of the Church, and could not conduct Mass. To perform that necessity, two priests came every day from the nearby monastery. No good road connected the cloisters, only a rough forest path through a wilderness reputed to be filled with wolves (though I never heard their howls) and savage boars. I have noticed that children and women both are often regaled with tales of the ravenous beasts that fill the forests. The world builds so many walls around us, coils so many chains about our limbs to keep us from straying too far from home.

These priests, though, must have been too tough or gamey for the wolves to trouble, for they made their daily trek unmolested. Different men came at different times—old Father Ignatius, who looked like the sort of thing you'd give a dog to gnaw on, or Father Jean, tugged between the twin demons of sloth and gluttony. I knew straightaway I could not look for help there.

Whichever priest came, they always had a younger priest with them to shoulder the physical burdens while they carried on the spiritual ones. Lady Mary taught me to look for opportunity, and I found it in this young priest.

At the first Mass after my vows, I saw the stripling priest again, swinging the censer. Frankincense, myrrh, wood shavings, dried cow pats . . . what was in that smoke, I do not know. All I knew was that while I knelt in purported prayer and breathed that heady mix, I let my eyes slide slantindicular to him as he passed, and saw his own do likewise. Our gazes met for an incandescent instant, and I saw him stumble, the pendulating censer missing its orbit and smacking him in the knees. He caught himself straightaway, glazing his eyes toward the suffering Christ, and the moment passed. But in that gaze, I realized anew the power of all the things Lady Mary had taught me.

In that look, he cast me a noose and said, *Slip it around my neck if you will.*

In that look, I began carving the key that would unlock the great creaking convent door.

He was not lost then, you understand. Neither great passions nor great plots come to fruition all in a moment. Yet every oak was once an acorn, and I held the acorn cupped in my palm. It would need care lest it wither, but I knew then that if my mother did not come for me, this young priest was my best chance of escape.

It made me feel ill to think of using those manipulations taught to me by Lady Mary, but it seemed like my best weapon, so I steeled myself to wield it.

What did he think at that moment? Only, *There is a comely girl. Alas for my vow of celibacy!* Or did his mind project to my softness, to murmured words by moonlight, to stolen sweaty moments or years of placid, plump, domestic bliss? When the fish swims into the trap, he doesn't know he is caught. To him, it is still the same river he's always known, though circumscribed by a reed fence. Only when he tries to escape does he realize there is no egress where he found ingress. To follow the parable of fishes (and he was a bit like a fish, sleek and slim and supple, comely enough, but all told a bit floppy, staring eyed, and widemouthed), the barbed hook that slips in so neatly will rip and tear coming out.

Later, he swore he loved me at first sight. But I have found that men rewrite history to suit their needs.

"How will you do it?" Connie asked that night as we lay in our cots.

I would caution anyone contemplating malfeasance to never, ever make the mistake of cultivating a confidante. Those in the spy game often say the only way two can keep a secret is if one of them is dead. While I have entrusted a few people with a few of my secrets, it is almost always after the fact. A story told can be denied. But a plan revealed can be foiled. To tell of schemes in progress is a dangerous thing.

But ye gods, I was so alone! And Connie such a fun and sympathetic friend. She treated my plan like a delightful game, and we would sooner be caught by her giggles than by any untoward action. I confided in her, too, because after knowing her for but a few days, I was resolved to take her with me when I escaped.

If I could, I would have taken a great many of them. All of those newly minted Maries who had lost their own names, those women without a place. But I could see the folly of a dozen untutored women traipsing through the French countryside after a convent-break. The law would be on the side of the Church, and their families who had condemned them to its service. We'd be caught, and returned. But the two of us— clever, educated, adaptable—would stand a chance of making our way unnoticed to some distant land and there finding a new life for ourselves.

I wondered whether Connie should be the one to lure the young priest into her clutches. After all, she had a great deal more carnal experience than I.

"No, no," she said with a laugh. "I have no skill at seduction, no more than honey has skill at attracting flies."

"But flies notoriously swarm to honey," I said.

"Likewise to shit," she replied in her earthy way. "The men who seek something out will find me easily enough, and I will, no doubt, in my careless way, tumble into a convenient position for them to access whatever they desire. The men will think they seduced me. Their wives will think I seduced them. But with me, my dear, there is almost no volition. No more than with the leaves turning each fall, or the salmon surging upstream." She thought a moment, then hit upon the exact right phrase. "I am a natural phenomenon."

It was true. Though she would cheerfully do almost anything, she lacked the subtlety and guile for proper seduction of an unwilling man. And although I could clearly see certain natural urges at work within the young priest, his position was a ball and chain around his ankle. It would take the utmost enticement to make him exert the effort to drag himself to a woman's bed, however much he desired it.

So with the observant eyes of the Reverend Mother and sterner sisters watching me for any hint of sin, I began my subtle seduction. Lady Mary, villainess though she was, knew her business. My tutelage under her should allow me to entice any man. I entered my scheme fully confident that before long the young priest would be nibbling sweetmeats from my hand, ready to defy the heavens and do my bidding. Noble lords had complimented my beauty. Princes of both state and church had desired me. It was impossible that this novice priestling bursting with the rut of youth could resist my charms.

Yet resist he did.

At our nighttime bent-kneed vigils (for though we weren't caught plotting seduction and escape, Connie and I were scarcely ever out of trouble), I muttered my frustration to her between clenched teeth.

"I thought to be gone by now!" I fumed and fretted. "There is frost on the ground. Winter will settle in soon. Are winters here harsh?"

Connie shrugged. "I am from farther south, and I came here in the spring." She'd yet to see a winter here, but the mildest winter makes travel awkward, and as fugitives we must have both speed and stealth, each hard to accomplish when snow slows travel and marks the traveler's

trail so plainly. I did not fancy sacrificing fingers and toes for my freedom. Extremities rotting from frostbite are ugly and inconvenient things,
and I was practical enough to know that without family or fortune, our
beauty must sustain us. Stuffed gloves may conceal a missing finger or
two, but what if winter stole my nose?

"I cannot manage to get alone with him," I went on. "That's the rub."

"Get one good rub in, and he's yours," Connie said with a giggle.

I did not laugh with her. "No," I explained, "you fail to factor in the
power of guilt. If I do not play him exactly so, he will flee in mortification after the first act. Heavens, he may even confess, and where would
we be then? No, this needs far more than a grope in the vestry. I must
make him love me. Commit to me. Pledge to me his very soul!"

You see, I had been thinking on this matter with all the wisdom I'd
accumulated in my life. When I was set to prayer, I dwelt not upon the
divine but on mortal flesh, its strengths and its failings. The devil, they
say, makes work for idle hands, but what of brains? In setting me on my
knees for so many hours, the Reverend Mother only sharpened my wits,
strengthened my resolve, and gave me patience to carry out plans I never
could have at court. If I were a sword, Maman had shaped the metal,
Lady Mary tempered it to strength, but it was the Convent of St. Ursula
that cooled the steel and honed it to exquisite sharpness.

Just then the Reverend Mother came in to check on us before retir-
ing, and I believe even she was impressed with the ecstatic fervor in my
eyes at that moment.

"Why do we need him at all?" Connie asked when we were alone
again. "Instead of plotting his jolly corruption, maybe we should focus
on getting the key."

"Which is held by the Reverend Mother," I reminded Connie. "Her
and no other."

"So you will trust the wee priestie to wrestle it from her? I think you
stand a better chance."

"He is a man," I told her. "And a priest. He will come up with some
excuse, and whether she believes it or not, she will be bound to follow his

command. Perhaps someday he will come alone, without his seniors. And then . . ."

"Clarice, you don't even know his name yet! Nor he yours. Think you now, cozen Father Ignatius, tickle him under his tender wattle, and see what befalls. Or!" Her eyes lit up with mischief. "Perhaps the Reverend Mother herself is in need of a good rub. You can open with a discussion of St. Teresa of Ávila. Her ecstasy, they say, included a seraphim repeatedly thrusting his golden spear into her." She shivered deliciously, and shifted on her reddened knees. "Perhaps the Reverend Mother has a soft side that *you* could penetrate . . ."

Then at last I gave in to laughter, but inwardly, I was troubled. Heated glances under stern watch can only take one so far. The young priest was aware of me—acutely aware, I was certain. That he looked at me less than any of the other nuns at the convent was evidence of that. He was, in fact, constantly *not* looking at me in a very telling way. But try as I might, I could not contrive to snatch a moment alone with him.

During the day and those nights on my knees, I schemed seduction. But when I lay alone in my cot, the breathing of the other young nuns like the sighs of doves (or the snufflings of boars—one of the girls was adenoidal), it was not the young priest who filled my thoughts.

George. Oh, George. How often that bit of sacking stuffed with hen fluff they called a pillow was sodden with my tears. I had learned from my mother, and later from Lady Mary, how a woman can be two people at once. But in those weeping nights of misery and regret and yes, love, ever to my shame, love, I realized that a person can feel two deeply disparate things with utter sincerity.

I hated George Villiers with all my heart.

I loved George Villiers with all my heart.

The hate was rational, of course. I could have penned a learned treatise upon it, with proofs and formulae, *quod erat demonstrandum*, and been accepted (bar my gender) into any academy that demanded evidence of clear, level-headed thinking in its members. Blacksmiths and philosophers alike would understand the hate.

The love, though, perplexed me, infuriated me, made me fear for the soundness of my mind and soul. In desperation, I gave it another name—obsession. Yes, that fit. Hate, love, it all came down to constant mulling, to contriving phantom conversations with the object, to thinking how they would react to this or that. In those nights on my hard cot, George came to me, incorporeal, and I kissed his phantasm as often as I stabbed it through the heart.

I must be diseased, I thought, for against all reason, I came up with more and more fantastic ways to excuse him. Contrary to the usual order of things, my hate became a kind of faith, while my love strove for reason. Other people love irrationally, but my well-tutored little brain managed to come up with every excuse under the sun for George's perfidy. He was being blackmailed, threatened. He was protecting me in some way. He was making a noble sacrifice to save his family. To save the king. To save England! There must have been something I didn't see, I harangued myself. And so I crafted ever more implausible scenarios to excuse him.

And though I told Connie that I trusted my mother would discover from my father where I'd been taken and come to deliver me, even as I planned my own rescue . . . in my inmost heart I saw George riding on a roan charger, leading a dappled palfrey, come with any pretty excuse and a vow to save me and love me forever.

I think I had too much belief in myself to be utterly convinced I'd been deceived. Surely, I thought, I couldn't have been such a stupid little girl to believe some lying man's blandishments. There must be something I wasn't seeing. That picture he'd painted for me of the life we'd have together . . . there must be truth in that.

And then I would pinch myself hard on the thigh, the self-inflicted bruise mingling well with those given me by the Reverend Mother, and make myself hate him again as I should. I must be that stupid little girl after all.

Chapter 10

❦

ork and prayer. Work and fasting. Mortification of the flesh, volun-
tary or not. I suppose I have not made my time at the convent sound too
ghastly, with all the girlish giggling and romantic plots worthy of Ben
Jonson. But these were stolen moments in weeks of misery, beams caught
in a storm-tossed sea, clung to but a moment and too soon snatched away.

I was used to work, and enjoyed being useful. But imagine an airless
cloister with small windows and hardly any congress between outdoors
and in. All of those women, and so little dust, so few footprints to clean!
Yet clean we did, endlessly scrubbing the stone floors and plastered walls.
When I asked why we spent so much time cleaning that which was already clean, the Reverend Mother said that the convent was the soul of
the Church, and it must be cleansed daily of its sins.

"Perhaps, after all, she has a penchant for young women on their
knees," Connie quipped as we scrubbed side by side. She wiggled her
plump, upturned buttocks.

There was a garden, of course, and I yearned to help in its tending.
When I offered my services early on, I let too much enthusiasm light my

eyes, and the Reverend Mother, seeing what would make me happy, naturally used it as a weapon. Thenceforth, she would dangle the possibility provocatively before me, letting me think I might earn the privilege of working the soil as I did with Maman, if only I scrubbed harder, prayed longer, subjugated myself to her will, abased myself a bit more. I would have hope, and then she would snatch it away from me for some small slight.

It was only much later that I learned how to manipulate her. I let her overhear me tell Connie how restorative the water and wax and lanolin in our cleaning potions was for my hands, how they were ever so much more supple and lovely now than when I used to have dirty cracked fingers from helping my mother in her herb garden. She sent me to the kitchen garden the very next day. Of course, it was winter, so I had little to do other than to coddle the last cabbages and mustard greens that lingered in the frost, and plumb the hard earth for what few mealy potatoes and turnips weren't yet in our cellar. I got chilblains, but they were the smug, self-satisfied chilblains of a small victory.

So you see, months had passed, with autumn's gold buried under snow, and still I was a nun. No one had come to save me, nor had I contrived to save myself, or Connie. When I was first ordered to my garden penance, I rejoiced, thinking that once I was past the convent walls, escape would be easy.

Not so. I was always attended by one of the senior nuns. The sojourns outside were short, for there was little to do, and I stayed in the garden only until my watchdog started to shiver, then in for the Reverend Mother to glance with satisfaction on my grubby, unladylike hands. I could outrun my keeper, of course, but then the alarm would be set at once. Also, I'd be leaving Connie behind, something I steadfastly refused to do.

And then, as always, where to go? Where was a woman alone to venture, without (or even with) money? I was bold, but also pragmatic. There is precious little work for women, the most common being both sides of the same coin—marriage and harlotry. I had no stomach for either. If I could find a position, I could be seamstress, healer, gardener, tutor, or (thanks to my recent teaching) scullery maid. But in which of these could I find enough to live on as I wished? In which of these would I not be raped, as my father had raped (or near enough) any unprotected woman beneath his own station.

I did not just need the priestling to free us. Much as it vexed me, I needed him to accompany us. Traveling with a man would give us at least the most basic protection as we made our way to my mother, or Paris, or whither we decided so that it was away from here. It was an unfortunate truth. Though I had the skills to travel and support myself on any journey, I couldn't travel free from harassment or persecution without a man.

I tried every technique in Lady Mary's arsenal, adapted to my situation. Once, coming in late to Mass, I scurried under accusing glares to my place and, when nearest to the young priest, enacted the Elegant Stumble. For a second as I tripped I saw his eyes widen, his arms jerk toward me with a yearning to save me. But he controlled himself, and, out of practice, I wound up twisting my ankle in earnest. In the public view, I knew not much could come of it, but I thought if only I can get him to touch my bare flesh, however quickly and perfunctorily, the noose around his neck would tighten.

The only physical contact I got was a beating for tardiness.

I speak of these beatings lightly, but they were wretched, dehumanizing, and all too frequent. Later in life, I'd meet people aroused by the pain of others, or by their own suffering. I cannot say for certain whether the Reverend Mother was such a person. There was nothing overtly lascivious about the beatings. Yet the Reverend Mother, and a few of her choice underlings, seemed to take definite pleasure in administering them. Should they ever change their vocation, Mrs. Fox would put their penchant to very profitable use. The sisters wouldn't even have to change their garments, though perhaps vary their instruments. Some men are fond of birch switches, I'm told, while others prefer the hairbrush.

Some of the beatings were impromptu, like that on my first night.

Others—and these were the worst—were scheduled. When I interrupted Mass, for example, the Reverend Mother hissed to me that my reward would come the following day after vespers. So I would sleep on thoughts of my chastisement, wake to the same fear, and have to endure a long day of dread for eventide.

And then, to receive holy words all the while. The Reverend Mother alternated between the scourge being a kind of scouring implement to scrape the pitch from our sinful feminine natures, and an ecstatic joining with the suffering of Christ. We were wicked, dirty, disgusting harlots, lazy sluts so debased that only the whip could teach us. We were holy objects, Brides of Christ, whose pain would uplift us so we could truly glorify our creator. Convention and modesty would not allow us to be nailed to a cross, but we could share in our savior's suffering nonetheless. It was, I must own, confusing. I would have preferred it if she had simply said it is the way of the world, that the strong beat the weak.

If I'd abandoned hope of release, I might have fought back. I might have yelled and railed and cursed, so that if I was to be beaten, it would take the effort of three sisters, and they would share in my protesting, un-Christlike suffering with pinches and bruises and bites of their own. But, believing that this was temporary (you see, I did learn a species of faith in there), I decided to endure. I did not struggle or cry, and though at first this seemed to spur the Reverend Mother on to further violence, after a time she seemed to have lost some of her vim, and there was a resigned, dispirited air to the chastisement, so that as winter deepened it became yet another meaningless ritual like the Masses and vigils.

"Do you know," Connie said one day as she rubbed the chilblains on her red, rough hands, "I used to examine myself in the mirror for hours at a time. As other people look at a landscape or a fine painting, I vow. Of course, we had no books in the house, and besides my stepbrothers, there were few diversions. I haven't seen an image of myself since I left home—until today." She gave a low moan such as the most pitiable and adorable ghost might utter.

"I thought for certain the Reverend Mother must have one, for her cross is always so devastatingly centered between the sag of her bosoms. And I was right! Sister Marie Justine had a coughing fit just as she was bringing the Reverend Mother her bouillon, and sent me instead into that holy lair."

I paused in my work, highly interested. Her personal quarters were the one part of the convent I'd not yet seen, and they might play a part in my plan. For I'd determined that if I could not win over the priest by high summer, we would hazard the escape on our own.

"Three rooms, and if I did not know better, I would call one of them the dressing room of a vain spinster who still nurtured hope. Her habits are draped like priceless furs, and there is a mannequin bust of ivory upon which hangs the glory of her pectoral cross. On a table, a pair of ivory hands hold her crosier. And oh! In the corner, just as I predicted, stands a cheval mirror as tall as she is, catching the sunlight and dazzling like you wouldn't believe! Only . . ." She hung her head, and I saw a tear drop into the sudsy scrubbing bucket, popping the largest bubble.

"What is it, *ma chérie*?" I asked, alarmed—the dimples had vanished!

"I looked in the mirror!" she said, then buried her face in her hands. Between her fingers I heard her say that absolutely no one, not even a stepbrother, would so much as look at her now. "The grease! The smuts! And a spot, on my chin just so, which I never would have known about but for that cursed mirror. Oh, misery."

She was laughing now through her tears, and the dimples returned. I think half her vanity is for my amusement.

I patted her head, which seemed to remind her of more cause for complaint. "And my hair! Such scraggly locks, with my ears peeking through like vagabond urchins in the marketplace. They have ruined me, these sisters. How I hate them."

I reassured her that she was still surpassingly lovely . . . which was *almost* true. A sapphire in dirt is still a sapphire, though perhaps it takes a subtle eye to pick it out.

Hesitantly, I asked her how I looked.

Connie wiped her eyes and looked at me with frank appraisal. "Well . . ."

"Tell me!"

"You are . . . gaunt. And red. Except where you are pale. Or dirty. And your hair!" My coif had slipped from my head while I scrubbed. She giggled. "Forgive me, but it looks like the down of a duckling. No, don't despair! A most delectable and golden duckling. Any priest would eat you up, with orange sauce."

But I realized I would have to do something about my person. In Yorkshire, I never thought about my looks, though I was always neat and often clean. At court, after my momentary astonishment at realizing I had that coveted and obscure thing, beauty, I took it for granted. Now, I assumed that beauty would shine easily through the suffering and grime.

"God, what a sight I must look!" I cried. "No wonder he avoids me."

Connie fixed me with a stern look. "He avoids you from fear, not disgust. Cover you in offal, and you would be appealing."

But with a shaking hand I pushed aside the bubbles in Connie's bucket and, when the water stilled, gazed at my ghostly reflection. Even given that dingy bucket water is not the most flattering of mirrors, I was not happy with what I found.

I stood up, throwing down my sodden rag with extravagant drama. I did it to amuse her, but I was sincere. "I will become lovely again!" I swore. "I will be the loveliest nun in Christendom, and when I am finished, the monks will line up to escort me from this place in a full ecclesiastical parade, carrying me on a litter like a relic of the Madonna!"

And so in that late winter, I ceased despairing, and took my fate more firmly by the reins. I had given it its head far too long. Whereas before I moped over my meals, I now dug into my tasteless gruel like it was manna. I wheedled my way into the kitchen and made for the waste pile, snatching up apple skins discarded from the Reverend Mother's luncheon, cramming the rosy peels into my maw before the pigs could get them. Greedily, therapeutically, I ate the whiskered tails of carrots, rusty heads of beets, the weirdest pared-off deformities of pale radishes, trying to force some tonic into my system amid that uninspired grain-based diet. I did not manage to grow quite plump again on this menu, but I looked less sunken, and my skin cleared. Whenever I could, I pressed my face to the tiny arrow-slit windows, catching as much of the wan winter sun as possible.

Bathing, though, was a greater problem. However much cleanliness was reputed to be next to godliness, standards fell sharply in winter when the well did its level best to freeze over every night. Trips to the well became onerous things. In the summer, we could fetch a modicum of water to wash our hands and faces. Now, though, we were confined indoors, and we began to reek. When once I held my nose at a den of stoats, Maman told me animals have such high smells as a means of conversation. Aromas advertise friendliness, fertility, or alternately, aggression and taciturnity, with no doubt a myriad of more subtle communications amid the muskiness. Perhaps if I had a more subtle nose I would better enjoy human ripeness, but our sapient stench spoke of nothing to me but dank pits and lice.

At meals, I would pour small beer onto my hem and scrub my cheeks. I was tempted to pour a measure over my hair, and risk smelling like a brewery all winter, but didn't quite dare under the eyes of the senior sisters. When I cleaned the floors and walls, I always splashed my face with the first water, but I could never achieve the privacy needed for any more complete toiletries. When, in frustration, I squatted over a bucket and attempted to wash my privities, I was caught by Sister Marie Margarita, accused of perversion, and put on bread and water for a week. And not, incidentally, enough water to bathe in.

Candlemas came, and the back of winter was broken. Not that one would know it there. Snow still lay thickly on the ground, and the celebration was so dour that I could not reconcile it with the merry pagan festivities we had at home. Officially, we celebrated the Presentation of Jesus at the Temple. In practice, though, the peasants were thoroughly heathen, and Maman and I took jolly part, cooking golden pancakes with last year's wheat, symbols of the burgeoning sun. Farmers carried torches through their fields, praying for fertile earth, and though the name they called aloud might have been blessed Mary, they might as well have been beseeching Brigid or some other old goddess. The village natural even dressed up in a moth-eaten bearskin and chased the virgins through the frosty commons. It was a veritable Lupercalia.

Here, though, they merely lit a candle, reminded us that Christ was the light of the world, and went on with cleaning, praying, fasting, and beating, in succession or simultaneously.

Out in the woods there may have been hints that winter had reluctantly admitted there would be such a thing as spring one day, but in the convent it seemed as freezing and drear as ever. The only good to come out of it was a blizzard. For three days in late February, snow fell ceaselessly, and when the gray heavens were exhausted and the sun shone brilliant in an azure sky, it still did not melt. The high, pristine white banks made Sister Marie Justine lose her smallest toe when she ventured out to the well in sandals, but it also imprisoned Father Ignatius and his young acolyte in the convent for a solid week.

Here was my chance! For a priest at night is surely more susceptible than by day. Secret shadowed corners, whispered promises, the tenderest caress, in darkness or by moonlight reflected on snow, when the body is weary and the defenses are down . . . I was certain I could trap him as surely as the snow, and more warmly.

And then, on the second day of us being snowed in, it happened: the chance I had been contriving for months. I was alone in the crypt, where the bodies of the more important members of the order had been laid in marble. Extinct reverend mothers—reverend grandmothers—lay cut in rough effigy on their tombs. I had been sent, as punishment, to clean their carved crevices. It was considered among the worst jobs, for not only did the girls fear restless spirits, but the crypt was so cold the washing water froze against the lifeless marble eyes as I laved them, making their gazes glassy and sinister.

Worse yet, in the back, piled like discarded cockleshells in a haphazard mound, were human bones. Connie told me that when the Convent of St. Ursula was built a few centuries ago, it replaced a much older convent some leagues hence. Rather than leave the contents of its crypt unattended as the old convent walls succumbed to worm and vine, the bones were relocated here. That was as far as anyone's ambition went. They were never reburied, nor was any attempt made to divide the bones and match each set to one owner. No, they lolled in an ivory orgy, limbs intertwined, pelvises pressed against skulls.

As I scrubbed the tombs in the far corner, I heard the heavy door swing open, and who should enter but the young priestling, mercifully alone. I held my breath, fearful he'd flee if he saw me right away. Peeping over the sepulcher, I saw that he carried a skull gingerly in his hands. It looked rather fresher than one could have wished.

Then, like Hamlet with the skull of Yorick, which I saw enacted by traveling mummers, he soliloquized.

"Alas, poor woman," quoth he. "They said you were elderly, but you must have been young once, and comely. Oh, will I never get any nearer than this?" Then, fumble-fingered with emotion, he dropped the skull. It landed with a crack on the stone floor, and he scooped it up with a most unclerical curse and traced the dome's fissures, trying to reckon if any were new. Then he shrugged, and proceeded to the rear of the crypt. He laid the skull reverently atop the pile, then with a look of distaste brushed off his hands on his robe. As soon as his hands were clean, the skull, precariously balanced, tumbled down the bony pile with a clatter. He cursed again and tossed it to the center of the jumble, where it settled, grinning lasciviously at him. He sighed, shuddered, and turned to go. It was then that he spied me.

I rose gracefully to my feet, and with a gasp of surprise, he backed to the most shadowed recesses of the crypt, as if I were a dangerous wild beast.

I was, of course.

I placed myself between him and the exit, forbidding him escape, all the while making sure to look like meeting him here was the most natural thing in the world. To feign shock or titillation might overwhelm him. No, better to pretend that priests and nubile young nuns met in such circumstances all the time, that there was no hazard in it.

"Good evening, Father," I said. It was scarcely past noon, but *evening* sounds so much more provocative. No tittering, no lowering of the eyes. I did not look innocent. Innocence is for people aware that guilt exists. Like a seraph, I was beyond innocence. Here are two perfect beings, my stance and clear gaze seemed to say. We may commune freely.

"Who was she?" I asked, indicating by an evocative dancer's gesture the skull with bits of matter still clinging stickily to it.

"I, er . . ." he began. I stepped closer.

"Was she a great and devout lady, whose last desire was to be interred among these holy sisters?" I deepened my voice ever so slightly on the word *desire*. Lady Mary had taught me a coded way of speaking, inserting eroticism into the most banal conversation, so that saying words such as *body*, or *hard*, or *wet*, or *need*, even in the midst of a discussion of the weather, can arouse, when they are uttered in a meaningful tone. The object may not even be aware of the subtle emphasis placed on those words, she told me, but they will sink into their soul nonetheless.

"She was," he squeaked, then cleared his throat to continue with an air of bravado, "a nun-errant."

Without even acting, I clapped my hands in delight. Here was a youth who had read romances! He would know of the heroic and romantic deeds of knights *sans pareil*, of Arthur's men, and Orlando's comrades, of the lovely, pure ladies they served. What beguiling charm, to call her a nun-errant, like the wandering knights. I knew at once what he meant. Even aside from my schemes, I took to him because of this.

"She found her calling on the road," I said, then frowned, worried this might smack too much of prostitution. I think, though, he was himself too untutored to catch it. "She was one of the nuns who travel from village to village, helping the poor, or who journey with pilgrims, saving souls on the highway?"

"Yes, exactly," the young priest said, relaxing a measure. "She had been traveling with a small group that was set upon by bandits, and she was . . . slain." The pause made me think other things happened before the slaying.

"Nearby?" I asked, alarmed. Yet another reason to travel with a masculine guard, even one as inexperienced as the priest. At the very least, he could provide some distraction while Connie and I fled.

"A few days' journey from the monastery. The survivors wanted to carry her body there, but . . . an animal came in the night."

The prospect of running away looked grimmer and grimmer. "Wolves?"

"The pilgrims did not know. They heard a snarling, and her body was dragged away."

"Oh!" I breathed, and drew nearer to him.

"They found her skull, no more."

I looked up into his troubled eyes and tried to think of something pious to say about parts being reunited on the Day of Judgment, but couldn't quite formulate something appropriate. "How sad," I said instead.

"So they brought it to the monastery. But then the brothers decided it would not be fitting to have a woman in their crypt."

Surprised by this, I tried but could not quite contain a laugh. It came out as a snort. Perhaps a charming one. I clapped my hand over my mouth and tried to look demure, but to my delight, I caught the amusement in his eyes. He steadied himself, but the moment had happened. No music and moonlight, only dust and bones and a persistent whiff of decay from the nun-errant, but it sufficed.

"Her skull might be a corrupting influence on the buried brothers?" I asked.

"They would turn in their graves," he replied.

I could not resist adding, "For a better look."

He drew in breath to laugh, then pressed his lips together. Careful now, Clarice.

"I can see no harm in it, myself," I said. "Why, here we are, warm and alive, together in a crypt, and nothing ill has befallen either of us."

I smiled up at him, as guileless as a marigold. "Small, mean minds make up scandal where none dreams of existing."

He nodded fervently. "I've been told not to talk to you. Not to be alone with you."

"With *me?*" I asked. I thought I had been more careful to allay any suspicion.

"Not you, in particular. The nuns. I've only just taken my vows, and Father Jean says it is a dangerous time."

I laughed aloud then. "Do I look dangerous to you?"

I thought it would be as good an excuse as any to rake my body with his eyes, an invitation to examination, but he held my gaze and said with a sincerity I hadn't heard since George's vows of love, "No, when I look at you I see only beauty and goodness."

I turned coquette. "Have you looked at me before now?"

"I see you sleeping and waking," he said, fevered and fervent. "You walk beside me."

Then the poor boy gulped, shoved his way past me, and fled, leaving me to the ice and decay.

For another three days, I tried without success to get him alone. Even a moment would do, to stoke the fire. I could whisper my name, give him something to cry out in his solitary cell at night. I could pretend not to see him, and softly sing a country song of love and heartbreak. I could slip him a note, bold and incriminating to have evidence in my own handwriting, but it would give him something tangible to kiss, and he could imagine it carried my scent (lye and sweat, at that time).

But whether through his will or happenstance, no maneuvering of mine succeeded in getting us alone together for even the space of a breath.

He would make more of an effort if I could fix myself up, I thought. My ragamuffin hair was covered by my coif, but the golden tendrils I coaxed out at my temples and the nape of my neck would make him

envision bountiful skeins flowing down my back if I ever removed it. I
had no cosmetics, but my skin had cleared, and I touched my lashes with
soot, and bit my lips to redness whenever there was a chance of seeing
him. My cheeks were rosy enough from the cold to not need pinching.
The rough habit and thin smock beneath it made me look like a shape-
less sack, but when the Reverend Mother or her minions weren't looking,
I could cinch my belt in to show off my figure. I had done all for my
beauty that I could.

Except bathe fully. If only I could be thoroughly clean all over, he
would not be able to resist me. After that good start in the crypt, I believed that it would only take one more rendezvous to secure his promise
of help.

Connie told me I was being silly. "My stepfather went so far as to
instruct me to bathe less. He would root about my body like a suckling
piglet, sniffing and snorting. Do you really think the priest shuns you
because you have not had a bath? None of us have. When all stink,
none stink."

It was easier to have a scapegoat, and I felt less a failure when I could
blame my lack of success on my lack of a full tub. I began to despair . . .

And then, when the snow showed the first signs of melting, on the
first day of March, spring launched its most concerted attack on winter.
Purple clouds tumbled across the sky, rumbling like bilious gods, and the
heavens opened up in torrential rain. Biblical rain! It washed the snow
away, and turned the world that I could see through the arrow-slit windows into slush, then mud. I cursed the elements, thinking the priests
would be able to travel home, now that the snow was gone. But the rain
never stopped. I heard the sisters say the land was now even more im-
passable because of the rain. It would swallow a man and a mule up
more swiftly than snow. I sighed with relief. I would have another few
days, at least.

But still, I could not trap him, and he did not seek me out.

On the second day of steady rain, we had gathered for Mass when
one of the sisters cried out, "Holy Mary be praised! Jesus weeps!" She

stood, pointed to the statue, and immediately swooned, and so didn't find out until later that her miracle was no more than the first sign of the roof leaking. Another drop fell splat on Christ's thorn-crowned head. Father Jean cleared his throat and continued Mass, while the young priest stood discreetly in the background, still not looking at me. Father Jean went bravely on while the drops became a stream, then many streams, and at last there came a great groaning from the ceiling.

Connie shrieked, and ran for the door, dragging me along with her. "The roof is about to collapse!" she cried. "It happened at our neighbor's house, just so. The roof was weakened from snow, then when the rains came, something blocked the drains and gutters, and the weight of the water brought the roof crashing down. Come! We must get outside!"

But the door was barred. Frantically, I ran up to the Reverend Mother and told her what Connie had said.

"Nonsense," she replied, "nuns cannot leave the convent unsupervised. It would be chaos." She murmured something about God protecting us and started to make for her private quarters on the far side of the nunnery, a wing of newer construction and probably safe even if this side collapsed.

Furious and heedless of her power and bulk, I ran after her. Away from the others, I caught hold of the Reverend Mother's sleeve and hissed, "They will take it as a sign that God does not favor you as abbess. You will be removed! Another will wear that priceless pectoral cross you treasure."

She stopped, as still as if she'd been clapped in the stocks. Then she struck me hard across the face, sending me staggering against the wall. But then, mercifully, she pulled the heavy key from the mysterious folds encompassing her lower half and went back to the shrieking and mewling others, and let us all out.

She handed the key to my young priest, saying, "As soon as the danger has passed, lock them up inside again." Then she went back inside, not from any act of heroism, I later discovered (to no surprise), but to fetch her valuable crosier from her room.

Freedom! Frigid, sodden freedom that almost instantly made my toes numb. But as we piled out, all of us instead of the one or two at a time who were allowed in the garden, there was a festival air. We gasped and held our faces to the torrent, looked at one another and grinned, and shivered, and hugged, half for celebration, half for warmth. It was obvious we couldn't escape, not in those conditions. The thought surely never crossed any of our minds. But I can see how the Reverend Mother would fear to give us any taste of freedom. Even at its worst, life is better outside of walls.

"It is only a matter of time now," Connie said, looking up with detached interest at the roof. "It was poorly constructed, and if the gutters are blocked . . ."

Despite the heavy rains, the carved faces showing the seven deadly sins that served the building instead of gargoyles did not spew water from their gluttonous (or slothful, or lusty) mouths. The water was trapped, the roof like a great fish tank.

"Could it be stopped? Could someone unclog it?" I asked.

Connie shrugged. "Mayhap. If someone were to climb up and remove whatever leaves or dead rats are blocking the drains. But who would dare such a thing in this weather?"

I hated that place. But it was shelter. It was freedom from starvation and safety from bandits until such time as I could brave those risks on my own terms. And though I hated the Reverend Mother and her particular cronies, many of the other women had become my friends. I could not let the convent fall. I had to save the place I loathed.

"Ladders!" I called . . . and was ignored. I shook Sister Marie Margarita by the arm and shouted to her that the roof would collapse and possibly destroy the whole convent if we didn't do something soon. She shook me off and told me to mind my own business.

Then, through the pounding of the rain, I heard a voice behind me. "She speaks truly, sister." My priestling! "We must act now to save the convent."

A man spoke, and suddenly everyone hustled. Sister Marie Margarita dispatched nuns to fetch our two ladders, mostly used to reach our prized small piece of stained glass. They propped them against the wall, where they almost reached the roof, and my priest summoned Father Jean to help him.

Father Jean did not quite laugh, but scoffed, "Me? Up there? You jest."

My priest looked over his bulk. There was something to what he said. The ladders were made of saplings bound with sinew, used to holding feminine weight (but not that of the Reverend Mother, who neared Father Jean in girth and surpassed him in height). "You must," he decided. "We must help them." But the fat priest shook his head.

Huffing in frustration, I swept past them both and was halfway up one of the ladders before anyone could protest. I could feel their stares on me. A woman! Acting! Active! It was no different than Maman stanching a gushing wound. Should she stop and think, giggle, wonder if it is unladylike? If God would approve?

But oh, I can feel the coldness to this day, a chill that seeped to my marrow. I hiked up my habit and pulled myself over the edge of the roof, into an arctic sea. Two steps, and a tile gave way underfoot, making me fall headlong. I had my bath at last, I thought deliriously.

Then my young priest was at my side, helping me to my feet. There was no time for romance. We were laborers with a fixed purpose that precluded gender. With hands numb and clumsy, we fumbled in the flood, searching for obstructions, knowing all the while that if the roof collapsed with us atop, it was a coin toss whether crushing or drowning would do for us first. We hurled leaves and branches—and yes, dead rats, and a dead cat—from the rooftop, unmucking as best we could, until at last, when I was near dead with cold and fatigue, there came a gurgle and a sucking sound, and a gush of water spewed from lust's lascivious lips. We cleared another, and another, and the pool began to drain through the seven deadly spigots. When it reached my ankles, I decided we had done enough and made my way down the ladder.

Halfway down, my body gave way, and I fell into the mud.

All that water, wasted.

And for a long time, that was the last I knew . . .

I dreamed of drowning. In the tossing sea when I was thrown, bound, into the channel. In sucking mud that oozed insidiously into my orifices.

I drowned in a kiss, one that started out so sweet but then changed its tenor, the unseen man sucking the life, the very soul from me.

I woke to find lips on mine. Gentle lips, feather light, and before I could formulate what was in my best interests, I shrank back and turned my head, feeling sick. And then I was sick, copiously, into a basin held for me. When I fell back, my head was swimming, and I saw stars. When my vision cleared, I saw my young priest looking down at me with worry and, I believe, devotion.

"What happened?" I asked.

"You took a chill," he said lightly, although when I pressed him for details, it seemed I almost died. I'd been feverish for days, delirious. He'd carried me to my bed, then to a cot away from the others in what was nominally our infirmary, but which was mostly used for drying herbs. They hung above my head in clusters, mint and artemesia and rose-mary.

"You tended me?" I asked weakly.

"My father was a physician. I was supposed to follow in his footsteps, and at times would accompany him on his rounds. I knew what to do for you. Your good Reverend Mother tried to tell me it wasn't appropriate, but Father Jean stepped in and swore he could vouch for my purity and good intentions. Your friend Marie Cecilia was here most of the time, acting as chaperone."

It took me a moment to recognize the name Connie had been given when taking her vows. "I know I have nothing to fear from you, Father . . ." I still did not know his name.

"Felix," he said, and his beaming face made the name appropriate. "And you are Sister Marie Anne, I am told?"

"Clarice," I whispered.

He spoke my name after me, making it sound like a caress. "Clarice..."

I looked into his pale gray eyes, and found that I had no need of further tricks or seduction. All unwilling, I had enacted the Lovely Invalid, and his care for me in extremis had bound him inexorably to my side. Accidentally, I had won him. And more than that, I discovered. Delirium had done what craft might not have.

"You spoke in your fever dreams," Felix said at length.

My eyes flew open. The things I might have said!

"You said that your father sent you here against your will, that you waited for your mother to come for you, but she never has. You were forced to take vows against your will. Oh, sweet girl, so was I!"

He told me how his father, tending to the local baroness, slipped when bloodletting and severed an artery that could not be stanched. The scandal ruined his career, and his sons, suddenly a burden, were forced to abandon hopes for medical careers of their own and fend for themselves. "My older brother, a dear soul but one who never had any medical calling, had mostly been useful for holding patients down or setting obstinate dislocations. He turned his strength to smithing, and to . . ." He broke off, and I wondered what shameful sideline his brother might have.

"And I, without useful skills beyond reading, was sent to the priesthood. It was never what I desired. I have no calling. But once sworn, there was no going back."

"No," I said softly, "there is only going ahead in this life. What people forget is that they can always choose a new path."

Felix nodded. "In your dreams, you begged me to save you. Me! It was as if God had summoned me to your side, laid you like a wounded bird in my lap. As you rambled, you spoke of traveling with me, of making a new life far from here. Oh, Clarice!" He caught up my hand and pressed it to his lips. "I will! I will save you!"

My wildest dreams, my every ambition for the past months, suddenly brought to fruition. It was enough to make me . . . suspicious. The gods do not give us our fondest dreams very often, except to make sport of us.

As we talked in the few moments that remained before a senior nun came to check on us, I realized that my dreams were his, that he was a romantic looking for an object—any one would do, very likely, if I had not come around. Further, he had been plotting his escape for months, just as I had. All he lacked was courage, and what is better for giving a man courage than a woman? (Some will say liquor, but the effects of womankind last longer, and tend to yield better results.) To this day I wonder how much of his seduction was my own doing, how much was accident, and how much was him. I am called a master schemer, and yet I have found that the random twisting of the universe in its weird convulsions ofttimes gives such results that the most meticulous planning will never render.

"But how will I . . . we escape?" I asked. "The Reverend Mother keeps the key on her person at all times."

A slow grin spread across his pale, beatific face as he pulled a chain from his pocket. At the end dangled the key. He swung it as he did his censer. "I told her I lost it in the snow and mud," he said. "Which is completely true. Is it a sin that I neglected to tell her I found it again?"

There was still much to discuss. He must, of course, agree that Connie would accompany us. Then there was the question of where to go—and how? How would we travel? How would we eat? But there was time enough for that, I thought, as relief and lingering fever made me sink back into my pillow. It would still be too muddy and cold to travel easily for weeks. And the fever had left me too weak for a rigorous journey. But the foundation was set, and I rested easy knowing that my château of dreams would be built by this lovestruck young priest.

Chapter 11

1628

*W*e are somewhat limited by the language of our birth. I am perhaps a rare creature, having been weaned on both English and French in equal measure, and now think and feel equally in both, but most people only feel what their native tongue encourages them to feel. Anything else is too subtle. The English, therefore, are a linear people. A thing happens, and it is consigned to the past, never to be repeated. Each mistake or victory stands alone.

We French speakers, however, have déjà vu, and know that each life has a motif, a melody reprised again and again through the magnum opus. Crucial experiences in our lives repeat, albeit often in disguised form. Curse or blessing, I cannot say. Are we doomed to relive subtle moments throughout our lives, realizing just too late that we should have known what was going to happen? Or by having patterns in our existence are we granted the power to one day take control of those endless ripples? For déjà vu is only a realization of repetition in the moment, not foreshadowing.

When last I ran from this convent, I left with joy and hope. Look what that brought me. Now tonight I flee from the same convent. As before, I ride a panting horse hard through the wooded trail. This time, though, I ride alone.

I once swore I would never leave my friend behind. This time, though, I cannot go back for her.

That sense of life's cycles does little to reassure me. Perhaps other mad gallops, perhaps other people left behind were but premonitions of this moment, the echoes somehow coming before the blast.

Enough of this! Life is not a prophesy, nor yet a play. Nothing is written. I trouble myself needlessly by waxing philosophical now, at the end of things. All my life, I have been a woman of action. Introspection and retrospection are for the quiet moments. Tonight, my only purpose is to run from the Musketeers who would kill me.

I shake my head, freeing the loosely pinned locks. Hairpins tumble over my horse's flanks, making him shy, and his sudden stop and buck almost unseat me, a thing that hasn't happened since I was three and on my first pony. Steady now. My end must come in a prescribed manner, or all is lost. I cannot die of a broken neck in the middle of the woods.

I make myself breathe deeply, and the horse (a skittish beast, not of my choosing) settles into an uneasy walk. His ears flick at every woodland sound, but after a time he calms, and we continue on to Armentières.

At the inn, I attract a certain amount of attention by seeming to not desire any. I dismount out of view and lead my horse, for the sight of a woman riding, alone, commands notice. A deep hood conceals my face, and even when I ask the landlord for a private room in the back, I keep my countenance in shadow. It makes him look all the harder, picking out details he might otherwise have missed—the exact hue of a loose curl, the opal jewel I wear on my smallest finger, the husky, persuasive timbre of my voice. He will be able to recount the minutiae to anyone who comes in search of me.

No matter, I am weary, and a few hours of sleep will not change the outcome. Better to face what is to come well rested.

Before sunrise I am away, and when I reach my destination, the sun is climbing brilliantly over the curve of the river near Erquinghem. Past the ford stands a little cabin, hardly more than a shack, but cheerful yellow curtains waft in the open windows, and a curl of smoke rises from the chimney. It has been made ready for me.

A quickset hedge as high as my waist rings the house except where it meets an arched arbor. I feel a frisson of fear as I pass through, but no, no one is lurking on the other side. I've not been betrayed. I must yet be discovered.

Inside, bread has been left for me, still warm, along with a hunk of veined cheese, a small pot of honey, and a bottle of decent Rhenish. I leave the wine, though it seems to be safely corked, but dig into the bread and cheese like a peasant. And do you know, it is the best thing I have tasted in months. They say a condemned man gets his best night's sleep just before his execution, and eats a hardy meal if offered. I always thought that strange, for wouldn't he want to savor his last few hours, and not waste them in slumber? And wouldn't fear make the food dry and tasteless?

But I slept like the dead last night, for the first time in weeks. And now, this simple repast tastes like ambrosia.

I am ready.

They, alas, are not, for the long day passes alone . . .

I don't hear them coming, a sure sign that I am giving up on this life. It rained just after dark, and the ground is moist and silent. Lingering raindrops ping on the roof and drip musically from the gutter, and the last growls of thunder roll across the land. Lost in thought, I sit in a wicker chair with my elbows on the table, propping my head up as I wait. And wait. And wait. Lord, but I will be glad to be done with this life of endless waiting.

Outside, a horse squeals, the sound a beast makes when it has had the spur one too many times. I sigh. He is ever the same, having no thought of his underlings. I believed, once, he could be different than his endless series of forefathers.

Suddenly, there is a face in the window, a pale face, intense even through the clouded glass. The face is replaced by a fist, smashing through, and I leap to my feet with a cry. He kicks away the rest of the shards and tries to leap through, but age and drink hamper him, and he has to clamber inelegantly.

I dash to the door, far faster than he, and fling it open . . . only to find D'Artagnan barring my way. Seeing him makes caterpillars crawl across my skin, a prickly, unbearable feeling. I could stab him in the throat, whirl, and fling my blade into Athos's heart. But Athos has drawn his sword, and D'Artagnan his pistol. I stand at the intersection of their vengeance.

"Uncock your weapon," Athos says, with that old tone of authority that even hotheaded D'Artagnan can't deny. "We are not murderers. Leave that title to Milady. This demon must be judged, not slaughtered. Judged, found guilty, and executed for the countless crimes she has committed."

"A strange sort of trial if the verdict is predetermined," I say.

Athos ignores my protest. "Come in, gentlemen. You will have your satisfaction ere long."

The room is small, and I back up as much from necessity as terror as the others file in. Added now to my jury are Porthos and Aramis, and a greater pair of rogues you will rarely meet. I've taken care to find out all about them. Porthos is a glutton, gambler, and braggart. Aramis pretends piousness while cuckolding half of France's nobility. Joined with Athos, who was ever cruel, and that arrogant little Gascon with his slippery ways and cunning wiles hidden under the face of a square-jawed buffoon, what hope do I have? They point their gloved fingers and decide I must die.

Ah, but those are not the only members of my jury. Adding themselves to the press come two more figures. Here is Lord de Winter, known by some as my brother-in-law, who once served the cardinal but was ever fickle in his allegiance, selling himself to the highest bidder. Who might that be, now?

Behind him is a tall man robed and cowled all in red.

I shrink at the sight of his demonic form. "Who is this?" I gasp.

Athos smirks. "In good time, Milady. First, gentlemen of the jury, present your accusations."

D'Artagnan steps forward, two high spots of color dotting pallid cheeks. "Before God, and these honorable men, I charge Milady de Winter with killing the innocent Constance Bonacieux by poison scarcely a day hence."

I collapse in my chair, and hold out my arms as if to ward off the very words that tumble tremblingly from his lips. "No!"

"We testify to her crime," says Porthos, as Aramis nods in agreement. "We witnessed her death."

"Come, Milady," Athos says in his glacial voice. "There is no use denying it. You are a cur backed against a wall. Snap all you like; the end will be the same."

"Yes! I gave her the tainted tea! Wolfsbane and foxglove. But I had ample reason for it." I glare with burning eyes at D'Artagnan. "You loved her, and you sinned against me, so yes, I killed the woman you loved. But tell them what you did to me!"

"Whatever trifling offense you imagine D'Artagnan committed against you," Athos says before the Gascon can speak, "it cannot justify killing a lovely young woman who has done you no wrong." D'Artagnan flushes, and looks immeasurably grateful that his crime—his intended crime—is not revealed. "Tell us, D'Artagnan, what other crimes she has committed."

He gulps and stammers before choking out, "She sent me poisoned wine. My servant drank it, and died horribly of gripping guts." For just a second he meets my eyes, and I see a deep shame. Now that the end is near, I wonder if I should offer him forgiveness. No, better he toss and turn at night, recalling how his crime killed his love. Or rather, how his imagined crime killed his contrived love. What men believe becomes their truth.

"Speak, woman!" Athos barks. "Is this true?"

"He deserved it!"

"Poison, bah!" Athos spits like a peasant on my floor. "A coward's weapon. A woman's weapon. What a monster you are! I testify to this crime."

"And I, and I," echo Aramis and Porthos.

"This is more than enough to condemn you to death in any court, Milady. Yet this is not the end of your misdeeds. Musketeers, recount what else this treacherous woman has done."

Porthos, tipsy fool that he is, pipes up, "She stole the diamonds from Buckingham!" Athos looks at him sharply, while Aramis nudges him hard in the ribs with his elbow. "What?" he demands, rubbing his flank. Aramis leans close and whispers something in his ear, and it is all I can do not to laugh.

You see, France's own Queen Anne gave the English Duke of Buckingham a set of priceless diamonds given to her by the king. I stole four of them back to condemn the queen, to give the cardinal leverage over her. But to charge me with that crime would be tantamount to charging the queen with adultery, in wish if not in deed. That accusation against me was quickly withdrawn.

Lord de Winter steps forth, and in his gravelly, badly pronounced French, says, "She killed my brother."

I gasp. "How dare you say such a thing? I loved . . . I . . . respected your brother. I would never . . ."

He turns to the Musketeers. "Of this, I have no absolute proof, but I know my brother died not long after marrying her, and drafting a will that left her the bulk of his property even beyond her allotted jointure. I thought he died of quartan ague, as they said, but with all this talk of poison, I now have my doubts."

Athos sighs at the way the trial is deteriorating. "No matter. There is enough to condemn her already."

"Wait, my lords," cries de Winter. "I know of another crime, most terrible. She has killed His Grace the Duke of Buckingham!"

They gasp, for the news has evidently not reached the Continent. Perhaps soon the besotted queen will be weeping her eyes out.

"I never killed him! I swear it before God!"

"We shall add lies and blasphemy to your crimes," Athos says.

"Are they capital crimes, too?" I ask archly.

"A man who lies to me may well die."

"And a woman, too," I breathe, "however guiltless she may be, beyond that lie."

De Winter tells them the most fantastic story, of intercepting me in England, holding me prisoner under care of his most trusted lieutenant. How I twisted that lieutenant around my finger, turning him from jailer to assassin. Like a man in a trance, he stabbed Buckingham, all at my bidding, and now lies in chains awaiting execution.

"Never have I heard such an unbelievable tale!" I gasp hysterically. "I vow after that testimony you must declare a mistrial! What do you think I am, that I can make a man, a stranger, kill for me? This is a farce. And even if it were true, I never harmed Buckingham. I demand you take me to the cardinal, to the king, and let this be decided by courts royal or ecclesiastic."

Athos pulls a paper from his breast and flaps it open in my face: the letter of marque granting the bearer of that missive free rein to act as they will with the cardinal's blessing. "You see, this is indeed an ecclesiastical court. On the authority of your master, we try you. Now, gentlemen, the accusations have been made, vouched for as facts by honorable men. How do you find this woman?"

"Hold," said the man in the red cloak, and all heads turned to him. "All accusations have not yet been made."

"Athos, you have brought this stranger here without telling us why," D'Artagnan says. "I am anxious to hear what he has to say."

"He can say nothing!" I wail. "He is a stranger to me. Who are you, sir, to speak against me?"

He steps forth and with a dramatic flourish strips his red hood from his face. His countenance is still half-covered by a mask, but I know it nonetheless. It is a face I see in my dreams nearly every night.

"You sent my brother to his doom, witch," the man in red snarls. "I am the executioner of Lille."

Part 4

Chapter 12

***

1616

A week or two later, when I had just gained enough strength to start scrubbing floors again (and the improving weather and muddy gardening duties meant there was finally need to), little Sister Marie Celeste ran up to me, tripping on her overlong hem, and told me that a woman had come to the convent door, asking for me.

I dropped my sudsy bucket and was gone before the splashes could hit my legs. "Maman!" I cried. "Maman, I'm here!"

But when I got there the door was locked—the Reverend Mother had a duplicate, as it turned out, but they were still searching the grounds for the original—and there was no Maman, only a stern-faced Reverend Mother striding angrily past me. Heedless of any possible punishment, I trotted after her. "Where is she? Is it my mother? Has she come for me?" She gave no answer. "You must let me see her!" I grabbed hold of her sleeve, but she shook me off roughly. Unlike the last time I was so bold, though, she didn't strike me. I took that as a good sign. If Maman was here, she couldn't hide her handiwork, and if I was bruised, she'd be questioned. It could lead to trouble for the order. Emboldened, I kept following her all the way to her private quarters, pestering her for answers.

Only at her doorway did she turn and say, "You have no mother. You have no family. They were left behind the moment you spoke your vows. You belong to the Church, now and forever." Then she called to her attendant for pen and paper, and slammed the door in my face.

I ran back to the door and shook it until its hinges rattled, screaming for my mother. I pressed my ear to the door, but there was no answer.

For the next two weeks, I raged (as far as I was able, for I was still weak from my illness) and wept and begged. I was never struck, which gave me hope, but after making a nuisance of myself, I was locked in a room for three days, given nothing but stale bread and water. Though I made every one of the younger sisters swear to listen hard and tell me any news, they all reported that no one ever came asking for me again. I quizzed Marie Celeste until she wept, but her story was the same: she'd been cleaning the door brass when the knock came. The Reverend Mother had shooed her away before opening the door, but she'd clearly heard a woman ask—no, demand—to see Lady Clarice Paget. Beyond that, she heard nothing else clearly, only sharp, elevated voices, and the slamming of the heavy door. She saw no one.

For a while, I lived in certainty. Then, I lived in hope. After a time, though, the cold fingers of despair began to creep over me, poking, pinching, violating. Maman had not come to court, though she'd promised to follow me as soon as she was able. She had not come here. I was alone, except for my wits, my friend . . . and Felix.

Felix had become my loyal swain, and showed a surprising aptitude for deceit. Like a practiced seducer, he quickly learned the art of slipping notes secretly into my hand. He developed the stealth of a hunting-master, the cunning of a general, as he sought out the most secret lairs and arranged for us to rendezvous undiscovered. He was pure, though, and a gentleman. He never claimed more than my hand (and no, not for that—only for him to caress and kiss) and said that when we escaped together we would be married. Only then, he declared, would he allow himself the true bliss that has been the blessing of every couple since Adam and Eve.

I was tempted to say that the primordial pair are not the best example. How can it be true love, physical compatibility, when there is no choice of partners? Discounting Lilith and her ilk, of course. And the question of sinful incest among Adam and Eve's descendants. One cannot be both devout and rational. One or the other must give way.

But I engaged in no theological discussions with my Felix, nor did I ever contradict him when he spoke of marriage. For myself, I had no idea what the future would bring. I thought it foolish to plan too far beyond escape. That was in itself such an uncertain thing. I was much relieved at his views on letting me be pure until marriage, though. I cannot say for sure whether I would have yielded. I was so married to my plan of escape, that if he made my virtue (such as remained to me) a condition, I might have acquiesced. Or, perhaps, I would have introduced him to what Armand was kind enough to teach me. There is such a charm, such a fetish about virginity, that it seemed a great thing to give it up.

My only small conflict with Felix was my insistence that Connie elope with us. He thought me pure, innocent, mistreated, for my beauty has always been of that kind. I have a pathetic and angelic look about me, I think, when I am not roused to passion (and I certainly never was with poor Felix). No one could ever look at Connie and see the angel in her nature, though. Every curve and angle of her, from her freckled, ever so slightly retroussé nose to the piquant tendrils of her hair, spoke—nay, shouted—of illicit activities. In short, Felix did not trust her. I made it clear, though, that I would not go without her, and in the end he praised my loyalty and agreed she could come.

Our plans grew, and I began to believe that the story of a woman asking for me was no more than a myth. The land grew warm, spring crops were planted, and I hid dried beans and hard biscuits in secret crevices for our flight. Soon, very soon, we would be ready to fly.

Fortune favored us. The traveling trader the Reverend Mother had been expecting at the first sign of spring never came, and she had the clothes and hair of last year's novices to sell. Hearing of her plight, Felix nobly volunteered to take them to the nearest large market, where, he said, he could surely get a better price than at the one in the closest village. By rights, he should not have been allowed to go alone, but he asked in the presence of Father Jean, and he certainly wouldn't stir himself on such an arduous commission even to help a sister order. So it was decided on the Monday next, he would take the clothes and hair, mine included, on donkeyback.

"Perfect!" I cried when I found out. "We will have our clothes, so we can travel without attracting attention. I will have my . . ." I almost mentioned my dagger, but caught myself in time. "The rosary my mother gave me. See if there are any sturdy shoes in the lot. When I was taken, I had on slippers for court. And oh, if you can sell the things and then fetch us, we will have money enough to reach Paris. Or do you think we should go to a smaller town? They might think to look for us in Paris first, but then, people in small towns see everything, and love to gossip. In Paris we would simply be a few more fleas on a large dog, unnoticed."

I found him looking at me in a peculiar fashion. "You want me to steal?"

I realized I'd have to tread carefully. "It isn't stealing. The clothes and hair are ours by right. At least, some of them are."

"But those of the other nuns. It all belongs to the Church." He looked pained.

"What is the Church but an institution of charity? Its mission is to help the poor, the unfortunate, the lost. This convent has lost its way. Have you seen the priceless pectoral cross the Reverend Mother wears? Why, sell that, and you'd have means to fund a thousand pilgrims, to feed the poor, to convert the infidels!" I was not sure how an infidel could be converted by money, except perhaps by bribery, nor had I in fact any true idea what being an infidel entailed, but it sounded good, and seemed to strengthen him. More so than I ever could have predicted.

A few days, then, would secure our freedom. He would set off, separating such clothes as we needed and selling the rest. He would leave the key with us, so that when he returned, with money and donkey, we could escape and meet him some distance from the convent. I would leave a vague note of despair on my bed, naming Connie, and hinting at the well. It may be some time before they realized we had not committed suicide. By then we would be anonymous travelers on the road.

Perhaps they would not search overmuch for us. We girls were paid for up front, with no monthly stipend, and our absence would only mean two more spaces for other unfortunate girls. I had high hopes.

Felix stayed the night on Sunday, and planned to leave before matins the next morning, leading his burdened donkey.

Late Sunday night, though, there came a knocking on the door. We were at prayer, and with the walls between us, and the chanting, it came to my attention like the clicking of a deathwatch beetle, so that for a moment I was scarcely aware of it. But it grew, commanding first the attention of those nearest the door (the elder nuns, who could more easily slip away to the privy mid-service) and causing a sort of undulation of interest to pass through their ranks. It continued to escalate until it became a martial pounding, as if by battering ram. The Reverend Mother, always a little deaf, heard it at last and a look first of alarm then of stubborn determination crossed her face.

"No one move!" she cried as she hustled for the door. But I was faster. Even as I told myself no, it cannot possibly be her, I shoved the older sisters aside and raced for the door.

"Maman!" I cried, though it was obviously not her pounding on the door. She was a strong, formidable woman for all her beauty, but this was the sound of a man, or even men, a soldierly beating upon the door. I called for her again, but heard no response, only the continuous knocking that made the very beams shudder.

And then I thought: George. He has come in force, with soldiers from the king himself. He has repented, he has bargained or forced or cajoled a way to claim me, and he brings men to fight for my freedom! Ah, stupid girl, I chided myself. It wouldn't happen, and I wouldn't wish it to. If I saw him, I would stab him in the heart for what he did to me.

But at that moment, with the Reverend Mother huffing up behind me, my idyll gained credence when the knocking suddenly stopped and a deep, loud voice commanded, "Open in the name of the king!"

We both froze, the Reverend Mother and I. The king! Could it be possible? My hatred melted, I was prepared to pardon everything for the man who had repented and come all this way to rescue me. The Reverend Mother stared in confusion at the door, as if through superhuman effort she might bore through it and have her questions answered without opening it.

Whereas I knew it must be men from the king of England, she no doubt thought they must be from the king of France. But at that time, there hardly was a king of France. Little Louis, the thirteenth of that name, was technically the king, and had been since his father was assassinated when the lad was nearly nine. Since then, his voluptuous, carelessly scheming mother, Marie de' Medici, has ruled as regent.

The Reverend Mother waited as long as she was able, but there was no getting around it—she'd have to open the door eventually. I could see her compose herself, pull herself up to her full and considerable height, straighten her huge, unwieldy cross . . . then with all the dignity of her position, she flung open the door.

Two fighting men, not quite soldiers, wearing a livery I did not know flanked a third man who carried himself with light grace despite his size; a sandy-haired warrior with freckles across his unbearded face, a small, light sword on either side of his hips.

It shames me today to say I had not thought much about my childhood friend these past months. That youthful kiss, that stunning rescue when the captain of the guards was choking the life from me . . . they had all been relegated to some lost past in the moment of George's betrayal. He had crossed my thoughts in an abstract, wistful way, the same way I remembered Maman's garden, or Isolde's last egg. He was a relic.

Now he stood here in the flesh: Denys.

And such flesh! Had he filled out so much, or was it only that in my memory he was a boy? Now he was a man, undoubtedly, and even the

Reverend Mother, her feet planted firmly on her own territory where she was queen, quailed a bit before him.

"I've come for her," he said briefly, nodding toward me. He did not greet me, though, did not smile.

"You will not dare violate this sacred space," she replied. "This is a sanctuary for the Brides of Christ."

"Abducted brides, like the Sabine women," Denys said. "Jesus will not miss one of his concubines."

The Reverend Mother went scarlet, and started to huff objections, but the two men—mercenaries, I decided—stepped past Denys and into the convent. Behind me, I heard feminine gasps of excitement. They were all gathered there, watching the spectacle. Denys followed, ignoring the Reverend Mother and holding out his hand to me. "Come," was all he said. It sufficed.

I took his hand, and felt such warmth as I had not known since I ran free on the Yorkshire moors. He felt like the summer sun.

"No! I forbid it." She'd recovered her powers of speech, and was promising Denys and his men eternal damnation, excommunication, imprisonment if they dared steal away an avowed nun. Denys held out a parchment, and she squinted to read it. "An order . . . from His Majesty? It is not possible! Why would the king . . . ?"

"Ours is not to reason why, madam," Denys said curtly. "Come, Milady." He pulled at my hand.

"But . . ." I began. I had yearned for this moment, and yet now my feet felt heavy. I looked over my shoulder. "My friend Connie must come, too," I whispered to Denys. "I promised her."

"I'm sorry, but the royal order is only for your own person."

"I can't leave her behind. I won't!"

He ignored me. This was not the Denys I knew, but a stern soldier. "Fetch her things at once. We must away."

The Reverend Mother stomped her foot, but already little Sister Marie Celeste was running to the storeroom. She came back a moment later and handed me my bundle—travel-stained dress, the dancing slippers I'd last worn in court, my red-beaded rosary, my sweat-darkened bodice. I didn't dare look, but I felt within the bodice. Yes, the wooden busk was still slipped inside. And yes! My fingers touched the cold metal of the hilt well-concealed within. I felt powerful again.

"She has been given over to my care," the Reverend Mother insisted. "This is criminal! Her family . . ."

"Who do you think arranged for her release, ma'am?" He gestured to his men, and before I knew quite what was happening, I was being bundled out the door.

"Connie!" I cried over my shoulder as I sought one last glimpse of her. She stood among the other girls, a brave smile on her face. She was happy for me! Was there ever a better woman than Connie?

As they pulled me along and perforce tore my gaze away, my eyes raked over Felix, standing alone, half collapsing against the wall. I thought to see sorrow, thwarted lust, perhaps. Maybe even just a touch of relief that he'd been saved from my mad scheme.

Instead, in that farewell flash, I saw something I've since seen on the faces of maniacal killers, on lunatics, on religious fanatics. His eyes bored into me, and they *burned*.

Then the door slammed behind me and I was out in the cool spring evening. A dove cooed, a low, soothing sound that proclaimed the bird's belief that (save for hawks) the world is a peaceful place.

Somewhat in shock, I stumbled, speechless, up to the horses they had waiting. Denys mounted, and his men helped settle me on a cushioned pillion behind him.

"Hold on to me," he said. I needed no further prompting. I wrapped my arms around him and let my cheek sink against his back. He still smelled like my childhood. Without a sound or a shudder, I wept, for all that had happened, for the hope that it was truly behind me now.

For where there was Denys, there must be Maman.

As I clung to Denys, I didn't ask any questions, nor did he offer any information. I felt almost afraid to make an inquiry. It was too good to be real. For all I'd dreamed of rescue, after I'd been in the convent for a while, I never really believed it could happen. Now, the dream seemed on the verge of coming true, and I didn't dare ruffle it in any way for fear I would wake.

We rode along the path that led to the nearest village some ten miles away. Midway along, we cut off on a forest path and rode some way until we reached a woodsman's cabin. By moonlight I could see a curl of smoke rising from the chimney. As soon as Denys reined in his horse, I tumbled off the pillion and ran to the door.

I smelled her before I saw her. Oh, perhaps it was the smell of anyone's mother, a smell of domesticity, but to me there was no mistaking it. Inside, someone was cooking. Onions, garlic, fennel, red wine. And bread, not the yeasty smell of bread rising, home baked, but bought bread warming near the fire. It could be any woman inside, but I knew it was not.

Maman, just on the other side of that door. I paused. I froze. Why? She had come. That should be all that mattered. I should not mourn that she had not come sooner.

Denys came up behind me and laid a hand on my shoulder. "Your troubles are over now, Clarice," he said. "You will be as you were meant to be all along."

"What is that?" I asked, bewildered. Would I go home and be the wife of a man with so many sheep, mother to his children? Was that what I was meant to be? Would I be a child again, innocent in the gardens and the moors, untouched by the terrible world? We were meant to be thus, before the fall.

"You will see," Denys said, and reached around me to open the door. I stopped his hand as it touched the knob.

"I've missed you," I said simply.

Then, there it was, that wide, delightful boyish grin on that startlingly manly face. Though he was so different from the boy I knew, there was still the familiar falconer inside. His fingers caught mine, and for a moment we stood like that, with the promise of my fondest hopes just on the other side of the door. In that instant, I had no desire to open it. I was content where I was.

Then he released me, and I pushed the door open . . . and saw no one.

The pot bubbled, swung on its iron arm over the fire, and as my nose so clearly told me, there was the baker's bread, in small, uniform loaves, basking like happy tortoises in the fire's glow.

"Maman?" I called softly. The hearth was the only light, and it flickered confusingly around the single room of the cabin. Then, in the corner, I saw a bundle of blankets in the bed. They stirred, and rose to make the shape of a woman.

"Maman!" I cried, and flung myself into her arms. For a second, as I buried my face in her hair and felt her hands caressing my head, I was whole, in a world without sin. Then I noticed, and pulled away.

"Maman, you are all bones!" Never fat but always robust, Maman was what the locals referred to as "a fine figure of a woman." Strong, upright, bosomy, she was like a Valkyrie, an Amazon.

The woman I held, though tall and broad shouldered with the carriage of a hussar on parade, nonetheless felt like a tree in winter, all sticks and angles. My face fell as I pushed her gently to arm's length and examined her face.

For a moment, it was all there naked before me. The violet smudges under eyes that were peculiarly, unnaturally bright. Cheeks pallid beneath her traveling tan, skin that looked almost transparent. Hair witchy and brittle, the gold shot with stark white.

By some trick, she suddenly pulled herself together. She could not add flesh to her meager skin and bones, but by sheer force of will seemed to layer health on top of sickness so that what I first perceived seemed to be an illusion. Her face brightened; the tension of its contours relaxed. The white in her locks now seemed mere silver among the gold, matter nearly as precious.

"You are ill?" I asked uncertainly, and was perfectly happy to accept her word when she told me she'd suffered from a particularly bad winter ague, but was very nearly recovered.

"Fear not for your old maman," she said brusquely. Old? I reckoned up in my head. I was just turned nineteen, my mother married not long after that age herself. I was a late child, with twelve years between my nearest brother and me, but still, she could not be much more than fifty.

Her eyes raked over me in a strange frenzy, as if they were eating me up. "My only thought has been for you. Oh, my sweet girl! How cruel this time apart has been. How I have suffered without you."

"*You* have suffered?" It burst out, unbidden, shamefully. All the self-pity I had been fighting for the last months, the fear of being left to make my own decisions, the lack of Maman's guidance and advice, suddenly bubbled up in a flash of resentment.

"You have suffered!" I cried again. "I was in a den of vice and vileness, a lair of liars and schemers and whores of all genders and stamps who would sell bodies and love and honor and scruples for a pittance. Do you know what they made me do?"

"I know," Maman said with utmost gentleness. "Denys told me."

I glared at him briefly. "He does not know the half of it," I assured her. "George . . . he made me love him! I loved him, Maman." I faltered, seeing George's golden face in Lady Mary's garden, hearing the tender words whispered in my ear afresh, the promises. "For his sake, I poisoned a man and stole from him, Maman. I poisoned a woman and condemned her and her cohorts to death. And then he . . . he . . ." Even to her, I could not speak of it. "I killed my heart for him, all but the part of it that loved him. I killed my soul, Maman, and did things no natural woman would ever do."

I was weeping now, such a hiccuping, red-faced, unattractive flood of tears as would make Lady Mary wince. One tear, she would council— a precious diamond spent on a good cause.

"There is no such thing as a natural woman," Maman said. Her voice is so soft, but hoarse, and I think she is using the technique Lady Mary taught me. Loud words are easily ignored, she said. A quiet voice compels attention. "Nor yet a natural person. We are all corrupted from what we would be were we not tarred by the world's pitch. In every man, and in every woman, is the capacity for all things. Nothing you have done makes you unnatural, *mon cœur*."

I was weeping openly now. "I did what they asked of me, Maman. What they asked, and more. I removed Robert Carr; I made a place for George. I was their instrument! But he sent me away. All of that sin, for their sakes, and when he found me with . . ." My eyes flicked to Denys. I would not say that before him, either. "My father did not care how I erred, how I pawned my goodness, my soul, so long as I did so to his liking. A danse macabre, so long as it was to his own tune. And so I refused to be used any longer, and then he caught me . . ."

Maman was beside me, holding me in her frail arms like a child, stroking my hair. Exhausted in spirit, I leaned against her. Somehow, she supported me.

"It is over now, and you are absolved," she said tenderly.

"Would God ever absolve me?"

Maman tut-tutted. "I absolve you. And God, they say, is love. Furthermore, he is unfathomable, so why trouble your mind about what he will think or do." Her voice had become light, between teasing and teaching as it had been in the gardens, on the moors, in the sickroom. I scrubbed at my wet eyes. "Now we must look to the future." She drew me back onto the bed, and I thought it was for my comfort. I did not notice then how she almost collapsed onto the hay-stuffed mattress, nor yet how her hands trembled. "And for you to decide upon a future, you must know about my past."

Puzzled, I asked, "Decide?" Decisions are not part of rescues. I was to be swept up and carried away. Nurtured and protected. She was supposed to make me a child again.

She nodded, and started to speak, but the words would not come. For a moment, it looked like her breath was caught in her throat, and a spot of red appeared high on each pale cheek. She pulled a handkerchief from her sleeve and turned away from me, making a sound like a low growling. She coughed once, a small cough stifled by the linen. Then with a great attack the coughs seemed to be ripped from her throat. She stiffened, trying to hold them back, but they erupted, shaking her body, unstoppable, so violent I thought she'd faint.

"Maman!" I cried. I'd helped her treat so many sick people, but I'd never seen her unwell, and it shook me.

At last her coughing ceased, and for a moment she was still, breathing shallowly with intense concentration, the handkerchief pressed to her lips. Then she stuffed the bit of cloth under her skirts and turned again to me, smiling reassuringly into my wide and startled eyes.

"Only the remains of my ague," she said in a calm but ragged voice.

"Mullein, dried and smoked," I said with authority. "Hyssop and plantain leaves. Cowslip in a strong decoction . . ."

She waved away my concerns dismissively. "It is damp in this cabin, that's all." It was not. It was dry and toasty. But I wanted to hear what she had to tell me, to know what decision awaited me. And so I did not press her as I should have, but only prompted, "Your past?"

Mothers are . . . mothers. I suppose we tend to define all people by their relation to us, but this is particularly so with mothers. Maman was first and foremost Maman. She had never been a little girl, except in an abstract biological way. She'd never had hopes or dreams or doubts that did not in some way concern me. In short, before I was born, she existed only as an expectant cipher, awaiting my advent. After my birth, of course, she existed wholly for me.

When she told me of her past, it was an utter shock. And yet, each bit of information she gave me seemed to be bricks that filled an incomplete edifice. It made sense. It was plausible, and explained a great deal that I had never thought to question. Still, it didn't seem quite real. I would not fully believe that a mother can be anything but a mother, first, until I had a child of my own. Then I realized that the child is only the brightest thread in a vast tapestry.

"I was born in France," she began prosaically, which of course I already knew. But she was setting the scene, easing her way into a difficult topic. "Papa was of the *noblesse ancienne*, the oldest hereditary nobility. Little in the way of land by then, hardly any money, but a name, oh, what a name! We lived on that name. We ate it. Maman, though . . ."

She told me things I dare not repeat here, but the long and short of it was that her mother served the crown as that peculiar mixture of courtesan and spy and femme d'affaires. The most beautiful and clever woman of her generation, she served in a visible way that won her the frowns of wives and the admiration of everyone else. But she served the crown in a less public manner, too. She revived the old friendship between Scotland and France by arranging the marriage of little Francis with Mary, Queen of Scots, and almost made Scotland into French territory, were it not for the work of bumblers. She prevented disaster by foiling the Huguenots' plot to kill the teenage King Francis. And, Maman added, she may have poisoned that young king, and later his brother, when they both proved intractable and unpopular, leaving their mother Catherine de' Medici to govern through her youngest and favorite son.

"Hers was the delicate, jeweled hand behind the most important events of the 1550s and '60s. And she taught me all she knew."

How to take mere beauty and turn it into the magical loveliness of a goddess. How to appear to have a different nature to different audiences. How to dissemble. How to kill.

"She raised me to follow in her footsteps," Maman said. "Dainty little footsteps, they were, and each one filled with blood."

This sank in slowly. "You were a spy?" I say at last.

She shrugged, which I was coming to learn was a very French thing. She was reverting to her old ways here in her home country, speaking the language of her childhood. "It was a family trade," she replied. "Butchers' sons become butchers, no? My brothers became soldier-spies, but my sister and I were trained to be like my mother: lovely and dangerous weapons, bodkins of the finest point."

"I have uncles and aunts?"

"Had," Maman whispered, shaking her head. Old wounds still pained. "It is a dangerous line of work. One brother was executed for treason. He died protecting the name of the king who signed his death warrant. Another brother simply vanished. My elder sister . . ." She looked into some balmy past, nostalgia just curling her lips, and I imagined Maman as a girl, an older sister combing out her fine golden hair. Her face grew serious once again. "My sister was strangled by English agents while she was trying to bring about the marriage of Queen Elizabeth to the Duke of Anjou. I only found that out much later." She reached for her handkerchief to dab her moist eyes, but there was none up her sleeve.

"I was the youngest of the brood, like you, my chuck. Perhaps my mother was sentimental with me, the last of her blood. Or perhaps those she worked for ordered it. Whatever the reason, I was groomed to be a silent spy, one who would to all purposes lead a normal life, a wife, a mother. But all the while I would be waiting. Waiting, every moment, for an order that might never come. I wonder if my mother hoped it never would. Perhaps that was the best way she could think of to give me a normal life. I never could fathom her. In any event, I was trained as my brothers and sister were in the subtle and seductive arts, in poisons and codes and the anatomy of death, and under guise of a pretty young virgin, I was married to Lord Paget and sent to England. Paget, a modest noble, whose rank would allow me to move in court circles if required, but whose absence from court would never be remarked. I became a commonplace nothing, all of my light concealed under a barrel. In all my years in England, I never heard from my contacts. They may have forgotten me."

Maman, a spy? I glanced at Denys. Had he known? Was it unwise to speak of these secret things in front of him?

Maman caught the flick of my eyes and said, "Denys's father was my ally, sent to England to aid me, should I need it. As a young man, his skill with hawks and falcons gave him entrée to the most noble houses. With me, he lived a kind of retirement. He married a local girl, as you know, and as I have said, it is a family business."

I gasped. This was somehow even more surprising. Denys, a spy, too? Yet what else could explain his skill with the two swords, his appearance now.

Pettishly, I asked, "Has everyone in my life deceived me, then?"

"Deceived, protected," Denys said from across the room. "Head and tail of the same coin. Your mother sent me to court to protect you."

"What a wonderful job you did of it, too," I said with dripping sarcasm, thinking only of my poisonous imbroglios. Then I remembered the captain's hands around my throat, and I blushed and lowered my eyes.

"There was only so much he could do," Maman said with the hint of a smile. "It didn't help that you have a natural aptitude for the spy trade, my dove. You led him the very devil of a time, trying to follow your plans and actions. The things he reported to me—duels at dawn! The crown prince in your quarters!"

Quickly, she sobered. "And the other things, which he learned after the fact. I am sorry that you had to endure all of that. It was not what I meant for you; at least, not unless you . . . But if it is any consolation, you handled difficult situations with aplomb. You achieved your goals, and you survived. You did what other people could not."

"I . . . achieved my goals?" I stammered after her. "Did you not hear what I did? I poisoned people! I used them."

She spoke softly, as if soothing a horse. "You poisoned a foreign agent, that Armand du Plessis—yes, I know all about him. But you knew enough not to kill him, and he is none the worse for it. And as for the ones who poisoned Carr, well, even if one does not take sides, there is no dispute that those executed were involved in the plot. You took extreme means to uncover it, but the truth is still the truth, however it is unearthed. You condemn yourself too harshly."

It is what I had been secretly hoping for all long—someone to tell me I wasn't as bad as I thought, nor as cursed as I feared. I wanted to believe her. But she had taught me better than that. I was not one to be soothed by sweet words when I could plainly analyze the enormity of my actions. Rather, I believe my good opinion of her fell because she tried to excuse my conduct.

"You may hate what you did," Maman went on, "and you may have suffered, within and without for your actions. But you survived deadly court intrigues. Carr and his wife, the captain of the guards, they could have killed you. Yet here you stand. It should not have happened. I would give a great deal for it not to have happened." Her voice lost its caressing cadence. She'd lost patience with my self-pity. "But it happened, and it is done. Do not wear the pain of the past like an ornament. Now you are in a position to make a choice. We are free, from this moment on, and I will be entirely guided by you. What say you, then? Do you want to be a lady, innocent and pure? A wife and mother? Do you want to have a life as predictable as the harvest . . . and count for nothing." Her eyes were blazing now, and despite her gauntness, she looked strong again. "Or do you want to do things that will change the course of human history?"

Of all the thousand questions I had, of all the myriad things that troubled me about everything she'd just said, one matter leaped to the fore.

"Maman, you said you had been sent to England to await some mission, an assignment that never came. Tell me, what was that mission?" I could not imagine. Would she have been tasked with seduction, with stealing some state secret, with passing a coded message or arranging an assignation?

Her lips curled, first the left side, then the right. Inexorably, a dimple appeared in her gaunt cheek. Then, as casually as if she were telling me the time of day, she said, "If I ever received the signal, my mission was, within three days of receipt, to kill the king of England. And all your life, unbeknownst to you, I was training you to take my place one day."

"You were training me?" I asked Maman after she revealed the secret of her life.

"Do you think every young girl learns the intimate details of anatomy, how to ride astride, and coax a mettlesome horse?" Maman asked. "Most young women learn to garden, and know what is poisonous so that they don't put it in their stew, but do you think everyone learns doses, from medicinal to deadly, down to the last grain and dram?"

"I never knew," I told her.

"I never meant for you to know. Not until you were ready. All your life, my love, in ways you never saw, I taught you. Some of it was simply giving you freedom. What nobleman's daughter would be allowed to swim in deep ponds, or explore caves? You taught that boldness to yourself. I only gave you license. You became strong in body and in spirit. Your mind sharpened to the finest point. Soon I was going to teach you to defend yourself. You knew where to slice or stab, but there is a world of difference between theory and practice. If your father had not ordered you away, if I had been able to follow . . ."

Yes, she taught me all of those things. I never realized how unlike other girls she had made me. She had sharpened her weapon, but she never meant for my father and Lady Mary to wield it. Who, then? Did she herself plan to use me, as they had?

Frowning, I said, "You taught me many things, but did you teach me the right things? Poison and boldness! Why did you teach me that, but never a word of what people are like? What men are like! Why did you not tell me there are rakes like my father, and sly manipulators like Lady Mary?" I went to the window, so they would know only my strong voice, not the weakness of the tears that welled, and fell. "With all of your knowledge and vast experience, why did you not tell me about heartless liars like George Villiers?"

"My sweet, did you truly love him?" she asked.

I could not answer that and maintain my strength. "One word, Maman. One moment on the moors when you could have told me, beware the pretty words of men. Beware their promises. Don't give your heart away. Everything I did, I did for love, Maman, and that love was a lie! Why didn't you tell me the world is so?"

I could see the silver of my tears in the window glass. They striped me like a subtle tigress.

I was young. I was hurt. I had held all that pain inside of me for so long, it felt good to let it out now. I did not see how I hurt my mother with my carelessly barbed words. I didn't mean to lay the blame in her lap. I only knew that it was a catharsis for me. Better out than in, Maman used to joke when our servants or tenants were plagued by worms or the gripping of the guts. I spewed out my filth, and as it purged me, it sickened her.

"Forgive me, my child," she said. But she did not plead. She did not look contrite. She had seen too much of the world to truly wish I could have stayed a tender grub buried safe beneath the sod.

I could not face her yet, and turned to Denys. "What now, then?" I asked him. "Do we proceed from here, a family of spies and agents, off to poison and kill in the king's name?"

He smiled. "Not the king's name. Perhaps in France's name. Perhaps in mankind's name. There are bigger things than kings, you know."

"Clarice," Maman said, sitting very straight and proper, her hands folded in her lap. "This day, this moment, is a new dawn. I was never given a choice. I was trained as my brothers and sister were. I was told what was expected of me, and knew the consequences if I failed."

"And what were they?" I asked, still looking away from her, out the window and into the darkness.

"If I refused, death. If I revealed what I was, what my family was, death. If I did everything that was asked of me, and was careless or unlucky, death. I was fortunate, though. In truth, I lived that life only for a few years, until my marriage. Still, I was trapped, in a foreign country, in a loveless marriage, waiting for the order. My children were some consolation, but of course my sons left me early. They belonged to their father. You, though, my treasure, were the only thing that brought me happiness all those drear years in Yorkshire.

"But you must understand," she went on, "despite the danger, despite the hardship, society could not exist without people like us. There are things that are seen—monarchs and laws—and things that are unseen. Agents like me, like Denys, like my mother stop wars before they start."

I shrugged, staring at my reflection. "Kingdoms fall. Such is life."

"So cynical, so young," she chided. "Kingdoms fall, yes, and soldiers die. But who else dies, eh? Mothers and grandmothers, little babies? Do you think girls are raped in war? Do you think boys of ten are skewered on pikes because they would otherwise grow up to be warriors? Crops are burned; people starve. War does not care if you carry a sword." I hug myself, but don't turn.

"As an agent, you can stop wars before they start."

"How?"

"A thousand ways. Pass a message, stop a message. Sink a ship, slit a throat, delay a general for a night. But to do this, you must know the secrets of the kingdom. You must watch, and wait, and know."

It seemed so farfetched that one person, not a king or queen but just a person, could have so much effect on the world.

"Think of a chess match. Do you think it is won in the final move? No, it is won ten, twenty moves back. In fact, it may be won with the first move. But who sees that, eh? The common man sees a knight take a king and thinks that is the story. They don't realize that a pawn sacrificed long ago made it all possible."

I felt something stirring within my breast. I will call it only interest at that moment. A spark. A curiosity. But in truth I know now that it was more. When, later, I carried my child within my womb, I knew I was gravid very early on, but it was not real to me until I felt that first fluttering inside me. It was like that—when Maman spoke to me that day, a new life stirred within.

"You still have your dagger?" she asked. "And your busk?"

I pressed my hand to my breast, but did not take it out.

"What does it say on it?" Maman quizzed.

"*Un pour tous*," I said. "One for all."

In that moment, I remembered so clearly what Maman had told me almost a year ago. *In the tide of great affairs, it is not the many who make the crucial choices, but the individual. Mobs do not decide the fate of the world, nor even armies. It is always one man—or one woman—often unknown to history, working in secret, dedicated to a greater good, who shifts the tides.*

"If you choose the life of an agent, a spy, the outside world will never know you. Not truly. You will appear to be one thing, and actually be something else entirely. You may seem a lovely courtesan, a charming widow. Or your name may be blackened beyond repair. You may be called wanton, whore, witch. But none of that will be the real you. The things you have done at the English court, they trouble you, I know, but they are not so bad. If you are an agent, you will do that and more. That and worse. But you will do it all well. I see that clearly in you—your ability, your boldness, your cleverness. If you choose the life of an agent, you will do great things. But they will be known by very few. Myself, and Denys. Your spymaster. You must be content with having no glory for your work. The things you do may appear cruel, selfish, heartless. But you, and those who truly matter, will know you serve a higher cause."

"But not the king?" I ask, turning to her at last. "Not France?"

"Not exactly. You could say that we serve goodness. Rightness. Perhaps we serve the angels. Perhaps we only keep the demons in check, barely." She gave a little laugh. "It can be a hard life, but should you choose it, you will never doubt for a moment that you are *alive!*" Again, her eyes had an unnatural glow, their bright blue vivid and glassy against the bloodshot whites.

"When must I decide?" I asked, keeping my voice cold so it did not quaver—and all the while thinking that this is what a spy would do, stay calm, dissemble.

"Today, tomorrow. We need to quit this place soon."

"Why?"

She just shook her head. "If you choose to follow in my footsteps, we go to Paris. I will teach you everything I know, and guide you to those who can teach you more. You will be one of those with the true power in France, in Europe. You will do great things." She fixed me with a knowing look and said a thing calculated to appeal to the Clarice she knew so well. "You will be a heroine in a novel, though your true name will be forever unknown."

I drew in my breath. How often I had envied those interesting women in my books. But for the most part, all they did was fall in love and get rescued. Only the sorceresses took action, turning men to swine and such (as if they needed much help). What Maman proposed would make me like the heroes and heroines both—beautiful and courted, adventuresome and powerful.

"And if I don't choose that life?" I asked, forcing down a fierce joy that against all reason was burgeoning within me. Why do her words stir me, I wondered? All I want is safety and comfort and love after my terrible ordeal.

"We will head in the opposite direction, away from Paris. We will go to a small village, like our old home in Yorkshire. Or perhaps we will leave France entirely. North to the Netherlands. Or if you prefer city life, with masques and balls and a thousand beaux at your feet, perhaps Florence. I have great sway with the Medici line. We will change our names, invent a plausible tale, and live in happy obscurity."

"And the decision is entirely mine?" I asked. She and Denys both nodded.

I knew what I *should* choose, but not yet what I *would* choose.

"Whichever I decide, there is one thing for certain," I said. "I made a promise to my friend Connie, a fellow nun at St. Ursula's. We had planned to run away together." Briefly, I told them about Connie, and my scheme. Maman and Denys, clearly pleased by the plan, exchanged a look that plainly said see, she is ripe for the life of a spy. "Now that I have been fortunate, I must share my fortune. I cannot leave without Connie. I *will* not." I believe I even stamped my foot.

"Ah . . ." Maman began hesitantly, and Denys looked at his feet. "You see, this is not a life that allows friendship, particularly not on short acquaintance. I'm sure she is a lovely girl, but if we are to survive, we must trust no one outside our immediate circle. We can't allow an outsider in."

"But she is my friend, whatever you might say! I promised her. She stood by me at the convent, comforted me in my suffering, listened to my woes."

"You told her what you did at court?" Maman asked sharply.

"No . . . not exactly." I'd probably revealed more than I should have, for the lure of a confidante is sorely tempting, but shame more than wisdom kept me from telling all.

"Good. If she knew, we'd be forced to . . ." She bit off her final words, and my eyes widened. Did she mean . . . ? I couldn't even bring myself to ask.

"It can't be that hard. If you are an agent, why not forge a letter releasing her? Bribe the Reverend Mother. Break in and spirit her away. Or send Denys and your mercenaries back to take her from them by force."

Denys frowned at me. "Violence is not a thing to be taken lightly."

"Then why carry those long knives? Why hire thugs? Maman, I beg of you!"

Her voice was firm, unyielding as she said, "No, Clarice. We leave tomorrow, for Paris or elsewhere. You, Denys, and me. We can trust no other."

How had my rescue turned into strife? I should be weeping tears of joy, embracing my mother and my beloved childhood friend. But there had been hardly any of that. Revelations, anger, argument . . . why could I not have a normal life?

Maybe I could have won her with tears. Maybe I could have told with exquisitely pitiable detail of my time in the convent. I could have convinced her of Connie's merit, of my need for a bosom friend.

Instead, my voice grew cold, and I said, "So you want me to abandon her to the cruel world—the same way you abandoned me?" My heart broke as I said it, and I wished I could drag the words back into my mouth. Maman's composure faltered, and again I saw the frailty of her. She looked so much older, weaker than I remembered.

"I'm tired, Maman," I said with chilly dignity. "If you don't mind, I'll go to sleep now." I took the only bed and turned my face to the wall.

For a while, they whispered together, words too low even for my keen ear to catch. The bed depressed, and I felt Maman's hair tickle my cheek as she bent over to kiss me. I pretended to be asleep. "We do not know what the future may hold, however carefully we try to prepare for it, my love. I know you're not sleeping. If I should . . . if I'm not able to . . ." She sighed. "Should you ever wish to embark on the life of a spy, with or without me, at any point in your life, go to Paris, to the church on the Rue Poisson, and tell the priest there, '*Je m'en vais chercher un grand peut-être.*' From there, you will be guided."

She kissed me again and stroked my arm. A bit later I heard Maman go out. Denys followed her, and I heard Maman start coughing, wrenching, bestial coughs suddenly muffled when the wooden door slammed shut.

I lay there, with the patience I learned in prayer. The sisters at St. Ursula's taught me that much, at least. She came in an hour later and made a bed for herself by the fire. Denys came in near midnight. I heard him standing over me, heard him sigh, once, then lie down on the bare floor as far as he could get from Maman and myself.

After that, I waited an hour, then an hour more. Finally, when all was still, I crept out of bed, silently opened the door, and began walking back to the convent.

Chapter 13

I took a horse, leading him away from the cabin and riding him with a bridle but without a saddle, fearful the sound or delay would mean my discovery. The night was warm, clear skied, and moonlight brightened my path. I made good time. The key was within my pocket, my dagger snug between my breasts.

I wish I could claim that some special skill taught by my mother aided me that night. With spy craft on my mind, I would have liked to come up with an ingenious plan. But it was only luck that won my goal. I had the key, of course, and simply crept inside in the small morning hours. I almost went to the bare little cells where we slept, but some instinct told me that on this of all nights Connie would have done or said something untoward. I pushed open the chapel door, and there she was on her knees.

She didn't look up, thinking me one of the sour old nuns, but pretended to be deep in prayer. "Are you thinking of handsome young men, or honeyed marzipan?" I asked her, and in an instant, she was on her feet and then in my arms.

"Oh, my friend, they let you come to say goodbye!" She did not say one word of reproach, displayed not an ounce of jealousy at my release. See, Maman, I wanted to say. She is good, and trustworthy. A friend to cling to.

"No, not to say goodbye."

She looked puzzled. "You mean, you aren't leaving?"

"No, silly—*we're* leaving. Come, we have no time to waste. My mother and her men are a few miles hence. We must get there by daybreak."

She flung her arms around me, and together we crept out of the convent. I helped her up onto the horse I'd tethered in the woods just out of sight, and we started down the path.

"Wait!" came a cry, and even as I drew up my heels to kick the horse into a gallop, I recognized the voice of Felix. I had not spared him a single thought all night. He had served his purpose, and then became unnecessary.

Unfortunately, he did not realize that.

He led a huffing donkey up to us, worldly goods and virgin tresses strapped to its back. "I was coming for you," he said, nerves making him as breathless as the elderly donkey. "I thought I could follow your trail, that you would not go far before night came. Oh, my love! You returned for me! I thought, what if I can never find her? What if I am doomed to wander the globe, searching for my lost love?" He looked up at us with those romantic mooncalf eyes . . . and I felt nothing but irritation and the slightest frisson of fear. To be looked at with that fanatical adoration! That is for saints' knucklebones and icons of the Virgin paraded through the street. Men ride into holy wars wearing that rapt expression. That is how misers look at their gold. When that gaze settles on mortal flesh, it is not at all comfortable.

I did not want this dangerously lovesick boy. Yet I could not disappoint him now. Not within earshot of the convent. He might not love me so much that he wanted me to be happy, if it was without him. Few can love like that.

So I smiled down at him, the benevolent goddess smile that Lady Mary taught me, full of promise, and said sweetly, "Come. My mother awaits."

Together we went down the path, my horse carrying his two light girls easily, while Felix dragged his reluctant donkey behind us. I had to hush him a hundred times, first because of the real danger that we'd be heard, and later, as we got farther along the road, from sheer weariness at his obsessive prattle. He praised me; he made plans for our life together. He painted such a rosy picture that at last I snapped, "And how do you propose to pay for this pretty chateau, this brook full of trout, these elegant gowns?"

He grinned at me, his pale eyes bulging, fishlike, and said mysteriously, "I have come into a fortune, my love. Together we will . . ."

Just then I noticed the first pearling of dawn peeking through the trees. Enough of this. "My dear, my maman will be so worried about me. Forgive me, but I must ride ahead, lest she become distraught. Follow at your own pace. It is not above five more miles."

I urged our horse into a trot, and Felix called after me, "Where is she? Where is the turn? Wait! Wait!" But I pretended I could not hear him, only blew him an encouraging kiss as Connie's hair streamed into my mouth and I pressed my thighs to my horse's flanks until he broke into a gallop.

Ah, how free I felt, leaving behind all annoyances, all fears. With dawn breaking and the wind kissing my face, I realized what a beast I'd been to Maman. When I got back, I would fall on my knees and beg her forgiveness. Poor Maman! How worried she must have been for me. Her fears even weakened her physically, diminishing her. I vowed I would make it all up to her. The spy work that had tempted me in my hot anger last night had no appeal for me now. Once she met Connie, she would adore her as I do, and together all of us would vanish from the harsh real world to a realm of our own, where we would live simply, happily, safely.

And I'd been almost as horrid to Denys, too, hardly greeting him like the friend of my childhood. Oh, what a merry time we would have in our new life! He would climb a cliff or the tallest pine tree to pluck a pink chick from its aerie, and we would raise the unfledged raptor to be the scourge of hares and pigeons!

As we trotted along, leaving Felix behind without a qualm, I gushed disjointed visions of what our life would soon be. I was as bad as that lovesick priest. "I'll teach you to ride properly," I told Connie (for she was bouncing uncertainly on the broad dappled back). "I'll teach you about the healing herbs. No, Maman will teach you, for she knows far more than I. Oh, you will love Maman!"

"What is she like?" Connie asked, though in our nightly vigils I'd told her a thousand stories of my mother. It was real, now. Maman would be a part of her life.

"She is like a goddess," I said without hesitation.

"Which one?"

Lovely Aphrodite or wise Athena? Queenly Hera, or Artemis hunting in the wilderness? "All of them!" I forgave her for not coming for me. That didn't matter now. Maman was perfection. Maman was love. At long last, everything was right in the world.

I have since learned not to offend the gods with such thoughts.

Denys was waiting for us in the clearing beyond the woodsman's cottage.

"At last," he said, grabbing the reins.

"I was just . . ."

"I know what you were about, and you were told she couldn't come." His voice was a strange mix of anger and sorrow. "You shouldn't have left her, Clarice." I thought he meant that I shouldn't have left Connie, and I was about to upbraid him for his inconsistency. "Stay!" he said when I started to dismount, and pulled my horse's head, making him turn with dancing hooves so I couldn't easily get off. "Don't go in. Not yet."

"You think to deliver a lecture? If anyone must, let it be Maman." I pulled the horse in a sharp circle, jerking the reins from Denys's hands, and hopped down. "Stay here, Connie. I promise I won't let them send you back. Our fates are bound now."

Denys looked like he wasn't entirely sure what he should be doing at that moment, which you can be certain I took full advantage of. Dodging around him, I headed for the door, calling, "Maman, I'm back! Don't be cross."

Denys caught my shoulders, gently, holding me immobile. "Clarice, wait. I must tell you . . ."

"Is she that angry?" I asked. "I said things I shouldn't, and for that I am sorry. But let me talk with her. She'll understand."

"You can't go inside," he insisted.

I frowned at him, our old ranks returning, so that I was the lady, he the lowly servant. "Take your hands off of me," I said coldly. Abruptly, he let go, and I marched to the door, throwing a smile over my shoulder at Connie.

Maman lay on the bed. I knew. I knew at once, but I did not let myself believe it.

"Maman," I called softly. "I've returned." She did not reply.

My vision blurred, but still, I spoke as if all was well. "I've brought Connie. I know, you think she is a danger, but you raised me well, Maman. I see the risk and accept it." Slowly, so slowly, I crossed the small room until I was standing at her side. Her eyes were closed, which made my self-delusion easier.

There was blood on her chin, on the bodice of her gown. On the floor, her handkerchief, covered in gore. I could not see any wound.

My legs trembled, and I almost sank to my knees at her bedside. I caught myself halfway down. There had been enough kneeling of late.

She lay there, her face so white against the blood on her chin and chest. I smoothed her hair away from her temples. She was still warm, a sheen of sweat still on her brow. I put my cheek to her lips, feeling for the slightest breath. Nothing.

For a moment, I closed my eyes, not quite in prayer. Then I opened them and examined her body, all Maman's clinical teaching steadying me. I heard Connie sniffle in the doorway. Denys came up behind me, his shadow falling over us.

"There is no wound on her," I said at last. "But the blood . . ."

"From her coughing, Clarice. She'd been bringing up blood for months."

"From her winter ague, she said, but that had passed. Her lungs were weak, no more."

"No, Clarice. It wasn't the ague. It was the white death."

"No!"

"That's why she didn't come to you. She was sick when you left."

"That can't be. Maman was strong; she was healthy." I thought back to our last weeks together. She'd had a little cough, perhaps, but she still worked in the garden, still rode.

"She'd known about it for nearly a year, but kept it from you. You're right, she was strong, and because of that the progress of the disease was slow. But after you left, it struck her down. She took to her bed the day after your carriage rolled away, and she never recovered. After you left, I managed to ride back twice. Each time, she was weaker. But when she learned of what had happened to you, she found some hidden reserve."

Denys told me how she would instruct the servants what plants to gather from the garden, how to brew them into healing drafts, what leaves to throw into the fire so she could inhale their curing smoke.

"She couldn't risk traveling in the winter, but she said if she could only hold out until the spring . . . I don't know how she lived so long, Clarice. Sheer force of will. She lived for you, long enough to save you."

"And I cursed her for not coming sooner." Why weren't my eyes streaming? I wondered. I'd cried enough for myself, tears of fear and self-pity. Why, at this, the greatest loss of my life, were my eyes dry?

Maman had taught me to be strong. Now, in her presence for the last time, I owed it to her not to give way to the abject misery I was feeling. The tears were easy to fight back. I couldn't do as much for the inner parts of me. I felt like I was melting away, a hollowed crustacean. My pulse fluttered, and I felt weak, supported only by my will. Everything inside me was liquid, a body filled with tears.

Oh, merciful heaven, Maman had been my life! My other self, my guide, my light. Even when we were apart, it was to her my thoughts always turned in both joy and tribulation. I wanted to curl into a ball and mourn for what felt almost like the loss of my own soul . . .

But there was much to be done, and even as Maman taught me not to flinch when cutting for gallstones, or turn away from blood, now I had to seem unmoved so that Connie's future and my own could be decided, clearheaded and clear-eyed. The tears would have to come later. "Clarice, you must not torment yourself," Connie said. "A mother always understands. A mother always forgives." I let her hold me, soothe me for just a moment.

Then, for I was my mother's daughter, I shook her off and straightened myself. "What do we do now?" I asked Denys.

"We bury your mother, and then we must leave, immediately. As for your friend . . ."

I grabbed Connie's hand. "She's coming with us. I made a vow to her. And now you must make one to me. Swear to me that you'll protect her and keep her safe, even as you would me. Even more so, as I intend to protect myself."

"Clarice, do you really think it is wise to burden ourselves with a stranger at this time?"

"She is no stranger, and no burden! She is clever and resourceful and loyal. We have enough horses. She . . ." I could not quite find the words to tell him that it might very well prove useful to have a companion who would cheerfully fornicate her way out of any difficulty, but perhaps as he looked Connie over, marking the mischief of her mouth, her boudoir eyes, he guessed as much.

"Very well, she can come."

"And you swear to protect her?"

He was in a hurry, and this made him take the oath lightly. "Yes, of course," he said as he shoved his things into a sack. "Now come, we have no time. The royal order was a forgery, of course. When flying under false colors, one oughtn't linger. We should leave this morning."

"You mean we must bury Maman here? In unsanctified ground? No, we must have a priest, a church."

"And risk getting caught? I stole you from a convent, and now you've doubled my crime with the addition of your friend. No, Clarice, life is a ledger, in red and black. The debt to the soul of burying her here is more than countered by the profit of saving our three lives. It is hard, I know. But then, the life she chose is hard."

"I do not know that she chose it," I said.

"*You* will have a choice," Denys said firmly. "That was all she wanted for you. But we will speak more of that once we are safe. For now, we must get as far from here as possible."

I didn't like it, but I could see the reason behind his words, and reluctantly agreed. We left Connie to prepare Maman's body. She said she had done the same for her mother when she died. In the woods behind the cabin, Denys and I dug and talked.

"Why didn't she tell me?" I asked as I hacked at the hard top layer of earth. Manual labor never bothered me. I liked to see things ordered, cleaned. I felt like I was back in the gardens. I would be planting her like a rare root. Only, the thing that would grow from her had already sprouted: me. It was not right, that the seed should plant the root.

"She would have, eventually. I think. All of your life, she was torn. Because to be a spy, to take those actions and have that knowledge, it is a remarkable power. She wanted greatness for you. But she also wanted safety. You must remember, this is not a choice of being a dressmaker or milliner. To tell you of her work would be to expose you to the dangers of it. Once you knew, it would be harder to not choose it; do you understand? To have secrets is to be a target for those who want them. To have information is to want to use it. If she told you, could you truly find happiness in the only alternative open to you?"

"I wish she had told me, though. I wish she had taught me more.

When I went to court, I didn't know what to guard against." It sounded feeble even as I said it. Did I need a mother to tell me not to poison and seduce? Should I not have figured that out for myself?

"And you?" I asked. "What was your job?"

"My father was mostly a messenger between England and France." I remember when I was younger he would occasionally cross the channel. To advise the next generation on the art of falconry, he always said, or to collect some raptor remedy from a fellow falconer. Sometimes Denys would accompany him. "I was—am—an assassin."

I left my pick buried in the earth. "What!" Not Denys. Not gentle, sweet Denys with his flop of sandy hair and freckles like spilled cinnamon.

"Only three times in my life have I killed someone. No, four. I forgot about your captain. Three executions." He leaned on the shovel and gazed into the trees. What memory was he seeing?

"That's why you can wield those blades so skillfully."

"One of my many skills," he said without modesty.

"But when? You were always at home."

"Was I? You did not see very much of me, in the last few years. You never noticed when I vanished for a week or two. Never asked where I had been."

"I'm sorry."

"No matter. It only shows it was the perfect cover. Who pays attention to a servant or lowly employee? Under-falconmaster at a rusticated manor. Even the person dearest to me didn't suspect."

It took me a moment to realize he meant me. The kiss loomed fresh in my mind. I'd forgotten that for years before that we had grown apart. No, I let us grow apart. As enlightened as I thought I was, I still let the disparity of our rank separate us. I felt a pang over that lost time now. With Maman gone, he was the only connection to the happiness of my youth.

"Will we go to Paris?" I asked him.

"That's up to you. Your mother insisted . . ."

"I'm asking your advice."

He walked around the half-dug grave and took my hands. "I am not only an assassin, Clarice. I had another job. One I relished much more. It was not official, not from my handlers, but from one I respect even more. Victoire asked me—not commanded, but asked me—to keep you safe." He brought my hands to his lips. "It was a task I welcomed. Perhaps I didn't do as good a job as I should, but I will do it all my life."

I didn't know what to do or say. I stood there dumbfounded, with my hands in his, my mother growing cold inside the cabin. His words touched me, and yet . . . they were not real somehow. Denys was my friend. He was the falconer's son. He was not a lover. It was not part of the natural order of things. Pigs do not fly, nor should they. It would be good for neither the pigs, nor those below them.

I didn't pull my hands away—I needed that comfort, as confusing as it was—and I asked again, "What do you think I should do?"

"I cannot leave this life, Clarice. I have obligations. People will die if I fail them." So noble, that face. "Come with me. Come to Paris and become an agent."

"Maman was giving it up. She was going to run away with me and start a new life."

"She had been inactive, waiting, for so long, she had no one else depending on her. I am part of a web. Snap my strand, and the whole web could collapse. But if you come with me . . ."

I thought about it. I truly did. There seemed to be a tingling across my skin, prickles that urged my body to action from the outside, rather than from inward impulses of brain and nerve. I had learned so much from Maman and Lady Mary. Just a little more, and what a power I could be!

"And if I don't?"

"I can get you money. Not much, but enough. You and your friend can set up a household in another country, where no one will ever know who you are. And I can visit you, perhaps. Every few years, no more. You can do as you like. Marry, or not." A shadow crossed his face. "You can have a garden, keep geese."

I laughed, which shocked me over my mother's grave. "Geese *are* very attractive birds."

What a small life it seemed after all the possibilities that lay behind and before me. How safe, how . . . dull.

Under my breath, I whispered those words Maman had told me while I feigned sleep. "*Je m'en vais chercher un grand peut-être.*" I am going to seek a grand perhaps. Those words were the key to a life of infinite possibility.

But then, the danger. Maybe after all I had experienced, simple and dull were best. Like rest after a long illness. A lifetime of rest. Life seemed to stretch so endlessly long out before me in that moment.

I didn't know which life I wanted. And I didn't know if I wanted that life with Denys. I felt like declaring for my mother's trade was declaring for him. So many men had admired me. How was he any different than any other fellow who saw pretty blue eyes and a fine bosom? Was that even what he wanted? He is just one more person who deceived me, I thought. Another liar, even if it was a lie of omission, even if it was for my own safety.

I would have gone with the smiling falconer's lad. I trusted him.

I did not trust the spy and assassin. The smile was the same, but now I had an inkling how much it hid.

Before I could commit myself, we heard an agitated nicker from the front of the cabin. Denys ran 'round the side. "What manner of foolishness is this? A skinny priest on a fat donkey?"

My heart sank.

"Clarice! Oh, Clarice, thank heaven I found you!" Felix cried when I stepped into view. "I almost despaired, then I told myself no, the divine powers could not thwart a love as pure as ours."

I glanced at Denys, and the look he gave me was such a mix of annoyance and amusement that I'm afraid I smiled, which only encouraged Felix. He tugged his unwilling donkey up to me and knelt at my feet. "Whither thou goest, thither go I, even as, er, Naomi said to Ruth. Or was it the other way around? No matter, my priest days are behind me." He sounded like a caricature of a lovestruck fool performed by an unskilled actor. Perhaps he had read one poem too many . . .

"Felix, you have to leave." I did my best to look like I was thinking of his welfare, but I was only concerned with my own. He was a burden now, superfluous.

"Of course, at once! Where are we going? Hello, who are you?" He looked at Denys with faint hostility.

Denys gave a none-too-patient sigh and shook his head. "Come, Clarice. We bury you mother and leave."

"Your lady mother is dead?" Felix asked. "You poor child! I will say a prayer for her. Though I'm a priest no longer, I may do that much, I think. But, I will say it on the road, if you'll forgive me. We must hurry!"

Two men with common purposes.

"You can't come with us," Denys said, sparing me the trouble. I was thankful. I wasn't in the mood to salve Felix's feelings.

Felix tried to square his shoulders, but they only seemed a narrow oblong next to Denys. "Clarice and I—and her friend, for I vowed—are going to parts unknown. You, sirrah, whoever you may be, are not needed."

I gritted my teeth. "Felix, someone will be after you any moment. If you don't leave . . ."

"I know they will. I heard the alarm sounded, but the horsemen passed the turning on the road. We have a while before they find the path."

We bustled back to the cabin, ignoring poor Felix as he pursued us. He saw my mother in her bloody bed and crossed himself. "The abbess has summoned the abbot, who sent a rider to rouse the town guard." He unslung his sack and spilled out its contents with a slither and thunk.

"Oh!" I said.

There, on the straw-strewn floor of that humble shack, lay the Reverend Mother's ivory and gold crosier, and a king's ransom in gold and rubies in her pectoral cross.

"You stole from the convent?" Denys asked as he came up beside me.

"Well, there was nothing much in my own order except a few saints' knucklebones. I could find a buyer, I'm sure, but I thought gold was more reliable."

Denys caught him by the scruff and shook him. "You little fool! You'll have them at our doorstep!" Felix flopped like a rat in a terrier's jaws, but he didn't seem frightened. He looked like a man in a holy daze, as a Christian might look strolling out to the lions while the Romans jeered, certain of his heavenly reward.

I was to be his reward, I realized with a shiver.

Men will do anything for you, Lady Mary had said. They will steal, and lie, and kill, all to get what you deny them, and she made it sound like a splendid thing. Now I saw that fervor in the flesh, and it terrified me. I thanked heaven I'd be free of him shortly.

Still, he could be trouble, so I tried to be clever. "Let him go, Denys. Felix, it is too dangerous to travel together. We will set off first; you head in the opposite direction, and we will meet . . . Where, Denys? Where will we meet in three days' time?"

Denys didn't smile, but his lips twitched as he named a town.

"But why can't I go with you?"

"You love her, no?" Denys asked. "If her safety is the most important thing to you, it must be so. If you want to see her in prison, by all means, travel together."

Though it pained him, Felix nodded.

There was a sudden cry from Connie, quickly muffled. I raced for the door, but Denys shoved me aside and beat me to it. "Damn! Too many. They've cut the horses loose, too. Curse you, priest!"

Even now, the only thing I fear is the mob. A man can be reasoned with. A man—or woman—can be charmed, seduced, tricked. But a mob acts as a single animal, and its whims are near impossible to fathom. There are some who have the measure of a mob, those who can stand before a crowd and bend it to their will. I am a prodigy of changing a single mind, but I have no sway on the hive, the herd. A mob is an ugly thing.

When they were home, they were farmers and smiths, men who worked hard, loved their wives, dandled their children on their knees.

They were good, homely country folk. Some were even clever, or hand-some. Until they were roused by the abbot with words of hellfire, whipped into a killing frenzy, and sent after the priest who had defiled their religion. I saw murder in their eyes. No, something beyond murder. They were ready to tear Felix apart with their bare hands.

They were not expecting Denys. There were a dozen villagers, and half again as many priests. The village men were armed with the tools of their trade: shepherd's crooks, sickles, and in the meaty hands of the butcher, a shining cleaver. Denys came at them like a whirlwind, his twin blades here, there, faster than my eye could follow. He disarmed them, he poked and sliced their extremities, but he forbore to kill them. I could see the crazed fire die in each man's eyes as he was wounded and thought how the poke in his shoulder might keep him from hauling carcasses or threshing his grain. One by one they fell back, came to their senses, realized this was not mob justice but a war they could not win.

I watched from the doorway as Connie clung to me and Felix prayed behind me—Denys was like a god, his blades flashing in the sun. I licked my dry lips, and felt a tingling in a place I'd scarcely thought of since Armand lifted my skirts.

Even vastly outnumbered, there was no doubt that Denys would win. Soon the eight or so still in the fray would fall back. We'd recapture our horses, and ride away, leaving poor Maman unburied. I hoped her soul would find peace. Surely, the holy brothers would treat her remains kindly.

I reckoned without the monks. I thought they would be peaceful bystanders. Instead, unarmed but still angry men, they slipped around the fighting unnoticed and crept up to us before I even saw them, so intent was I on the battle. I threw myself against the door, but they barged past me and seized Felix.

"Blasphemy!" one cried.

"You'll burn in hell," said another.

A third, more practical, added, "Burn here on earth first. Or do you think they'll draw and quarter him?"

They dragged him to the door, not seeming to care about Connie and me. We were not in our habits, and neither Father Jean nor Father Ignatius were among them. Maybe they thought we lived here, or that we were harlots the thief hired in anticipation of wealth? All would have been well had not Felix called out at the door, "Fear not, Clarice, my beloved! I did this all for you, and we will be together again, if not in this world then in the next!"

I heard them mutter the word *accomplice*, and they set upon us, not caring which of us was his well-beloved. They made bread and beer, those monks, and were a hardy lot. I fought them as best I could, but they overwhelmed us with sheer numbers, pinning Connie and me close together. We were surrounded by a bulk of priestly flesh, two little pasties trapped in dough, ready to be carried to the oven. There were so many hands on us that I couldn't strike, couldn't even reach my knife.

"Denys will save us," I breathed in her ear. But when the priests bustled us outside, I saw Denys was battling a big farmer. The man flailed at him with a long, wickedly curving scythe wielded with strength and precision. He couldn't touch Denys, but nor could Denys get past him. He was held at bay while we were pushed to the forest where the priests' horses were tethered. The trees closed around us, and though I could hear the battle, I could see nothing.

He didn't come. Not when my hands were tied in front of me. Not when I was hauled up onto a horse whose bridle was held by one of the monks.

It is only in storybooks that someone comes to the rescue, I decided in that moment. No one had ever come for me, save Maman, too late, and never again. As I was held tight by a dozen clutching priestly hands, I realized that I would have to be my own hero. I would have to save myself.

They got Connie onto the other horse, and a monk climbed up to sit behind her. I let myself be placidly flung astride another horse. When a monk came to mount with me, I threw my head back as hard as I could, striking him in the nose so he screeched and fell back off the horse. It wasn't, perhaps, the best idea. His nose spilled more blood, but my head got the worst of it, I think, with a lightning bolt of pain and then whirling silver stars that clouded my vision. I flung my leg over and landed between the horses, then grabbed the priest behind Connie and pulled him from the saddle. He landed on top of me, and I screamed and kicked out, accomplishing one goal—spooking Connie's beast so it broke into a sudden gallop—but not managing to escape. The last thing I saw was Connie clinging desperately to the horse's neck, racing through the forest.

Then another terrible blow to my head, whether from the monks or a horse's hoof, I didn't know. Blackness. Eternity.

Then, some hours or days later, splitting pain and a mouth like sawdust.

I opened my eyes and saw a spider crawl across a shit-stained stone floor. Beyond the spider: iron bars.

The gate creaked, and an official-looking man came into my cell. He wore a gold chain draped from shoulder to shoulder, and a furred cape too warm for the season, which seemed designed only to show that he could afford ermine. A mere jailer, less sumptuously clad, stood behind him.

"Rise for the magistrate," the guard barked. "Show some respect!"

My mother dead, my friends vanished, it was easy to form the image of pitiable beauty the magistrate expected to see. I stood, shakily, but with a carriage that plainly showed I was a lady, and said, "Good sir, why am I here?" I had to have enough dignity to show him that I was worthy of the utmost respect, while still groveling enough to remind him that I was within his power, a lovely wounded dove. He looked me up, and down, and then up just a bit, staring at my bosom so hard I feared he could see my knife. But no. I bowed my head in pretended modesty and confirmed my clothes were all intact, deadly busk and all.

"You've been charged with stealing valuable Church property, corrupting a priest and a novice nun, and breaking your own vows." He looked very sternly . . . at my breasts.

I inhaled deeply and said in a husky voice, "My lord, do I look to you like a woman who is capable of such things?"

To my breasts, he replied, "No. But just to be on the safe side, I think I should get to know you a little bit better. Guard, you're dismissed." The bars clanged shut behind him . . .

Chapter 14

⟬❦⟭

The next morning, I sat in a shaded pavilion at the edge of the village green at Lille. It was a pleasant place on a late spring day. White butterflies skipped across the grass, and a gentle breeze blew golden tendrils across my cheek. The magistrate, sitting beside me, tucked an errant curl behind my ear and offered me a syllabub. I smiled and graciously accepted. If only he'd offered me brandy or fortified wine! I needed something stronger than a syllabub to help me through this unpleasant farce.

I could still taste the magistrate. Yet it was better than the alternative, I suppose. And more efficient. I could have spent days in that cell, working my wiles, manipulating him to get my freedom. Instead, he straightforwardly presented his offer, I countered it with a reasonable and equally pleasing alternative (*I am a virgin, and would not, could not . . . but the sisters in the convent told me that a maiden might yet . . .*), and we struck a bargain.

Justice is a strange thing, like a lean greyhound. Have you ever met one of the beasts? On their own, the most sluggish and lazy curs imaginable. A greyhound will not move from the hearth except to eat or piss . . .

save for those rare moments when life dangles a rabbit in its line of sight. Oh, then it is a bolt of lightning! Most of the time, I have found that justice crawls at a snail's pace, meandering, often getting lost on the way. Cases linger, witnesses wander, prisoners molder, and nothing much is accomplished. But there are some cases that make the public's ears prick up. A thrilling story, quick capture, eloquent priests, and a pile of holy gold and jewels made this a sensation. Felix was tried and convicted within twenty-four hours. His sentence was carried out immediately thereafter. Five hundred lashes to be spaced fifty a day at one-week intervals. Branding. Ten years' imprisonment. He was lucky to escape a death sentence. I believe the magistrate's good mood might have had something to do with the mitigation.

Now I was the magistrate's guest as all of Lille gathered to enjoy the spectacle of a man's pain and degradation. I cannot say I have not enjoyed similar moments myself, but they were always private, and for better cause. If a man has wronged me, I delight in his suffering. But Felix had done these villagers no personal harm. I had no wish to be among this mob, but the magistrate insisted on my company. I was free to leave immediately after.

The syllabub took the taste away, a bit, but its creamy white consistency made my stomach turn.

The magistrate stood and read out the charges. He kept it simple. What he did not understand—my mother's death, the mad two-bladed swordsman—he ignored. Mankind can do worse, I suppose. My own tale I'd told with near truth. A relative had falsely sent me to the convent while my mother was ill, and she obtained a royal order for my release just before her death from the white plague. As for Denys, I professed no knowledge of him. A man hired by my mother to protect us on the road. He did his job zealously, and disappeared. The magistrate didn't care. The neat narrative of the corrupt priest was enough to keep him in favor with the populace.

Felix stood, lean and trembling and confused, beneath the instruments of torture that mar so many pretty village greens. There was an oak, ancient as the old gods, spreading shade in the middle of the open meadow. The hanging tree, bare of fruit today. Beneath that, the stockade, where lesser criminals were pelted with old cabbages, and more serious offenders had their ears nailed to planks. Beside that, a simple post with rings fixed at different heights. There all manner of people could be whipped: children, women, men, giants.

He was still dressed in his priest's robes, defrocked in name only. They wanted to see him in the uniform he had betrayed. It was a mob again, but they wouldn't be roused to violence as long as another did that part for them. I recognized some of the same men who'd come to capture him. They had no weapons but their voices, and they shouted and hissed at Felix as he looked at them, dazed. Women had joined the mob, tidy in their aprons and caps, lusting for blood.

Suddenly, the spectators hushed. A stranger was among them. Oh, as in all towns, they probably knew full well who he was, by his build and manner, by marking who was absent. But officially, the executioner's identity was supposed to be a secret. He was a townsman, a tradesman, often a farrier or blacksmith. For the rest of the year he lived among them, a common citizen. But occasionally, he was called upon to don his mask and his red-hooded cloak, and legally commit the acts it would be death for another to do. He was the executioner of Lille, ready to hang a man, or behead him if he were noble enough. The executioner might take down a man half hung and cut open his bowels, drawing them out before his living eyes. It was he who built and lit the pyre for a witch or a woman guilty (or at any rate accused) of killing her husband. The magistrate's servant could handle putting someone in the stocks, or a simple ear-nailing. One round of whipping, too, could be delegated. But five hundred lashes, even divided, could kill, and it needed a master to lay them hard enough to rip open flesh and muscle, light enough not to open arteries and bone. It took an artist.

"A fine specimen, no?" the magistrate said, leaning as close as he could to my décolletage. "New to the town, and the trade, but he took to it like a trout to a brook. In short, swimmingly! The prisoners are so cowed, they don't even squirm when the brand descends. His marks are always clean, never blurred. Freezes them in his gaze like a snake!"

He certainly struck terror into my heart. Huge, his arms bare and veined under the swirl of his red cloak, he looked like one of those Yorkshire nightmares that keep children indoors after dark. The flayed giant, his exposed muscles scarlet, livid, coming for little maidens who tarried in the gloaming to meet their lovers.

Someone had already started a fire, and the brand rested in the low-burning flames. The executioner donned a heavy blacksmith's glove and caught up the brand. Others pushed the priest forward and bade him kneel with a kick to the back of the legs, then ripped off his robes. The executioner approached, the tip of the brand, in the shape of a fleur-de-lis, glowing brightly even in the morning sunlight. He looked like an emotionless mountain, a faceless force of nature. In front of the priest, he paused. Felix looked up at him.

The executioner raised his brand . . . then he stopped. At first, I thought it was part of the routine. Perhaps the brand worked better when it cooled slightly, charred the flesh with a more pleasing cicatrix. Maybe the waiting was just part of the torture, anticipation being half the joy or fear of any future event. A murmur through the crowd told me otherwise. Something was wrong. Was the executioner refusing to do his duty?

He waited so long, the brand's fiery crimson glow went dull and russet. The executioner looked at it, then a shiver passed quickly through him, like the skin of a great draft horse when a fly lands on its flank. He strode heavily back to the fire and plunged the brand in. We all waited a long moment until it was fiery hot again. Then without more ado, he took Felix behind the neck with one hand, and with the other pressed the brand against his breast.

The sizzle was drowned in the cheers of the crowd, but when the wind shifted, I smelled cooking flesh, which, in the peculiar manner of natural philosophy, made my stomach growl with hunger. What did my stomach know? Only that it had not eaten breakfast, and it smelled something very like charred bacon.

Felix didn't scream. His eyes found mine, and held them. I half rose, to escape, but the magistrate put his hand on my thigh and coaxed me down. Leaving his hand there, and even a bit higher, lest I be overcome by maidenly pity again, he said, "They don't feel anything, really. Not after the first bit. They're like calves and foals."

I found the magistrate years later, bound him facedown on his bed with a sack over his head, and branded him with my initials on his left buttock. When he squealed, I reminded him that he didn't really feel anything after the first bit. Then I branded his right buttock, too. From the sounds he made that night, I believe he had been in error.

The crowd wanted screams, and were disappointed. But I was proud of Felix. He did not look it, but what resolution was in that skinny, fishy frame. A voice whispered in my head, *You used him shamefully. You let him love you, and look what he has come to. In the end you didn't even need him, you discarded him, but still he suffers for your sake.*

Whose voice was this? When that whispered angel urged me to better behavior before, I always thought it was Maman. But she was a spy, trained to be cold when need be. She would not urge me to have pity on Felix, would she? No, surely, she would say that he made his own choices. That it wasn't my fault or concern.

They tied his wrists to a high ring, stretching him out. His bare body was slimmer than I imagined. I could count his ribs. Didn't they feed those priestlings? The older brothers were sleek on bread and beer. He needed porridge with butter, cream poured over gooseberries . . .

I pinched my thigh (the one not in the magistrate's possession) to bring me back to my senses. How strange the vagaries of the mind, to be thinking some woman should fatten Felix up, when he was doomed to maggoty bread and water for the next ten years. Henceforth, I decided, I would think only of my future. The executioner took up his whip, water-soaked and supple, and as he raised his arm for the first stroke, I thought of my next steps. With my friends' whereabouts unknown, my best choice was Paris. Even if I didn't choose spy work, when I entered the church and spoke the password, surely, they would help me find Denys. From there, I could decide.

It would be a long and lonely road to Paris, I thought as I watched Felix's back convulse under the first lash. A fine red line appeared, then seemed to widen as blood oozed and dripped. Another lash snapped down, placed precisely below the first. I did not relish the idea of such an arduous walk and wondered if I could beg another favor from the magistrate. No, I decided, as I heard the sharp report of the third stroke. His price was too high for a ride in a turnip wagon, and besides, I did not want anyone to know my destination. I would fend for myself.

In this way, I watched the lashes, all fifty of them. After a time I could see no skin, only blood. By the tenth stroke, Felix's strength crumbled, and he screamed. By the fortieth, it disintegrated entirely, and he slumped in his bonds, insensible to the final lashes.

He woke and screamed again when they threw a bucket of salted water in his wounds, and then a measure of brandy. Good, I thought, less chance of pus and rot. I stood, prepared to go. But when they cut him down, he found the strength to stand and located me once again. His mouth moved, though I could not tell what he said. But that burning look! That fanatical devotion! I could not look away. Nor did he, as he shuffled painfully back to his cell. Not until they dragged him out of sight.

For a moment, I stood dazed. Then I gave a little sigh and straightened my garments. That chapter of my life is behind me, I told myself, and smiled down at the magistrate.

By noon I was on the road, having let drop a mention of relatives in Bruges. Later, I looped south for Paris.

There is a strange sort of freedom in having everything taken away from you. I was not lighthearted, you understand, yet somehow, I was still light. I was reborn, and if the birthing had been painful and tragic, well, here I was, happy to be breathing if not actually happy. I shut off everything behind me—the pitiable torture of that poor boy, the way I'd degraded myself—and looked only ahead. I did not even allow myself to dwell on Maman. I watched the road for holes; I looked to the birds swooping from branch to branch. I thought of my next meal, and where I would sleep, but not, somehow, in a worried way.

I thought, at the time, that I was being incredibly strong. Looking back, I think I had lost my mind, for a while. The details of that journey are hazy in my memory.

I walked along that road like the village natural, singing Yorkshire songs to myself, never thinking that a highwayman could be around every bend.

Never thinking there are worse things than highwaymen.

I kept to the main road, assuming it would be easier to get food that way. I could stop at a farm, perhaps, trade my skills (no, my other skills) for food and a night's lodging. I could physic any minor ailments, write letters for the illiterate. And I was not picky about my quarters. A hayloft is better than a prison cell, or even a cloistered cot.

It was ridiculously easy for him to find me.

Dusk was falling, but I wasn't tired—luckily, for there wasn't chimney smoke in sight. I was just considering the possibility of sleeping beneath a hedgerow when I heard the clatter of a cart behind me. Good. He likely lives nearby, or can at least give me a ride to a nearby cottage. I stepped just off the side of the road and put on a humble, winsome face.

It was a light covered cart pulled by a Frisian whose high-stepping stride made the long hair on his fetlocks dance. He was a charming horse, reminding me of the light draft horses we used at home, relics of war-horses that used to carry a knight in full armor, and seeing him made me smile and think my fortunes were improving.

It was the last time I smiled for a long while.

A man was driving, a large young man, and I thought, good, he will be easy to bend to my will. Young men will do anything. He brought the wagon to a halt and saluted me without a smile. "Need a ride, mademoiselle?" he asked.

"Yes, please," I said, and climbed aboard. To my surprise, he did not offer to help me. Perhaps he was shy, or in awe of a domineering wife.

No matter. If he would aid me without flirtation, so much the better. "Do you live nearby?"

"Not far, but in the other direction. You need lodging?" I nodded. "I can carry you to the home of a friend. There, you will be received as befits you."

I thanked him, and he clicked his tongue at the horse. I didn't mind that he was taciturn. He looked like a lump of muscle, and there are some who say that the larger the arms, the smaller the brain. I saw dirt under his fingernails, or perhaps soot, and that together with a certain smoky and metallic smell about his beard and ragged dark hair made me mark him as a blacksmith. I would have liked to talk to him about forging swords, for I knew little and wished to know more, but decided a village smithy knew more about shovels and scythes than swords, and held my peace.

Dusk deepened, and darkness came. "Are we close?" I asked the silent man.

He didn't answer for a moment, then said, "We'll not make it there tonight. I'll not risk laming the horse in the dark. I'll pull to the side."

At last, I got a bit nervous. Was this his game, then, to get me alone at night on the roadside and have his way with me? Looking at him, it didn't seem likely. A man less troubled by lust I had yet to meet. He looked like he was brooding on some deep trouble, as if he hardly knew I was there. If he attempted any familiarity, I always had my tongue—for arguing and persuading, foremost—and as a final recourse, my blade.

He walked the horse a little way off the road and hopped down to unhitch it. "You can sleep in the cart," he said without looking at me. "I'll make a fire."

So I crawled in the back and settled myself down to rest, hoping he'd brought provisions and would cook something nice over the fire. A rabbit, maybe. Lacking that, bread and cheese and wine would do. Singing under my breath, I let my hair down and listened to the crackle of the fire outside. I yawned, and stretched out on the empty sacks. If he didn't call me, perhaps I would skip dinner and just sleep . . .

I must have dozed. The next thing I knew, I was being dragged from the cart by my hair.

He pulled me out to the trampled grass, and when I drew my blade, he caught my wrist and wrenched it so hard the knife went flying. He picked it up and looked at it dispassionately, then traced my jawline with the tip. "Not yet," he said, to the knife, not to me, and stabbed it into the silvery bark of an aspen. "We have the whole night."

My feet dug into the earth as he pulled me toward the fire. I'd counted on that knife. Ever since Maman gave it to me, ever since she spoke of the secret of possessing that blade being a type of power, I'd let it comfort me. If the worst should happen, I'd have her knife to succor me. Well, the worst had come to pass, and my knife was a joke compared to his hideous power.

I fought him. Oh yes, I fought with every ounce of my strength, with my fists and claws and teeth, for all the good it did. I batted at him as a moth beats its wings against a child's cupped hands. The moth has no say in whether the child opens or squeezes those hands.

This man squeezed.

He tied my arms behind me with a leather cord, wrapping them over and over so I was bound from wrist to elbow, my flesh squeezed like a sausage. Then he flung me down beside the crackling fire.

"Do you know me?"

Trials and terror had taken away my senses. Now, I'm ashamed I hadn't marked him at first glance. But the last days had been like a bad dream, and I'd let myself toss in and out of awareness as if delirium was a sort of drug that eased my broken heart and ravaged soul. I stammered some answer, and he turned his back to me to take something from his satchel.

He turned back to me, and I knew I was lost. Only, I didn't understand why.

He wore a black mask over his face. As I watched, he swirled a scarlet cloak around his shoulders. He was the executioner of Lille.

My first and natural thought was that he had spied me spectating, and determined to have his brutish way with me. I can talk my way out of this, I assured myself, trying to stop my trembling, forcing myself not to pull against my bonds. He wants something. Of course, every man wants something. This is a negotiation. He has all the power now, but I must claim some for myself. I'll have to give up a great deal, but if I'm clever, he may not get everything he desires. It became a question of degrees. It was possible I could escape even now unmolested, unharmed. But at the very least, I could minimize whatever happened next.

I thought he was just a man, you see. I didn't know he was a Fury out for revenge.

"Of course I know you now," I purred at him. "I shouldn't confess as much, but how I admired you this morning!"

He sat down opposite me and took a long swig from a brown bottle. "Our father was a prosperous man," he began, as I did my best to figure out how anything he might say could be turned to my advantage. "A doctor. I was never that way inclined. My brother, though—he has fine, tender hands. I've seen him mend a duck's broken wing. He cured a pig of foot rot. It all but killed him when he had to abandon medicine."

"Oh God!"

I remembered now, the priest's whispered words that I only half paid attention to. His brother who'd become a smith and . . . Felix had broken off. He knew of, but didn't want to confess, his brother's secret, shameful sideline.

That long pause before the branding. How had he done it? How had he burned and whipped his own brother? I knew then that I had no hope. A man who would mark flesh of his flesh would not stop because I begged or cajoled or offered him the most extreme liberties with my person.

I looked into his eyes and saw only hate and iron will. "I've always been a rougher sort," he went on, holding his hands up for my inspection. "Big hands, good for wielding a hammer. Or a whip. Or an ax. I didn't bring my ax today. I don't intend to kill you. Though when I'm done with you, you'll wish for death."

He laughed then, and for a moment, I had hope that there was a flesh-and-blood man behind those cold eyes. "I'm joking, of course." His large mouth suddenly pressed into a tight line. "You'll wish for death long before I'm through with you."

Then those big blacksmith hands dug into my décolletage and ripped my gown from my breast. He unlaced my bodice, tearing through the cords when they stuck, and flung me back down to examine my naked flesh. I was weeping hysterically then, all reason gone. There was no craft in my tears, only hopeless desperation. Lady Mary would have been ashamed of me. But then, Lady Mary was never violated by an executioner.

He stared at my nakedness, but I realized he was not looking at my breasts, quite, but at my skin. His eyes wandered over the topography, and he talked to himself as he lingered on each spot. "It would be most visible there," he murmured, looking at a spot just below my collarbone. "But perhaps the skin is more sensitive there." His eyes went to the center of my throat. "But no, I will let you hide it from the world." His gaze settled on my left breast. "Not from your lovers, though. No man will see you naked again. Is that how you seduced my brother? Gave him a flash of your dugs? Poor lad didn't realize they're as commonplace as udders in a cow pasture, to be seen for the asking, or the taking. My brother was so innocent. He'd never been with a woman. I brought him a harlot once, and do you know what he did? He read her poetry, and took a splinter from her heel."

He went back to the cart and disappeared inside for a moment. I tried to scramble away into the bushes, but he kicked me back as carelessly as a boy who wasn't done playing with his beetle yet. In his fist, he carried the brand. By the firelight I could see a ragged bit of flesh adhering to the end.

"I hope he enjoyed you," the executioner said, looking over my body now with the idea of his brother's hands upon it. "I hope he has something good to remember as he sits in jail for the next decade. I would curse you, but he, poor fool, says he loves you. What witchery did you use to turn that gentle boy into a thief?" He lay the brand in the fire. "The courts did not find you guilty, but you and I know the truth. You and I, mademoiselle, know there is a debt to be paid." He stirred the brand in the flames, and I saw it start to glow.

"Please, no," I begged.

His lips curled, and it somehow reminded me of his brother's gentle, loving smile. *Did I truly wrong you, Felix? I never said I loved you. I never said I wanted to live with you. You said all that. We only both wanted to escape. I never asked you to steal for me.*

"It's not my fault," I said. "Please, don't do this."

"You corrupted him. He was a good lad."

"He didn't want to be a priest."

"He didn't want to be branded or whipped or condemned to prison for ten years," he spat. "You brought him to that."

I could have argued as long as I had breath. Nothing would convince him that I was anything other than a temptress who had set Felix on the road to perdition.

"I'm not going to hold you down," he said. "If you flinch away, the brand won't be perfect, and I'll do it again. And again, until there is a perfect fleur-de-lis on your skin. Even if I have to burn it all to achieve it. Can you keep still, do you think?" He brought the brand closer to the round flesh of my left breast, and closer still, until I could feel the heat. An inch away, and it was painful. A fraction away, still not touching, and the pain was so intense I couldn't help myself. I screamed and jerked my body away. The red metal touched my skin, and I heard a fleeting sizzle.

But he didn't plunge it down. He kept it there, hovering so near to my breast, and leaned close to my ear. And then—oh, it was worse than any pain! I lay there on the dirt, bound and helpless with that huge man over me as he whispered the obscenities he would practice on my person. In the most vivid, cruelly imaginative detail, he breathed it all into my ear in the murmured tones of a lover. As he elaborated, his hand began to tremble, so that a description of something particularly vile was accompanied by a searing pain as the brand touched my skin.

At last, he rocked back on his heels. "It will be a long night," he said, and lunged at me with the brand.

I flinched. Of course I flinched, as he knew I would.

He stopped midway as I cowered. It had grown too cool.

I learned valuable lessons that night, ones that helped me a time or two in my career. As he dragged out the night, I understood the exquisite torment of anticipation. I've never done that for a simple assassination. Death should be swift, like butchery. But when I knew I would let them live—when I was settling a personal score—I have taken the executioner's lessons to heart, and lingered.

He returned with the glowing brand held in his heavy mitt. "And now, mademoiselle, we begin."

It was almost a relief when at last the red flower pressed against my breast.

I didn't flinch. I didn't pass out. To my regret (at the time), I didn't die. We were as close as lovers, breathing each other's breath, smelling my flesh cooking. Like a pied mask, his face was divided. His brow was a mask of consternation, deeply furrowed, fearing God and the law and no doubt remembering that his mother, too, was a woman. But his mouth was twisted into a smile.

Only when he jerked it away from my skin—it stuck, ripping the wound deeper—did I scream again. My breast throbbed with an agony like being stabbed over and over again by a precise and unimaginative murderer. I writhed and whimpered, and thought, good, there is one consolation. Nothing can hurt worse than that. Whatever else he would do to me before the dawn, those sickening things he'd whispered in my ear, I was sure I wouldn't even feel them. After this, any pain, any degradation would be no more than a stream feeding into the vast ocean of my torment.

Did Felix feel so, just before the whipping started?

The executioner understood his work, though. "I'll let that ease a bit," he said, leaving me in the dirt as he rifled through his satchel. "You think the pain will never stop, but it will go numb in a while. Just for a time. The agony will return before long, so intense you'll want to rip your own teat off."

And, apropos of this, he brought out some kind of blacksmithing instrument, a sort of grasping claw. He set it beside me. "Consider this," he said. "I have a terrible thirst. We'll continue soon."

He left the flickering circle of the fire, and I let my head fall back with a moan. The cords cut into my arms; I couldn't reach anything but my own tailbone. Even if I could find a knife, a sharp rock, it was hopeless. Some part of me screamed to try, to do anything rather than succumb like a dumb beast. Scoot to that iron claw, see if there's an edge sharp enough to work on the cords. Crawl, roll as far away as possible. Maybe he'll trip on a branch and break his neck fetching you. Grasp at anything, the slimmest hope!

But despair had seized me. I lay there, sodden with tears and sweat, and waited for my doom.

I heard him speak from the darkness. "Who goes there? Oh! But how . . . ?" Then there was a thunk, and a crash, and uneven steps came toward me. For a moment, I shrank back from the shadow that loomed on the edge of the firelight. Then . . .

"Felix! My love!" I said those words without thought, without guile. I'd have loved Lucifer himself at that moment if he'd been my salvation. Perhaps, after all, he was.

He didn't run to me, didn't take me in his arms. He stared wonderingly at me, at my breasts thrust upward by my bound arms. Not, I think, at the livid wound on one of them. He looked at my belly, the curve of my hips just exposed above my torn and tumbled skirt.

Then he looked away.

"Did my brother . . . did he . . . violate you?"

Are you daft? I wanted to scream at him. Look at me! Look at the way I'm bound and helpless, exposed for the world to use as it wants. Look at the burn on my breast, and tell me if I have not been violated!

But I knew what he meant, and with my heart sinking—for I thought he was better than that—I said, "No. Not yet."

He sighed in relief. "Then we can still be man and wife."

"Truly?" I gasped. He did not take my meaning. He thought he was doing me an honor. You see me here tormented, and the first thing you think of is whether I'm still pure enough for you? Whether I've been ruined? In that moment, I hated him more than I hated his brother. At least the executioner was motivated by revenge. It is a better guiding light than stupidity and selfish pride and heartlessness.

"Of course, my love. I have always seen the purity in your soul. I thank God it is preserved in your body as well." And he left me there, long enough to get a cloak from the cart. Edging up to me sideways, his eyes half averted, he tossed the woolen cape over my nakedness, and only then did he cut through the cords, freeing me.

"They let you go?" I asked.

He shook his head. "I escaped. It was the town saint's day, and the guard was drunk, and careless with the bolt. I don't think anyone will notice I'm gone until tomorrow. Here, I will excuse myself so you can dress."

Those knightly tales of romance and chivalry he'd read had served me well, for they motivated him to perform great acts for his ladylove. But those same stories made me a cipher for purity—an ideal, not a woman. I did not want this stupid boy. Though I could see from his tentative, wincing movements how much worse his own wounds were than my own, I frankly could no longer muster up any pity for him. How disheartening it was, to discover he lacked real human warmth.

Very well, if I was to be his pure maiden, then I would remain untouchable. I would use him as I saw fit, let him be my knight. Knights are useful, and disposable. They often die protecting their ladyloves. If he had acted otherwise, gratitude might have made me embrace him. Now he would be just another pawn.

"What are you going to do with him?" I asked when I was dressed and Felix could bear to look at me. Heaven help him if the sight of my mutilated bosom urged him to sin. His brother was stretched out on the sod, a knot at his temple, but he was, alas, breathing.

"When he wakes, I can explain to him . . ."

"No," I said firmly. "He branded and whipped his own brother. Do you think he'll show you any sympathy, or mercy? We should . . ." We should kill him. That was plain enough. But I didn't want to ruin my image of maidenly innocence by suggesting such a thing. Perhaps I could push Felix toward it without seeming to? "We should tie him up, and take his horse. We'll cover distance better that way than in the cart. But, when he wakes . . ."

I tried, subtly, to convince him, but I was too subtle or he too dense, and we left the executioner of Lille before he revived, alive. Before we departed I pulled my knife from the aspen's silvery bark and concealed it from Felix.

We took to the road, riding as fast as we could. I suggested cutting through the forest, for if Felix had been able to find me, surely, any competent pursuer could catch us now. But perhaps the gods had for once decided to pity me. We rode on the main path for the better part of the day—making good time, for the executioner trade paid fairly well, and the horse was young and strong—before turning to ride across open country. We lived off plants I gathered and fish he tickled, supplemented by milk and eggs given by kindly cottagers I would approach alone. It was not much, and we grew lean. But Felix's wounds didn't fester, and the farther we got from Lille, the more confident I grew.

All along the way, I hoped that Denys or Connie would find me. Had they even escaped? Were they together? As I slept uneasily in the damp hedgerows, I dreamed that they would be there when I woke. I looked for signs of them, but didn't dare ask any cottagers if people matching their description had passed by. There was a price on all of our heads now. I could only hope that they had escaped, and plot my own way forward.

The executioner had not lied. When the numbness passed, the pain of my brand seemed to cover my whole chest like stinging bees. But I saw how Felix whined about his wounds, and made myself uncomplaining.

In fact, I did my level best to feel nothing. With all my power, I forced myself to be numb in body and spirit. I didn't hear the birdsong, could not smell the freshness of the mowed fields. What little food passed my lips was tasteless. I rode, in the uncomfortable sidesaddle pillion Felix thought more appropriate than astride, swaying with the horse's gait, or else trudged to spare the beast, without any real awareness of what was going on. My only sincere feeling was annoyance at Felix's incessant prattle about our future. I had to get away from him, but I didn't quite dare without a firm plan.

One night, by moonlight, I sat a little apart and pulled down my bodice to look at the crusted, angry wound. "What will I do?" I murmured to myself. "I am marked for life. I am cursed."

Felix came up behind me. "It doesn't matter, my love. No more than my whipping scars do for me. I know the truth of your innocence, and I will be the only one to see . . ." He gulped. "To see that particular part of you. You've suffered like a martyr, and like a martyr, you'll be blessed."

Suffered because of you, I thought, but there was no rage there, not anymore. It was like an echo in the back of my mind. The emptiness inside me frightened me, when I noticed it, but this fear, too, I shoved away, leaving nothing, nothing . . .

I hated him, but I was bound to him. I didn't know what else to do. Paris seemed so far, and when I thought of traveling on my own, something inside me shut down. Every night, I thought about creeping away in the blackness so he'd wake up alone. But every morning, I was still there.

At first I urged him to go to Paris. But he was a small-town lad, and the idea of that vast metropolis intimidated him. I couldn't convince him. So we wandered aimlessly, escaping from one place but not actually seeking a new one. I somehow could not bring myself to plan. I went where he led me, did what he bid me, without volition.

Well, no, not entirely. This man who so treasured my purity had no qualms about bedding me himself, so long as it was the marriage bed. Or something close enough to it to both suit his naive ideals and coincidentally satisfy his lust.

"I look upon you as my lawful wife," he told me on the second night—evidently thinking one night was sufficient to recover from the trauma promised, and inflicted, by his brother.

"But the law does not look upon us as such," I countered.

"There is a higher law," he tried to argue, saying in short that God, as a man, would be on his side. "In His eyes we are man and wife. As therefore it is fitting and proper that we should . . ." He made to embrace me.

"God gave laws to man for a reason," I said, shoving him away with far more passion than I'd shown for anything, even breathing, lately. "I am not you wife until we have been married by clergy." Which will happen over my dead body.

That same tedious routine, every night. He, justifying his right to have me. I, pretending modesty and piousness was the only barrier, declining. Somehow, I didn't stab him in his sleep, but it was only because when I thought of drawing my knife, it seemed in my imagining so impossibly heavy.

I barely slept, staring at the tree canopy with stars winking through, not thinking. Oh, how much effort it takes to not think. I have been told that in the Far East there are people who make a lifelong study of it, and only achieve complete absence of thought after years of devotion.

And yet, though sleepless, come morning, I would lie on the leaf litter that was my bed and refuse to get up as the sun climbed higher.

"We must be on the road," he would say.

"Where? Why?" I would reply before reluctantly dragging myself up to resume our weary pilgrimage to nowhere.

What would I have done without him? I wonder. Would I have lain down beneath some hedgerow, never to rise again? Or left to my own devices, would I have found my volition, taken charge of my life again? I don't know. With him there, I did whatever was easiest. I was in such a state that if he had been forceful instead of pious, he might have had his way with me. Fortunately, he was too timid and untutored to know precisely what that way entailed.

Although there was no sign of pursuit, we were careful. After the second day, we sold the horse for a fraction of its value and traveled by foot. He'd be too easy to trace back to his owner.

We stuck to fields and small paths when possible, and if on a larger road, we'd take to the trees if we heard anyone approaching. Four men fighting over one small pouch of coin make a considerable noise, so we were forewarned of the brigands ahead of us and were well hidden by the time they passed, cursing and debating the relative merits of two local alehouses and the wenches therein. When all was still for a quarter hour, we crept out, and it was not far down the road that we found the curate.

There was no need for them to bludgeon him, to kick him until his ribs shattered. He was young, with a sweet face. He probably would have given them all his coin, with his blessing, and called it Christian charity.

They left him in a roadside ditch, his clothes disheveled from searching, his papers, of no value to the robbers, scattered in the timothy grass. I ran to his side, but soon saw there was nothing I could do for him. His ribs pierced his lungs, stabbing the life from him with every shallow breath. His eyes were already looking in different directions, unfocused. The back of his head was a pulp. They could have finished the job, at least, slit his throat cleanly. If I told them that, they probably would have looked aghast and said, *We're not murderers.* No, only indifferent brutes.

I had no herbs to ease his suffering. Sometimes, though, simply being there at the end is enough. He grew calm when I sat beside him. His hand clutched mine, weakly, and he murmured something about his sister.

"You must give him last rites," I insisted to Felix. But the sight of blood unnerved him, and he'd retired behind a bush, retching, when the beaten man breathed his last.

With a sigh at life's harsh vagaries, I gathered up the curate's scattered papers to leave tucked in his jacket for whoever found him next. We couldn't risk involving authorities, who might ask us questions. It crossed my mind to search him in case the bandits missed a coin or two. Any small amount would be helpful.

Then, I skimmed over the papers and saw that I had a treasure worth far more than coin: a means to escape Felix hounding me for my body.

He had papers identifying him as Pierre de Breuil, and orders of ordination from his home in Rouen. There were papers for an Anne de Breuil, along with a lock of fawn-brown hair bound with a pale yellow ribbon. His sister, then? The lady had apparently perished on the road from Rouen. Here was a death certificate, naming her a mademoiselle.

Then, there was a letter of introduction, addressed to the Comte de la Fere. It was from François de Harlay, archbishop of Rouen, wherein he commended the good and worthy Pierre de Breuil to his lordship, and had every faith that the young man would prove himself an excellent curate in one of the small villages attached to his lordship's estate. Though new to his vows, the archbishop said, de Breuil is a fine scriptural scholar who nonetheless does not confine himself to book and candle, but is always going about the neighborhood doing good deeds. Along with his unmarried sister, Anne—a good and modest girl—he will surely be a boon to the poor and suffering of his lordship's demesne.

It was the first stirring of life I'd felt since the executioner ripped my bodice down to my waist. It was the first time since beholding my mother's corpse that I felt certain of my direction in life.

I ran to the dead curate and hooked him under the armpits. "Help me drag him farther from the road. Quickly! Before someone comes along." Felix was baffled, but complied in an ineffectual manner, still shying from the blood.

"Why are we hiding him?" Felix asked.

"Anything suspicious might lead the authorities to us. He will be found, but not for a few days. By then we will be long gone." Or, one of us will.

That night, I rebuffed his advances more kindly than usual, hinting that the day might be near when I would yield. This put him off more successfully than outright denial, and he was soon asleep with a smile on his face. I slipped away just after moonrise, leaving him snoring.

My torpor, my stupor had passed. What did I care if I was alone? Alone was better than traveling with a lovesick fool who might at any moment press his case too far. He was a liability. I was better on my own. As an Englishwoman escaped from a convent, I was at significant risk.

But as Anne de Breuil, the respected sister of a respected clergyman, I was much safer. The road would still be a hazard, but once I reached the demesne of this Comte de la Fere, I could present myself as a legitimate gentlewoman, alone after her brother's death and in need of sanctuary. The lord of the land would provide. I would be pitied, succored. For a time, I would rest, without fear or suspicion. Ere long I'd probably be given money and transport.

I could make a new life for myself in de la Fere's village. Or when I had rested and gathered my mental and physical strength, I could go to Paris and speak Maman's words. I still didn't know what I wanted, but I had bought myself time. I traveled all night, and at sunup asked for directions at the first cottage I saw. The lands of the Comte de la Fere were only two days away. However, they were so vast that it may well take another two days after crossing the border to reach the comte's castle.

"What is he like?" I asked a cheerful milkmaid with cowpox scars on her forearms.

"The comte? Oh, very old and gouty, though he used to be a terror, my grandmother told me. We are outside of his seigneurial reach, but within his lands, the de la Fere nose is seen from hovel to manor house."

I said I was glad to hear he was hindered by gout, and no longer a nuisance. "Ah, but there is a young vicomte, his only surviving son. Little is said of him, but who knows, he may one day surpass his father. He is rumored to be young and handsome." Yes, because good looks make a young woman not mind giving up her maidenhead to a man who thinks it his rightful possession. I would have to look out for this gouty comte and his son, the unknown quantity. Still, I hoped a curate's sister—even one now alone in the world—would be exempt from their attentions.

Chapter 15

1628

The executioner of Lille looms nearer, seeming to glide under the grisly crimson robe. He towers over me, then slowly reaches out an ungloved hand toward my neck. A fingertip touches my nape, sending shivers down my body, and I close my eyes . . .

"Wait!" Athos says. "This must be legally done. We still need to pronounce the penalty."

The whisper touch retreats, but still the man in red stands close to me, ready to do his job.

"This is murder, plain and simple!" I tell them. "Disguise it in legal mouthings all you like; it is a mockery of justice. Bring me to a tribunal, let me defend myself. If you knew the story of my life, the facts behind these partial truths you charge me with, you would not condemn me."

"Athos," D'Artagnan begins, "maybe we should listen . . ."

His mentor whirls on him, hand on his pommel. "She has the devil's tongue, boy." D'Artagnan flushes. In his drugged delirium, I made him believe I did very devilish things with my tongue, and I can tell he's recalling it now. I begin to think he may stand up to the Musketeer.

But Athos goes on. "Every word out of her mouth is a lie. She can taint even the truth. She can touch gold and turn it to ashes, receive love and turn it vile." His voice catches, and I take a rash chance.

"You have yet made no accusations against me . . . Athos."

For a moment, the entire shack is hushed, save for the distant murmur of thunder. In the pause before his sobriquet, he clearly hears the phantom whisper of another name, one I once spoke with laughter, with happiness, with trust. What a powerful drug memory is. It paralyzes him. What a powerful poison . . .

He shakes himself loose of recollection's shackles and points his pistol at my face.

"Not my face," I say in my Lilith voice. "My heart." I clutch my bodice, pulling it down to reveal a swell of bosom, rising and falling swiftly with agitation, and the first bit of pink scar from my brand. Inwardly, I curse. I have used that very line on him in our last meeting. What is wrong with me? I'm slipping. But he doesn't seem to notice. He is mesmerized—by skin or scar, I cannot tell—and the pistol wavers.

"The penalty for her crimes shall be death," he intones, and shoves the pistol back into his belt. "What say you, gentlemen?"

"Death," says Aramis, no doubt wishing this was over so he could return to Paris and the arms of his lovers.

"Death," agrees Porthos, yearning for claret and a haunch. My final moments seem to bore him.

"Death," says that man for hire, Lord de Winter.

We all look to D'Artagnan to speak, but he stands mute as I watch him with my eloquent eyes. He has been raised on tales of glory and heroism, of the kind of honor that bids him rescue a woman from cruel fate, not condemn her. Save me, I plead without words, with only my body and the long line of damsels in distress that came before me. He is wavering.

"D'Artagnan!" Athos barks.

He gulps, and the word, "Death!" forces its way past his lips. He looks like he'd give anything to have remained home in Gascony, with his bullocks and turnips and simple wenches.

The executioner of Lille nods, and before I can even think to flinch away, he snakes his hand into my hair, clutching a fistful close to the scalp. I would call it the hand of fate, but Maman taught me long ago that we make our own fate. He drags me outside where several lackeys await, fascinated by this mummer's show put on by their betters.

He releases me with a push that makes me stumble. "Walk," he instructs, and what choice do I have? Six men, as many servants surround me. If I try to escape as a wild beast would—with surprise and speed—I'll only be beaten and bound.

My feet sink into the sodden ground, dragging me back with each step, as though the earth itself is reluctant to let me obey my executioners. Or, I think with a chill shiver, it is impatient to have me buried forever amid its muck and worms, and tries to drag me into its maw all the quicker.

The moon has not yet risen, and the overcast sky dims the stars. Flashes of lightning spark from the storm lingering on the far horizon, each burst illuminating the faces of my persecutors with a sickly greenish witch light.

"Where are we going?" I ask, but the men are talking among themselves. Two of the servants are nearer to me than the others, and to these I turn my melting eyes. Think of your mothers, my eyes plead. Your sisters. Think of every woman you ever yearned for, and see her in me. "This is wrong," I whisper. "I am innocent, and even were I not, this is murder."

They look to each other uncertainly.

"I will give each of you a thousand pistoles if you distract your masters so that I may escape."

"We dare not," one murmurs, scarcely audible.

"Where is the money?" asks the other.

"I have allies nearby who will meet me. They have the money. If you let them murder me, though, those friends will avenge me most terribly."

They bite their lips and think, not of justice and virtuous womanhood, but of a life of rising late and having a servant of their own to beat, of devouring meat every night, sleeping on fine linens, and walking down the boulevard with a swagger. One thousand pistoles' worth of the good life, all for tripping up their masters, for being the bumbling fools their betters always accuse them of being.

But Athos has heard our voices, and guesses at the exchange. "Hold your tongue, woman! Send these lackeys away, to the back of the retinue. They've heard her temptress voice, and can no longer be trusted." He sends them away with a hard cuff each, replacing them with two others, who also get hard blows in anticipation. "Tell me if she speaks, and I will tear out her tongue."

And so we proceed in silence to the grassy banks of the Lys. Touched by the starlight, the river is like mercury. The executioner of Lille ties my wrists together in front of me with a leather cord.

Suddenly, my legs give way, and I fall to my knees, holding out my bound hands. In a piteous voice I say, "You're going to drown me? Oh God, no! I beg you!"

This weakness—which is what most men really want of us—moves D'Artagnan, and he, too, falls to his knees, so we look like fanatics sharing faith among the infidels. He claps his hands over his ears as I moan, "Please, if there is a man among you, a true and honorable man, put a stop to this now!"

The executioner of Lille picks me up and slings me over his shoulder. "No! D'Artagnan! D'Artagnan, save me! Remember that I loved you!"

He looks up at me with an impassioned, tormented visage, and jumps to his feet, drawing his sword. "I cannot stand it! No woman should die like this. Release her!"

The executioner sets me down, but now Athos has his sword out and growls between clenched teeth, "One more step, my friend, and we become enemies. Your compassion and sense of honor are misplaced here. Were she a real woman, I would not be doing this. But she is a demon, a wolf. Wolves must be hunted and slaughtered, and demons banished to hell. Sheathe your sword, D'Artagnan."

With a despairing wail, he obeys, and turns around so he won't have to witness my end.

"I will ferry her across the river," the executioner says. "There, you will see true justice carried out." He moves to pick me up again, but D'Artagnan, openly weeping now, turns back and bids him wait.

"Milady," he chokes out, "I forgive you. You attempted to kill me, you murdered my only true love, but I forgive you, and commend your soul to the Lord."

"What?" I cannot help but say, and even the executioner pauses and eyes D'Artagnan strangely.

Like a chorus of ninnies, the others pipe up. "For the poisoning of my brother, and for killing a duke of my realm, I forgive you," says de Winter in his most pompous tone.

"May God have mercy on you," says pious Aramis.

"I forgive you for . . . for . . ." Porthos takes a swig from his flask and hiccups, then flings his arms wide, spraying drops of brandy as he hits on the perfect finale, "for all of your sins."

"Hypocrites!" I cry to them. "By such mouthings do you think to absolve yourselves for this gross miscarriage of justice, for this . . . this assassination?"

They stood there, looking sanctimonious.

"Even bound and helpless, I have more dignity than any of you curs," I say, standing straighter and tossing my disheveled hair. "You call me a witch and demon. Very well, then. I lay this curse upon all of you. You are hailed as heroes, as valiant warriors and honorable soldiers, as gentlemen. And because you will buy the ale and tell the tale, people will believe it of you, for a time. But I vow to you this: one day, the world will know the truth of what dishonorable brutes you are. Libertines." I look to Porthos. "Hypocrites," I cry to Aramis. "Rapists." I frown upon D'Artagnan, who squirms. "And you, Athos, standing there dumb. You have not even accused me. Do you fear to speak the truth of your past before these men? You drink to forget, but there are those who will make sure everyone knows, and remembers for generations to come."

Athos is breathing hard now, though he stays mute. I can see his shoulders heaving, his fingers clenching and unclenching. I wonder if there has ever been a day, a moment, when he has not thought about me.

"Mark my words, gentlemen," I continue. "Those who now admire you shall learn what you are really like, and your names will be spoken with derision. Your children will shame to have you as forebears. Change your sobriquets, Musketeers, for these are blackened by your deeds. No!" I jerk away from the executioner as he makes to pick me up. "Unhand me. I will walk to my doom under my own power."

They watch me, amazed, as I step elegantly into the partially ground boat waiting in the water weeds. I settle myself in the prow like a marble figurehead, looking away from these men who, along with an endless line of others almost exactly like them, have filled my life from the moment I swore my fealty to Cardinal Richelieu and his spy ring. Looking at the far bank of the broad, deep Lys, where the tedium and terror of my life will at last come to an end.

There is a commotion behind me, and I hear the executioner cry out, "No! It will only be legal if I . . ."

Then the boat pitches so violently I'm almost tossed overboard. I turn, and see that Athos has shoved the executioner aside, taken his huge two-handed sword, and clambered into the boat with me. "Hold him!" he orders the others as the executioner tries to reach the boat.

Then Athos shoves off, and we two enter the current together, unexpected eddies grabbing the boat and whirling it around. And for what may turn out to be the last time in my life, I am surprised . . .

Chapter 16

1616

The little village burst upon me in a golden glow of morning sun. The path had been rising steadily, bordered by forest, but suddenly it cleared, and before me spread the most charming valley one could imagine. A little creek ran through it, sparkling. The village was on the near side, a cluster of cottages and shops, with orchards stretched out beyond. Across a picturesque arched bridge to the lightly wooded far side stood a small church. A little apart from it was a stone house overrun with vines and flowers. As I overlooked that village from my high vantage point, I felt a suspicious sense of peace. Suspicious, because it couldn't be true, could it? It must be like the heavy hush before a black storm rolls over the hills, like the sudden quieting of birdsong when a wolf lopes through the forest.

But no, as I descended to the village, the birds kept singing.

Carefully, meticulously, I donned the mantle of Anne de Breuil. How to approach this little community? Country folk are a canny lot, and suspicious. Even with the saddest tale, they might look askance at me. Look at that hoyden traveling with her brother from Rouen. What is wrong with her that she's not married? Is she really the curate's sister, or his secret lover? How did he die?

I could tell my tale convincingly, I thought, but what if they manufactured scandal nonetheless? A hint of discrepancy, a shadow of doubt, and someone might write a letter to Rouen. What if someone here knew the curate? What if he wrote ahead describing his raven-haired beauty of a sister? Any little unknown could undo me.

Who should I approach? I had to choose my opening salvo with care. If the first person believed me, the next would likely follow suit. Would man or woman, youth or elder best suit my needs? There would be a tavern in the center of town, no doubt, the focus of leisure, but at this early hour, it would be empty of all but the most degenerate drinkers and raconteurs. Perhaps a simple householder? The village residents probably mostly worked in the orchards but lived in town.

There was a bakery on the edge of the village, yeasty deliciousness wafting on the breeze. After days of foraging, the smell made me feel faint.

I smiled as the perfect solution struck me. I put so much effort into being strong, that I forgot it might be to my advantage to appear weak.

I slowed my pace, let my steps stagger. A rosy-cheeked woman with flour to her elbows stood in the bakery door, but I affected not to see her, glazing my eyes. I stumbled, caught myself, and walked on.

"Miss?" she called, but I didn't hear her. I needed every last drop of my energy to walk. I was at my end, so traumatized and abused that I hardly knew where I was. Only animal instinct had guided me to this sanctuary.

I managed a few more steps, just enough to get myself deeper into the village with a bigger audience. Then I quite literally threw myself on the village's mercy. With a pitiful cry, I collapsed in the dust, and did not move again.

Let them discover me, search me, find my papers and draw their own natural conclusions before I could utter a word. I could judge the most compassionate by the first to my side. I could listen to their remarks and modulate my story to fit whatever they already seemed to believe.

I could show myself to worst advantage to the women—who might otherwise be jealous of a pretty newcomer—with my slack face, tears, and filthy clothes as I lay helpless in the dirt.

I could show myself to best advantage to the men, my limbs loose and sprawled, an object of their free gaze and desire, helpless in the dirt.

The best actors can play to many audiences at once.

The first to reach me was a woman with a rough but tender voice. She carried with her the smell of flour and yeast. A little out of breath from running up to me, she shook me by the shoulders and said, "Mademoiselle, awake! *Sacré Dieu*, do you live?"

I kept my eyes resolutely shut and let my head loll.

"Who is she?" asked another woman. I could tell almost to a certainty from her suspicious tone that she was standing a little way off with her arms folded, looking disapprovingly down her nose.

"I do not know," the baker said. "She looked in a daze, so weak she could hardly walk, and then she fell all in a heap, the poor pretty."

"A whore on the run from her pimp, no doubt," the second woman said. Other footsteps now joined them, women and heavy-footed men. "Or a maiden who got herself in mischief," I heard her spit, and tried to compose my unconscious features into something more innocent.

"Enough with that filth, Romy. Just because your sister . . ."

"Hist!" a man said sharply. "I trust you will both have plenty to tell me in confession this Sunday regarding ill thoughts and words. Stand aside, and let me see the poor creature."

I felt the priest's gentle touch on my brow.

"Is she alive?" the baker asked.

"Yes, and I feel no fever. She is exhausted, I think. Madame Romy, will you be so good as to fetch a basin of water?" The woman went off with a grumble. "Mademoiselle?" He slapped my cheek lightly, and pried an eyelid open. "Perhaps a splash of water will revive her."

Though I wanted to look pitiable, I didn't want to descend into outright degradation, and I knew the drowned kitten look is not at all becoming. So with a low moan I let my eyelids flutter and uttered, "No, Pierre, don't leave me!" My hand clenched on his surplice, and I seemed to faint away again.

"Pierre?" the priest asked. "No, it cannot be. Madame Capucine, would you see if she carries any papers?"

I felt the baker touch my pocket and, when the documents crinkled, delve in. The priest took the papers, and mumbled half aloud as he read.

"Pierre de Breuil!" He had found my feigned brother's papers. "Anne de Breuil!" And mine. I had, of course, destroyed the document that declared me dead. "And a letter to the comte. Why, this is the sister of the young curate we've been expecting these many weeks, the one recommended to me by my old seminary friend in Rouen. Oh, what tragedy has befallen?"

So much better when people tell their own story, rather than have it told to them. When a person speaks, they believe their own words at once, while there is always some little gap between reception and credence when you hear the tale from another. The priest had declared my identity, hinted at terrible happenings . . . and he believed it. In these little villages, popular opinion followed the cloth. All that was needed was for me to come prettily awake and fill in the details.

That I did, rousing in bewilderment, modestly pushing down my skirts before I was even aware of my surroundings, betraying my confusion even as I tried to stay stoic. When I realized I was safe among friends, that I had made it at long last to the very place that had been prepared for me, I wept tears of relief, which turned to sorrow as I recounted how my brother had been set upon by ruffians.

"How did you escape with your virtue intact, then?" asked the skeptical Romy, clearly believing I hadn't.

"I was . . ." I blushed. "I was answering nature's call deep in the woods where I could be sure of no prying eyes. They attacked while Pierre waited on the roadside.

"They beat him to death, and took everything—our money, my clothes, the Bible our father gave us before we departed."

"Why were you traveling with your brother if your father was alive, eh?" Romy quizzed. "I could see if you were an orphan, but . . ."

I lowered my eyes, but not before I saw an eager gleam in her eye. She was as hungry for calumny as a cat is for plump mice. "My intended died of a fever before we could wed. There was too much sorrow in Rouen to remain." I sobbed. "Sorrow has followed me here, too!"

This won Madame Capucine over entirely, for she called me a lamb, and a duck, and a host of other tender and delicious things, and shooed the others away. "She needs a fireside and fattening up. New bread and fresh butter have cured many an ill. Can you stand?" She helped me to my feet and, with an arm around me, led me back to her fragrant home.

And so my life in the Comte de la Fere's village began. I stayed the night with Madame Capucine, and she and her plump and jolly husband made much over me in a way intended to let me be at peace, but which actually consisted of checking if I needed anything every time I managed to relax.

In the morning, Father Leo called on me and, with a certain amount of diplomatic hemming and hawing, offered me the use of the cottage that had been intended for the new curate and his sister.

"It is a designated clerical residence," he said, "and is supported by certain proceeds from local fields. For you to stay there is without precedent, and it may be that the bishop will . . . But never you mind that. This is my flock, and I can . . . Ahem, though I will eventually be granted a new curate, and when he arrives I'm afraid . . . though it may be months, or more. You understand?"

I was being granted a home, and an income of sorts, but on a temporary basis, until the new curate arrived. I was not to think that I could live out my life here, but they would care for me as they would have my brother, for as long as they could.

My eyes welled with unfeigned tears. I had hoped for a bit of charity. Perhaps a garret room. Perhaps the congregation would take up a collection to send me home. I had never dreamed that I'd be allotted my own little household, my independence. "You are too good. I don't deserve . . ."

"Nonsense," Madame Capucine tutted as she patted my hand. In a carrying stage whisper, she added, "Don't worry about a new curate, my dear. Father Leo is a lazy fellow, and it will be half a year at least before he thinks to even write to the bishop about it. Surely, by then such a dove as yourself will find a suitable . . ." She broke into a girlish giggle that made her matronly jowls jiggle.

"The poor girl is in no state to think of a husband," Father Leo chided. But he, too, gave a worldly little chuckle that told me he thought as much himself.

That evening, Madame Capucine took me across the bridge to my new little home. For the only time in my life, I fell utterly in love at first sight. It was a small, squat house, made of the same weathered golden stone as the bridge and the church. I had lived in a grand estate, in a manor house, and even in a palace, but none of them grasped at my heart as did this humble house that was to be all my own. I forgot about the time limit, and started planning seasons and years out. I would put a pear tree on that wall, an asparagus bed there in that sunny spot . . .

The house had not been lived in for a year or more, and there was a garden on one side, overgrown with weeds, but I could tell at a glance the earth had been well tilled and nourished before that. Once planted, it would yield all the better for having lain fallow. There was an herb garden, too, gone to seed, but I could already see what I would keep, what I would add.

I pulled open the door, tearing a morning glory vine that had bound the entrance. There was a slight musty smell, but no real sign of damp or rats. There were three rooms and a little kitchen. One room had a small bed and a number of sconces and candlesticks, another a desk and even more candle holders. Shelves nailed to the wall held a collection of dusty books.

"The last curate died?"

"Yes, how did you know?"

"No one who read so much by night would leave his books behind willingly."

"Quite the sorceress you are," she joked, and commenced dusting as she sang a country song. But her words gave me pause. Maman would never have stood for such a thing on her estate, but I knew full well how easy it was for a woman alone who was clever, or peculiar, or angry to be accused of witchcraft. I had to be careful. All it would take was for Madame Capucine to make a joke about my prescience, for one to think my herb lore a mite too good, another to hear me talking to myself in the garden. Perhaps there would be a jealous girl, an old woman with a taste for mischief, and then rumors would begin, fed by troublemakers like Romy.

Suddenly, the sanctuary seemed less safe. What if . . . Oh, but I was being a fool, fearing dangers that had not yet reared their heads and probably never would.

All I wanted was peace. Would I find it even here? I was so welcomed; no one had given even a hint of real malice. Yet suddenly, it seemed like a dark cloud (albeit of my own imagining) loomed on the horizon.

"Are you all right, my dear?" kindly Madame Capucine asked.

"I . . . I just need a breath of fresh air."

I ran out, flinging the morning glories aside, and found myself practically under the hooves of a glossy roan stallion. He capered in alarm, and without thinking, I hooked my fingers under his bridle and steadied his head firmly. "Easy," I whispered, and stroked the long curve of his jaw before I looked up at his rider.

He was a nobleman from the plume of his hat to the polished toes of his boots that probably had their own dedicated attendant. In a strange way, he reminded me of my mother, the supreme confidence and ease she displayed on her own estate (when my father was absent). It was a casual but absolute kind of power, wielded lightly because it would never be challenged. When I saw him, I realized that every noble I'd met at court had been in a state of high anxiety every moment of their lives. Oh, they mostly maintained a look of superior, refined languor, as if any worldly cares were beneath them. But inwardly, they were always plotting, planning, scrabbling, and it left a mark on their countenance.

Here was a man utterly at peace. Nothing in the world could ruffle him—because nothing ever had.

"Tell me what you flee from, mademoiselle, and I will save you from it," he said, so lightly, but behind the tone, there was no doubt that whatever was required, he felt able to do it.

"I . . ." I dragged my brain for something plausible. "There was a rat in the cottage. I cannot go back inside while it is there."

He dismounted smoothly and stood with the horse's head between us. "This charger has been trained to kill men in battle, to dash out their brains with his hooves. Yet you handled him as if he were a child's pony. And you say you fear a rodent?"

"A horse would never scurry up my skirts, my lord," I replied. I looked this young nobleman in the face without the slightest trace of wantonness, so that he didn't know what to think of me. Sometimes the best defense is not even admitting the possibility of an attack.

He cleared his throat. "I will seek out this marauder, and slay him for my lady," he said with joking gallantry. "You will be the curate's sister?"

I curtsied, taking care to make it a country curtsy, not the deep and elaborate debasement of an English court obeisance. Then, seeming to remember myself, said primly, "We have not been introduced!" and turned as if he suddenly ceased to exist. Holding myself very straight, not swinging my hips even the slightest bit, I disappeared around the side of the house. For who else could this be but the vicomte, heir of the Comte de la Fere.

And I had referenced things going up my skirt!

The last thing I needed was for a man to pay attention to me. They were nothing but nuisances at best, outright dangers at worst. I didn't need Felix, and I certainly needed nothing from the vicomte but to be left alone.

I wandered in the derelict garden, desperately wishing to be a fly on the wall inside. Was the vicomte asking about the hoydenish creature passing herself off as a curate's sister? He was more sophisticated than the villagers. Would he notice some detail of accent or manner that would reveal me as a fraud? If my plan was foiled so soon . . . It crossed my mind that I could steal that magnificent horse and make good time away before anyone could muster a pursuit.

At last I heard the door open, the horse nicker at the front of the house. Then the pounding of hooves, urged quickly to a gallop. Why so fast? Was he fetching the law? I went inside, anxious, but Madame Capucine was all smiles and began a glowing and detailed description of the wonderful vicomte.

"He was so embarrassed. Have you ever seen a great lord blush? He didn't know about your poor brother, and greeted you lightly without any trace of condolence. He thought to find your brother within. Oh, he was so full of apology, swore he and his father would do all they could to soothe you in your lonely state."

"Oh, how kind, but he shouldn't . . ."

"He said he will send you an abundance of squash, and game every week. Can you fathom the kindness? And he said that one day he would have you for dinner at the castle. You will need better clothes! Such wondrous condescension. He treats you almost as an equal."

I could have told her that he does not treat me as an equal. Rather, he treats everyone beneath him as if they are equal to one another, because they are so far beneath him that they might as well be. When you stand on a mountaintop, elephants and goats seem the same size in the valley below.

I used to dream of falling. Maman told me once that she often dreamed of being able to soar like a hawk, still and effortless in the rising heat of an updraft, but I've never been fortunate enough to have that dream. Instead, I would without preamble suddenly be plunging from some vast unknown height. There was no story behind my fall, no logic. I was never chased to a cliff's edge. Perhaps the soaring bird in my mother's dream had been carrying me in her talons, and released me mid-sky. In any event, the first sensation of falling would bludgeon me in the gut with a horrid, lurching jolt of fear. Some nights I would wake then. But if I survived that first fear, I would settle into a comfortable weightlessness, the air rushing around me, my body without volition, powerless yet accepting.

In my dreams, I never landed. At the slightest hint of ground, my eyes would fly open, and I'd lay in bed, breathless, giddy with relief but with a lingering, tingling thrill.

For months I had been falling. Now, at last, I crashed.

On the road after being first imprisoned and then branded, I was almost catatonic, with the world passing by in a haze. Now that I had settled, the world was vividly sharp and I was clear minded. It was torment.

Every moment of my past seemed to crowd upon me from behind, jeering at me. Before me, an army of futures, possible and impossible, mobbed me just as cruelly and then, one by one, tauntingly took their leave.

You could have lived in Yorkshire forever, happy with your maman, said one possible future. If you had stayed with her, maybe you could have cured her. She wouldn't have driven herself to death with fretting and her long journey. That future thumbed its nose at me and skittered away.

You could have married a nice man, someone your mother approved of, someone you loved. Or if not loved, at least respected. A simple man, a man of the land who had no interest in politics, no impulse toward treachery. If you did not love him, you would have loved your children and raised them to be clever, brave adults. But no, that future said with an evil chortle, you've mucked up any chance of that, too.

Every possibility, from the grand to the humble, mocked me and fled. Marry an earl. Be mistress to the prince. Grow old and ugly as a spinster lady-in-waiting to the queen.

One by one, they left me alone with my past, until only one future remained, watching me like a carrion bird hunkered on a dead tree, waiting for me to drop.

Maman kept her secret life from me because she wanted me to have the choice that she didn't have. Most people are doomed to follow the family business, be it butchery or spying, and she was no exception. But she wanted me to have a life that spread before me like the azure sky, open and limitless. The training she gave me might have prepared me to be an agent for France, but it also meant that I'd excel at many other avenues.

Now only one road loomed ahead of me. It might have been the one I'd have chosen anyway. But it frightened me. It seemed dangerous and lonely. I remember when Maman gave me my dagger, and the scabbard marked with the words *un pour tous*—one for all. One person can serve all of humanity, she'd said. One person, often faceless, anonymous, can change the course of the world. It was a thrilling prospect, and when I thought of it that way, I felt huge and powerful, like going to Paris would be a significant step in becoming who I was meant to be.

Then I would remember her recitation of our family tree— grandmother, uncles, aunt, all in the spying trade, and all dead of it. Then I would wish I had any other alternative.

But there was nothing else for me. Maman's dream had died with her. I had no choice but to go to Paris, speak the words, and become a spy.

Unless . . .

Over the next few days, I settled in the village. Mostly I worked around the house, dusting and tidying. I preferred to be out in the garden, where the buzzing of bees competed with the droning of regrets and vanished possibilities.

The village folk were friendly. Curious and helpful, they all paid calls on me. No doubt prompted to Christian charity by Father Leo, most came with small gifts of food or household necessities. No one in the village was rich (except, of course, the comte and family), but the orchards thrived, and no one seemed in want. They brought honey and oats, apples and cider and salt. The pig farmer brought a ham, and a spinster delivered soap scented with lavender.

They carried with them gossip and small confidences, for they'd only had themselves to talk to for years. Familiarity is both the blessing and the curse of country life. I was a welcome distraction. The pig farmer and his wife and two daughters of thirteen and fourteen rumbled up in a cart and tumbled out, mobbing me with welcome and friendliness. The farmer mentioned an unmarried nephew who had his own acres— freehold!—just beyond the de la Fere lands. The girls wanted to know about Rouen, which seemed a great city to them. Before I could commit myself to any inaccuracies, the pig-wife steered me out into the kitchen, and we talked about the most nourishing food for children and pigs.

When they left, I felt a strange emptiness.

The spinster sipped discerningly at the tea I offered her, correctly identifying rose hips, chamomile, and nettles, all gathered in hedgerow and field. Afterward, we wandered out to the unkempt garden I was slowly reviving. Tentatively, she asked a probing question or two about herb lore, and when I answered to her satisfaction, she settled on a stump bench with a sigh and said, "Thank heaven you've come! I've a smattering of knowledge, and they've decided that since I'm unwed, and own a cat, I must have a plant for whatever ails them. Now I can send them to you. It is a relief that you've come, Anne."

I felt tears stinging behind my eyelids. She displayed no fear at being mistaken for a witch, only relief that someone more knowledgeable had come to relieve her of a duty. There must be no undercurrent of malice and superstition here after all. So that worry was allayed.

But more than that, I felt that surge of emotion because it suddenly seemed that there might be a place for me here.

It was something I hadn't honestly considered. This was to be a temporary respite, nothing more. A place I could rest, hide, and get a bit of money before moving on to Paris and the inevitable-seeming future. Now it occurred to me that there might be an alternative: Why not stay here?

Maybe I couldn't keep my charming stone cottage, but surely, I could buy or build another such one, perhaps on the outskirts of town, with sufficient land for a garden. I had skills enough to earn my keep. There was no physician or midwife in the village. Births were attended by aunts and friends, and the blacksmith drew teeth or roughly set bones. I could be useful. And beyond that, I could turn my hand to anything—jellies and cheeses, bookkeeping or beekeeping. Maman had taught me all the things a lady needs to run a household, the domestic tasks, and though I'd never thought to do more than supervise servants with that knowledge, I could now put it to good use myself if I chose.

What was there to take me away from here? Denys had his own life, and if Connie had escaped, well, he'd promised to look after her. Neither of them would come for me. This was a small, isolated village in a valley far from the main thoroughfare. It was not likely they would find me, if they were even searching. Nor yet would Felix discover me except by chance.

Out there, beyond the cobbled lanes and pretty cottages, past the friendly village folk and blushing orchard fruit, was a world of tumult and torment. Even if Maman had prepared me for it, why would I seek that out? Other villagers followed on other days, and after a while, I returned the social calls, helping one put up preserves, spinning last year's wool with another. It was predictable and homely and . . . safe. Before long, I was enmeshed in village life.

The only one who didn't visit me in the first two weeks was the vicomte.

Then one day while I was mucking about in the herb garden, spreading manure, a boy ran up with a note. "I'm to wait for a reply," he recited carefully, as if he'd been made to rehearse that line several times.

I slid my finger under the wax seal and read the letter. It was written on fine paper in a careless scrawl that took me a moment to decipher, but at last I realized that the Vicomte de la Fere requested the pleasure of my company for dinner that night.

I caught my breath . . . then instantly banished all those initial thoughts that flew into my head like so many summer starlings.

Men are dangerous, I reminded myself. Particularly when they are wealthy, and face no consequences for their actions. Certainly he had seemed kind, and charming, and . . .

I blinked as the starlings fluttered again. "No," I said too sharply to the boy. More calmly, I added, "Please tell your master that I am honored, but cannot possibly accept." I hesitated a moment. "At this time."

"Mademoiselle is honored but cannot accept," the little magpie repeated to be sure of the message.

"At this time!" I prompted.

The imp turned to go, but then looked back at me. "He'll be disappointed. He has a new suit in topaz." With that baffling remark, he scampered off.

What had his lordship's new suit to do with me?

Much of the reason for my refusal, I must admit, was sheer vanity. I only had my old travel-stained dress. Even the undiscerning eyes of the villagers marked it as having originally been something far beyond the reach of a curate's sister, so I concocted a tale about a lady in Rouen donating it to me for my journey. We had a good laugh about a refined lady's idea of proper traveling attire, and in exchange for the frippery attached to it—lace and pearled buttons and such—the local huswives helped me turn it into a serviceable working dress. They marveled at the number of petticoats and other underthings, and once we'd scrubbed them and soaked them in chalked water, I was able to concoct two shifts and a loose morning dress from the surplus linen, and still have enough smallclothes to be decent.

A week later, the lad came again, with a similar missive. This time I told him plainly that I was a simple woman who lacked the means to dress for such an august occasion. I made sure to send my thanks, but emphasized that castles and vicomtes were well out of my sphere.

The villagers absorbed me in their domestic activities to such an extent that I hardly thought about the vicomte at all. It would be ridiculous to have dinner with him, and presumably his father and assorted retinue, at the castle. Denuded of its excess, my dress was now plain in the extreme. A man was never out of place in a simple uniform, but a woman, however lowly, could not attend a social function if she owned only one solitary dress.

But I was too busy to care overmuch. My life had settled into a satisfying routine of medical and social visits, gardening, and domestic work. One of my new acquaintances was with child, and all the village women were gathered at her mother's house to sew miniature dainties in anticipation of its arrival. When I walked home that afternoon, there was a package wrapped in rich cream-colored paper, propped by my door. Curious, I carried it inside and tore it open to reveal a large sandalwood box. Its scent filled the cottage.

Inside was a dress. Ah, such a dress!

I do not care for clothes, per se. Left to my own devices, I'm happiest in something comfortable and simple. Yet I know that clothes make the woman. Put on one outfit, and I am a fishwife, poor and overlooked. Don another, and I am a high-born lady whom people grovel to instinctively. Clothing might as well be a pedigree and bank account pasted to the body—it tells the world exactly who you are. Or who you are pretending to be.

This dress, on the very gimlet tip of the mode, would make whoever wore it a walking goddess.

It was in the languid, looser style the more a la mode ladies had just been adopting at the English court when I was banished. Gone were the low, pointed waist, the snug sleeves, the lace. Instead, this gown positively billowed. I held it up, marveling at the way the silvery blue silk flowed like mercury. The sleeves were gathered, puffed, gathered again in a deep blue spangled with faceted silver teardrops. The underskirt was that same crepuscular shade. The square bodice was low, so low that I wouldn't be able to conceal my busk/scabbard and knife in my décolletage. So low that it would show off my criminal brand.

There was a note in the box on the same creamy paper it had been wrapped in. In an aristocratic scrawl, it said only, "Please expand your sphere."

I could not help but smile. The boy must have delivered my message to the vicomte exactly.

I admit, I briefly considered the possibility. But no, a ship flying under false colors does not put in to shore. My only desire was to be unnoticed until I could leave by my own terms. A nobleman was more likely than a peasant to suss out my heritage. A difference in accent, a dropped reference to something beyond their ken could be easily explained to the cottagers. They knew nothing of the wide world, so the customs of my pretended home Rouen were as alien as London or Yorkshire. But with a nobleman, I might slip into an English word, or drop a reference that showed my Englishness, and all could be lost. I might not be connected with the runaway nun, or the English court scandal, but it would open up the certainty that I was more than the simple curate's sister I seemed. No, I could have no intercourse with the handsome vicomte.

Though the dress was very beautiful . . .

I decided it could do no harm to try it on.

Oh, how heavenly it felt after the rough habit and my old reworked gown. Wearing it, I felt cherished, caressed by life.

There was no mirror, of course, such things being rare here, but I looked down at myself, pulling up the bodice to hide the still-aching burn, and twirled my hips to and fro. I remembered the power of having every eye on me (and the terror, too), and for just a second, I felt an urge to know that power again.

But as soon as I had that costly gown on, I realized why he had sent it. It was not an act of pity, or charity. He had not done it to honor me. No, for that he would have sent a dozen yards of fabric for me to make something up myself, or a woolen dress suited to my station.

Surely, the vicomte sought to buy me with this rich raiment.

A moment later, I was tearing the gown from my shoulders, tugging it roughly down, crumpling it on the floor under my bare feet. It was thus, scowling and disheveled, with his costly present disdained beneath my heels, that the Vicomte de la Fere discovered me. He later claimed he knocked, but I don't believe it. The first I knew of him was his face pressed against the window.

Another woman might have screamed or tried in vain to cover herself. I reasoned that my shift already covered up all my vital parts, so why should I . . . and then I *did* give a little shriek, for I remembered the criminal brand that might be visible above the low neckline. To slap a hand over it would only draw attention, so I whirled around, giving him my back, snatched up my own dress, and stalked away. Just before I disappeared, I snuck a glance to confirm that the glass was as ridged with imperfections as I thought. Yes, he'd stepped back from the window, and his form was blurred enough that I was quite certain he'd seen me no better. Tossing my head in indignation, I slammed my door and got dressed.

There I would have stayed in an agitated huff, but eventually, I realized I would have to give him back the dress. Could I ask a friend's help? Perhaps Madame Capucine? But no, I didn't want the village to know I was the subject of such attentions. Better to make my position clear myself. I didn't think then that staying hidden would make it clearest of all. To me, sulking in my bedroom seemed a coquettish act, and that was the last thing I wanted him to suspect me of. I gathered up my dignity, then the dress, and went outside to confront him.

The vicomte was standing in the middle of a new-planted bed of pennyroyal, his legs wide apart, arms akimbo, taking up as much space as was humanly possible. Yet for all that grand presence, he wore an abashed half smile. He looked both ashamed of his actions, and unable to desist.

I looked at him coolly, then sank into a deep curtsy that also served to put the dress box on the ground. "There must have been a mistake. This package was delivered to me in error."

I started to turn, but he said, "From what I saw, it seemed to fit, though perhaps it was rather snug at the . . . shoulders." Only, he looked a bit lower than my shoulders. Inwardly, I sighed. Of course it had to be like this. They are all the same, priests, magistrates, and nobility.

Suddenly acutely annoyed at his presumption to intrude on my quiet life, I cleared my throat, dragging his eyes higher. "Every woman has them," I snapped, "and they were not crafted for entertainment purposes. That you and every other man should look on them with such worship is as ridiculous as if I fixated on your ears as a source of wonder. They already have a function, and it is not the cynosure of lust!"

The last thing I saw as I whirled around in retreat were his eyes widening in shock. No lady would say such a thing. But then, in this guise, I was no lady. A curate's sister, though, should probably be even more controlled than a lady proper, and as I stalked through the front door, I berated myself for losing control. I should have blushed and stammered like a ninny and simply refused his gift.

Just before I slammed the door, though, I heard him say, "Blight me, but you're a rare one!"

For a moment, I leaned my back against the closed door, breathing hard. Then I shook my head, clearing it of any thought of the Vicomte de la Fere. I was quite certain after that little show I would never set eyes on him again.

For three days, nothing. Then on the fourth day, the messenger boy came to me cursing and bleeding, carrying what looked like a bunch of thorny sticks in a burlap sack. "Christ's wounds, but these are a torment. Here, the vicomte thought you might like this." It was a rosebush, though it looked like no more than dry, thorny sticks protruding from a clod of earth.

I took up the bush and checked the branches, making sure they were quick, then unwrapped part of the root ball. It was moist and well developed.

I wanted to toss it in the rubbish heap, but I'd spent many happy hours tending Maman's roses. Frivolous, overblown things with a cloying scent, she'd said, but I knew she secretly loved them. She went on about their medicinal use, the way rose hips could prevent loosening of the teeth. Yet I noticed she always chose the most beautiful cultivars, not the most prolific.

So, in her memory, I planted it in the back, in a well-tilled spot with just the right amount of sun. I could not visit her grave, but I could kneel before the rose and think of her.

That, plus idle curiosity to see what color rose he'd chosen, prompted me. Nothing more.

When at last it bloomed, it was, surprisingly, a yellow rose with its petal tips just touched with ocher. It annoyed me that I couldn't interpret it. Red, the rose of passion, I could have scoffed at. Pink for young love, white for pure friendship. But what did he mean by cheerful golden roses that looked like they had been dipped in blood then left to dry?

Nothing, he meant nothing. He probably had no idea which rose he sent. He told the gardener to dig up a spare specimen for a cottager.

All that time the rose was sending out its leggy new growth (I didn't prune it as I should, anxious to see the bloom all the quicker), I didn't see the vicomte. I didn't ask any of the villagers about him or his whereabouts, because of course I didn't actually care, except perhaps to avoid any unwanted attention. But the weeks passed without a sighting, and eventually, he never even crossed my mind. Not more than once or twice a day, at any rate. And then only as one would think of an adder spied once in the garden. It may never be seen again, but one is always waiting for it to reappear.

It was late summer when the first gift appeared beneath my now-flourishing rosebush: an emerald-colored velvet ribbon, tied to one of the branches. I smiled and reached for it . . . then let my hand fall. How dare he! What did he think I was, to be swayed by trifles. To be swayed by anything.

It is astonishing how easily we can argue ourselves into the basest foolishness. It might not be from him, I thought as I stroked its kitten-nose softness. Maybe one of my new friends left it for me, in appreciation of some herb or minor doctoring. (For I was getting a reputation. When the miller's son wrenched his shoulder out of the socket, or when the baker's infant daughter had hives, I found they called me straightaway. The poor benighted fools were treating the baby's rash with arsenic powder, for heaven's sake!)

So I wore it in my hair when I went about on my errands and visits, waiting (so I told myself) for some friend to tell me it was from them. Instead, they eyed it and smiled, turning their eyes deliberately from the ornament. Finally, after I'd been wearing it for three days, Cecilia, the miller's wife, pulled me aside and said, as if it were the most natural thing in the world, "Take care not to fall with child. At least, not for a while. He is always generous in the beginning, less so after a whelp, I'm told." She bounced her firstborn on her lap. "She's the miller's. I'm sure of it. Just look at that nose!" She kissed it, making her baby giggle.

I'm normally quick, but it took me a moment to catch up with her. Even then, knowing full well, I thought it better to say, "I'm sure I don't know what you mean."

"Your ribbon is lovely. He gave me one in light brown that wasn't nearly as pretty. I tried to tell myself it was gold colored, but . . ." She shrugged, and put her little one to the breast.

I should have thrown the ribbon away in the stream. But some transient whim bid me tie it to the rosebush. (I couldn't pull up the rose. It wasn't the rose's fault that a wicked man who abused his power once owned it.) Almost lost in the foliage, it perched in a piquant bow.

A week later, it was joined by another, in a bright yellow that matched the petals perfectly but would have looked horrid in my hair. I left it untouched.

The week after, a pair of diamond earrings dangled from a slender branch.

Those made me hesitate. They could fund my journey to Paris, or enable me to live comfortably there while I considered my options. But though they were exquisitely made, I didn't have enough experience with gems to know if they were real or expert paste, and I didn't want to compromise myself for worthless fakes. I left them on the bush.

Late one night when I couldn't sleep, I crept down and took one earring, hiding it well in my room. If it were real, it would bring in a nice little chunk of funds even without its mate. The important thing was that he would never see me wear them, would know I had no interest in them. If he were ever bold enough to ask, I'd disavow all knowledge, and guess that a magpie must have stolen one.

Utterly piqued at the vicomte's attentions, and glad that at least he did them by stealth and never showed his face, I counted the pittance that I had managed to save, and thought, though less and less often now, of the road to Paris.

Then the vicomte sent me a gift I could not refuse.

This time, the boy was nervously leading the most beautiful mare I'd ever seen. She was rich, creamy white, a color that Maman made sure to teach me early on was properly called gray. True white horses, she said, have blue eyes and pale skin beneath their coat, and are often inbred and weak. A creamy gray has pure white hair but dark eyes, and when you brush them, you'll see dark skin under their regal ermine coat.

This mare must have had Spanish blood, with her strong arched neck and elegant head. She capered on impossibly trim ankles, and had a look of good-natured mischief in her eyes.

I caressed her neck, breathed into her nose, dug my knuckles lightly into that place where mothers nuzzle their foals. "For you, for today only," the boy clarified as he handed over the reins and sidestepped the prancing hooves. "I will return in the midafternoon to collect her. My master recommends you ride in that direction." He pointed away from the village. Of course, did he think I was a numbwit? Was I naive enough to flaunt his attentions to everyone?

I shouldn't have. I never should have touched her velvety muzzle. But it had been so long since I'd ridden hard across open ground, the wind tossing my hair (which had not yet grown long enough to properly stream), feeling the breath of a galloping horse like a bellows between my thighs. The mare rolled her eye at me, impatient. Very well, I thought. For your sake. You look like you yearn to run free as much as I do.

Still, I could not treat this as a gift. "Tell your lord I will happily exercise his horse for him—for three livres per session."

The lad looked astonished. It was two or three times what he would earn in an entire day. But he nodded, and I mounted the mare and adjusted the fullness of my skirts. If I was going to do this often, I'd have to shock the village with trousers, or make myself a more suitable riding habit to accommodate riding astride.

And then I was off. Oh, it was like riding the wind! Her hooves scarcely seemed to touch the earth as she skimmed fluidly up the rise at the edge of the valley. For a few paces she faltered when the ground grew steep, but she soon found her new pace and picked her way speedily through the broken woodland until we reached the clear higher ground out of sight of the village below. She gave a little nicker and tossed her head, then with the lightest touch of my heels, she galloped headlong across the open ground.

Almost at once, I heard hoofbeats behind me. I turned and saw the vicomte on his roan stallion, gaining on me. Leaning down over my horse's neck, I urged her to greater speed, and she gamely found a reserve of strength, stretching her body with each stride. I hazarded another glance behind me and saw the vicomte's hat fly off as he bared his teeth in a look of wild animal glee. I had no idea if this was a chase or a race, but I was determined to best him.

Suddenly, a hedgerow loomed ahead. Could my mare take it? I shifted my weight, ready for the jump, and without the slightest hesitation, she sailed neatly over it. I couldn't ask for more from the gallant little beast. Her flanks dripping, I wheeled her around in a slow circle, then let her pick her own pace as she slowed to a walk and finally stopped, bending her head to nonchalantly pluck a clover with her lips.

The vicomte trotted up, and I found I was too breathless and happy to berate him for following me.

"Three livres, eh?" he asked.

"Five, now that I know how you like to train her. I get extra pay for jumping."

"I would give you anything you desired."

I swear I don't know what came over me. Some vestige of Lady Mary's tutelage, no doubt. There was no truth behind the words when I said, "There is only one thing you could give me that I would accept."

"Oh ho? And what is that?"

But I wouldn't answer, and he caught my meaning. The only thing—or at any rate the first thing—a lady can accept from a gentleman is an offer of marriage. Other gifts may come only after that.

"Are you offended at my gifts?" he asked. "I should think a mere ribbon would be acceptable. I know my vassals have given you gifts, too." He seemed genuinely baffled. What a strange manner he has, I thought: both bold and shy. As if he'd gotten everything he ever wanted all his life, but had never tried to win a woman before. I seemed to shake his confidence in some unfathomable way.

"If you had given it to me simply because you knew my clothing had been stolen and wanted to preserve me from getting my hair in my eyes, I would accept it as an honest gift." I narrowed my eyes at him. "But the other village women who have received similar gifts from you assure me that it is anything *but* an honest gift."

He looked at me, baffled. "But I have never given a ribbon to anyone else! I send grapes when a villager is sick or lying in, and sometimes linen for a birth or a death, but . . . oh!" He looked chagrined, then laughed, then quickly sobered. "My father. He . . . Good Lord, what you must think of me!"

Shame and mirth battled so manfully on his face that I softened. He told me about his father, the notorious rake whose only hobby was seduction. "His infirmities have nearly taken away his ability to act sinfully, but I'm afraid the will is still there. He cannot go out on the hunt, as it were, but he does his best to lure the game in to him. Occasionally successfully, I'm afraid. Yes, he sends little presents to the village women from time to time, hoping one will slip her foot into his quite obvious snare. A good many still do, I believe."

When he was a boy, he told me, he had no idea. Later at school, he was not in a position to notice or object. Since he had returned and taken over governance of the estate, he had found it easiest to turn a blind eye. "I am ashamed of him, but at his age and condition, any

woman who goes to him is at least mostly willing. I hope you don't conflate me with my father."

"I will withhold judgment until I know you better."

He gave me a huge smile, and I asked why. "Because you plan to get
to know me better!" I turned the mare homeward, but it would have
been criminal to make her run again so soon, so perforce, the vicomte
traveled beside me. It would have been rude to not reply to his conversation. Maman raised me better than that.

No more of Lady Mary's ploys came out. We spoke of the weather,
of the crops, and mostly of horses. He was impressed with my knowledge, and I too hastily made up a tale of my father being a skilled horse-
man.

Later that week he had the mare sent, and twice again the following
week. Each time he would meet me on the high ground beyond the
valley and we would race.

Our conversation remained innocent until one day he said, "I know
why you always best me in our gallops."

"Why is that?"

"Because you are forever chaste, and so can never be caught."

I couldn't help but smile, though I lowered my head to hide it. "You
would not pursue me if I was not . . . chased," I replied. "It is a truism."

"I cannot escape your logic. And you cannot escape . . . me." He
urged his horse nearer mine with a twitch of the reins.

"Take care, our legs will be bruised between the horses."

"Anne," he said breathily. "Beautiful Anne."

Lady Mary would have been ashamed of me for being caught off
guard. Of course I knew that every moment since our first meeting had
been flirtation. Of course I knew our relations would not be static, that he
had some end in mind. Yet these days together had been so pleasant that
I had almost believed none of those other complications would surface.
We were friends, companions, and I was content. Now he no doubt believed he had put in enough time and was justified in launching his attack.

Now the simplicity of our interaction was over. I was prey, and he had pounced. I felt a lump in my throat.

"No," I said firmly. "You must not speak to me so."

"Anne, I dream of you . . ."

"No," I insisted again. "Oh, you stupid man, now you've spoiled it all!" This time I didn't care about the mare's heaving sides, but kicked her hard and forced her to an unwilling gallop. I didn't hear the vicomte after me, and I would not turn around. When I got home, I dismounted and left the mare wandering free. Inside, I flung myself down on my bed and wept, though I hardly knew why. I wished I had one friend, one ally to confide in. One person who would tell me either that I was being foolish to think of the vicomte for a moment, or that there was no harm in being lonely, or intrigued by a man's attention. Connie could teach me how to refuse him in a way that didn't cause offense . . . or else encourage me to embrace the offer he was surely about to make when I fled. But I could not speak of all that to the spinster, or Madame Capucine, or any of the simple, good women I knew and loved here. They would not understand what it was that I feared.

I didn't want to be a mistress, a lover, a whore. Surely that is all the vicomte wanted of me.

The following week, the boy brought my mare as usual. But when I rode out of the valley, the vicomte did not meet me. For long and listless hours, I ranged in the same small place, not admitting that I was waiting. He never came. I would not deign to ask the lad, but handed the mare over without a word. He in turn silently gave me a purse of coins. Five for each day I had ridden. I'd almost forgotten about that agreement. It seemed like a jest. I'd forgotten I was simply exercising the mare.

I was disappointed, but I shouldn't have been surprised, I suppose. Court life, Felix, and almost every experience since leaving home had taught me that a man will seek to possess any woman who catches his eye and is unprotected. No other woman in the village would ride alone with a man. What else could he have expected? Now that I had put him off, and because I would not be his whore, I could not be his friend.

That night, nestled in the softness of my bed, my body suggested another solution. As the sheets brushed my bare skin as if in a lover's caress, I remembered other touches. Denys's kiss. George's embrace. And oh, the attentions of that lascivious bishop's clever tongue! It was easy enough to picture another's head hidden beneath my skirts. Perhaps those sensuous escapades had come to nothing, or brought pain, but in themselves, separate from their consequences, they had been delightful.

I could be that kind of woman, taking lovemaking easily and joyfully. He would give me money, no doubt, and clothes. Perhaps even bestow on me that spirited mare. I could enjoy a span of time, and when I grew tired of it, take my gleanings and go where I wished. He was a wealthy man. With what he could give me, life as a spy following my mother's footsteps wouldn't be the only option.

Other women had done it. Why not me? I fell asleep easily after that, but woke to a grim certainty that fantasy could never match reality. A woman could not give herself to a man, and yet keep herself for herself.

I couldn't stay in his village if he was going to continue to pursue me.

It would have to be Paris and the Rue Poisson after all. That was the only way I could maintain my independence. I counted my money and calculated a pawnbroker's rate for the earring. Spring was the best time to travel, but the prospect of a dreary winter in this valley suddenly enervated me. All the charm of village life seemed to have fled. It was early fall now. If I left in the next few weeks, I'd have ample time to reach Paris before the roads grew dangerous in the winter. This was no kind of life for me.

Twice again the mare was brought, and I ceased to expect the vicomte. I forced myself to enjoy the speed, the flowers, the butterflies. I discovered that *force* and *enjoy* are incompatible words.

The first little coolness had come to the land when I brought a tincture of clove and thyme to Mathilde, who cooked and served in the tavern. Having done the job myself, however briefly in Dover, I felt a particular affinity for the girl, and stayed in the kitchen to chat with her in the intervals between serving the regulars.

She came scurrying back with her face aglow. "You'll never guess who is here!"

Of course I could. Who else of all the world would spring to my mind right then? But I smiled and shrugged.

"The vicomte! He's sitting in that corner table just outside the door with another man, his cousin, I think. I've seen them riding before. I had to walk right past him now, just inches away! I could have reached out and touched his cheek. Not that he'd touch *me*." She sighed. Mathilde's face had been fearsomely marked by smallpox. "Though I don't believe half the tales they tell of him. He's not his father, you know. What is he doing here, d'you think, drinking our swill when he has the best wine in his own cellar?"

I had no idea, but instead of sensibly bidding her farewell, I waited for her to go back to her skillet and then crept as near to the door as I could, cracking it open silently.

He was so close that I could hear his voice clearly. I'd gotten to know it well on our rides. It was a warm, rich voice, one made to speak of love. No doubt he had perfected it, as a man with an army of guards between him and his enemies might perfect a pretty flourish of his blade, knowing it was all decorative.

"She's driving me mad, Luc. I accomplish nothing, all for thinking of her."

I hazarded one quick peek, and saw him picking at his teeth with a knife blade. As I ducked back, I saw him reverse the utensil and gnaw on its end like a cheroot.

"You know as well as I do what would make you stop thinking of her," the other, presumably the cousin, said. "Bed her once and be done with her. You don't hunger for the mutton you've already eaten."

"That's not what I want from her."

"Come now, I know you better than that!"

"Well, that's not *all* that I want from her!" he said with a laugh. "Yes, she is lovely, and when I look at her, when I'm near her, it is all I can do not to . . ."

Luc chuckled. "Ah, my cousin is a man of flesh and blood after all. And there I thought you were above such things."

"She is a remarkable woman. A simple, pure, gently reared curate's sister, but at the same time, she speaks like a man."

"I didn't know your tastes ran that way," Luc jested.

"Can you be serious for one moment? She is the only woman who has never bored me. When I think of all those pudding-faced countesses my father has proposed for me."

"Sleep with her, cousin. Her enchantment will fade."

"She's not willing."

"Every woman is willing. Some just take more convincing."

The vicomte lowered his voice so I could scarcely hear it. "I haven't been with . . . many women. And only peasants. When I look at her, I think how different things could be."

"Then I revise my first advice. Have her more than once. Make her your mistress, build her a little house of her own."

"No, she would never submit to that."

"You are obsessed. Has she bewitched you? Will she visit you at night in the form of a succubus?"

"You don't understand," the vicomte said with sober contempt. "You've clearly never felt this way."

"What way?" Luc scoffed. "Engorged with lust?"

"No," the vicomte answered. "In love."

"You jest!"

"Cousin, I have given it a great deal of thought. I mean to marry that woman."

"Have you gone mad? Your father will disown you."

"He can't. The estate and title and fortune are all entailed to me."

"Then he'll die when you tell him."

The vicomte was silent for a moment. Then, just barely, I heard him say, "All the better. It is a cursed thing to be ashamed of your father."

There was the sound of a chair being shoved back. "Then I bow to you, Comte de la Fere!"

If the vicomte was a more clever man—if, for example, he was a woman—I would think he had orchestrated the entire thing. Paid Mathilde to feign a toothache, set himself and his cousin in the proper place for eavesdropping, trusted my curiosity to let me overhear. But no, I am convinced it was pure luck.

I had thought it mere desire. I had thought him no better than his father, than thousands of other men who wanted one thing only. It was as if I had spent years digging through the mud and was suddenly rewarded with a diamond, pure and shining. When I rode with him, I seemed to see a man who valued my mind as much as my breasts, a man who wanted to talk with me as much as he wanted to ravish me. And now, in those simple words—*the only woman who has never bored me*—I seemed to read a world of respect. Could the vicomte be a true partner for me, one who would see me as an equal as I'd always dreamed?

He said that he loved me. Was I swayed by it? If I was, despise me—I command you. And then despise yourself because you have been as uncertain, as conflicted, as young as I was. We are all of flesh. We all have a heart, however cruelly it has been used, however we beat our heart to callus it. I admit that word *love* had an impact on me, particularly since it was confessed to a scoffing cousin rather than me. I'd seen that word used as a precise tool before.

But think you this: What if it was not the word *love*, but *marriage* that made virtues of his coincidental lust for me? What if I was not a foolish chit, but a clever and ambitious one?

I was storm-tossed in the world, and though I could swim, I was far from shore. I had this cottage, this small life to cling to for now, but perhaps not forever.

Secure as you are in your position on dry land, you cannot quite understand that the vicomte was a sleek little schooner approaching on the horizon. Afloat for the nonce but with an uncertain future, should I hold out for a galleon or frigate? Should I trust a boon wind to carry me to shore? Or should I seize what might be my best, my only chance to have a good life? The vicomte was rich, titled, young enough to be malleable, and he had told someone other than me that he loved me. From what he said unguarded, he was not, after all, a lecherous noble who would take any woman who didn't outrank and couldn't outrun him. But I wondered, was he too swayed by lust to know what would make him happy, or truly care for my happiness? Was the love, the respect genuine, or a mere symptom of lasciviousness? A plague victim does not die from his spots. Those things I treasured might vanish once lust was slaked. Experience, and Lady Mary, had taught me to be cynical, to think that emotions are transient, love is an illusion, people are liars, and everyone looks after themselves first.

And oh, how could I ever marry when I carried on my breast a brand unjustly marking me a criminal, which only a lover would see? He claimed love, but would that be strong enough to stand against a small fleur-de-lis scar? I was not sure I could trust him with my secret.

Weighing all these things, I slept uneasily. The next day when the boy brought my mare, I bade him keep the five livres for himself if in exchange he would tell me where the vicomte was riding this day. He was happy enough with the bargain, and within the hour I was on the road to the next village, at the edge of his estate. I saw his look of shocked pleasure when I rode toward him. A few lengths away, I reined in my horse and very deliberately pulled the emerald ribbon from within my sleeve.

He watched, entranced, while I slowly removed my bonnet and shook out my hair. It had grown almost to my shoulders, and glinted bright gold in the sun. Then, watching him with a sly smile all the while, I tied the ribbon around my hair and made a neat off-center bow. Without a word, I wheeled the mare around and galloped away.

Of course he chased me.

When we lay on the grass that afternoon—chaste and clothed, I might add, arm's length apart—he reached out and touched first the ribbon, then my abbreviated hair. "A bit bedraggled, isn't it?"

"It has been out in the elements—as you well know."

"And your hair. Very charming, very gamine . . . if anything could make you boyish."

I could have told him that a jerkin and breeches had done that very thing, well enough to fool a prince, but I only smiled demurely and said, "Before I left, I donated my hair to a convent. They sell it for wigs for great ladies, and the money it brings helps their good works."

"Great ladies, eh? And what are they?" He twined a lock around his finger.

"They are . . . not me."

"But you could be."

He did not ask me that day, and I did not press it. I still didn't know if I wanted it. So I set him a secret task. If he attempted the slightest familiarity with me—a kiss, a caress of the bosom—I would cut him off entirely, never so much as speak to him again. So he said I was different? Let him prove it.

I did not think he could.

But three weeks later he proposed to me, and I accepted.

I didn't love him. Love was behind me—the moth who burns her wings. But I liked him, esteemed him. And I was certain he esteemed me, too. When I spoke, he listened as if he valued my words. He asked me questions about things large and small.

I could envision a life with him, an equal, running the estate, helping the tenants, being the sort of great lady my mother was.

Well, the sort of great lady she had pretended to be while she waited for orders that never came . . .

Chapter 17

The vicomte was like a schoolboy who escaped his tutor. He'd sent for a priest from Paris who would perform the ceremony without the usual prelude—paternal permission, the reading of the banns—for an extravagant fee. Highly suspicious of human nature, I might have doubted the priest's credentials and the legality of the marriage, but the vicomte had also invited a dear friend of his to serve as witness.

"He is a jolly fellow, the Comte de Wardes. Our fathers grew up together, and the comte recently inherited the title. He's lived abroad, in England mostly, but he, and until his death, his father, would travel often to France and stay with us every year or so. You'll like him, Anne. He's a champion swordsman, and rides a horse like a centaur."

"Do centaurs ride horses?"

"You know what I mean, you vexing girl," he said, giving me a quick kiss on the cheek for my pertness. It was the first, and I blushed. A true blush, none of Lady Mary's counterfeits. "Now de Wardes is a representative of Marie de' Medici, the queen regent. My father and I have been negotiating a trade deal with England, and . . . some other matters."

"What kind of matters?"

"Nothing for you to worry your pretty little head about. Suffice it to say that not long after we are married, you will have a chance to prove yourself as chatelaine of the castle when the English representatives come here to parlay. Don't fret, all you'll have to do is look beautiful and modest. You'll be fine. Drat the man, where is he? I have a wedding night ahead of me!" He gave me a vast anticipatory grin, as if I were all the cakes in the world and he was waiting for leave to gobble me up.

I smiled, and touched his hand briefly, but inside I trembled. Soon, I would be Vicomtesse de la Fere, secure in position and title forever. It would not matter what was revealed about my past. He could not know about my life and deeds in England. Soon I would be lawfully married. He could not cast me off, and his love would surely let him see the truth, the purity of all my intentions. So I told myself, over and over again.

And so there I stood in the deserted chapel, waiting for the Comte de Wardes to witness our secret marriage.

The chapel was dark, and darker still to me through my veil. My vicomte didn't want to risk attracting attention. He was still a little frightened of his father, I think. I stood by his side, shivering, afraid with more than the terrors of a virgin on her wedding night. I looked to the vicomte's shadowed face, just barely visible by the light of the three slim white candles burning on the altar. He was chewing absently on a heavy golden chain that hung around his neck, anxious for his friend's arrival, and no doubt for the long-awaited consummation.

He caught my look and dropped the chain to kiss my brow, pulling me close. How strong he was! I clung to him as the creeper clings to the oak, knowing I was latching on to someone powerful who would protect me. Once I was his lawful wife, nothing could touch me. Not Felix, not the executioner. The vicomte and I would survive any awkwardness, and grow into a comfortable relationship. What a brave, good man he was after all, to marry for love. Yes, I thought as the flickering candlelight softened his face—in time I might come to love this strong, honorable man.

Honorable, I called him. I did not know then what a tricky double-edged blade honor can be.

When the chapel door burst open behind us, I almost fainted, irrationally thinking it must be Felix, or the nuns, or my father. It could not be that I would truly find safety and happiness.

But the vicomte cried out, "De Wardes!" and spat out the gold chain he'd resumed chewing on. "There you are, you rascal. Hurry, I want this done. Stand here. Priest, are you ready? The introductions can come later. Begin, at once!" He was bouncing on the balls of his toes, and took my hand, squeezing too tight, grinning like a child. I caught a glimpse of a man in dark clothes move to stand behind my lord, then the priest began.

He vowed, I vowed, and it was done. The vicomte swept me up in a kiss and whirled me around, his favorite new toy. Nothing can touch me now, I thought.

"De Wardes, may I present my bride, once Anne de Breuil, now the Vicomtesse de la Fere."

I lifted my veil and held out my hand as the man stepped into the light. Only Lady Mary's teaching, only my memory of strict court protocol kept my hand midair, held aloft by a nerveless arm, when I beheld before me Denys, dressed in severe, elegant finery.

"Comte . . . de Wardes," I said, the name as strange as the title.

"My lady," he said, bowing over my hand and kissing the knuckles lightly. He stayed down a fraction too long, giving the shock of seeing me time to evaporate from his face.

"Careful there, my friend—she belongs to me now. And you better be trustworthy, because I'm leaving her in your care while I prepare the bridal bed. Two reliable servants are setting up a room fit for a princess in a charming cottage on the estate, where we will pass the night." His eyes met mine, and he blushed like a boy. "So that at least we will have a few hours of joy before I have to face my father." He kissed me again quickly and was away. The priest, having no desire to be caught by a furious comte, followed close on his heels.

The moment we were alone, he asked not, *Where have you been?* or *What happened to you?* but, gazing down at the ring on my finger, "What have you done?"

"I . . . I have married, as you see."

Attack-fast, he blew out the candles and pulled me to the darkest corner of the chapel that even the moonbeams through the stained glass did not touch. "I was coming for you. I was looking for you, all this time! You vanished."

I told him of my adventures after my arrest, quickly, but omitting nothing.

Though I couldn't see his face, there was admiration as well as bitterness in his tone when he said, "Your mother's daughter."

Charged with Connie's safety—and knowing I could look after myself for a while—he took my friend to the house of an ally and then doubled back for me. At least, he thought, he'd know where to find me. That is one benefit of being arrested. But when he got there the next afternoon, I was gone, rumored to be heading north. He knew nothing about the escaped priest, but rode hard on the road to Belgium, certain a girl on foot must be easy to find. But when days and weeks passed with no sign of me, he had to assume I was lost to him forever.

"I had word with every connection I have for a hundred miles in every direction—and I have many connections here. This has been my base since I first joined my father on his work."

"Your father, the Comte de Wardes?" I clarified, still astonished.

"My late father," he said.

"How I loved that old man," I said. "But . . . a count? He was a nobleman and was content to live in my mother's mews?"

"He was an agent, like your mother. Like your grandmother, whom he loved, who never knew of his love." There are stories everywhere, I thought. "And he was passionate about falconry. That was no spy's acting. He'd be pottering about the mews at his own estate either way. Better to serve France in England and be close to your mother, the child of his heart. We returned to France often, boarding the ship in rags, departing in velvet."

"I never knew," I said wonderingly.

"No one did. That's the whole point. But, Clarice, what were you thinking marrying the vicomte? How could you? Didn't you know I would find you eventually?" He took my face tenderly in his hands.

"How could I know that?" Against my will, tears welled and fell, cascading over his thumbs where they caressed my cheeks. "Tell me, what in my lifetime of experience could possibly teach me that the men I know will use me well, that the people I care for will not abandon me?"

His hands dropped. "Clarice, you know me." His voice was wretched, ragged.

I gasped a sob. "I knew Denys the falconer's boy. Who is the swordsman? Who is this Comte de Wardes? My own mother lied to me. You lied. George lied." I willed anger to best self-pity. "Who did I have to depend on but myself? Tell me, what was I supposed to do?"

"You could have waited," he said bitterly.

"For what? For you to take me to a life of danger? Everyone in Maman's family has died of their trade. You want that for me? No, thank you, I'll be a vicomtesse."

"Do you know what kind of man he is?"

"Well enough. He is a man. I am trained to deal with men. Will you speak ill of him? He calls you his friend."

"We were boys together, when I visited France with my father. He is . . . not a bad man." Somehow he made that faint praise sound like the deepest condemnation.

"Have I the right to ask for more? You know what I've done. You know what I deserve."

"You deserve happiness," Denys said softly. "You deserve real love, with a worthy man. Not . . . not him."

"And what is wrong with him, pray?"

"He is a proud man, and vain. He has had his way in all things. Now he has you, his for the asking."

"It was not like that. He courted me for a long while."

"Does he know you? Does he value you?"

"Yes!"

"You go to your bridal bed soon. What will he do when he sees the criminal brand on your breast?"

"He is a man of honor, a gentleman! He will hear me out, and understand." But inwardly, I doubted, and trembled.

"Yes, and he will be a gentleman as long as everything goes his way. As long as no one opposes him."

"I opposed him," I said, lifting my chin. "I denied him, refused his gifts, and yet he loves me."

"Who has ever countered him before? You piqued him. He values you because he sees that you are rare. Take care you don't lose value. When he was a boy, we were eating porridge one morning, when his spoon scraped a bit of gilding from the dish. When he saw, he frowned, and hurled the dish into the fireplace."

"A child's tantrum, no more," I said, though I felt a deep foreboding. "I know what I'm doing. I chose this path with open eyes. It is what my mother wanted for me—a choice. Are you vexed that I'm not following you into a life of danger?" I cocked my head at him. "Or are you jealous?"

I saw his nostrils flare, but he did not rise to my bait. "This is no life for a woman such as you, Clarice. What, a backwoods broodmare? You are made for finer things, a knife honed to the sharpest point . . ."

"I am a woman, not a weapon!"

"Come with me, Clarice. Before he beds you. We can get the marriage annulled. Or simply disappear with me. He'll never find you."

"Go with you and do what?" My hands were on his chest, clutching his doublet in the dark. "Tell me, what future do you have for me?"

"Why, what your mother intended."

"She wanted me to have a choice!"

"You have no other choice now. He will find out, and you will be ruined. Come with me, become an agent for France."

"With you?"

"Who else?"

"I mean, are you asking me to come with *you*? Or are you asking me to become an agent?"

There was a long silence in the darkness. Say it, I willed him. Say it and I will come.

He said nothing.

I let go of his doublet and walked toward the moonlight streaming faintly through the cracked chapel door. Oh God, what had I done? I was young enough, conventional enough to believe that marriage vows bound me. I took a deep ragged breath. The vicomte is a good man, I told myself. If he has faults, I will manage them. If he has a temper, well, then I shall myself temper it. I was taught to read and control men. "No, I have made my bed. It is the vicomte's bed. Now I must lie in it." But I trembled and cursed the day, and wished with all my heart that Denys had come an hour sooner.

"Clarice, please."

I stopped, but he didn't go on, so I went outside to await my lord. He followed me, and soon we heard hoofbeats in the still night. My lord was returning.

"Come to Paris, Clarice. Please." Not *come with me to Paris.*

But then the vicomte was there, looking so boyishly thrilled at being a bridegroom that I was convinced Denys's warning must be sparked by jealousy. I stepped away from Denys without looking at him again.

And there I left my childhood friend, my last connection with home, and happiness.

The vicomte carried me across the threshold, kissing me all the while; carried me to the bed bestrewn with rose petals. *Our* rose, gold tipped with blood. Laughing, he tossed me down and hovered over me, kissing my throat, my shoulder, the first swell of my breast.

I took his face in my hands, stilling him, forcing him to look at me. "Are you sure you made the right decision?" I asked, and he thought I was asking him.

"Too late to think of that now," he said with a low laugh as he searched my face. "You belong to me, my own darling wife."

How strange that word *belong* made me feel. To belong was to be safe, cherished, a part of something bigger than myself. As a nobleman's wife, I was fulfilling my natural destiny. I would be the wise and generous chatelaine of not only a castle but a village. People would come to me for advice and help. I would preside over my husband's table, and also mingle with the village women. I would be respected, have friends. I would belong.

But I would belong to him, and that is the part that troubled me as I lay in his arms. To give myself to another! By law I was his property now. Denys, who had known him longer (though I did not like to think better) than me, had hinted at a darker personality. But what nobleman was not proud, selfish. It was a question of upbringing. It was nothing I couldn't manage.

But what if, after he owned me, things should change? The things that charmed him early on might pall in my new position. What if he decided his possession shouldn't ride fast horses, or visit the baker's wife, or grub about in the garden? What if belonging to him made me that cowed woman Maman appeared to be whenever my father was home?

He took my hands in his and gently removed them from his cheeks, kissing each in turn. "Do you know how proud I am to call you mine, Anne? To have found such a pure, untarnished woman, with such a lively mind, so bold and yet so ladylike? You are everything I could desire."

He kissed me, and his nearness, his devotion, the large, safe, masculine presence of him drowned out all of my fears. Save one. When he pulled at the neckline of my bodice, I turned away from the candlelight to put myself in shadow and said, "Have a care, Olivier. This is my only good gown."

"Tomorrow I will have a thousand gowns made for you," he said. "And every one will show off your glorious breasts. Oh, how beautiful you are. How perfect, how pure."

Oh, merciful heaven, I found I could not risk it. What if all his love and devotion and protection melted away the moment he saw my fatal brand? I had entered into a marriage of deception, and it poisoned the happiness he offered in his arms.

"My love, you're crying!"

"Tears of joy," I insisted, then broke into ugly sobs that made him sit back.

Uncertain, he reached for my bosom, but with an animal sound of despair I pushed his hand away. "I can't!" I wailed, and threw myself to the ground at is feet. "Oh, my lord, my husband, forgive me. I have deceived you!" I felt his hand descend to my shoulder, tighten, not quite painfully, but almost. Careless in my grief, I pressed my face to his loins and writhed in a wanton ecstasy of misery— to great effect. The hand unclenched from my shoulder, and made a low guttural sound.

"I cannot lie with you, my lord. I am unworthy to be your wife." I looked up at him, and for all the sound effects, I'd taken care that my actual tears should be strategic and few, so that although my eyes were large and luminous, they hadn't reached the red and puffy stage. Real, unattractive sorrow can inspire sympathy, but I needed far more than that from the vicomte.

"Tell me what you mean," he commanded, trying to keep his voice stern, though my hands now clutched his thighs in the unconscious abandonment of my dismay, pressing and teasing tantalizingly high.

I shook my head. "He said he would kill me if I told."

Was this too much? No, I could see the flame spark in my husband's eye. A threat to me, his property, was by extension a threat to his own noble person. Without even knowing what I would say, a little murderous fire was already kindling in him.

So, with hesitation and a few more calculated tears, spent as wisely as diamonds, I told him how the late curate—my stepbrother, not my true brother at all—said that the Church must always claim its tithe, the first fruits.

"When we were some weeks on the road, we slept in a field. It was cold, and he came near to me, saying he would warm me. I never suspected. He had been like a true brother. He lay down beside me and he . . . he . . ."

"Say it," the vicomte insisted savagely.

"He embraced me, and I thought . . . I didn't understand. Then suddenly he pushed me back on the grass and threw my skirts over my head, and I couldn't breathe! He pressed down on my mouth, and I choked on my own garments, and it was dark and I tried to scream, but there was no one to hear me." I pressed my head down into his lap again, rolling my cheek against his cock in abject misery.

"Did he . . . possess you?"

Now, here I was uncertain. I wanted to create a reason why I had to refuse my new husband, a trauma so great I could not give myself to him. And yet men, with their obsession with virginity, can be unpredictable. Felix himself, who lusted after me with every molecule in his body, had expressed disgust at the thought that another had stormed the breach before him. If the vicomte believed I was not a maiden, would he renounce me?

"I couldn't breathe, and the world grew black. When I regained my senses, there was something wet on my belly." I widened my eyes to their most sincerely innocent. "Then he said no matter, since we would be living together in the Comte de la Fere's village, and a bed was more comfortable than grass. My lord, I don't know quite what happened, but I know he shouldn't have done that." Was this expressing too much naïveté? No, he believed it. He did not expect a woman to know the details of sex until he showed them. It seemed ridiculous to me, but my biological confusion was entirely plausible to him.

"You must send me away, or get the marriage annulled," I tell him again. "I don't think I am . . . pure. And I am afraid! When you touch me, I think of him, and I grow cold inside!"

He pushed the curls away from my brow and said, "You are not at fault, my love. It only happened the once?"

I nodded. "He was attacked on the road the next day."

"My poor tender flower. I will show you that all men are not like your stepbrother. What is a sin to a maiden can be a great joy to a married woman, and I promise I will teach you to feel the warmth of trust and passion."

Oh, what a good man I have found! "But not tonight," I hastened to add.

"You belong to me," he reminded me. "We have all the time in the world. Only when you are ready, my love." Then he shocked me by saying. "We will indeed begin tonight."

I recoiled, but he only reached for my hand. "Remember that a beginning can be a very small and tender thing."

Lightly, he traced the outline of each finger, sending unaccustomed thrills along my arm. He made a snail shell shape on my palm, tracing calluses from gardening and leather reins. He calmed my next shiver with a firmer touch, pressing his thumb into the heel of my hand, massaging toward the fingertips. I closed my eyes, never having dreamed that such an innocent-seeming touch could both soothe and arouse to such an extent.

I mewed a little protest when he dropped that hand, but he reached for the other and gave it the same ministrations.

"See," he said when he released me. "Slowly."

You were wrong, Denys, I thought as he curled his body chastely around my back, his hand on my hip, his face nuzzling my hair. Olivier, the Vicomte de la Fere, is the best of men.

Why, then, did I spend a sleepless night in his arms, stiff and uneasy, wracked by guilt and fear?

I had hoped to find something real in my marriage to Olivier. But as I lay in my marriage bed, a virgin still, I realized that I had wholly committed myself to a life of lies. I could not be that innocent, sweet girl he thought I was. I'd done too many horrible things. But he must never know. Are all wives actresses? I wondered. Do all women play a part, hiding their true selves? So I took truth, and honesty, and wrapped them in silk and placed it in the most secure reaches of my inmost heart. It was there, waiting, a precious treasure that I did not dare touch for fear I would tear it open and wantonly spend it.

When he touched my hands and nothing else, I think I began to love that man. Or, to care for him, to respect and admire him in a way that I clearly saw could lead to real love. And it broke my heart that he could never know me fully and completely.

Perhaps I could solve one problem, though. Olivier had left an hour ago to confront his father. Scrubbing my cheeks tear-free, I crossed to the fireplace and stirred the logs with a poker. All could be ruined if the vicomte ever spied my brand. Perhaps I could explain, perhaps he would understand, but I thought it better not to put it to the test. I could not undo the burn, but I could obscure it. It might still arouse his suspicions, but if other things were aroused at the moment of unveiling, I thought I had a chance of allaying any doubts. But I'd have little hope if the brand showed a livid fleur-de-lis freshly scored.

The poker, basking in the fire, glowed a salamander red. Don't think, I told myself as I unlaced my bodice. Just act. Don't remember the pain, the fear of being tied up, held down. This is your own volition now. One moment of pure will, and it will be done.

I pulled the poker from the flames, but it was a long, unwieldy thing, and when I juggled it to bring the burning tongue to my skin, I shifted my grip too near the tip and burned my hand. I dropped it with a yelp, and the poker seared a line along my skirt as it fell. Ah, the hellfire burn of even that small wound! I unclenched my hand and looked at the little blister, a pittance of a wound beside my brand, and still unbearable.

I couldn't do it. Twice more I heated the poker, and I couldn't force myself to come even as close as I did the first time. My body shook, my mind rebelled, and I became again a helpless, bound thing at the mercy of the executioner of Lille.

"You coward!" I hissed, throwing down the cooling rod.

Well, there was no other choice. I simply could not let my husband see my brand.

That first week was a whirl. The old Comte de la Fere was not pleased, and the vicomte kept me in the bridal cottage until he'd spent the bulk of his ire. The second night of my married life, Olivier again paid fealty to my hands, but on the third he ventured to reach for a foot. The foot became an ankle, then a calf . . . but when his fingers touched my thigh I gasped, and he snatched them away. I did not have the words or the courage to tell him that I gasped because I wanted him to go higher still.

"We will be moving to the castle soon. My father is slowly becoming accustomed to the idea of you. I'll send a dressmaker to prepare a suitable wardrobe. And I have this for you." Without ceremony, he pulled a glittering bauble from his pouch and slipped it onto my forefinger. It was a sapphire, huge and placid, surrounded by scintillations of diamonds. "The first of the de la Fere jewels, all of which shall be yours, my lady." He kissed me and departed.

I had a harder time with the dressmaker and her assistants than I ever did with the vicomte. Twittering with tales of the latest mode in Paris, they tried to kit me out with low square necks, low scooped necks, practically nonexistent necklines barely covered with transparent gauze. Adamant in their taste and expertise, it was a struggle to convince them that I wanted demure high-necked gowns.

"You're a lady now, not a curate's sister," the head dressmaker snapped testily, deprived of her chance to shine.

I had to play the mighty lady with her then. "And I will have the finest gowns you can craft," I told her, fingering the material. "But they will be cut to my specifications. Send this lace from my sight; it is second-rate. I prefer Flanders point. And though I like the color of this bolt, the material will never do. Find something in this hue in moire silk. I'll have the sleeves striped with cloth of gold."

Overawed by my demands, and by the coin they would require, I gradually dominated her entirely. She dressed me in the most splendid fashion in gowns that showed less skin than my nun's habit, and neither she nor her assistants ever saw me without my high-necked shift tied tight at my throat.

The old comte cooled, and I was presented at the castle. He saw the product of much rehearsal, a woman who, despite his protests, he could be proud of. My pedigree (fabricated) might be lowly, but he could not deny that I carried myself like a countess and apparently had the morals of a saint with none of a saint's dourness (for I think they are a singularly humorless lot, those saints, and how else, when they are always being pressed beneath stones or broken on the wheel?).

When the Comte de la Fere died a few weeks after my establishment, there was little sorrow, and loud rejoicing about my husband's ascension. We were now the Comte and Comtesse de la Fere.

Weeks, then months passed, and my husband still came to me every night. Every night I refused him, but he touched what innocent parts I would allow, proving night after night that when it comes to skin, there are no innocent parts. He was aroused, and frustrated, but oh, was I not just as much? To be caressed every night—*almost* intimately—and yet never able to allow myself the satisfaction of fulfillment! For I was sorely afraid. Things were going so perfectly. Just one glimpse of my brand, and everything I'd built for myself would come tumbling down.

Or, the hopeful sliver that remained in me said, perhaps if you tell him the truth he will understand, and forgive, and then you can live an honest life at last instead of this taut-nerved existence plagued by fear. I would have to relent one day. Someone would jibe him about an heir, and he might forget his gentleness and compassion, and insist. I could only hope to control the script well enough to set the act in the dark. My modesty and reluctance might buy me years before he ever saw my naked body in full light. We slept together in darkness, and if I did not rise before him, I lazily stayed abed until he left, so that he never saw me unclothed. I rejected every offer of a lady's maid, and dressed myself in my fine and modest garb. Everything becomes commonplace eventually, even fear and guilt. Gradually, those terrors subsided under routine and something very close to happiness. I didn't think about the future, but only managed my husband and new household from day to day. I was as busy as a scullery maid, for to run a castle and help manage an estate is a huge undertaking, even with an experienced steward and staff. Thanks to Maman's training and example, I excelled. As long as I succeeded in the moment, there was nothing else.

Once, when I was bathing, a maid came in unannounced and almost saw my brand. I turned away quickly and slipped into a robe, quite safe, but I distinctly remember an unexpected thrill that coursed through me at the moment of near-discovery. I didn't want to be caught. That would be foolish—who could possibly want that? Perhaps it was like a carbuncle, this secret, ever growing. No one wishes to be stabbed with a lancet, but what a relief to have it drained and gone! There was a strange excitement at the thought of being found out.

Perhaps that was my better angel, muttering about what I deserved.

Things went on quite placidly, as I collected clothes and jewels, and presided over dinners and parties with our nearest noble and almost noble neighbors. I never made a move that wasn't calculated as I performed the needful things, yet despite that, I seemed to move through the world almost without thought.

And inside me, I kept my secret self, soft and kind, regretful and lonely, and wondered if it would wither.

I got to know Olivier better, for a husband is a far different thing than a courting man. I wonder what our marriage would have been like if it wasn't based on deceit. Perhaps if he had gotten a better woman than I— or if I was in truth the person I pretended to be, arch, clever Anne de Breuil—we would have been sincerely happy. As it was, it seemed to me that we were two expert actors giving a stunning performance of happiness. The castle staff, the villagers, our neighbors all applauded our act, but I knew that it was hollow.

He was kind, and loving, and patient with me. He gave me everything

I wanted, and much that I didn't—jewels, clothes, a carriage. His patience only began to fray when men would ask jocularly about his first son, when women would not-so-subtly look sidelong at my belly, searching for thickening. Everyone speculated, as they will a few months after a wedding.

Every night he came to my bed, and I had no reason to suspect he visited another's. In time, though, the loving words became fewer, and sometimes he even snapped at me, though never in public. He was always contrite, and a jewel would follow, another piece of the de la Fere parure. I immersed myself in his life, and took care to be his helpmeet even if I could not be his proper bedmate. Together we rode about the estate, checking the crops and orchards, helping those in need, and in general maintaining that overawing lordly presence that is all that keeps the downtrodden from rising up.

One morning, when riding at the distant reaches of his estate, we came upon a mean little hut. It was the sort of thing I was constantly taking care of. The old comte had been negligent in his duties. These were his tenants, and if they had to give him yearly rent and tithes, he should have kept their homes in decent repair, and tended to them when they were sick or old. It is the bargain we make. But I had found a great many cottages in disrepair, and was using my influence to convince my husband to reduce his own spending a bit to help his dependents.

As we rode up, we saw one of our under-cooks enter the hut, carrying a live chicken under his arm. Olivier called to him, and the man came out with a beet-colored face (and without the chicken) and stammered out that these were distant cousins of his. The father had died, and four of the five children were sick. "They have nothing, my lord."

"And whose chicken is that, then, if they have nothing?" Olivier asked.

I turned to my husband, expecting jocularity, thinking only to chide him that it wasn't the appropriate time to tease, planning in my mind the bone broth and apples and blankets I would bring to help the family. But when I looked, I saw him in a red rage.

"Please, your lordship, I know of your lady's generosity, and I knew she would not mind if I helped them."

"Whose chicken is that?" he repeated between clenched teeth.

"Why, your lordship's." The man began to see the danger he was in.

"By whose leave did you take it?" Olivier gripped his sword hilt.

"I . . ." He looked to me pleadingly. But before I could help him, before I could laughingly say that I'd given permission, the fool said, "No one, my lord. I thought you wouldn't mind."

"In other words, you stole from me."

"Olivier," I interjected, nudging my horse to his side and laying a hand on his arm. "I don't think he meant . . ."

He shook me off and dismounted, grabbing the poor cook by his scruff and striking him. He threw him to the dirt. The man raised a desperate, bloody face.

"You have committed a crime against your rightful lord. You know what the penalty is."

He raised clasped hands as if to his maker. "Please, my lord! I will pay for the chicken. Your lady has helped so many. I thought she would not mind."

"Really, Olivier, I would have told him to take the chicken," I said, still half thinking this was all his idea of a joke. A damned chicken!

My husband ignored me. "By the law of the land, I sentence you to death for stealing from your lord. The sentence will be carried out forthwith." He drew his sword, and at once I slid off my horse and grabbed his sword arm.

"Olivier, what are you doing?" He tried to shake me off, but for the first time, I showed my strength. "Are you mad? If you have charges against him, bring him to the magistrate, or try him yourself during public audience. You cannot kill him here: witness, victim, and judge and jury all at once!"

His face was red, sweating, veined, making him monstrous, but I kept hold of his arm until at last he sheathed his sword. He looked like a man awakened from a daze.

"Of course, gentle Anne. I only wanted to make a point." To the cook, he said, "Go, present yourself to my steward and tell him what has happened. If you run, your family will be imprisoned."

The terrified cook tugged his hair and bowed jerkily, then ran off.

"Poor man. You were not right to frighten him so."

"There are ladies of the manor to be gentle, and lords to maintain order," he said as if explaining to a child. "Feel free to send them food or a nurse. But the cook must answer for his crime."

"His crime? He took it upon himself to do something that either of us would have given him leave to do!"

"We will not speak of it again."

"But . . ."

Something in his look silenced me. I felt as if I had lived these last months with a tame leopard, all velvet softness, never thinking the beast would one day remember that he had teeth. For the rest of the day, I trod carefully, but his mood seemed to improve by the next morning. He rode out early, and when he came back, I asked after the cook.

"Oh . . . he ran off."

"No! But his family!"

He petted my hair. "Don't worry, my sweet, I won't harm them. That was all an idle threat. Well, the fellow is gone, so I have one less criminal on the estate. It all comes to the same thing. I doubt we'll see that thief's face again." He chuckled, and I let him embrace me, grateful that I had taught my husband greater kindness than his own father.

For all I had seen, I was so naive, still. It never occurred to me what had truly happened.

Despite life's little abrasions, I felt like my decision to marry Olivier had brought more good to more people than any other choice I could have made. I had made great improvements to the management of the estate, increasing efficiency and income, and the tenants were already profiting by it. Soon there were no more huts like the one we'd found before, dank and in disrepair. I had the estate carpenters and masons scurrying, and if Olivier sometimes grumbled about the expense, or pointed out that peasants *like* dirt, he could not help but admit that fewer laborers dying of typhus or childbirth kept the workforce steady and the rents coming in on time.

Was Olivier happy? In the main, I think he was. Every marriage has some little challenge. With ours it was chastity. Now there was a mournful look of resignation on his face when he caressed my hands and feet, and he nevermore ventured beyond my wrists or ankles, afraid of rebuff. The stalemate had to break one day, but I forced myself not to think of it. During the day, the laughter and the deep discussions made up for what was missing in the privacy of our chambers.

One morning, after he had drunk particularly heavily with guests, I was up and dressed before him and headed to the stables to make my rounds. I was going to visit a pregnant woman whose last child had died at birth. Already, I didn't like the way her ankles were puffing. Then I'd see how the construction of a new row of well-drained cottages was coming along. Finally, I'd pay a visit to Madame Capucine, for no particular reason other than the pleasure of her company, and the smell of her bread.

I hadn't yet mounted, but was walking my mare off the immediate castle grounds, when I was accosted by a beggar. At least, that's what I assumed him to be at first, with his dusty, hooded clothes and filthy bare feet. I was already absently thinking what I would supply him with— boots, rags to wrap around his legs, perhaps a place in the hayloft for the night.

"Clarice," the beggar said, and tugged back his hood.

I didn't scream, but my emotions were transferred through the bridle to my sensitive mare, and my sudden tension on her leathers made her snort and caper.

"Felix! What are you doing here?"

"I've searched for you for months. They say in the taverns that the Comte de la Fere has a new bride, the sister of a curate killed by highwaymen. Is it true?"

I found myself speechless.

"What happened to you, Clarice? When I woke you were gone. I thought the bandits had found you and . . ." For a moment he had seemed the devoted, trusting Felix I remembered. The foolish Felix it would be easy to manipulate. Then I watched his face grow hard and canny.

"But you weren't stolen away from me, were you? You *left* me." He edged closer, and I felt frozen on the spot. "I stole for you. I betrayed my vows for you." His voice was rising, and I looked around to see who might hear.

"Let me explain, Felix," I began. "If you'll meet me away from the castle, I'll tell you what really happened." We were in full view of half the castle windows out here. Why, our own bedroom overlooked this courtyard! Olivier could be watching at this moment. If only I could get Felix away from witnesses, I felt sure I could manage him, whether by cajoling or threats or . . . My hand strayed to my bosom, where I used to carry my dagger. I hadn't of late. There had been nothing for me to fear, I thought.

I couldn't let Felix upset this life I'd made for myself. Imperfect as it was, it had become precious to me. I thought of Olivier's dear face crumpling if he heard the truth of me from this ragged man's lips. I would tell him myself, I vowed then. Better to do it myself under exactly the right circumstances than to chance a reveal like this. I would pay Felix handsomely to leave and never trouble me again, and then I could begin anew with my husband, my conscience clear. I could be a true and honest wife to him.

Never had I cared for Olivier so much as I did right then, when our tentative happiness was threatened.

"You belong to me, Clarice," he said.

"Hush! This is not the time or the place . . ."

"I gave up everything for you! You owe me." There was no more talk of love. He was so close I could feel his breath on me. I couldn't back up; the mare made a solid bastion behind me. With one spindly finger he pointed to my breast. "That mark makes you mine. Does your comte know he married a criminal?"

"I'm not a criminal! You stole the holy relics. You! All I wanted was my freedom. Leave me in peace!"

"I'll tell him everything, and he'll cast you out. And when you are a bedraggled wretch, a starving harlot on the streets, I will snatch you up, and you'll be glad of me." How my besotted priest had changed. The outstretched finger loomed closer, and I flinched away. I wanted to scream at him, beat him, choke him with my bare hands, but I couldn't do that until we were alone. Thank heaven he kept his voice low. Any witness might well believe he was only a mad beggar.

"You have the mark of the devil, but I don't care. I've given up everything for you, and I will have you!" That finger touched my brand through my gown . . . and suddenly, Felix was snatched away.

"How dare you lay hands on my lady wife, you cur!" Olivier shouted, and punched Felix twice before letting him crumple to a heap on the ground.

Through blood and spittle, Felix shouted obscenities at me. "Whore! Witch! She seduced me, my lord. She is not as she appears! Slut! Harlot! Criminal! Look at her breast, my lord!"

My husband looked at me, red faced, a vein in his forehead throbbing. I knew he was hungover, parched, tired, edgy—in a perfect state to act rashly if I wished him to.

Send this poor, mad beggar to the coast, I could say. The navy has need of dim-witted men who can follow orders. Leave him for your underlings to manage, I could tell him, and take his arm, leading him back to the bedroom.

Or I could confess, tell him who this ranting, dirty man truly was to me. Purge all the secrets at once.

But I said nothing. Always let the other speak first, Lady Mary taught me. Then you will understand how to guide or goad them.

With a flash of insight, Olivier looked at the man's clothes, the ragged remnants of clerical garb hardly recognizable in the torn and dirty rags. "You told me he was dead."

"I thought he was," I said, then caught Olivier's hand, pulling it to my breast, the breast only he had the right to touch, the sacred place this other man had violated. I let him feel how my heart fluttered like a terrified bird. "I hoped he was. Oh, my love, don't let him touch me again!"

I saw Felix's eyes go wide with shock and sudden understanding.

I let two tears fall, and Olivier pulled his hand away from the tender nest I'd made for it.

And then, my husband made part of my story true.

"This man is a vagrant and a criminal, who has assaulted the comtesse," he called to the curious onlooking servants. "Restrain him." They needed no other explanation. The comte was the law within the reaches of his estate. Shocked and silent, they dragged Felix away.

"Olivier," I began, but he shook his head.

"We will not speak of it. It is behind us." Then, "Bring me a rope!" as he turned and stalked away after the struggling young priest.

Afterward, by day he was his old self, attentive and respectful. But he did not come to my bed that night, nor any of the nights that followed.

After Felix's death, a chill seemed to settle into me. I felt as if I had looked into my own soul, and found a stranger looking back at me. How cold she was, how calculating. She would stop at nothing to stay safe, to maintain this lie.

I had been so close to telling Olivier the truth, to freeing us both so that we could find true happiness and fulfillment in our marriage. Now I never could. I was committed to the lie. I would have to hide my body from him, even as I hid my past and my true self. Even if we became lovers, it would be an act of strategy, not abandon.

I was trapped in this lie. There was no escape for me. No peace.

Still, we maintained the illusion, Olivier and I. Part of my role as wife lay in charming special guests. I was adept at this, of course, keeping my conversation light and amusing and just on the right side of flirting. This one can give me an excellent price for my wheat, the comte would tell me, and that one supplies muskets to the king's troops and might be able to redirect part of his wares to the Turks for the right price—and a finder's fee to my husband. The comte seemed to have his finger in far more financial pies than was considered proper—or even legal—for a nobleman, who was supposed to make all his income from his land.

And of course he dabbled in politics. I entertained a pert little Italian nobleman, slim and sharp as a rapier, who wanted some concession from the French crown and convinced the comte to act in his interests. A Russian came, complete with his bear, specifically to discover what sort of present would best please the Queen Mother. Although my job was mostly to smile, and leave the room at the right time, it felt almost like spy work.

Then, some three months after our still-unconsummated wedding, the comte informed me that a very special guest, a high-ranking nobleman from England, would be arriving the next morning. "There will be a representative of the queen regent speaking on behalf of France, and I represent our king, while our guest represents England. If we can work out this treaty, we will present it to our respective monarchs, and England and France will both prosper. I withhold judgment until our guest tells me the details, but if I find out it is something I can support, it might be a very great thing for our two countries. It is of the utmost importance that these talks proceed smoothly. Can I count on you?"

I kissed him chastely on the edge of his mouth and assured him that I would do everything within my power. Inwardly, though, I made plans to come down with ague, or worms, or pox, or anything that could keep me from meeting an English nobleman. The risk that he'd know me was just too great. I'd keep abed and wait until whoever it was departed.

Knowing I'd be confined for the next few days, I took advantage of my momentary solitude to wander the gardens, always my favorite haunt. The castle gardens were splendid, of course, though a bit too refined for my tastes, and too dominated by ornamentals and tortured boxwoods.

Foliage does not appreciate artificial geometry, and every shrub on the property looked like it bore a grudge against humanity.

I'd gone some way toward de-civilizing the herb garden, though, adding less common cultivars gleaned from village women, and loosening the arrangement so the flowers did not look like soldiers on parade, squadron by herbaceous squadron. I had just bent to see if two tender leaves new-shot from the earth were the hoped-for mullein (which I'd use in a tea for persistent winter coughs) or an unwanted weed. When I stood up, I saw the god of my past standing before me, staring at me.

In that instant of recognition, I bifurcated. One of me wanted to kill him; the other wanted to fall at his feet, embrace his legs, never let go. As I couldn't very well do either, I stood there, waiting for him to recognize me. It took surprisingly long, all of five seconds, perhaps. He had not been trained as well as I, though his mother was our teacher. Everything darted across his face like the swallows of summer: shock, nervousness, and last of all, subtle craftiness.

"There you are!" said my lord and master, coming up behind me with a crunch of boot, taking my arm. "Our guest came early. He can have the Swan Room, I think. Could you see to it? Oh, forgive me, my lady, may I present George Villiers, Duke of Buckingham. My lord, this is my lady wife, Anne."

George collected himself and made an elaborate courtly bow, while I returned a calculatedly awkward curtsy, not looking at him but saying to my husband when I rose, "I will attend to it directly, my love."

I fled with straight shoulders, without a quaver, and no one saw how my eyes darted from side to side, picking out the plants that, in strength or combined, could kill.

In my chambers, I fumed. He will die tonight, at our table. I will give him yew berries and foxglove, henbane and mistletoe, a salad of death. How dare he show his face in the sanctuary I tried so hard to create for myself?

You'll appreciate the depth of my agitation when you know it was only after some moments of deciding the exact fitting poison for his demise that I realized what must be happening at this very moment. What a distracted fool I was! What a child! To think Maman had believed I'd be suitable for the spy trade!

Of course George must even at this moment be telling the comte exactly who I was. He would frame it innocently, casually mentioning how I was the belle of the last season. This to the nobleman who had no idea I was English, for I had never let a word of that tongue slip past mine, never faltered ever for an instant in that perfect court French accent Maman insisted on. Even if George didn't do it maliciously—and I had no doubt that he'd act from the worst intentions— one little slip would unravel the warp and weft of everything I'd woven. Then the truth, bad as it already was, would seem so much worse for having been concealed.

I should have killed him on sight! Shoved the most deadly plants down his throat, run him through with . . . no, I haven't carried my dagger since my wedding night. I must remedy that. Very well, I couldn't have killed him outright, but I could have drawn my husband away before George could reveal anything, or stayed with them to direct the conversation—anything but run away.

Now I'd have to run farther. I looked around the room in a frenzy. What to wear? What to bring? I grabbed up the busk from the sandalwood box where I kept it hidden and shoved it down my front, then tucked Maman's red and black beaded rosary into my pocket. There was no time to change. Could I make it to the stables before the vicomte decided what to do with me? Denys's warning about the comte came back to me.

Too late! There were footsteps without, and I drew my dagger just as the door swung open, hiding it behind the swirl of my skirt as I whirled to face him.

But it wasn't my husband.

George ran, staggered, stumbled across the room like a drunkard, pitching forward at my feet, gasping, looking up at me . . . with tears in his eyes?

He reached to a hidden place at his side, and my fingers clenched around my unseen blade as I imagined any treachery. He pulled out a ring, an oval of milky fire, an opal unadorned by any other gems.

"Forgive me," he sobbed. Are they real, those tears, that heaving chest? Lady Mary taught us more subtle, delicate emotions. Nothing ugly, even in extremis, she said. There is no situation, however dire, that calls for red eyes and a snotty nose. Not even a broken heart.

"I had no choice." He prostrated on my hem, and I looked to the door, still half ajar. Reckless boy, that tender part of me thought. The stern part slapped it silly. "What a flimsy excuse that sounds," he said, looking up at me with a wry smile through the tears. "We all have choices, no? You chose to be strong, and brave, and true. I chose to be weak and faithless. But my love, my beautiful Clarice, he said he would kill you!"

I let him speak uninterrupted, biting back all the questions, the cynical doubts.

"He loves me with an unnatural affection. I didn't understand it at first. As you might imagine, such a thing was completely alien to me." He gave a little chuckle. "There I was thinking innocently of marriage and babies with you, so happy that the king was taking an interest in me. He plucked me out, talked to me, admired me, asked my opinions, and I was such a vain, stupid boy that I never guessed his intent. I thought I was rising on my own merits!" He shook his head. "Then one day he kissed me, and . . . What could I do?"

A woman may always hide behind modesty, he said, and it is true. If the king had kissed me, I'd lose none of his respect by refusing him, particularly at first. More important, the king himself would risk nothing in the proposition. If I carried tales of his attempt, and his failure, it would be no more than the jibes men exchange when stag hunting or drinking. Oh ho, the wench slapped me in the face, and henceforth kept her homely sister always between us!

But the moment a king kisses a man, that man is doomed, George explained. To say no is to call the king unnatural in his desires. To say no is to threaten to tell the world of His Majesty's proclivities. The proposition is its own deadly secret.

"If I'd refused him, he would have sent me away from court at the very least. If I'd refused with the slightest look of disgust, or had ever spoken of it to anyone, I might have been tossed in the Tower. And, Clarice, I thought of you all along. Give in, I told myself, sacrifice this little thing for her sake, and you will be able to take care of her and love her forever! And it is a little thing, is it not? Bodies, friction, release. A mechanical act. A physical exertion. If my king told me I had to chop down a forest to be with you, don't you think I'd do it? Muck out the Augean stables? Every hero has to perform unpleasant, arduous, even impossible tasks to win his ladylove. I hated myself for what I had to do, but I thought it was a worthwhile sacrifice if it got me you."

The knife became slippery in my anxious palm, but I said nothing as he knelt at my feet, gazing up with hope in his eyes.

"And then, I don't know how, he found out about my love for you. He flew into a rage! He stomped and swore and hurled his goblet at me. Then he grew unnaturally quiet and told me very plainly that if I had anything to do with you, he would have you killed. She'll walk into her quarters one day, he said, and a knife will find her throat. Can you picture all that pretty golden hair matted in blood, those blue eyes staring? He was deadly serious, Clarice. And he's the king! He can do things like that, end anyone at a whim! I begged, I pleaded, to no avail. I thought of plunging my face in boiling water, to disfigure myself so badly his desire would flee. But he seemed to read my mind. He touched me, in that unnatural way of his, and told me that if I ever showed you the slightest affection again, you would die." Then, when I discovered him in flagrante, he had no choice.

"It killed me to treat you so, my love. To tell you I never loved you, that I used you? I'd have sooner ripped out my own heart. I can't bear to remember the things I said to you. But I did it to save you. And it worked! Your father told me you went to France to stay with your mother's family, and now look at you, a lovely bride in a castle all your own."

He pressed his lips together in a thin, tortured smile. "I'd like to be happy for you, Clarice. Truly I would. Are *you* happy?"

I couldn't answer, not yet. Instead I asked, "Did you tell the comte that you know me?"

"Not a word," he vowed. Then, looking hopeful for the first time, he added, "I thought it best he didn't know we had a history if there's the slightest possibility you'll run away with me."

My bones dissolved, and my heart gave one mighty thump and declared, *On this beat I die.* The world went liquid, George and myself the only solid things remaining in a bubble of rarefied air.

Lies, lies, lies . . .

Happiness. Vindication. Reward for my suffering.

I heard footsteps in the hall and hissed at him to get up and compose himself. In a breath, he looked as calm and lovely as ever, so that I wondered if I'd imagined it all.

"When your husband is away, I will come to you."

"Tomorrow night," I gasp out, for the comte would be riding out to buy a stud bull early the following morning, and he didn't trust such important things to underlings, no matter what diplomatic crisis was looming. He was decidedly a farmer at heart.

"Until then," George said, and slipped the opal onto my finger. Then he was gone.

He was getting sloppy, forgetting what he'd learned at his own mother's knee. Always be wary of being followed, she'd taught us. Whereas my own maman had taught me to stalk as quietly as a cat, and I did not forget her lessons . . .

Such politeness you have never seen! The excessive courtesy between George and myself that night and the next day was nuanced to a hair, neither too formal nor too familiar. One could be as revealing as the other, but we played it perfectly.

That night, as we sat down to an intimate family dinner, George thanked the comte, and me, his lovely wife, for our kindness in hosting this meeting. Though the comte had not decided whether he would support George's proposition, if he did, his courtesy as host would go down in history as a key factor in more deeply uniting the two nations.

"Between you and me," George told my husband in a voice too low for the servants, "His Majesty is most keen for this treaty to come about. If I can persuade you and the other French emissary, the king will be so delighted with my success that he will grant me any boon I desire. Not," he added, "that I do it in hopes of reward."

The comte laughed. "Perhaps not, but kingly rewards are always appreciated, if all too rare. If you could ask a boon, what would it be?"

George's eyes flickered toward me, fast and bright as the twitch of a candle flame.

"My heart's desire depends on the whim of another, so we shall see."

The comte, not really listening, said, "Land is always good. Better than titles. Well, I will tell you fair, I have not decided in your favor yet. But you may make your king's proposal when our friend arrives, and we shall see."

The French emissary wouldn't be arriving until the day after next. George stole one moment with me, not really alone, by my side looking out the window at the grounds. He spoke loudly of garden design, then quietly arranged the time and place of our tryst the following evening.

"Let me claim what should have been mine all along, my love. I swear I have lain with no woman. I'm saving myself for you."

The next morning, the day of our scheduled liaison, I kissed the comte goodbye as he went to examine his bull. Afterward, I noticed that George went for a walk. As it was a pleasant day, I did, too. I find that a day spent traipsing through the outdoors is never without reward. There is always something interesting to discover. Afterward, I went home to write several letters. Or rather, one letter, several times.

That evening, bathed and refreshed after my long, solitary hike, I snuck and skulked to my rendezvous in the castle library. It was a small place, and the only room in the castle I could guarantee my husband would never enter.

How my hands trembled as I waited for my old love to come to me! How my heart fluttered when the little-used door squeaked open, and there he was in all his glory before me.

I flew into his arms, and in a frenzy kissed his cheeks, his jaw, the little mustache he had grown. "I have thought about this moment for so long," I murmured into his throat.

"You thought about me?" he asked. "Even after all that I did to you, you still could harbor a fond thought of me?"

"George, I loved you from the first moment I saw you, wholly and truly, and I never wavered. You crushed me, broke me, but despite my better judgment, I never stopped loving you. It shamed me. I made myself curse your name, wish all manner of ill on you. But through it all, like a whisper in the darkness, was the little hope—no, the faith—that we would be together again. That the ending I had long dreamed about would finally come to pass."

"What you say fills me with joy. It is beyond my wildest dreams!"

"I have done bad things in my life, George. More than even you know. But if you can forgive me, if you can take me away from all this, I can erase my past. Oh, George, can we be the children we once were, in that garden of innocence? Will you pluck a perfect flower for me once again?"

"I will," he said, not remembering how that ended. "But . . . if these negotiations fail, I can do nothing. If I cannot convince your husband to sign his approval, the king will never follow suit. My success, and our future happiness, rests in the result of the meeting tomorrow. How helpful it would be if, when the queen regent's emissary arrives, your husband is already persuaded. I trust it would be an easy matter then to convince the queen regent's man. The comte is well respected. His word, his opinion will hold great weight."

He paused, and I said nothing.

"Your husband loves you."

Still, I said nothing.

"If you were to . . . Oh, my love, if anything goes wrong in this we can never be together! Wouldn't it be a sin to come this close to finding happiness, only to lose it through your husband's stubbornness. If I go home victorious, my reward will be your annulment. We can marry, at last!"

"Is it possible?" I asked in awe.

"With the king's favor, anything is possible."

"He will let you marry? I thought he promised to kill me if you didn't forsake me."

George smiled ruefully. "Kings are fickle things. There is a handsome young man newly come to court, a black-haired, blue-eyed devil who caught the king's eye. I believe the king would happily put me aside."

"And we can marry?"

He nodded. "But only if this treaty succeeds." He took a deep breath, girding himself. "Will you help me? I know a woman in bed can sway a man as the best-argued case cannot. Oh, it pains me to think of you in his arms. But, for our sakes, can you not find a way to sway him with your infinite charms? Is there not some special trick, some request you have heretofore denied him, that might make him lend his support to this treaty?"

He looked at me in a way that made me feel beautiful, cherished. I nodded. "After what you have done, of course I will do anything within my power to make sure you and I both have the fates we deserve."

"Oh, bless you, my love!" He clasped my face in his hands and kissed my forehead, then lowered his head to my breast, kissing, biting through the fabric. "You will be mine now, won't you?" He pulled at my bodice, but it was a bit too high to be shifted.

"Here," I said, eagerly offering him the laces. I was flushed and panting, excited by what would come next. It seemed to me that the most pivotal moment in all my life was at hand.

A tug, a muttered curse of frustration when the cord snagged, and then my bodice was loosened enough for him to tug it down and cup his hands beneath my breasts, lifting them like prize treasures.

Then he froze, staring at my left breast.

And smiled, and dropped them like they were lumps of foulness.

"You have had some adventures since we parted, then. I take it your husband doesn't know."

I bowed my head, shook it.

"You've only bedded him in the dark? Had him lift your skirts, or taken you from behind, while you stayed dressed? Is there no end to a woman's guile? I wouldn't think it possible that a fleur-de-lis criminal brand could be hidden after consummation. But you must have, for if he knew, he would have cast you in the gutter." He took my chin in his fingers, pinching cruelly, and made me look at him. "This simplifies matters considerably, my sweet. Your situation is thus: you will find a way to persuade, or force, your husband to support this treaty, or I will strip you bare before him and let him know he married a criminal."

"You wouldn't!"

"My future rests in this treaty. That was no lie. If it fails, I will destroy you."

My lower lip trembled. "But . . . you love me!"

"My mother told me that you were clever, Clarice. Do try to dredge up an ounce of sense. Love you?" He laughed.

I looked at him with glistening eyes. "I will do as you ask," I told him. "What choice do you leave me. But I loved you once, you know. Truly loved you, and believed in you."

"The more fool you."

"So, the other emissary comes tomorrow, and you will negotiate for two, three days? I will make sure my husband takes your side." Did he notice how calmly I was talking? He should have been alarmed at the lack of hysterics. He was that secure, was my George. "Only, if you stay that long, do you think you can beat the letter back to England?"

I batted my dry eyelashes at him, and he regarded me, nonplussed.

"Well, not one letter, of course. The beauty of having a rich husband is that you can hire several riders, send them by different roads, book them passage from different ports, instruct them to deliver the letter to different people. But one letter? That would be foolish. And you did advise me to show sense, didn't you? Oh, how nice to have a clever man like you to advise me."

"Letter? Letters? What letters?"

"Why, the ones detailing how as soon as you have support for this trade treaty, you plan to sell the advance information to Spain, and Portugal, and the Turks. Oh, my weak little woman's head can't quite grasp the details, but if I have it right, I believe that knowing a price of some commodity is about to drop for two countries with a new agreement, and rise for everyone else, can be used to make a profit. Particularly if one knows about it before everyone else. I admit numbers were never my strong suit, but treachery is, and you were planning to sell advance knowledge of this very secret treaty between England and France to the highest bidder. And the second highest, and the third."

"You lying cunt, it's not true!" He lunged at me, but I'd already corrected my recent negligence, and in a trice, my dagger was at his throat.

"Steady, my love. Do you think the king will be pleased when he finds out?"

"You can't tell him. You wouldn't dare." He looked suddenly crafty. "And I'll tell you why. You might want to destroy me, but you could never live with yourself if you condemned"—he paused for dramatic effect—"your own father!"

Then he waited for my shock.

Poor George. It is hard to see masterful plans crumble. "My father, the man who sent me to a convent-prison? My father, the man who set me to falling in love with *you*? Oh no, it would wound me to the quick to condemn him." His gaping mouth was a joy to behold. Even the most beautiful man loses his looks when wearing that expression.

"How did you know all this?" George gasped.

"You were too secure. I simply followed you, and listened at your window. How lovely to see you and my father in partnership again. What kind of ass sets up his partner on his adversary's own estate? You wanted to get the news out the moment the treaty was approved, right? If only

you had left my father twenty miles away, you would have been successful. Why, I might have even been swayed by your false apology. But you
had to run to him and tell him about me. You weren't secure enough
to just carry out your plan without guidance." I shook my head. "Your
mother said you were clever. Do try to dredge up an ounce of sense. Trust
you?" I laughed and poked the dagger against his throat.

"Go now, without a word of explanation. Let my husband and the
emissary believe you were called back, or were murdered, or anything
you like. Only go. You may yet intercept the letters, if your spy network
is any good. There are only so many ports, so many ships to England.
Perhaps you can stop them all." I prodded until a scarlet drop welled. "If
you leave now."

He was red and frantic, huffing and ugly and distraught. "You can't
do this! Call back the letters, or I'll tell your husband."

I smiled slowly, wickedly. "Tell him, don't tell him, it matters little to
me. He is no danger. Do you think to threaten me? Tell me, George,
how many men have you killed?"

He said nothing. "I thought not. Now scurry along, and do your best
to survive the terrible things that love can bring you. I have. Will you?"

He gasped and shook, tried to speak, but in the end he stormed out,
and when I returned to my room, I looked out my window and saw a
lone figure riding away.

I could have bluffed. It would have worked just as well if I had not
actually sent the letters. But I *had* sent them, and the next morning at
breakfast I imagined the possible fate of the two men who betrayed me.
The penalty for treason is drawing and quartering. First, they would be
hung, not with a sudden drop to break their necks, but lifted with a slow
strangling, the most terrible death. But the executioner (a terrifying one
like my own executioner, I hoped) would watch them carefully, cutting
them down when they had suffered to the extreme but had not quite
expired. Then, oh, then their bellies would be sliced open and their guts
drawn out hand over hand before their very eyes. A skilled practitioner
could keep them alive even through that. Then, the butchery. For dra-

matic effect, each limb would be tied to a horse, the traitor torn apart. Other times, though, in the name of simplicity, the body would simply be hacked to bits and displayed around town. Had I wished, I could soon make a quick jaunt to London to see my former love's head on a spike, see my father look down on me one last time.

I felt almost nothing at the thought of my father dying. He had not been a father to me. I felt no affection for him, nor yet, in truth, all that much hate. In that deliberately calloused mind-set I'd forced myself into, he was just a man who had wronged me and had to be dealt with. I did not dwell on the barbaric horror of his possible execution, did not revel, only crossed him off a mental list.

As for George, well, I remembered the fate of Robert Carr and didn't really think the king's lover would be executed. Enough that he would be frightened, perhaps deposed. For George, the newly minted Duke of Buckingham, a fall from grace would be worse than death.

When I thought of George, his pretty face stricken with terror as he tried to lie his way out of disgrace, I could not help but laugh aloud. My husband, returned from his bulls, glanced up from his accounts. "What is it, my sweet?"

In that moment, he looked at me with such a simple, distracted tenderness, a kindness, that it struck me to the core. I thought how patient he had been with me, far beyond what could be expected of any virile man who needed an heir.

Was it the thought of his tenderness that decided for me? Or was it the thought of my revenge so perfectly executed? The image of George, that bastard, suffering on the gibbet, his parts sundered, made me ready.

"Tonight," I told my husband.

"What?" he asked, distracted by figures.

"Tonight," I repeated. "I am ready."

I had all of his attention now. "Truly?"

I felt powerful, indomitable . . . and aroused. My breath came hard, and my skin seemed to tingle. "On second thought," I told him, and saw his look of hope start to crumble. It felt like the greatest gift I could possibly bestow when I told him, "On second thought, why not right now?"

Laughing, incredulous, he threw aside his accounts, forgot his numbers, and swooped me up in his arms. I don't think his mouth left mine all the way to our bedchamber. A bemused steward tried to waylay him with some task or another, but Olivier waved him aside.

"I will tell him you are engaged in more pressing matters," said the steward with a conspiratorial smirk. I think our tenants loved seeing their popular lord and lady happy, and I knew this bawdy sight would be fodder for many a tavern joke. I didn't care. At last I felt safe enough to abandon myself to joy with my husband.

He carried me into our room and tossed me lightly on the bed. "How delightfully you bounce," he said, eyeing my softest parts hungrily. But on the last bounce, before he could pounce, I sprang up entirely and drew the heavy curtains over the single small window.

"Leave them open," he protested. "I want to see everything you've been hiding these last months."

"No, no!" I said, laughing. "I would be too timid in the daylight. It must be as night."

"I will shoot out the sun!" he cried in his glee. "I will shake my fist at it so it hides its burning eye! Oh, Anne, at last! How I love you!"

"The fire, too," I insisted before he could resume his caresses. With a mock-annoyed grumble, he heaped ashes over the low hearth flames. I was glad these old castles were built for defense rather than light and comfort. The window was little more than a slit with a grate to keep out bats, and even at midmorning, the curtained room was dark.

"We're exposing parts that don't care for the cold," my lord said.

"Then you will just have to find some means to warm them," I purred, and at last lay on the bed and pulled him to me. His sigh as he tenderly unlaced my gown made me feel like I was a good woman again. Perhaps my definition of goodness did not match his, but what did that matter? I was strong and clever, loving and loyal and passionate. If I lied, it was to protect his happiness and mine. Where is the sin in that?

I was exposed, open as my body enveloped him, melted into him. I had feared that loving him would be demeaning, a kind of surrender. But I found it was like surrendering yourself to a galloping horse, yielding to the rushing thrill, being carried off . . . not powerless, but a part of something greater than yourself.

When we lay slicked with sweat afterward, limbs intertwined, he kissed me like a benediction and said, "You have given me all the happiness I need for my entire life. I shall never know a finer moment than this."

The wind shifted the heavy curtain, and the warm sweat dried with chill prickles on my skin.

We were going stag hunting that morning, my husband and I, but our revels delayed us until past noon. Reluctantly, with promises for that night, Olivier left me abed while he went to tidy up affairs before the hunt. There were always petitioners to see, papers to read, accounts to balance. People think a great lord leads a life of cream and honey, and there are some who use their position only for decadent pursuits, but a proper nobleman must work for his pleasure and continued prosperity, and labors as many hours as a bricklayer.

A bit sore in unaccustomed places, and flushed with a languid heaviness in my limbs, I almost wanted to stay abed. But the prospect of a thrilling ride roused me. It would be like the earliest days of our courtship, racing across the dales on our lathered horses. I smiled at the thought of the secret looks we would exchange at the memory of our morning. God help me, I blushed!

I perched on my lovely gray mare, waiting for my lord. His groom held his mount, not the roan war-horse today but a lighter dappled gelding who could better handle the jumps. It pranced with high-strung nervous energy as we waited for him. We were the only nobility, but the lawn was crowded with minions to flush the stag, kennel men to handle the dogs. They held the eager hounds on long ropes. They were elegant coursing hounds who would chase the stag while we pursued on horse-back, then hold it at bay for the comte to kill. The death didn't matter to me, but I was excited to ride, with my husband at my side. I felt like a new life had begun.

At last, Olivier burst from the castle, looking darkly distracted. Of course, he must have learned that George Villiers had left, and believed the negotiations ruined. And the French representative due to arrive this very afternoon! I had no interest in the negotiations, these fortunes made and lost among nations. I only cared that it mattered a great deal to my husband. Well, I would charm the French ambassador this evening, who-ever he was, and do my best to smooth things over. I thought it counted for very little in the grand scheme of things. After all, what had I to do with grand schemes anymore? All I wanted was this quiet, happy life—peace, punctuated by the excitement of the hunt . . . or the bed.

Well, the ride would do him good, and if he needed more distraction from the cares of rule, I could provide it tonight. I blew him a kiss, but I don't think he saw, occupied as he was with tightening his saddle straps and chastising the groom. I thought I could read him well, and deter-mined to let him fume for a while until he'd galloped off his ire. We could find a moment alone on the hunt when surely I could smooth his ruffled feathers. How delightful it would be to make love under the open sky. Impossible, I knew, but maybe some moonless night by the palest starlight . . .

It was almost winter again, and the ground was damp from the light frost just melted by the sun. Never had I seen such a perfect cloudless sky. It was as if heaven had finally condescended to look down upon me. I hoped the view was as lovely from above as it was from below.

Everything felt fresh and new, the crisp coolness and the feeling of renewal more reminiscent of spring than creeping winter. In the transi-tional times, who can tell which season is fleeing, which stalking forth?

We rode for the pleasure of riding, and before long, the horn sounded. A stag had been spotted. We wheeled and raced for the sound, dreaming of death. Then, far across an open field, I spied the stag, a huge, pale beast, tossing his rack defiantly. He heard the tumult of hounds and men and was alert, but not yet afraid. Confident in his towering strength, the sharp tines of his antlers, he never dreamed that he was prey.

Between us and the open field was broken ground, hedges, rocks. "This way!" the comte called out, indicating a long way around over flat turf. But I was thrilling with life, aroused by the speed, the heaving horse beneath me, and I tapped my mare with my heels, heading for the shortest path.

"Wait!" my husband cried, but I thought he just wanted to win, so I leaned low over my mare's neck and whispered encouragement. We took the hedge like a falcon, swooping at speed without a jostle.

The rocks, though . . .

She caught her hoof and went down with a scream. Have you ever heard a horse scream? I loved that animal, and when I heard that sound, I knew it meant her death. She might rise, but she would never do so on four good legs. That's what I was thinking of when I went flying over her head, when I saw her huge body flipping over me, heard the crack of breaking bone.

A thud and a crushing, and then blackness . . .

I awoke to a scratching at my throat, and thought it was the grass. When I opened my eyes, the azure sky was looking dispassionately down on me through the branches of a tree.

"What happened?" I asked blearily, then it came back to me: the screaming horse, the tumbling. My head hurt, and when I breathed in, there was a sharp pain in my side, but I thought I could stand. Soon.

"Your horse went down, and when I reached you, you were unconscious, gasping for breath." It was hard to see him against the brightness of the sky. His voice sounded so distant. I shaded my eyes to see him more clearly. "Lie still," he said.

My head was ringing, throbbing, and his words barely registered. I felt like I was about to vomit, and my main concern was to combat that indignity. I scrolled through all Maman had told me about head wounds and broken ribs, and tried to tell Olivier what to do, but he hushed me with three fingertips over my lips.

"Oh, that mouth," he breathed. "That sensual, lying mouth."

"What?"

"You told me he was dead. Your priest. The man you called your stepbrother. That was enough lie to condemn you, but I forgave you because of the pain you said he had inflicted on you. I was glad to kill him myself, for your sake. To kill the man who had harmed my beloved, who told such lies about you. Do you remember what he said? He called you a whore, a criminal. Calumny, I thought. No, not thought—knew! I trusted you with all my heart, for of all people I knew that you would never betray my honor."

Dimly, my mind registered alarm, but I was in such a daze it seemed like a dream. "Lies," I said weakly. "Let me explain."

"I would have, my love. I would have heard any excuse you had to give, and welcomed it, just for the pleasure of having you in my bed again. If you had told me, then perhaps . . . But you made me kill an innocent man!"

"Felix? He was not innocent. He . . ."

"I executed him for his accusations against you. Beat him to death with my own hands, because he called you a criminal."

I struggled to sit up as bolts of pain and light seared across my eyes. That tickling, scratching sensation at my throat grew more irksome, but I reached my hands toward him, not to my throat. "Thank you," I whispered. "Now we can move forward and forget . . ."

"I did not believe he spoke the truth," my comte went on. "If he was lying, I had to punish him for those lies about my wife. And if he was telling the truth . . ." He leaned closer to my face, and I felt the scratch of his cheek, the stubble that had delighted my skin only an hour or two before. "If he was telling the truth, then the world could never know."

"I'm not a criminal! I swear!"

"And then this morning, a letter, unsigned and in a disguised hand, slipped under my door. I didn't find it until I left you, after . . ." He swallowed hard. "Do you know what it said? 'Your wife is a murderess. Beware the dagger at her breast, and the viper in her tongue.' The duke and his entourage rode off into the night without a word, so I can only guess who wrote the missive."

"Last night he was drunk, and he . . ." I could not concoct a lie fast enough. Damn his eyes, I should have killed him when I had the chance. What a fool I was. If he believed himself ruined, what did he have to lose by exposing me?

"Ah, Anne, I would have believed you if you said the sky was the sea and the devil my savior, as drunk as I was on the pleasure of your flesh. You could have fobbed me off with any tale. But then you fell from your horse, and as you lay gasping for breath, and I thought my love was dying, I cut the strings of your bodice, loosened your dress."

He loomed into view, and I saw him clutching a rope loosely in his hands. My fingers leaped to my throat, and I found the other end of the hemp rope around my neck. "What are you doing?"

"I've sent everyone away."

"What? Why?" I sat up, and my hands, falling nervelessly from the rope, brushed the bare skin of my breasts.

He had seen my brand.

"Justice has been rendered," he said, so flatly. "The courts of France have tried you, and found you guilty. You have been marked as a criminal. Now justice will be executed."

I felt a tug on the rope as he flung his end over a looming tree branch.

"My lord—my love! Don't do this. It was not the court but a merciless fiend acting alone who branded me. Let me explain!"

"There's nothing to explain. You tricked me into marrying you. And if he told the truth about you being a criminal, are you a whore, too? While I thought I was protecting a traumatized woman, were you cuckolding me with every man on my estate?"

"Don't speak so, my love. You sound like a stranger. You can't mean it!" He looked at me like I was a thing, an object, and jerked the rope. I yelped and came up to my knees, my ribs stabbing.

I reached for the knife in my busk, but my fingers found only empty wood.

"I found your weapon." He brandished it, then dropped it so it impaled the earth between his feet.

"My husband, please!" I gasped, desperate. "Yes, I hid something from you, but if you'll give me but a moment, I can make everything clear. I'm truly not a criminal, I swear. It was the priest! He stole from the Church, and his brother accused me."

A vicious jerk cut off my speech, and until I scrambled to my feet, I couldn't breathe. "Shut up," he said, in that same icy, flat voice. "I thought you pure, Anne. And yet, now I think on it, you were such a wanton with me this morning, I should have known then that you were a harlot."

For an instant I forgot about the rope around my neck. I lunged at him as best I could, a savage snarl curling my lips, kicking at him in a fury.

"You long for months to bed me, yearn for my flesh, my touch, and when I finally give myself to you with joy and abandon, you call me harlot for my enthusiasm? If I'd wept and lay still beneath you, would you have thought me pure now?"

I might as well have been a grub arguing with the plow. Without expression, he heaved the rope slowly, cutting me off with a gurgle. I stood on my toes, my mouth stretched in a breathless scream, my hands clawing at the hemp rope. "You are a criminal on my land, and as is my right by long custom, I condemn you to death." Another pull, a fraction of an inch, and the rope cut into me, burning like a brand all around the front of my throat. "You are my wife, my property, mine to dispose of, and I condemn you to death."

The ice in his eyes, the frost in his voice told me how utterly he believed what he said. He had loved me only as he loved his land or horses: he wanted the best, as a matter of pride, but if the horse went lame or the land barren, he would dispose of it. I had been blinded by the fact that he loved me after his fashion. I didn't realize until too late that his love had the narrowest limits, and I had stepped outside of them. He was just like every other man. The rage within my breast as much as the rope stole the breath left in me. There was nothing left to whisper those soft words Lady Mary taught me can sway a man, even if I could choke back the venom I felt. My bulging eyes and livid face could not be coaxed into a countenance to seduce him. My breasts, which all men stare at hungrily, were exposed, bearing the mark of my crime.

My toes dangled, striving for the earth. Above me, a hawk screamed. I had no air, but I mouthed his name: "Olivier."

He looked at me one last time, his face stone, and walked away while I kicked inches above the earth.

My life rolled before me, scenes on hillsides traversed by the fastest steed. Most fleeting was my youth, the only happy time. Everything else was sweet turned sour, or bitter outright. Love that was not love. Ambition that brought me nothing. Lovemaking without faith. Murder. Blood. Poison. Death. Lies.

All over now.

It had been a long day, and now night had fallen.

I could rest.

Chapter 18

1628

"To be killed twice by the same man—that is quite a feat." We stand some distance apart from each other, like duelists. Athos believes he is the only combatant armed. "But then, according to legend, Milady de Winter is capable of almost anything."

We stand on the far bank of the Lys. Athos holds the executioner's sword in both his hands, testing its heft. He is accustomed to lighter dueling blades, but this is a broadsword, a rude chopping weapon. "You have yet made no charge against me, husband. What say you now that we are alone?" My voice is a purr, my bearing as calm as if we were in his bedroom. Over the murmur of wind through the water reeds I can hear the executioner protesting, the grunts and thuds of an unequal struggle as he does his best to reach me. A true professional, he. The executioner will not be content to let another person do his job.

"You are a seducer, an assassin, a spy," he spits out. "Deny it!"

"I cannot deny it. But I was not so when first you killed me. I was a girl ill-used."

"A liar, a criminal."

"Your wife, and yet you never asked about my supposed crime—not even now."

"The brand on your breast is tale enough." His eyes linger there, and I hear a heavy breath that is almost a sigh. "Very well, then. We have time. Make your confession. It will be good for your soul." He shouts across the river to the other Musketeers, "Give the executioner his purse and tell him I no longer have need of his services. I will carry out her sentence myself."

The executioner breaks free and surges to the riverbank, objecting, fuming, but the Musketeers drag him back. "You cannot deprive me of my rightful vocation!" he shouts from behind his mask across the rushing flow. His sanguine hood has fallen back over his shoulders, exposing shaggy, sandy hair. "Else you commit murder, not justice."

How strange to hear my own words in the executioner's mouth.

Athos flaps the cardinal's letter of marque. "I have the approbation of heaven itself. Get yourselves back to Paris, my friends, and tell Cardinal Richelieu that his serpent has been beheaded."

They retreat, dragging the unwilling executioner back into the forest, and before long, the riverbank is still, save for the nightjars and distant thunder. We are alone.

I hold up my bound hands and shrug. "It is better than the rope, at least." Better than swinging empurpled, soiling oneself as one twitches in lingering agony. "Beheading is a royal death, reserved for the aristocracy."

"You were ever a lady, no matter your origins," he admits. "I was wrong to hang you. I was young, rash, hurt."

"Wrong?" I ask.

"Not wrong to kill you. But you deserved a gentler death. The sword will be quick."

You see, he grows by glacial degrees. The years have not taught him compassion or kindness, exactly, only a twisted, misogynistic sort of mercy.

"I never hurt you, never betrayed you, Olivier. It was your pride that suffered, your sense of honor."

"A man has no greater prize than his honor."

I laugh, wiping the tears from my eyes with my bound hands. "Honor? Pride? They are wax fruits! However much a man may eat, they give him no sustenance. You wrap yourself in that threadbare cloak and think yourself in princely raiment. What poor things pride and honor are compared to love." My scoffing voice grows gravid. "For you loved me, Olivier. And I . . . I loved you."

Did I? I could have, I think, if trust and honesty had blossomed. But I have never scorned a lie in a good cause.

"I won't be poisoned by your words," he says with effort, as the sailor shuns the sirens. Tie yourself to the mast, Olivier, lest you dash yourself on the rocks. I fall to my knees, holding out my bound arms in supplication, coincidentally offering my bosom at a better angle of inspection. His eyes do not disappoint.

"I could be a wife to you still, my husband." Absurd, you will say, but when death is creeping close, you will use any means to keep it at bay. Weave a fantasy, and death itself will stop its scythe in fascination. Scheherazade knew this lesson. Athos lets the tip of his broadsword touch the earth.

"Perhaps we were not suited then," I press. "You wanted an ingenue who was yet clever enough to match you, or even to best you. Poor lad, when you found me like an orchid among the country cowslips, didn't you stop to think I might be difficult, need careful husbandry? But now look at us. You are grown old and bitter, worldly and wise. You need a woman of power and resolve. Think what you could accomplish with a clever woman at your side. You were a child then. Now you are a man, ready for a woman such as me."

He takes a step closer, and I drop my hands and insinuate myself nearer to his legs. It is awkward to scoot seductively through the muddy turf with tied hands, but somehow, I manage it. "Because I appeared innocent in your eyes, you did not take what you wanted of me on our wedding night. You waited for me to come to you. Now I am your legal wife, and no innocent. You can have me now, legally, freely, and I have not the power to refuse. Do you remember how you yearned for me? The torture it was to deny yourself when I lay in your bed, bound to you, a fruit for the plucking? Yet you did not pluck until I was ready. You were a good man. An honorable man. You aren't anymore."

"You made me so!" he cries, and I thrill at the sound of despair in his voice. A broken man can be reshaped to any purpose.

"We are more alike than you care to believe, Olivier." My voice is husky as I reach for him. "Obey the law of God, and man, and take me as your wife."

"No," he breathes, but it is an argument, not a statement. He is begging to be swayed.

"The others are gone. Here and now, claim me as yours."

He looks around desperately for succor, but his Musketeers and minions have vanished, the masked executioner nowhere in sight.

"Had you but claimed me on our wedding night, seen my mark then, we would have reconciled. You know it, Olivier. Or if I'd told you after we at last made love. If you were lying sated in my arms, with my scent on your skin, our limbs intertwined . . . you think you would not have heard my sad tale to its ending, seen how I was ill-used and innocent, and forgiven me?"

"Tell me, then!" he says, reaching down to touch my brow as I kneel before him. "Tell me how the priest lied to me, how you came to be branded as a criminal."

But I smile and shake my head. "What does it matter now? Whatever we were then, we are different now. I changed you, but oh, the transformation you brought about in me, Olivier. When you killed me, I was resurrected! We are not Olivier and Anne anymore, but the cruel and brave Musketeer Athos, and the diabolical spy Milady de Winter. The time for explanations and innocence is long past, my love. Don't you see how the long, strange journeys of our lives have brought us together again? Now, when we fit each other like a dagger and scabbard." My eyes burn into his as he imagines the joining. My bound hands caress the exposed flesh of my throat, trailing lower, offering all.

"Athos, I am yours," I whisper as he throws aside his broadsword. His hand reaches for my breast . . .

And snatches out the dagger I was just about to sneak out and plunge into his thigh.

He grips my hair, wrenching my head back as he presses the edge below my ear. The steel tinkles in faint fairy song against the dangling ruby cluster of my earrings. "Your wiles won't work on me, woman. Other men may be the dupes of your fair face and soft body, but there is no lust left in me, nor love. You destroyed any chance of happiness I ever had. I am only glad to know I did the same to you. I see your life of scheming and cruelty, of secrets and poison, and I think: *Good. I may not have killed her body, but she has been a walking corpse, like me.* I rejoice that you never knew love, but only base mercenary seduction. I revel to know that you have been hunted, harried, without friends, without family, without comfort. And when you quit this life, at my hand, perhaps I can at last find all of those things for myself."

I look up at him with tears in my eyes. "Oh, Olivier, how wrong you are . . ."

The dagger presses, and I think madly, *Not edge, you imbecile. An assassin kills with the point.*

"Hold, in the king's name!"

I hear the slosh of water-filled boots, and there is the executioner of Lille stomping along the riverbank toward us, a masked demon. "You have violated the law of the land, Musketeer," he growls. "You have usurped the authority granted to me by patent of His Majesty himself, to render final justice in this land. What matters a scribbling from the cardinal? I am the master of death. You have pronounced sentence. Now your work is done. Killing is not vengeance." From beneath his mask, the executioner flashes me a hint of a smile. Oh, it is about vengeance, I think, and tremble to know that I am in the final moments of my life. So long it seemed once, how brief now! And when I think about what is coming next, now that the executioner is here . . .

I bow my head to hide my expression. The movement makes Athos's knife—my knife—slice a bit into my skin, but I no longer care.

"Begone, sir, and let justice be done," the executioner says, and I can sense his eyes on my body like a physical touch. Athos stands, and I feel his knees trembling against me before he staggers away a step. "I know this woman better than you. Her history has been revealed to me, her every action, and I know to an exactness whether it was excusable. I know her inmost heart. I more than anyone deserve to be the reaper who cuts her off from this life. Go. I will take her deeper into the woods where she may make her peace with God."

"No!" Athos protests. "I must see her die. The last time . . ."

The executioner grabs the great hacking broadsword and hefts it in two hands. "The rope may fail. The sword, never. In but a few moments, Milady de Winter will be gone. Up, woman!"

Like an automaton, I rise and move to go with my executioner. Then I turn back to Athos where he stands dumbfounded, still holding my dagger.

"I forgive you, Olivier," I say, and wonder if it feels as false and hypocritical to him as it had to me but a moment before when he deigned to forgive me. "Promise me one thing—that you will pray for me." Fumbling with my tied hands, I take the red and black beaded rosary from my pocket and slip it over his head. He flinches at my touch. "Carry it with you, always, and pray for the woman who wronged you, but whom you also wronged."

He shoves Maman's dagger into his belt and clutches the rosary. Then he brings it to his trembling lips and kisses it. "I will pray for your soul every day of my life. By Holy Mary, I swear it." As is his habit, his lips linger on the beads, mouthing them in succession like a ruminating cow telling the rosary.

I have nothing left of my old life. With resigned steps, I follow the executioner to the next life.

Chapter 19

1616

I should have known there is no rest for the wicked. Particularly if there is still someone left in the world who has faith in their goodness. Just when I was getting comfortable with the thought of death, I heard the telltale snick of a blade being drawn. A whistle through the air, and I fell in a heap on the earth.

Then hands were at my throat, mine and another's, my own getting in the way of more practiced help as I gouged my own flesh trying to get myself free of the choking hemp. The world throbbed in a red sea; my eyes felt like they would explode as my blood surged back on its proper course and my head cleared. It was a struggle to breathe, and I sucked in a fraction of the cool air I longed for as a voice said, "Easy, easy."

I looked up, and there was Denys crouched at my side, dressed in all the finery of his rank. A war-horse stamped and snorted nearby. Of course, he was the French ambassador come for the aborted negotiations.

I tried to babble out my tale, but he said, "Hush, I know. I saw."

He saw, and he didn't stop it? He saw the hurt disbelief in my eyes.

"I would have intervened sooner, if he'd stayed to watch . . . or if he had any knowledge of how to conduct a proper hanging." I grimaced, remembering the way Mrs. Turner's neck had snapped when she was dropped on the gibbet at Tyburn. "But he chose the lingering method, and I knew there would be time to save you. I could not do it sooner. It was better that he should think you dead. Now when we go, he will not pursue you, but only think the villagers who love you so well have cut you down and given you a secret burial. I will spread money to make sure it is so."

"Go?" I gasped, latching on to that single word. "Where?"

"Wherever you like."

"Paris?"

"Only if you wish it." He pushed my hair from my brow, then lightly touched the abrasions at my throat.

"You still want me to be a spy?" I asked with some bitterness.

He looked at me so tenderly it made my eyes grow heavy, welling with a feeling I didn't believe possible after my ordeals.

"I don't care where we go, or what we do," he said. "I don't want you to be a spy. I want *you*."

He kissed me lightly, not wanting to hurt me, but it was too tender a kiss for the violence of the emotions I felt at that moment. I had been reborn, a phoenix, and knew exactly what I wanted.

"We go to Paris," I declared. "I will go to Rue Poisson and say, '*Je m'en vais chercher un grand peut-être*,' and like Maman, like her mother before her, I will be a spy for France. I will be strong, and fearless, and wise. I will never be helpless again, nor ashamed of the choices I've made. No man will own me, not my body or my heart. No man will bind me so that I cannot escape. But, Denys, . . ."

"Yes, Clarice?"

I looked at the man who had been my friend all my life, who knew all my secrets. The man who always judged me justly, who did not let me be weak but lent me his strength if I faltered. The man I had laughed with, and fought with. The man I could not help but love. Anyone else would say the last thing he had to offer me was peace and security. I knew what the life of a spy, with him, would be.

And yet as I looked into those jasper eyes, I knew that whatever dangers lay ahead of me, there was a peace deeper than that, a security that went beyond physical safety. He was the deep breath after the long struggle, the cool flagon after a parched march. Whatever the future might hold, I could bear it, because he would be my partner.

"However, I may choose to bind myself to someone." I pulled him to me and kissed him, fierce and hard, then lingeringly, touching him in wonder, daring to dream of the future at last.

For a long time, we march through the woods. I listen expectantly, but hear no footsteps of anyone coming after us. At last, we come to a break in the trees. The executioner of Lille grips my arm, halting me and gesturing wordlessly toward the clearing where all I deserve awaits me. He unties the leather cords at my wrist, and I reach up to unmask him.

"How could he not recognize you?" I ask. "He was your friend in youth. How did he not see past a mere mask?"

"The world is blind," the Comte de Wardes answers, taking me in his arms. "It is easier for people that way."

Connie was right. Only death could free us from the cardinal's clutches, from the great and terrible duty of being the *one* fighting for the good of the *all*. But what could kill Milady? Only a fiend from her past, a brutal and heartless Musketeer bent on revenge.

A Musketeer who never would have known of my existence unless I willed it.

A man who never would have thought to kill me if I had not presented the opportunity to him.

A proud and stupid drunkard who never could have captured me if
I had not allowed him to.

Milady needed a nemesis, and the cardinal needed to believe I feared
for my life. No average man could hope to best me—the cardinal would
never believe it. So Athos and his Musketeers had to be built into veritable demigods, noble heroes of righteousness. I played them all, letting
them believe at each step that they had, through their own wit and daring, gotten the best of me. Slowly, I seemed to be the fox brought to bay.
But look how the hounds barked and bit to my exact order!

A trio of Musketeers and a half-grown Gascon defeat Milady de
Winter? Who would credit it? But now, thanks to my most subtle machinations, history will record the tale those men shall tell. In taverns
throughout the land, they will repeat the story of my treachery, and my
defeat. The innocent Connie killed through spite and jealousy, the no-
blest lords laid low, the monarchy itself manipulated. And fighting that
embodiment of feminine evil, the heroes whose names will survive the
centuries. No one will know the true tale of Milady de Winter, and when
she dies, only her most heinous exploits will be remembered.

Exactly as I want it.

Milady de Winter is dead. The story becomes the truth. Now I am
reborn.

The pink in Connie's cheeks is more champagne than strawberry, and
she moves more carefully than usual as she holds the gurgling, giggling
bundle who seems thrilled at this late-night adventure. Other than that,
I see few aftereffects from the herbs I dosed her with. It is the dose I
would give someone with a severe injury, slowing the heart and lowering
the body temperature to reduce blood loss, inducing a near catatonic
state so that I could sew or cauterize their wounds. To a rash Musketeer
looking for the worst, her pulse would have been undetectable for an
hour or so. They mourned her death, vowed vengeance . . . and were

away and after me by the time our friends the nuns were reviving her with cold well water and fortified wine.

I was vastly relieved to see her well. It is one thing to use such strong potions on a person already grievously injured, who would die without treatment, and quite another to dose one's best friend with a drug that, with just a small miscalculation, might kill.

Now Connie had joined the ranks of ghosts, too. Madame Bona-cieux was dead.

Denys will end his life soon as well. When he hears of my demise, he will write a lamenting letter and cast himself into the turbulent sea. His body will never be recovered.

It is something of an irony for an assassin to find death so liberating.

I take my infant in my arms, and place him to my aching breast, feeling a surge through my entire body as he latches on: maternal ecstasy, the sudden certainty that a world askew has just settled into place.

"Denys saved you again," Connie needles playfully. "What a damsel in distress you are, Clarice! First he swoops in and snatches you from the convent . . ."

"I had my own plan of escape well under way then, as you recall, and in any case, it was my mother as much as him."

"Then he hacks you free from death's hempen squeeze."

"I grant him that," I concede. "It was the one time I was unable to save myself."

"What of a certain captain of the king's guards?" he asks as I snuggle up to his side.

"I let him save me occasionally just to make him happy," I say as he slips one hand around my waist, the other cupping the pulsing soft spot on our son's head. The little beggar frowns at the interruption of his long-delayed feast. Goat's milk has no doubt begun to pall.

"In this instance," Denys says, "I was only the instrument. She wielded me like a knife, so I claim no credit. This remarkable plan was all hers. In any one of those other occasions, though, she could have saved herself." Denys saved more than my life the morning of the stag hunt. That moment had been the nadir of my soul. Other times in my life have brought me just as close to death, but never before nor since had I been willing to accept it. I remember the overwhelming weariness as the noose tightened, the flashing memories of the wrongs I had done. Were they mere wrongs of judgment, I had wondered as life slipped away. Or was every bad action of my life a sign of a deeper corruption, a disease of the inner self? As my face turned purple and my muscles strained against the rope, I decided I was guilty. I was a monster who deserved death. It didn't matter that the world had shaped me. As I felt my choked pulse beat ever slower against the hemp, I blamed no one but myself. I deserved to die, I thought, and begged only for the mercy of a sword to hasten my end.

The sword came, and the mercy, but not the end.

Denys made me believe that no person is static. We are not ponds, stagnant and unchanging, but great rivers that twist and rush, sometimes flooding, sometimes drying. We wash away cities, we slow to trickles, dry to cracked riverbeds. We are swift and deep, or broad and shallow by turns. A river is not defined by the one single place where you leap into it, no more than an entire life is defined by any one moment, or any dozen moments. It flows ever onward, ever changing.

We went to Paris, and I began my life anew. As a spy I did, oh, terrible things. But I did them with open eyes and a firm, decided heart. I set rules for myself so that the innocent would never suffer by my actions. When necessary, I lied to and defied my spymaster.

No life is easy. Every choice requires some compromise. I made the best decisions I could. What soldier, what doctor, what mother cannot say the same thing? To live is to cause pain. I did my best to make sure that it was mostly to myself. The three Musketeers have killed far more people than I, mostly in frivolous duels. I have killed, mostly, for the good of my country, for the good of humanity. History will remember that I have made a few widows and orphans, it is true, but it will never know how many women are safe and happy, their farms un-burned, themselves un-raped, their children un-skewered because of my ostensible crimes. One woman, one agent acting in stealth, for the good of all.

At least, that is how I will remember my years as a spy. How others will remember Milady, I find I do not much care anymore. That life is slipping away.

We stand together in the clearing—a family. Denys, though I have not yet married him, the man who I have chosen for all my life to come. Merry Connie, the sister of my heart, also chosen from all the world. And this little bundle in my arms, now sated and bubbling milk down his chin. Not for me any longer the selfish *tous pour un*, nor yet the selfless *un pour tous*, but rather *nous pour nous*.

Horses stand waiting for us, stamping their feet at the morning mist rising from the grass. We will ride them only a few miles—infants are awkward on horseback—and then meet an eight-horse coach that waits to carry us to . . . I don't believe I'll tell you where. Not anywhere in Europe, I think. It is much smaller than you would imagine. Can you picture us in China, though? Or Russia? Or perhaps salty and sunburned on Barbados.

I see myself growing sleek and content. Planting. Baking. Perhaps Denys will take up the pipe, and breed prize bullocks. Connie will have a string of lovers, or maybe, in her own contentment, just one. Or one at a time.

Or mayhap we will find strife. Or it will find us.

Still, better us than another. We, more than most, can handle it. And whatever comes, we will be together, and free.

As we set an easy pace toward the gold-glowing sunrise, Connie remarks that she thinks it strange that I did not exact the ultimate vengeance on Athos.

I smile and pull my son close, blocking his infant ears so he cannot hear of his mother's final act as the demonic Milady. "I leave his fate up to God," I say. To their questioning look I add, "I gave him my rosary, the chain of red and black beads my own maman presented to me when I left home."

"I'm surprised you would give up such a token," Connie says.

"I would not have, save that the beads are not carved and painted wood, but the seeds of an Indian plant. A weed, really, that sprawls across the roadsides in that spiced and scorching land."

Denys smiles. "Let me guess . . ."

I nod. "One single seed is enough to kill a man. Their shells are hard, and one might swallow a handful without harm, for they pass through undisturbed. But if a person were to gnaw on them, to crack the shell . . . if for example one had a nervous habit of chewing on anything within reach . . ."

So Milady may have her revenge after all.

Clarice the Yorkshire lass will neither know nor care.

She has found her happiness. She has seized it.

ACKNOWLEDGMENTS

I want to thank the three men who, in their own unique and ineffable ways, helped me as I was writing *Milady*. Luis Rodriguez, my paddling partner who reminds me to leave my laptop occasionally, but understands better than anyone when I can't . . . and who will soon set the screenwriting world on fire. Aaron McDaniel, who provided material for a particular scene (I'm not telling), and who better have his own manuscript finished soon. And Gregg Duszynski, for the way we were . . .

Milady has gone through several iterations, and wouldn't be the novel you hold today if not for some brilliant editorial minds. My delightful agent, Jason Anthony, was my first sounding board, and helped *Milady* find a happy home at Berkley. There, my editor, Amanda Bergeron, made me realize that there were still hidden depths to Milady that I hadn't fully explored. And when Amanda took a break to make a whole new beautiful little person, Jen Monroe ably stepped in and guided this novel through its own birth. I'd also like to thank my copyeditor, Marianne Aguiar, who has an even keener eye for anachronism than my own.

I owe so much to my family—Babaloo, Marla, and of course Buster. They are my biggest fans—and I'm theirs. Its good to have a tribe that completely gets you.

And finally, I'd like to thank my Brazilian Jiu Jitsu brothers and sisters at Gracie Barra Clearwater. Whenever things got hard, I could find solace in rolling around on the ground with my friends while we tried to choke each other unconscious.

MILADY

LAURA L. SULLIVAN

AUTHOR'S NOTE

Milady almost didn't come to fruition—simply because when I had the idea, I couldn't believe it hadn't been done before. After all, Milady de Winter is an iconic villainess, a character whose fame rivals the three Musketeers themselves. How could there not be a book depicting her origin story?

Usually I don't like novels that borrow other authors' characters, but I decided to make an exception with *Milady*. For one thing, the story was just too juicy to pass up! Then, too, along with the Musketeers, *Milady* has blurred the line between a historical figure and a fictional one. When I started the project, many people I talked with believed that Milady de Winter was a real person. It is only natural. The characters have become a part of our culture, and share the pages with real historical figures such as Cardinal Richelieu and Anne of Austria.

So, enraptured by my idea, I set about rereading Alexandre Dumas's *The Three Musketeers*, which I hadn't read since high school. I used Richard Pevear's engaging 2006 translation . . . and I was bowled over by what I found. Milady was raped by D'Artagnan, the supposed hero of the book! Previous editions had been translated with such coyness that I never realized this. Athos, Porthos, and Aramis, the Musketeers, are drunken brawlers, heartless seducers, completely ignoble. And far from being a villain, Milady is for the most part a competent civil servant employed by the effective head of the French government.

The king and the cardinal seem arbitrarily at odds, and their factions take sides just for the fun of having an enemy. Most of the plot is an excuse for a sword fight. At the end of all that bloodshed, when D'Artagnan finally becomes a full-fledged Musketeer, he promptly changes sides and leaves the king's service for the cardinal's.

This is a terrible book, I thought. At every turn I muttered, *No, Milady de Winter couldn't let that happen.* Then I remembered: the victors tell the story. Of course, with Milady dead at the end, the blustering Musketeers would tell the tale that puts them in the best (or in any case the most exciting) light. As I read and reread the book, I began to see where there could have been cover-ups.

And then as I studied the novel, and figured out Milady's history, I realized that she herself would deliberately conspire to leave a misleading legacy. The story doesn't fail her. It is simply the story she wanted to have told. To be underestimated—and presumed dead—is the best protection from one's enemies.

So I approached my book, *Milady,* not as an apologia—her defense of her entire existence—but rather a celebration of a woman who crafted her own life, and her legacy, very precisely. There are layers and secret motivations to everything she does. Even her failures are deliberate. In this novel with two timelines, you can see how her formative years turn Milady into a complex, powerful woman—one who is fully capable of writing her own story, Dumas bedamned! She is one of the lucky few literary characters who has taken on a life of her own.

(There's one other fictional figure I would love to write about someday: a secondary character from a beloved children's book that gets short shrift while all the main character's wildest dreams come true, an unfortunate victim of class expectations. Maybe next time?)

QUESTIONS FOR DISCUSSION

1. A constant theme in *Milady* is having multiple personas. Milady has many names, identities, and disguises. Her mother is also described as having two distinct personas, one when she is alone with her daughter, another when she is with her husband. That is necessary in the spy trade, but is it also something every woman has to do? Every person?

2. Milady is portrayed in *The Three Musketeers* as a sexual, seductive person who mostly manipulates men. Yet in the novel *Milady* it is her ability to form relationships with women that is her real strength. Did women need this to succeed in a world dominated by men? How is that relevant today?

3. Do you think Milady should have told the Comte de la Fere (Athos) her secret during their courtship or marriage? When, and what would have been the consequences? Knowing what you do of Athos's character, why do you think he acted as quickly and decisively as he did when he saw her brand?

4. Poison is sometimes called a woman's weapon, or a coward's. And yet, it can be argued that it takes greater subtlety and skill to use it well. As with Milady, a poisoner might also be a healer, using

herbs, chemicals, and knowledge of the human body for vastly different purposes. Why do you think poison is associated with female assassins?

5. Do you think that Milady believes herself to be a fundamentally good person? Is a person defined by their worst act, their best, an average, or what they are capable of?

6. Milady is a woman capable of profound independence and self sufficiency. When a woman of her habits and abilities chooses a partner, what does it take to make that partnership work?

7. Winners and the powerful write the histories . . . but in this book, *Milady* has taken control of her own story away from the men who have always told it so far. Have women and minorities been done a disservice by not having their stories told? How can this be corrected?

8. The fleur de lis is a symbol of France. As a brand on Milady's bosom, it is supposed to be a mark of shame and criminality. Yet in her career she served France's interests. Do you think that for *Milady* (and for the reader) the fleur de lis brand has any other symbolism? Who was *Milady* actually serving?

9. In *The Three Musketeers*, D'Artagnan, the supposed hero, rapes Milady by deception. He also seduces a married woman, and an unprotected servant. In this book, Milady is far too clever to allow that to happen. Discuss the sort of things people have to accept in order to see D'Artagnan as a hero in the original book. Is it acceptable because Milady is called the villain? Because she is al-

ready assumed to be promiscuous? Think about the mores of the
time that contribute to this, and whether they exist today.

10. Is Milady legitimately in love with George Villiers? If so, how does
this first love affect her future relationships?

11. This book contains many scenes of a woman bound and presumably helpless. Is it ever useful for a woman (or anyone) to pretend
to be weaker than they are, to allow themselves to be seen as helpless?

12. Discuss the phrase "one for all, all for one" as it is used in *Milady*,
and as it is used in *The Three Musketeers*. How are the usages different? How does Milady's final version of the phrase "*nous pour nous*"
or "us for us" sum up the theme of this novel?

FURTHER READING

If you enjoy historical fiction, and intriguing heroines, you might also like these books and authors, which are among my favorites.

Forever Amber by Kathleen Winsor introduced me to historical fiction. It's not a romance (no happy ending) but a bildungsroman of great vim with a heroine you'll never forget.

I'm a sucker for courtesan/prostitute/concubine narratives, and *The Crimson Petal and the White* by Michel Faber is my favorite. (Not a historical, but also try *Maia*, by Richard Adams, the man who brought you talking bunnies.)

For a long time, I'd only ever read one book by William Makepeace Thackeray—*Vanity Fair*, of course—and read it many, many times. For some reason I didn't try his other novels until recently, and I am absolutely delighted by such gems as *The Newcomes* and *The History of Henry Edmond*. Perhaps second only to Anthony Trollope in his depth of understanding of human nature, Thackeray reminds us that people don't change much through the centuries.

Written in 1901 and set in the 1890s, *Mord Em'ly* is an all-but-forgotten heroine that every woman should know about. A sharp, bantering slum kid who gets in street fights with other girl gangs, she manages to hold her own in a world that is against her.

And for pure happiness, the comfort-food of books, try any of Eva Ibbotson's romantic historicals.

After George MacDonald Fraser (the Flashman books) died, Laurie Graham took his place as my favorite living historical author. Her books are sharp, impeccably researched, and most important, hilarious. Try *Gone with the Windsors* or *The Great Husband Hunt*.

Ready to find
your next great read?

Let us help.

Visit prh.com/nextread